The NATIONAL Standard

THE NATIONAL STANDARD

Gerald Jay Goldberg

HOLT, RINEHART AND WINSTON
NEW YORK / CHICAGO / SAN FRANCISCO

 for NANCY

Published simultaneously in Canada by Holt, Rinehart and Winston of Canada, Limited.

Library of Congress Catalog Card Number: 68-12207

First Edition

Designer: RONALD FARBER

8685356

Printed in the United States of America

❧ CONTENTS

❧ The NATIONAL Standard

"*Je ne nie pas qu'il y ait, de par le monde, des actions nobles, généreuses, et même désintéressées. . . .*"
— A. GIDE

CHAPTER 1

Greetings!

Racing clouds in Confederate gray had been taking up their positions above the enemy since daybreak. At nine o'clock the sky still threatened the Hanover plain, but New England weather is changeable and the President was not one who held tradition lightly.

"It shall take place as scheduled," he announced solemnly when queried by the chief custodian of buildings and grounds, a man who allowed his efficiency to be hinted at by the tops of a half-dozen assorted pens and pencils peeping out of his breast pocket.

"But sir," the chief custodian addressed the chief, "the Boston Bureau says rain for this entire area today. Couldn't we maybe move the chairs to the field house just to play it safe? My men are ready any time you give the word. What do you say, sir?" He sounded like a small boy talking to a policeman.

"I say that in *almost two hundred years*—with but one infamous exception when the guest of honor, King Oomohamo of the island of Maui, arrived at the last minute half naked and President Winthrop, quite rightly, went indoors in order to keep things as quiet as possible—our graduation ceremonies have always been conducted, as it were, under God's eye. And, BY HEAVEN,

[1]

they will continue to be so during my tenure of office!" Slapping the palms of his hands down hard on the desk top before him, the President rose up shouting, "Cry woe, destruction, rain, and decay, the worst is death, and death will have his day."

The chief custodian was a feeler, one of those able to experience ideas best through physical exertion. In his effort to profit from what he had just heard, he drew blood from his lower lip.

"Shakespeare," the President revealed modestly, and taking his shaken visitor around by the shoulders, walked him slowly to the great door. "Besides," he added in a tone off the record and entre nous, his big hand poised with some authority on the gilded doorknob, "it's *not* going to rain." He rapped dramatically on the steel plate in his head, a memento of his World War I days with the AEF. "Not a peep out of it all morning. Don't worry, Bill, nature is on our side. We've won again! The exercises will take place as scheduled." With a flourish, the President threw open the great door and, smiling warmly, showed his uncertain visitor out.

On the lawn in front of the neo-Georgian façade of the library, a wooden stage had been erected and painted white. A tarpaulin, festively striped with the school colors of red and gold to hide its true meaning, had been set up above the platform. Stretching before the stage were countless rows of camp chairs divided by a center aisle lined with the flags of the United Nations undulating disconsolately in the moist air. Behind a still empty roped-off area reserved for the graduates, a gaily dressed crowd of invited guests were taking their seats. They waved excitedly back and forth with the joy of recognition that typifies the close-knit family of an old, distinguished institution. Only an occasional umbrella marred the texture of the scene, but the spring-green trees that established the outer perimeter of the lawn waited like sponges under the darkening sky.

At exactly ten o'clock, when the concussion from the last chime of the library tower clock still ruffled the air, the grand marshal made his appearance. Tall, and brilliant in his academic gown of yellow trimmed with ermine tails, he moved elegantly with the easeful certainty of the unobtainable. Although the graduates, eager to taste the world, pursued him hotly down the aisle rustling their somber plumage as they went, his step was unhurried, his palms dry. After a bit of shuffling, when seats finally matched seated, the school chaplain, a reformed Unitarian, delivered the invocation. It was a short message posted for Heaven, but its burden of prudent self-indulgence amounted to a clear return address. On the whole, all denominations seemed thoroughly pleased at the unequivocally moderate tone that had been struck at the outset and a murmur of approval went up on all sides as the audience settled back to enjoy themselves. And they did. For the pace and color of the proceedings, a touch of Mendelssohn here, a valediction there, constituted a well-ordered banquet delighting the assemblage not with novelty but good taste.

Even though it remained muggy, the weather did not alter the smooth rhythm of events, and by the time the President came forward to introduce the principal speaker, a ray of sunshine had finally filtered through the clouds. The President, grinning broadly, presented the sun to his audience as if it were his idea and waited for the good-natured laughter to die away before getting down to the serious business at hand.

"Famous son of a famous father who, praises be, did not prevail in his mistaken view that he had sired an artist, Warner Mumford Chub is no stranger to this campus. A College son, class of '18, distinguished member of The Mummers, his prowess as a Thespian during his four years here has become legend, and today students still speak of the time Chubby, playing Cleopatra, chased a heckler who demanded more leg out of the theater and into the night. Warner Chub has *always* resisted unreasonable demands, and one might say that his training for future greatness as the chief of the American delegation to the disarmament conference in Geneva began right here that memorable evening. How fitting it is that the cause of reason and world peace should be championed by one whose learning in the liberal arts is as profound as his practical knowledge of political science and whose preferences run to Mozart and Henry James rather than Wagner and Dostoyevsky. The pride you bestow on your alma mater is great, and accustomed

[3]

as you are to the vagaries—as well as the frustrations—of international diplomacy, it should come as no surprise to you when she, in turn, bestows upon you, Warner Mumford Chub, her Doctorate of Humane Letters."

The applause was deafening. It appeared that Mr. Chub was moved by the unexpected honor, but since his lower lip protruded and he smiled with a closed mouth, it was at first not easy for even the keenest observer to determine whether pleasure or pain was being registered. There could be no question, however, when, after momentarily becoming entangled in his new academic hood, he shook hands briskly with the President and approached the lectern with the look of a man who might conceivably loathe Christmas. Arranging his papers before him, he waited until he caught the eye of a thin-faced graduate in the front row who had been talking to someone behind him. The boy turned red and silent, his chest impaled on a sharply pointed chin, and Mr. Chub, brushing his steel-gray hair straight back, saw no reason for further delay.

"MR. PRESIDENT–GOVERNOR HENNEPIN–DISTINGUISHED GUESTS–GRADUATES–FRIENDS," boomed the speaker as if he had uttered a single word and paused to see how far along he was in his speech. After sizing up the situation, he removed his tongue from his cheek where it seemed to be engaged in relocating food particles and impulsively announced, "I've been where you are, so I'll get on with things and not mince words." Then turning back to his text, he read with the breathless urgency of a dying man. "As throughout life there are many diverse pleasures, so throughout this great country of ours there are hundreds of institutions of higher learning of diverse quality; and as this is unquestionably one of the most thrilling moments of my life, so, too, is The College one of the foremost bastions of learning, not only in the United States, not only in the Western Hemisphere, but in the entire world. A reputation for the highest standards in learning such as you have here is not easily come by, but perhaps more important is the school's renown for the men it molds—men of taste, men of conscience, leaders—and I consider it a real joy and a distinct honor to have been allowed to partake, if only for four years, of this rich tradition." Warner Chub snorted loudly.

[4]

Either it was an evaluative comment or the speaker a victim of chronic rhinitis. The audience seemed confused. The President, however, sensing the delicacy of the situation, began snapping his fingers enthusiastically, first with one hand and then both, as if in response to an unheard melody with an infectious rhythm. One by one, the graduates picked up the beat, snapping out The College's famous salute to excellence, and catastrophe was neatly avoided.

"I remember as a freshman"—the speaker ignored the tribute and plunged on, subtly implying that he could no longer be rattled by schoolboys—"the thrill of meeting my professors for the first time, all men of vast erudition and authorities in their respective fields, some of whom are still here today, still teaching their classes the very same way they did when I was a boy, still leading young minds from darkness to light, but never forgetting that there is more to a body than mind and more to an education than books. Will I ever forget the time . . ?" Warner Chub asked himself panting, and it seemed as if he never would, for the next fifteen minutes were spent in recounting it. Periodically punctuating memory with snort to the growing unrest of his audience, he described in detail the most amusing yet significant experience of his first year at The College.

"Then, as a sophomore, my most amusing yet significant experience occurred, surprisingly enough, in the locker room of the gymnasium."

There was a good deal of ribald laughter at this, but Warner Chub, oblivious, droned on like some large, simple machine digging a deep hole.

"It was a cold day in January and I was wearing my track shorts . . ."

A loud, continuous, throaty blast sounded—possibly an air-raid alert for it was not yet twelve o'clock. Warner Chub lost his place.

"Though it was far from easy to leave The College after four years," he persisted forcefully, "particularly when so many of my classmates were staying on to work in Administration, I knew I must fledge . . . fledge . . . fleh . . ." There was a puzzled, agonized look on the speaker's face as he ground to a halt and listened. It was as if he feared the sound he heard was coming from him.

People seemed to be looking toward the street and pointing. A young art instructor, his academic gown flying behind him in a baroque manner, came racing down the aisle and called the President aside excitedly. All eyes were on the President as he nodded sepulchrally, and brushing his informant to one side, stepped forward. Cupping his hands to his mouth in order to be heard above the din, he clipped out, "Will the owner of a new black Cadillac with Connecticut license D–A–D–D–Y have the goodness to attend to its needs at once?"

A stout, elegantly dressed, middle-aged woman wearing a chignon and a guilty face stood up and hurried to the car. She nervously removed a set of keys from her tiny beaded handbag and got in. But flustered, she failed to note the group of men who hovered over the exposed innards of the automobile in a grotesque travesty of the medical profession, and unable to stop the blaring noise, she raced the engine and roared off into the New Hampshire countryside, the car's hood a distress signal dipping wildly in the breeze.

The President showed signs of strain as he confronted his guest, whose face in adversity had contracted to the point where lip and nose were almost touching.

"Sorry, Warner," he said, grinning sheepishly, and slumped down into his chair bereft of muscle tone.

But Mr. Chub, unaccustomed to interruptions, was not easily mollified, and as he moved on in his address to describe the current problematical world situation, he managed by clever pauses and emphases to suggest that he knew exactly who was responsible. In fact, when he began to describe the difficulties encountered by his delegation in achieving a workable disarmament agreement with the Russians, his voice becoming louder and more strident with each obstacle recounted, he might have been haranguing card-carrying members of the Party. All fine distinctions seemed to have been blunted for him. Lashing out at his audience, he appeared content for the first time that morning as he condemned their delaying tactics and sardonically reduced their arguments to ashes. But his triumph was short-lived. Instead of grumbling outrage, his ears detected a groundswell of laughter, and looking up, his face turned white. There in the aisle before him a Great Dane had purposefully mounted a bitch and, circling the lovers, a pack of mongrel dogs of assorted sizes stoically waited their turn. A number of people were trying to separate them, but enthusiasm in any form is difficult to suppress and it took several minutes before the aisle was finally cleared.

"You've got your nerve!" Warner Chub shouted, shaking his fist at the departing animals, but, unsatisfied, he turned wrathfully on the President who cringed in his seat, an icon of despair. "Have you turned this place into a kennel?" he cried out in disgust, and feeling somewhat better when the poor badgered husk could do nothing but look back at him with panic-stricken eyes, he cheerfully returned to his task with new vigor.

At first his tone was coolly ironic. Gradually, however, it changed. A new note crept in. When he came to that part of his speech in which he said, "But these crises of our time may also be seen as challenges to those *sufficiently* mature to grasp the opportunities they provide and *sufficiently* equipped to handle them," it was with blistering sarcasm.

The audience by this time had become openly hostile and above their disgruntled murmurs some audible but indistinct remarks were heard. Warner Chub knew that the day was his. Snorting with pleasure, he broadly hinted that progress in a free society was impossible inasmuch as it depended on the creativity of individuals such as those whom he was addressing and, tongue in cheek, he relished his words despite the sound of a distant bugle.

With the possible exception of the speaker who continued his bitter, slashing attack under the guise of depicting the hope of the future, which he saw as a star-spangled flower safely plucked from amidst red nettles, everyone was alerted as the blaring bugle grew louder and repeatedly sounded its sennet. Necks were craned. People rose to their feet, shaking their heads incredulously and pointing to the road where, tires screaming, horn bugling, streamers flying, a long cream-colored limousine took the corner by Wally Simpson's Red and Gold Barber Shoppe on two wheels, shivered momentarily, righted itself, and roared down the block with the desperate abandon of a vehicle carrying perishable goods without refrigeration. In a trice it was opposite the speakers' platform and even before the brakes were slammed on, the door was thrown open and an Army major, a giant, square-jawed man wearing a skin-tight uniform on which gold braid glittered like scales, jumped out, tripped over an abandoned sprinkler, and went sprawling. Picking himself up disgustedly, the Major brushed off his pants and ran toward the stage. Three strides, a leap, and he was at the astonished President's ear. The frightened President, his mouth an open wound, appeared to be whimpering to himself as he shook his head lugubriously from side to side. But in time he was seen to give in reluctantly, and approaching the speaker with more decisiveness than might have been expected, he tapped him on the shoulder with tempered firmness.

Mr. Chub now saw clearly the scope of the plot hatched against him and responded to the touch like a thoroughbred. His pace, already prodigious, quickened, and with a monomaniacal concentration which reduced punctuation to medieval status, he sped onward, snorting out the promise of tomorrow. The President shrugged his shoulders in relief. He had done his duty and more could not be expected of any man. As he rejoined his honored guests who received him doubtfully, the secret hope that somehow everything would come out all right manifested itself in a silly smile.

The Major, however, was trained for victory. Resting a parental hand on Warner Chub's neck, he apologized grandly. "I'm sorry, sir. I have my orders." But when Mr. Chub shook off the offending member, disdaining appeasement, it might have been a declaration of war. Imperturbably efficient, the huge officer strode to the front of the lectern and placed the speaker in his shadow so that he could only be seen in cross section. Like a colossus the Major straddled the stage, towering over the audience, mocking perspective, and when he opened his mouth to speak, his voice, ominous and inexorable, rumbled spectacularly over Mr. Chub's darting syllables.

"The Commander in Chief of the United States Armed Forces sends GREETINGS!" The Major blinked nervously, a surprising hint of self-consciousness in his manner. Although lacking forensic polish, he had the audience eating out of his hand. "Greetings," he ad-libbed with aplomb. "In order to preserve our way of life, regardless of what others may think, this entire graduating class is herewith ordered to report to the second floor of the Seventh District Induction Center in Concord, 29 East Wheelock, north side of the street, tomorrow morning at 7 A.M. *sharp*. That is all."

The stentorian voice held the listeners transfixed. Unwilling to let the opportunity pass, although his mission was officially over, the Major shouted recklessly, "BUY SAVINGS BONDS!" and was gone.

When the sound of departing bugles had died away, Mr. Chub could be heard pleading with unashamed passion for peaceful co-existence. Pounding on the lectern, which shuddered under his blows, he called for "Reason and Justice! Yes, Reason and Justice. These are the hallmarks of all truly great civilizations of the past which have stamped their impress on time's tape recorder and which are twentieth-century man's usufruct. It is through Reason and Justice that America will be guided through the dangerous years ahead and take her rightful place in history's Pantheon. And it is in the world's exercise of Reason and Justice," screamed Mr. Chub hopelessly, "that universal brotherhood will replace universal distrust and international order will replace international anarchy. With Providence your guide, together, working hand in hand, the world is all before you." Warner Chub jerked his gray head up, gasped, snorted, and threw out his arms like a challenge. "Gentlemen," he cried hoarsely, "I give you the future!"

But before the audience could make up their minds what to do with it, a bolt of lightning zigged its way down the trunk of one of the surrounding elm trees, an electric finger pointing the way for the cloudburst that followed. As the rain came thundering down, cold, bleak, impenetrable, the chief custodian, who had been standing behind the speakers' platform, ran out and quickly started pulling up flagpoles in quiet desperation. Flashing back and forth in the aisle, he filled his arms with national standards, but the water poured down his face and into his shoes, slowing him up, and he was caught from behind by the audience charging for cover, knocked to the mud and, enmeshed in his burden, lost somewhere between Israel and Yugoslavia.

Warner Mumford Chub, from the security of the covered stage, surveyed the desolate scene before him with that mixture of exaltation and loss said to be common among those lesser primates whose young are brought forth stillborn. He stood hypnotized by the steady thrum of the rain on the tarpaulin above him, his eyes focused on an empty package of King Size Winstons riding the crest of a small river in imperial fashion until caught up in a large, amorphous pile of poles and wet rags from which extended a man's shoe. Inexplicably, two tears appeared in the corners of Warner Chub's eyes. Three boys had actually remained. They sat with their heads bent, huddled together against the rain like conspirators in an Elizabethan playhouse. Mr. Chub removed a white linen handkerchief from his pocket and wiped his eyes. Perhaps the future was safe after all.

CHAPTER 2
🌿 The plotters in the tower.

Ignoring the hurricane, Pearson Causley played his miniature cards close to the gown, somber, moody, wrestling with disaster. Blackjack was not his game. Gloomily contemplating the six he held in the hole, the frail stutterer vaguely remarked, "The Ar-Ar-Ar-Ar-Ar-Ar-Army—" and no more. An aborted burble of obscure significance.

His two friends exchanged impatient looks as the water rose up over the vamps of their shoes.

"Let's go, Pigeon," one of them prodded, a tall, dark young man by the name of D.C. Widdemore (Richard Courtney on his eggshell stationery). His easy and self-possessed manner told of gentle breeding and long happy hours with his mirror. "I'm losing my crease. Pull or stick?"

Although rain bombarded the top of Pearson's mortarboard and water coursed down the gulleys of his gown, he refused to be stampeded into error. He would make his error slowly, methodically, with malice aforethought. For whether he crawled or flew, the end was always the same.

"The Ar-Ar-Ar-Army—" began Pearson once again, straining to concentrate on his addition in the tempest.

Heavy with muscle tissue, Ivan Storch felt the camp chair beneath him slowly sink into the ooze. He was eager to move indoors. Reaching across with hands from Picasso's classic period, he confiscated the brooder's four cards and silently tossed them to Widdemore.

Pearson sighed with resignation.

D.C. glanced at the cards in his rain-shriveled fingers and counted twenty-three. "You're over, dammit," he observed sourly. "Now why did you have to do that for?" He grieved over the needless soaking his new knickers had taken as he quickly packed the miniature deck away in a cowhide case purchased at one of those chic Fifth Avenue shops that sells all of its merchandise, from flasks to reading lamps, leather-bound.

"But the Ar-Ar-Ar—"

"It can be worked out," Ivan calmly reassured him. Getting up, he shook the water out of the wild yellow growth that covered the lower half of his face and sloshed off at a gallop in the direction of the library.

By the time Ivan had entered the stacks his two friends had caught up with him and together they went up in the private elevator reserved for library personnel, a slow-moving curiosity that resembled a violin case. On the top level they got out and walked up a short flight of stairs to a locked door on which was stenciled: "No ADMITTANCE." Ivan took out his key and opening it led them through a dimly lit, cavernous storage room that was as humid as Africa and smelled of jungle rot. Arriving at another flight of stairs, they were about to ascend when a dumpy old lady confronted them. She wore a black leather apron and a shapeless felt hat and, with her troglodytic chum who hid in the shadows, she guarded the stairway like Roland at the pass. Not even dust could get by her without an explanation. Taking in Ivan's two friends, her face as white as the library paste she used in making book repairs, she asked peevishly, "What's with your bells *now*, dearie?"

"A farewell tuning," explained Ivan confidentially as he started up the stairs, his sopping friends close behind him.

"*More* yet!" she complained to the shadows. "They've been at those things *all* year. Always fiddling. Can't leave well enough alone. Tinker, tinker, tinker. They sound good enough to me," she called after them in a disgruntled voice.

"Layman," whispered D.C. and kept climbing.

Several more flights of stairs, a catwalk, a rope ladder, a trap door, and they were home.

Life was cramped in the clock tower for though large it was honeycombed with exposed oak beams criss-crossing the room from floor to ceiling. The clock's notched gears, as big as manhole covers and as small as caramellos, occupied one entire wall, and up against another was a squat, buff-colored metal cabinet containing the carillon. Admittedly there had been inconveniences in living here, but it *was* cozy and the privacy was unequaled anywhere on campus.

When at the beginning of his senior year Ivan had been appointed keeper of the mechanical bells because of his ability to handle the Burroughs 700 (a cranky old computer prone to electronic inflammations), he boldly moved in his few belongings and made himself at home. A good deal, but only "just passing" for a perfectionist. Confident that the authorities knew nothing of the housekeeping going on over their heads, Ivan, an ingenious developer, decided to sublet. It had been his novel idea to palm his tenants off as Master Bell-Tuners, a plan which the romantic D.C. found wickedly appealing.

"But w-w-why so much?" Pearson had grumbled when told of the rent. "*He* doesn't p-pay so much."

"You have the view," Ivan had informed him patiently, placing Pearson's inflated rubber mattress under the porthole-shaped window. "On a clear day you can see two states and an abandoned copper mine. Besides . . . *he* provides the entertainment."

And the entertainment had been Four-Star. Handsome D.C. was widely known in College circles as the S. Hurok of the Hanover plain, and by word of mouth, leaflets, and billets-doux, he plundered the available talent of the Seven Sisters—the Ivy League ladies' auxiliary. The bored young women who attend these schools, hungry for anything a trifle out of the way and reeking of a little harmless evil, flocked to the tower in droves. Bacchanalias were commonplace and also on weekdays. Their graduation party alone had lasted a fortnight with feverish couples taking turns in climbing out on the narrow wooden deck above the gilded face of the clock to cool off in the ticking darkness under the star-ridden sky. But now it was all over, buried, their bags packed, their wild oats inside.

Woebegone on his inflated mattress, Pearson listlessly started to untie the baggage tickets from his luggage, the long creases from the corners of his mouth giving him the look of a clarinet-player with a permanent embouchure. Chained to failure, he couldn't shake loose. It plodded after him from place to place like a dropsical, seedy, stale-mouthed bear. The few successes he had ever had he owed to his father. Reason enough to hate the man—a society doctor of such wealth and influence that he no longer had to wear white shirts or live with his wife. Pearson delighted in taunting him with his threats to become an M.D. and smirch the family shingle. "Over my dead body!" counseled his appalled father. Although it had started as a joke, the idea had given Pearson such status in his old man's eyes that he was determined to see it through. But after four years on probation, there wasn't a medical school in the country that would touch him. He was a confirmed low hanger, an academic basket case. When he had asked for letters of recommendation, teachers laughed until they cried and their arms flapped helplessly at their sides like broken shutters. Even diploma mills regarded him as a poor risk. Accordingly Pearson had decided to leave for less rigorous standards abroad where he could make a fresh start in a foreign language. But now the Army was about to filch his stethoscope. It was discouraging.

"Cheer up," said D.C. compassionately, and removing his gown he revealed a one-of-a-kind, belted, tangerine, Norfolk jacket—a College First. After wringing out his knickers, he combed his wavy black hair (which curled ever so slightly at the nape of his neck but was hardly conventionally long), lit up a Puerto Rican Bizarro, and looked himself over feeling sorry for other people. "Uniforms," he gagged. "The Army doesn't have us yet," he pointed out in a hopeful voice. "Ivan will think of something."

"W-Why should he w-w-worry?" cried the puny pre-med,

striking out thoughtlessly in his misery. "He only has one eye. But I'm in p-p-p-p-perfect condition."

"Stinko, Pigeon," accused D.C., full of righteous indignation. "You owe Ivan an apology."

Pearson fondled the baggage tickets in his hand. "I'm up-up-up-upset," he snuffled.

"Forget it," said Ivan offhandedly and gave up squeezing the squash ball in his pocket.

Strictly speaking, Ivan had two eyes, but only one was in working order. The other tended to float about aimlessly in its socket like a dark brown crouton and gave him an air of ambivalence that even his beard and crew cut didn't completely dispel. Yet nothing could be farther from the truth. Ivan had the focus of a giant telescope, the drive of a rocket, the determination of a Freedom Fighter. He was a Jason hot for America's Golden Fleece. Over three hundred years of energy had been deposited from coast to coast by dynamo men who had been burned up in the process of building American power, and Ivan, tired of the one-sided arrangement, intended someday to make a withdrawal. Although uncertain how to tap the conduit, he was eager to get started. Naturally this could all be explained by his childhood.

Every child deserves culpable parents. Ivan's problem was that he had only a pail. Upon closer inspection it proved not to be a pail at all but a cornucopic Shriner's fez of dramatic proportions. Too large for a Prophet or a Priest or a Rabban, it could only belong to the Supreme Insurmountable Refulgent Potentate himself and hinted tantalizingly at the young man's noble lineage. Nine months to the day after one of the most spirited Mystical conventions in New York history, Ivan was found in a bejeweled red hat on the steps of the Con Ed Co., 43rd Street branch, with a note tied to his tassel that read: "DIG WE MUST BUT WE'LL CLEAN UP AND MOVE ON." Pranksters! But, understandably, to the naïve, impressionable mind of a child which sets such great store by trivia it was an apodictic sign that he was destined for power from the start.

When contacted by the police, all Shriners claimed to be wearing their hats. And so it came about that by default and in order to protect their public image the Consolidated Edison Company of New York City became a mother. This unusual arrangement, however, lasted only through the third grade, for by then the publicity had largely died down and the Company felt that they could no longer afford to carry the waif under Accounts Payable.

Needless to say, an orphan's lot is not an easy one in any city in the United States with a population over 250,000, where there are countless agencies (both public and private) whose sole reason for existence is to seize upon the homeless urchin in order to pity him, protect him, advise him, and burden him with perpetual indebtedness for their generosity. And this does not include the thousands of nonaffiliated Christian souls working enterprisingly on their own out of missionary storefronts, so to speak, for whom a foundling is like a four-leaf clover. Ivan, an independent rascal from the start, did his best to steer clear of the whole benevolent pack, in daylight traveling between cars on the Eighth Avenue subway and nights sleeping under high-price beds in the Home Furnishings sections of some of New York's best-known department stores.

From fourth grade until his freshman year at The College, Ivan's education could best be described as hit-or-miss informal. Irregularly, he sat in on Shakespeare in the Park, Hobbes in the Great Hall at Cooper Union, Marx at the Militant Labor Forum, and Adler at the 92nd Street Y, filling the gaps with Sunrise Semester in Appliances before the department store in which he happened to be spending the night opened. Although casual, his unorthodox preparation proved to be ideally suited for the College Board examinations on which he scored so high that he received a Save the Refuse Opportunity Award to the institution of his choice.

A clever boy, Ivan became the intellectual darling of the Academy, their token oddball poverty case who dramatized the democratic impartiality of the Ivy League, and now his success at The College had been rewarded after four years by his selection for the coveted Thaddeus Tick Graduate Orphan's Scholarship to the Sorbonne. A signal honor that, if not for the money, Ivan would have cheerfully declined. He was frankly not interested in wasting any more time in formal education and didn't at all care to leave the country. But it was plain to him that nowadays it takes cash to become the top banana, the big cheese, the candied apple of Uncle Sam's jaded eye and his first order of business was to accumulate surfeit. If the philanthropic Mr. Tick wished to force him to go to Europe in order to collect his prize, Ivan would see that he paid for it—and with a clear conscience. For it takes two to make an exploitation, an exploiter and an exploitee, and Ivan had already been around enough to know that it's not always easy to say which one gets the most out of the arrangement.

Jamming his graduation gown into his luggage—a crumpled ditty bag containing his Py-co-pay toothbrush and a Dewey-decimaled book on physical culture that could be dangerous in the wrong hands—Ivan announced, "Our reservations are confirmed. The Army will have to do without us."

D.C. exhaled, filling the tower with the sweet smell of Bizarro. "That's fine as far as it goes," he commented dryly. "Now let's hear the details."

"War is a waste of energy," mused Ivan in a reflective mood as he yanked the zipper of his bag closed.

"It's an anachronism," D.C. contributed, mildly interested in the general theme. "But what about the specifics, the bare bones, the one-two-three? Where do we fit in?"

Ivan frowned at the impetuous youth. "I'm coming to that," he growled and sat down on the edge of Pearson's mattress.

"It's all o-o-o-over," moaned Pearson, more nasal than usual because he was gnawing on his knuckles. "It's all o-o-o-o-o—"

"Go ahead," D.C. urged Ivan, and drawing up his mattress, he settled down with an all-ears expression. "I'm listening."

The bearded plotter began in a low voice, his head bowed, intent, clandestine. He looked like a revolutionary in the shabby brown double-breasted business suit that he wore rain or shine, in sickness and in health. As the plan was laid before them, morose Pearson rallied in perceptible stages and D.C. snickered conspiratorially from time to time.

"How does that sound?" asked Ivan, glancing up when he had finished.

Inarticulated by bliss, the boys fell whooping on Ivan's neck, tugging at his beard gleefully and hugging him with joy.

"Let's drink to that," cried D.C. rapturously and passed out the paper cups. He loved any excuse for a celebration. Ducking his long frame under the beams, he went to the other end of the tower and located the Chianti left over from their last party. It was a bulbous bottle with a thin neck that was so long he had to pour it into their cups from where he stood, a dangerous balancing act that he dexterously performed. Taking his cup from Ivan, D.C. raised it high and toasted, "To FREEDOM! Academic and otherwise."

"To Freedom!" chorused his friends exuberantly, and though Ivan drank little and Pearson was busy pasting together the baggage tickets that he had mindlessly torn up in his distraction, D.C. continued to raise toast after toast.

Hssssssssssss. The rush of air from Pearson's deflating mattress woke D.C.

"What time is it?" he asked belligerently, sitting up and shaking out the cobwebs.

Rather than rely on his wrist watch, Pearson climbed out on the wet upper deck and glanced down at the huge clock. Precision was important for a future doctor and in his months in the tower he had come to associate size with accuracy. "Eleven–t-t-twelve," he reported—and then dropping his voice apologetically— "or thirteen. It's a b-bad angle."

"I guess that makes us A.W.O.L.," chuckled D.C., tickled pink. He hopped up eager for the day's adventure and critically examined his graduation suit which was neatly hung on a hanger from one of the beams. "What do you think about a scarf?" he asked Pearson's advice.

"Don't push it too hard," warned Ivan, coming up through the trap door. "You'll make them suspicious."

"Where have you been?" D.C. inquired, surprised at the early riser.

Ivan carefully produced a computer card that had been punched into lacy filigree and explained, "A farewell concert." Not especially fond of music, the brawny carillonneur had for a year been obliged to sweeten the air with Elizabethan ditties, Negro spirituals, Zarzuela arias, and *Chants d'Auvergne* in five-minute noontime snatches. Now he would have his revenge. He had programed three hours of original, random, uninterrupted, musical chaos.

"As long as I'm not around to hear it," said D.C., hurrying to get dressed.

When he had finished and combed his hair, he went about collecting his colorful reproductions of bare-chested women from the walls. He had first become involved with the undraped female bosom in preadolescence when, while riding his bicycle and quite by accident, he had come upon one staring out of a garden-apartment window on a particularly sultry Sunday morning in August. Although attaching little importance to the sighting at the time, he soon found himself longing for a miraculous power that would cloud men's minds so that undetected by Mrs. Flack, his sixth-grade martinet, he might visit the girls' elementary bathroom and see close up exactly what this was all about. But before long D.C. learned that good looks were better than invisibility, and since those humble beginnings he had had many opportunities for first-hand experience.

And for theory he had discovered art history. Encouraged by his reading of Sir Kenneth Clark's *The Nude*, D.C. was working on a long-term study, more specialized than Sir Kenneth's, that he had tentatively titled, "The Changing Shape of the Female Breast in Western Art from the Greeks to the Present Day," and he had already pinned down the early fourteenth-century "button" and the "half-moon" of the Renaissance. During his stay abroad, he thought he would look into developments during the Age of the Enlightenment, but he was reconciled to the fact that the complete study might take years and would have to be subsidized by either an indulgent foundation or a wealthy wife. D.C. saw his chance for the latter as more likely and Europe as a giant strainer in which well-to-do American girls would be conveniently sifted out so that he wouldn't have to waste his time on the well-dressed poor. "I can marry a rich girl as easily as an indigent," he frequently encouraged himself.

"What's she doing here?" Ivan irritably demanded to know. He had just locked his program into the carillon and was staring down at something on the floor.

"How should I know?" said surprised D.C. defensively, spotting a girl with long, straight blonde hair that almost covered her entire face huddled against the side of the carillon. It was Freckles from Smith. She wore her hair that way because her face was done in dots like a Pointillist painting, but she did have an uncommon bust which, though it was outside his primary area of concentration, D.C. had readily identified as a "narrow primitive dangler."

Freckles stirred. "It's almost time, isn't it?" she asked in a low voice, but it wasn't hard to tell that she was excited.

As Pearson started to climb up to the deck to find out for her, Ivan dragged him back. "Not now," he told him. "We're in a hurry."

Although D.C. couldn't understand how Freckles had been overlooked, she had somehow been left over from their graduation party. A kook, she had been so keen on the carillon that she had apparently decided to stay. On the very first night of the party he had seen her kissing it with stars in her eyes. D.C. recalled that she was a music major with pronounced religious interests of a cultural nature. Her big regret was that she hadn't yet been born at the time just after V-J Day when all the great American artists were converting. Right away she wanted to know his religion.

"Are you AC or RC?" was the first thing she had asked him.

"I'm D.C.," he replied suavely. "I get mine direct from the source."

They had hit it off at once. But during the course of the evening she had mentioned that she was putting herself through college by working as an exotic in The Pleasure Dome, a Northampton do-it-yourself glamour studio for amateur photographers, and even though she made a good salary, D.C. realized that there could never be anything significant between them. Besides, she was dirty. It wasn't Bohemian dirt, either. There were no sandals or pierced ears or pale lips or hip-hugging tormentors. She was just an unclean girl.

"You'll have to leave," said D.C. bluntly, trying to sound masterful, but Freckles loved the instrument and refused to budge.

"Shhhhh," she said. "Listen! You can hear the little hammers being primed. It's almost ready. O God!"

Chagrined, D.C. turned to his friends. "What are we going to do with her?" he asked helplessly.

Lifting the trap door, Ivan suggested, "Leave her for the next tuner. Let's blow." And he speedily dropped out of sight.

It was good advice and Pearson and D.C. scooped up their belongings and scrambled after him.

As the three graduates bolted out of the front door of The College library for the last time the tower clock tolled twelve and the initial crashing chords of the carillon split the air atonally like dynamite.

CHAPTER 3

✦ A partial success, or Pearson is bagged.

Concord (N.H.). In the afternoon city the scattered puddles in the street were depthless mirrors under a bright sky and perfect drops skimmed single file down the air from the lifted awnings of smart shops.

> I'm telling you boy I'm in a sweat
> My legs don't work and my teeth don't set.

Newly opened windows poured their hearts out to music by Vivaldi, and in the tootsie-roll-brown patches beneath the plane trees, the squirm of the worm was seen in the land.

> De man say come can't stay a-way
> Take my hand and we will play.

A small round woman wearing black stockings and an apron boldly declaring, I'M READY IF YOU ARE, came out of the basement of a brownstone house and judged the sky.

> Wi de bomb A, bomb H, bomb P

She fondled two frail leaves at the top of a wispy, enormous stalk with all the gravity of dark eyes and dreamed of avocados.

And learn to die in-stan-tan-eous-ly.

Hurriedly, she picked up her plant and hugged it to her bosom.

The three boys stopped, their arms wrapped about each other's neck, and as she vanished with her secret into the underworld, they gave her a harmonized calypso coda.

> Wi de bomb A, bomb H, bomb P
> And learn to die in-stan-tan-eous-ly.

Laughing and rolling from one side of the street to the other, they continued their giddy progress through the city, and despite mixed reviews, it was a triumph of noblesse oblige with waves and smiles for the old, the crippled, and the female. Not even the Gothic sternness of the Wheelock Street induction center, as wreathed with gargoyles as a nightmare, could dilute their spirits, and without foreboding, they marched fearlessly into the dank gloom past flanking owls that winked at them dubiously.

When they entered his poster-cluttered office on the second floor, the Sergeant on duty was sitting on top of his desk blowing Southern birds craftily through the gap in his incisors. He was short, bull-necked, and everything above his eyebrows had a fresh, unused look about it. He swaggered up to his visitors, his shirttail almost free of his pants but his shoes still held in protective custody. Cocking his head to one side, he was either trying to recall something or it was an earache. Finally, his lips puckered maliciously and when he spoke it was all croon, and dips, and rises, and mock surprise like West Virginia.

"You boys are late. Yes sir, I do believe you lads are tardy. Now shame on you. College boys and all."

"It was r-r-r-raining," Pearson offered glumly. A melancholy modern product of a broken home and visual aids, he wearily raised the large manila envelope he was carrying over his head and extended the palm of his other hand heavenward by way of illustration.

"And you didn't want to get your b-b-booties wet. Eh?"

Sensitive about his stammer, Pearson loathed the Yahoo. He turned to Ivan who stood off by himself in a corner of the room running his finger down the crease in the wall like a fastidious housekeeper and said spitefully, "He's so damned s-smart; I w-w-wonder how come they never m-made him a civilian."

The Sergeant, mirroring art, drew himself up into a poster attitude and sneered, "Listen, boy, cut the crap. I'm a *professional* soldier. Now you three—" The Sergeant's eyes, small vacant lots, sloped in the direction of the corner where Ivan, with legs and arms tightly crossed and a face reddened by the strain of his effort, was now trying to become one with the architecture.

Sensing danger, the Sergeant rushed to the front and, struggling, finally managed to turn the muscular Ivan about. "Now you just, you just cut that out," he admonished as he caught his breath. "This isn't going to hurt a bit. Besides," he added confidentially, nudging the conscientious objector, "I've seen beards a lot longer than yours try to beat the system and, believe me, you ain't going to make it. So why don't you just relax and be a good boy?"

Ivan, protected by the moat of his will, stood with his head bowed and thoughtfully said nothing.

"My dear Sergeant," D.C. intervened, placing the book he held under his arm and sidling up to the suspicious soldier. From the heights, he smiled down on the black fuzz camouflaging military intelligence. Bending over until their eyeballs were almost touching, he whispered ingratiatingly, "Aw, come on, you old sweet peter you."

Taking one step backward, the Sergeant carefully hooked his pudgy thumbs into his khaki belt and screamed, "KISS MY FILBERT!"

"Grand. I knew you'd see it my way, Sarge."

"Listen," the Sergeant whistled, his face black, his insides clotted with lunch. "Listen. You three are going to like the Army just fine. First, you do like I say. Hear? You just move your asses inside and drop your pants like good little boys. Now get the hell out of here. Move!"

"All right, Sarge," D.C. said, grabbing Ivan's unwilling hand and pulling him toward the door leading to the adjoining examination rooms. "But remember," he cried as they left, "without love it means nothing."

"You, too," shouted the angry soldier. "Move!" A violent shove sent the fragile Pearson flying after them, and the Sergeant slammed the door on his tormentors with the ruthless finality of judgment.

On the other side of the door, the three boys found themselves in what must have once been a gymnasium. It had been partitioned off into a maze of cubicles by white beaverboard walls that fell far short of the ceiling and established the public nature of the privacy they afforded in the manner of institutional bathrooms. The windows, long scars in the scabrous walls, were boarded up, and the only light came from widely spaced bulbs hanging half-way down from the ceiling on tentacular extension cords. The floors were covered with linoleum tiles counterfeiting marble and exuded a smell of ammonia that saturated the air.

Seated on wooden benches, the boys removed their clothes in cold blood and placed them in the provided receptacles, wire baskets to which clung the aura of last personal effects. Each of them seemed surprised and absorbed by the familiar articles piled before him. Indistinct voices could be heard coming from some-where in the maze, but they only accentuated the stillness. Reach-ing into the inside pocket of his neatly folded Norfolk, D.C. removed an envelope-size folder and held it out for his friends to see. Annoyed when they failed to look up, he threw back his well-shaped head and let loose with two tremendous foghorn blasts that shot to the ceiling, rumbled in and out of the rafters, and slowly died away.

"Just exactly what do you think you're doing?" grimly in-quired a thin-lipped man in the doorway, but it was hardly a question. His face, browned and bony, might have served as the figurehead of an eighteenth-century New England whaler called "No Nonsense," and the close-cropped gray hair on his skull bristled like barbed wire.

"D-Don't look at me," Pearson defended himself. "I w-w-wasn't doing anything."

Ignoring him, the man demanded, "What was that loud noise I heard?"

"So he crepitated," D.C. said nonchalantly, as if nothing short of a Bach cantata could win his admiration. "Big deal."

His voice ominously controlled, the intruder stood tight-kneed with all of his buttons closed and pointing to an overturned basket on the floor said, "Do you realize the penalty for tampering with government property is quite severe? . . . Let me further call to your attention that failure to report promptly at the assigned time upon receipt of an induction directive is punishable by either fine, imprisonment, or, in certain deserving cases, both. You're extremely fortunate that another doctor and myself happen to have remained late. However, should we have any further difficulty with you, I intend to see that you find yourselves among the deserving. Clear?"

"A window," replied D.C.

"Now take off your underwear and follow me."

The chastened candidates divested themselves of their last link with civilization and filed slowly into the adjoining room like mourners at a nudist colony.

"Come in, come in," called the doctor irritably. He picked up a clipboard and went over to a scale that occupied a niche between two glass-fronted white cabinets containing empty cream bottles. "Causley," he read off the top paper on his clipboard. "Which of you is Causley?"

Pearson, guilty of countless minor infractions in the backcourt of his youth, raised his hand instinctively.

"All right, step up."

As Pearson approached the scale, the doctor ran his eye over him and moved the large indicator from 150 to 100. "Whatever that is in your hand, get rid of it," he ordered.

"But these are my l-letters," he protested. Mounting the scale, Pearson opened the winged clasp on his envelope and withdrew a sheaf of papers neatly stapled together. "Th-They explain my c-c-c-c—"

"In good time," the doctor cut him off. "Now I want to weigh you."

"But it's unnecessary. I'm s-sick. Nine out of t-t-t-ten eminent d-doctors agree."

"Put those away," the doctor commanded.

"B-B-But . . ." Pearson was worried. Fumbling, he groped in his envelope and withdrew a passport-size negative which he held out uncertainly. "My lungs," he explained, and dropped his head as if humiliated by the prospect.

Without a word, the doctor snapped up all of the candidate's credentials and threw them down viciously on his desk. "If you think you can sway me, young man, you're sadly mistaken."

Frustrated at not being able to present his evidence, Pearson whined, "M-M-My f-father happens to be one of the l-leading ob-ob-ob-obstetricians in the country, for your information."

The unsmiling doctor closed his ears and went about his business as unruffled as a nail. He tapped the small indicator of the scale surely into place and with supreme concentration made a modest note on his clipboard.

"And m-my f-father says I'm not w-well. He's always said it. I'm a c-c-chronic bronchial asthmatic for one."

"Turn around." Although he had already taken the measure of his man, the doctor raised the beam to comply with regulations.

"And p-p-p-pernicious anemia. I've got that, too. L-Look at me. I'm not Army m-material. You need something better. Why st-st-stint?"

"Step down. Storch next."

"You're m-m-making allowances," screamed Pearson, burning with injustice.

"Storch," repeated the doctor, as crisp and cool as a frozen green bean. "Are you Storch?"

"Who?" said D.C. playfully, but the doctor would have none of it.

"All right, Storch," he peeved. "I give up. Where are you?"

No answer.

"Come on, Storch. I have no time for games."

Still no answer. But behind him he heard the rustle of bedding.

"Storch, what are you doing there?" asked the stunned doctor, who could see very well what Storch was doing there. Having quietly slipped beneath the examination table unnoticed, Ivan had pulled out the tucked in ends of the sheet that covered it and skillfully fashioned a tent in which he sat like a bivouacked Arabian monarch satisfying his needs with the eccentric abandon of royalty.

"Are you crazy, Storch? Defecating on government property! Get out of there at once," the upset doctor shouted, and reaching under the sheet, he grabbed a naked leg and tugged, and pulled, and tugged again. Finally winded, he turned to the tall boy who stood over him watching his efforts with unmasked skepticism. "Don't just stand there, you. Help me!"

"All right," D.C. condescended, removing his hands from his hips and reluctantly taking a leg. "But you people have no regard for privacy."

"Shut up and pull," insisted the doctor, losing his temper. "Now together, one, two, three, pull; one, two, three, P–U–L–L–L!"

Sitting upright, Ivan made a sudden dramatic appearance from under the sheet and slid smoothly across the linoleum to the middle of the room where he came to a full stop. Although he stroked his beard with the pure innocence of fresh laundry, the trail led unmistakably to him. His locomotion, however, had been so wonderful that even the doctor felt a sense of loss in its cessation, and it was with a touch of real sadness that he said, "Up, Storch. Up."

Ivan did as he was told, but slowly.

From a slotted pink cardboard box on his desk, the doctor removed a handful of tissues and presented them to the guilty party. "Wipe that mess up."

Ivan gazed down at the white objects in his hand as if they were nesting swans.

"Never mind," the doctor decided abruptly, snatching the tissues away from him in a wad and throwing them in the direction of a surprised Pearson.

"B-But I c-can't stand unpleasant smells."

"Neither can I," the doctor agreed. "So get busy." Pleased with himself, he took the hulking Ivan by the hand and led him gently to the altar. "Storch, I want you to step up on this scale."

Storch stepped up.

"Turn around, Storch."

Storch turned around.

"All right, Storch, you may step down."

He did that, too, and waited catatonically for someone to push another button.

The doctor meanwhile made his entries in the appropriate nooks and crannies of the candidate's application form, and then, as he glanced casually over the information already on it, his eye fell on something that was, *mutatis mutandis,* as unsettling as Sodom to Lot's wife.

"Just a minute," he cried loudly, and placed a restraining hand on the shoulder of the motionless boy. "You know, Storch," he confided good-naturedly, "we get all types of oddballs down here—imbeciles, morons, idiots, cretins, Mongoloids, and Kallikakian drivelers. But you're not like that. You're a bright boy. In fact, from the intelligence scores listed for you here, I would say that you are a very bright boy, indeed. Come on, what's the trouble, son?" the doctor inquired, his tone compounded of equal parts of such simples as honey, confectioners' sugar, intellectual snobbism, and gypsy violins. "Aren't you feeling well?"

The doctor's paternalism might possibly have won him converts among the other two boys, but his sympathetic words scraped across the bearded youth's nervous system like sandpaper. Ivan, an orphan both by fate and inclination, merely shook his head to indicate that everything on the inside of the capsule was go, and placing a small glob of saliva on the floor near his right heel, he proceeded to clean one square of imitation-marble linoleum tile.

"For your information, Storch, this isn't Hollywood. If you've got genuine emotional problems tell the psychiatrist when you speak to him and stop fouling up the floor with your leavings. Believe me, I'm only interested in your body, and it looks 1-A to me. Now you and your sick friend each take one of those bottles from the shelf and fill it up for me in the next room. Widdemore, next!"

When the doctor finished with him, D.C. appeared headachey and out of sorts. "I knew it," he groaned. "I've put on weight. Doctor, tell me honestly, do you think I've become grotesquely misshapen." He looked down at his buttocks and with two fingers gathered together whatever he could find, producing something the color and shape of a blister. "Don't spare me, doctor. I want the truth." It was Bette Davis, flanked by matching oxygen tanks and gloom as far as the eye could see.

"I have no idea," the doctor said dryly. He walked to the examination table and, bending down, picked up something. "Does this belong to you?"

"It's mine," said D.C., and rushed over to claim his property.

"Aren't you a bit old for this sort of thing?"

"What's the matter with fairy tales?" D.C. asked haughtily. "They happen to be the only viable literary form of our time. They represent the mythology of sanity in a fall-out world and a pox on Dr. Johnson's toe. Why, do you realize that in this country there are people everywhere huddled in two-dimensional simplicity within a cartoon square bounded by science, pragmatism, realism, and liberalism who are so emotionally cozy that they're dying of right angles? Did you realize *that*?"

"I should think they'd be more appropriate for children," sneered the doctor.

"For *your* information these happen to be by Oscar Wilde."

"The actor?"

"Oh, my God," D.C. cried, and threw up his hands. "Never mind. May I have my book back please?"

"Here. Get rid of it. Just take a bottle and get out of my sight."

D.C. was sorry that he hadn't worn the scarf after all.

The examination rooms were like railway cars with doors at either end; so it wasn't difficult to explain how shortly thereafter the doctor managed to sneak up malevolently behind them.

"No talking in here. That means you." The doctor directed their attention to the red signs that covered the metal trough running the length of one wall and the walls themselves. In fact, silence was encouraged on every vertical surface in the room by means of stickers, posters, printed signs, mimeographed notices, and woodcuts. The authorities, convinced that *pissoirs* operated very much like barber shops in their ability to stimulate conversation, were taking no chances.

"What's this?" Holding Pearson's bottle up to the light, the doctor scowled. The liquid inside was as clear and colorless as water.

"You s-see, I t-told you I'm sick."

The doctor sniffed. It was as odorless as water.

D.C. drew near and inquired anxiously, "Is it serious?"

"Stand back," cried the doctor, his rear end shaking in the face of challenge. Carefully he put one finger in and tasted it. His eyes narrowed like a cat choking on fur balls. "Water!" he announced.

"All you said was f-f-fill it up." Pearson shrugged his shoulders defensively. "So I filled it up. What's so t-terrible?"

"I don't care what I said. You knew exactly what I meant. Now take this bottle and fill it properly. The rest of you come with me." The doctor's jaw shot forward like a cantilevered balcony as he stalked off. Passing through several rooms crammed with spotless sinks and tongue depressors, he came to rest unexpectedly in one that was completely empty.

"Quiet. No talking. Storch, behind the yellow line and cover your right eye." The doctor turned on a light switch and a string-supported chart suddenly fell through a slot in the ceiling and jiggled puppet-like before the impassive left eye of Ivan Storch. "Read the top line, please."

Crouched behind the yellow stripe with his knees bent like a foul-shooter, Ivan strained. Slowly, with the painstaking deliberation of a murderer, he destroyed the first three letters and was grimly contemplating his next victim before the doctor's spirits were finally dashed.

"Stop it, stop it!" he cried, and approached Ivan menacingly. Although the aggressor was tightly knit, he was no match for the sturdy Storch, and having made this annoying discovery, like a father with a wayward son of adult proportions, he took the prudent course. "Frankly, I'm worried about you, Storch," he revealed, almost with tenderness. "That's a very bad eye you have there. Usually in a wanderer there's some vision but this doesn't seem to be true in your case. Do you have glasses?"

Averting the left side of his face in anger, the bearded Ivan said only, "Yes."

"Well, where are they?" inquired the doctor, not unkindly.

"There's nothing wrong with the other one."

"I don't care about that just now. I asked you where your glasses are."

"My right eye is fine. I'll read with my right eye," Ivan decided and, covering his left, he turned to face the chart.

"Storch, I want to know where your glasses are this minute," the doctor insisted shrilly as Ivan, monotonically, began to call off the letters one after the other.

"Try his pockets," D.C. advised, pointing to his friend's naked flanks, as hairless as mirrors.

"I didn't ask you. Keep your damn mouth closed," the doctor screamed. "And you shut up!" He slashed out at the beard like a razor, but Ivan was oblivious. He read on as though interested in the story, and only when he reached the last letter of the last line did he allow himself to drop his hand and expose his vanity. The silence that followed might have been something thrown on a potter's wheel.

At last, the doctor lifted his clipboard and made his mark. "Storch," he announced, his thin lips barely parting, "twenty-twenty. You're next, Causley."

The boys said little after that. But if their case seemed hopeless, they gave no indication that they intended to be good losers. Yet through it all, the doctor kept his head. He appeared now to be possessed of a new and nobler vision and hurried his charges from room to room. When the examination was finally over, he left them naked, breathless, dissatisfied, and disappeared behind a door marked "private." The boys dropped down limply on a bench. Placing their elbows on their knees, they leaned forward and toppled into the guilty silence of the losing side.

When the door opened again, a little elderly man came out carrying an open copy of *The New York Times*. He wore no jacket, and his white shirt—sleeves rolled to the elbow, open at the neck, and billowing about him in all directions—could have passed for a skimpy toga. There was a pink softness about every part of his small body, and even though his head was bald, it was so well fleshed that it sat on his shoulders like a ball of ice cream. He folded his paper and, looking up with a smile that Ben Adhem's angel might have envied, announced softly, "I'm Trautman, the psychiatrist. Who's first?"

Pearson leaped to his feet. "I'm s-s-s-saved!" he shouted, and sped to the door.

When the coast was clear, D.C. pounded his bearded friend on the back affectionately and whispered, "Don't fight it, Iv baby. Glad tidings from Zion."

But Ivan, expressionless, merely rubbed his large hands together and waited developments. They were not long in coming. In less time than it takes to peel a banana, almost as if he had entered a revolving door, Pearson was back, dazed and shaken, his head lobbing gloomily from side to side, on his lips a pathetic smile.

"Pigeon, what happened?" exclaimed D.C. amazed. He took his friend around and led him to the bench. "What did he say to you?"

"Next, if you please," called Dr. Trautman gently. He stood in the doorway beaming, Santa Claus waking a particularly good child for a personal interview.

Bewildered, D.C. walked hesitantly toward the doctor. But picking up his defenses, he minced the last few steps and entered the office with an admission. "I know I'm different from other lads, doctor. I've known it ever since elementary school and my first potholder. But you must take me. All those lovely boys in caramel pants. I simply will not be denied."

"Don't excite yourself needlessly," was Dr. Trautman's professional advice, and he closed the door behind them.

The boys left outside on the bench sat insulated from one another, two ice cubes in a freezing tray. Pearson shifted about uneasily in his misery and gave several little nervous coughs that fell somewhere between preludial throat clearing and sobs, but Ivan kept his eye fixed on the main chance and said nothing. Shivering involuntarily, he picked up first one bare foot and then the other and rubbed at them hard with both hands as if trying to restore life. But apparently no sooner had he revived his left foot than his right one began to fade for, like a conscientious lifeguard confronted by two unconscious victims, he went from one to the other with quickening desperation until, by the time the doctor's door had once more opened, he had worked himself up into a frenzy of kinetic activity.

Widdemore came forth haltingly with a face as barren and white as an empty bathtub. "Wait!" he cried, turning back to the cherubic Dr. Trautman. "I forgot to tell you. I'm an aggressive one. A love tiger, doctor, a TIGER! I stop at nothing. A 'no' to me is hardly more than coquetry. Are you *absolutely* certain they wouldn't mind someone like me in the shower room?"

Dr. Trautman reached up and patted D.C. on his forearm with a rabbinical air. "Believe me, my boy," he comforted, his Wedgwood-blue eyes twinkling benignly, "your happiness is my first concern. Don't worry. You'll fit in beautifully. All right, son," he nodded at the agitated Ivan, "I'll take care of you now."

There was nothing inside the office to suggest a tenant, other than one folded copy of *The New York Times* on a gray metal desk top and two colored photographs of Impressionist paintings Scotch-taped to the wall. The reproductions looked more alike than Coca-Cola bottles except that where there was land in one there was water in the other, but to Ivan, staring dumbly at them, they seemed to have the wistfully compelling fascination of travel posters.

"Do sit down." Dr. Trautman was all smiles as he settled himself behind the desk and waved his unheeding guest to a chair. "Please," he insisted quietly, observing the motionless figure with interest, "as a favor to me."

Ivan came over one foot at a time and slumped down into the chair, his thick arms swaddling his chest protectively.

Dr. Trautman, who played his hands like an instrument, turned his palms up and said, "See, isn't that better?"

It was the gesture of a magician, and Ivan watched closely for the surprise to follow.

"Now, don't tell me, let me guess. You're Ivan Storch, aren't you?"

Ivan's eyes crouched behind his beard in suspicion.

"Why be ashamed? It's a nice name." Dr. Trautman sat back, twirled his thumbs two or three times, and admired it. "I see you're wondering how it happens I'm acquainted with you. No mystery. My colleague, Dr. Bentley, told me all about you. He thinks you're an unusual young man."

Uncertain whether or not this was good news, Ivan shut his sphincters like drawers containing potentially incriminating evidence.

"Relax, Ivan. No one's going to hurt a big boy like you. You're going home."

Ivan looked up incredulously.

"My word is my bond," said the doctor happily, raising his right hand. He got up and came around to where Ivan was sitting. "And now that it's all over, tell me, just between the two of us, how come a smart boy like you doesn't want to do the right thing by his Uncle Sam?" Dr. Trautman laughed and poked at his visitor's beard good-naturedly with his index finger.

Whether it was the strain he had been under, the question asked, or the forced intimacy, he was afterward never able to determine, but confronted by the proximity of Dr. Trautman's finger, Ivan decided to take no chances and bit it.

Like a curious ink blot, the outlines of an agonized expression began to take shape on Dr. Trautman's face. His eyes widened to twice their normal size, and his mouth formed a perfect fathomless o. Ivan watched in fascination as the doctor opened the cocoon of his left hand to estimate the damage. Bent forward in their concentration, they might have been two scientists in search of truth. But Dr. Trautman's belated screams put an end to dispassionate inquiry. Ivan had not expected so much noise in the little man.

Suddenly, the small, unventilated room was crowded with people in motion—clothed, naked, yelling, and falling over one another in barrel-of-fun confusion. The smell of perspiration mingled with the ammonia already in the air to form something the color of nightmare, miasmatic and dizzying. In spite of the oppressive closeness, the noisy jostling about the protagonists continued, but in the now calm eye of the center, Dr. Trautman silently regarded Ivan like a knife-wielding Abraham who had at last made up his mind.

"Atten-n-n-tion!"

At the unexpected command, the Sergeant, who had been gamely trying to raise his knee to the height of Widdemore's groin, pulled himself together with Pavlovian speed. The others, too, desisted, but out of curiosity rather than discipline. Casually removing his elbow from the vicinity of Dr. Bentley's floating ribs which he had hoped to set adrift, Pearson looked up into a disturbingly familiar face. The experience was an instinctively unpleasant one, and as soon as he had placed the huge, square-jawed officer as yesterday's herald, he knew why.

Although no longer wearing his ornately braided garrison cap, the Major, within the confines of the tiny overcrowded room and close up, seemed even larger than he had the day before on the speakers' platform.

"Who's responsible for this?" he bellowed. In his hand he carried a long cigarette-holder like a baton, and lifting it to his lips, he nibbled thoughtfully at the end waiting for someone to crack.

"Major Gibble," gushed Dr. Bentley, relieved. "I'm glad you're here. I can tell you exactly what happened. I saw everything." Ivan gave the doctor the look of a cross-examining prosecuting attorney.

"Yes, *everything*! From under there." He pointed triumphantly to the desk, the one hiding place the room afforded. "We're not quite as simple as you seem to think. Would you believe it, Major, this young barbarian actually tried to eat Dr. Trautman? Are you all right, Isidore?"

"It's nothing," Dr. Trautman said coolly, and placed his hands in his pockets.

Walking over, D.C. examined the narrow space under the desk in wonder. "The miserable sneak!"

"We have our methods," Dr. Bentley said with a toss of his head.

"If that's the way you people play," D.C. announced, strutting toward the door, "I'm going home. I abhor deception."

"At ease, lightfoot." Although Widdemore was quick, Major Gibble was quicker, and with two well-placed taps from his cigarette holder he brought his man down. "Not so fast. Is this one free to go, Dr. Bentley?"

"Yes. Let him go. He's of no use to us."

"You see," D.C. addressed the Major accusingly. Surprised at the turn of events, he collected himself and presented the doctors with a final word of encouragement. "I think you're doing the wise thing."

The sea-shell pink of Dr. Trautman's face turned menstrual red as he started in anger to protest his colleague's action, but he was cut off.

"Rheumatic," Dr. Bentley reported definitively, and laid his hand pledgewise across his chest. "He's a sick boy." His stiff, tanned face wrinkled up like a shoe and something like a smile twisted his lips.

"What's that?" D.C. called from the doorway, his voice caught in a downdraft of reality.

"You're a sick boy," the doctor repeated with relish. "You've got a weakened heart."

"You're joking."

"No."

"Oh, come on, you are so."

"Not in the least."

"You're trying to needle me." D.C. looked uneasily at Dr. Trautman for confirmation but saw only an anonymously sweet face immobilized by years of nondirective therapy. A frightening sight under the circumstances. "Is this your sadistic idea of fun and games?" he began to shout sardonically, forgetting his elfin role. "The medical profession's revenge for being awakened at four o'clock in the morning? Hippocrates' darlings collecting a bit of emotional small change on account? —You know, the good old med school cheer, 'Eeny meany miny mass, catch the patient by the ass.' Well you can tongue mine because I don't buy it!"

"I think you'd better go," Dr. Bentley warned, his cheeks in spasm, "before I lose my temper."

"You heard the doctor." Major Gibble pointed disdainfully to the door. "Off the premises, four-efnik! Scram, weak heart!"

"On your way, fairy," the Sergeant put in, and out of the side of his mouth added, "ho! ho!"

"Who asked you?" boomed Major Gibble. The Sergeant threw back his shoulders in instant contrition having been in the Army long enough to recognize the sound of Congolese thatched huts and Arctic igloos. "Well, now," the Major found no other challengers. "Al-l-l-right. You heard me, cripple, beat it."

D.C. realized that he had been ungrateful. Since the Major was happy with the diagnosis, why should he complain? Once in a sterner age there were heroes who cut off fingers, pierced ear drums, and crushed feet in order to protect what they believed in. All he had done was let them give him a rheumatic heart that was invisible to the naked eye. And even if Bentley were right (which was preposterous), it was still a bargain. Head down to hide his change of heart, the discharged veteran shuffled rheumatically off to freedom and would have walked right into the Major had not that officer thoughtfully stepped aside.

"Double time!" Major Gibble ordered in annoyance, the words rumbling darkly in the barrel of his throat.

Once Widdemore had been disposed of to his satisfaction, Dr. Bentley addressed the Major. "You're welcome to these two. I think this one in particular," he nodded toward Ivan, "will be ideal for jungle warfare. He's already something of an animal."

"Good. We'll slate him for guerrilla training in the Double Counter Insurgency Operation. Who knows, he may even be able to keep his beard. The New Army wants happy soldiers. Sergeant, make a note of it."

"Yes, sir."

"No, I'm sorry, Sumner," Dr. Trautman informed his colleague regretfully. "I'd like to be a sport about this but, in good conscience, I just can't let you have Storch."

"But why, Isidore, why? You know he's only putting on an act for our benefit."

"True. But who's to say how much of Marlon Brando really is Stanley Kowalski?" Trautman ran his hands nervously over his head puzzling it out and smiled at the answer. "*Me*," he said modestly, not without a hint of surprise. "Look, Sumner, your field is the body, and if you tell me that that tall, homosexual faker is sick, I can't very well call your professional judgment into question, now can I? But my work is the mind, so when I tell you that this poor boy is a troubled spirit, that there's something wrong with anyone so desperate that he'll even bite a stranger's finger, do me a similar courtesy and kindly don't interfere. You're not the only one who can exempt a candidate, you know."

Dr. Bentley took the little man by the shoulders and looked deep into his soft blue eyes. "You're angry, Isidore. You're angry because I let Widdemore go. That's it, isn't it?"

"Nothing of the kind," Dr. Trautman said petulantly. "Nonsense." He pulled himself free. "I advise you to see a psychiatrist, Storch. Good-bye."

Convinced that the scrappy little doctor was holding up his end superbly without assistance, Ivan saw no reason to join in the debate and disappeared out the door.

"You can't do this, Trautman." Dr. Bentley valued his own judgment with the unswervable faith of the Albigenses, and esteeming psychiatrists only slightly more than chiropractors, alchemists, and astrologers, he stared at his adversary horror-stricken. "That boy is as sane as you or me. Don't think for a minute I'm going to let you and your kind get away with something like this. I'll have your license for malpractice. Depend on it."

"*My* kind, *my* kind," Dr. Trautman's neck puffed up like a goiter. "Anti-Semite!" he cried contemptuously. "It's done."

"Gentlemen, gentlemen," broke in Major Gibble, stepping between the two, "this is no time for petty professional jealousies. While you two bicker over personalities, today, at this very minute, right now, yes, even now, the enemy's submarines are poking their periscopes through our bedroom windows at all we hold dear. And what are you doing about it? I ask you, would you like your little girl to marry a Russian?"

"She's married," Dr. Trautman reported stoically.

"Damn it! What kind of an attitude is that? Shame on you. I want to see a little of that Camp David spirit here, understand? Now, let's get cracking. What about this man?"

"Take him," Dr. Bentley said feverishly quick, and glared at the opposition.

Dr. Trautman thrust his hands in his pockets and, serenely indifferent, turned his back. "Who cares?" he decided, disengaged, his motor idling.

"But-But-But-But-But—" His confidence undermined by a history of final selection for the baseball, basketball, punchball, stickball, johnny-on-a-pony, and steal-the-white-flag competitions of a lifetime, Pearson gave up and fled.

"STOP THAT MAN!" the Major raged, and the chase was on. The pursuers sped through the maze like Keystone Cops, undaunted by closed doors and minor obstacles, passing rooms like telephone poles, racing headlong into the void. Separating, coming together, parabolic curves gone mad, they sprang breathlessly into the dressing room from two sides and cornered their man with one trouser leg still to be filled. Caught in the anomalous position of believing in nonviolence in a violent world, Pearson was trapped.

"You d-d-don't understand. I'm g-going to the Sorbonne. L-Look," Pearson said, dropping his pants and removing a small folder not unlike the one Widdemore had displayed earlier. "My t-ticket. I'm g-going to study medicine for my c-country."

"Save the carfare," exploded Major Gibble. "The New Army has a place for you. Remember," he smiled slyly, tipping his hand, "they also serve who only stand and fight. Sergeant, the flag!"

The Sergeant flew, genuinely in love with his work, and when he reappeared, glowing like a debutante, the stars and stripes streaming overhead and snapping awesomely at his prickly crew cut, a sudden patriotic fervor swept the room and salutes went up on every side. Only the unhappy Pearson, who was frantically trying to get into his pants, appeared unmoved by the ceremony.

"Never mind them. Place your right hand on the flag," Major Gibble directed.

"I w-warn you. I'll be home-home-homesick."

"The *flag*," the Major threatened.

Pearson grudgingly took a fistful of cloth but, unseen, held on to his self-respect with one hand. On his face there was the hurt look of a wronged man, of Satan collared by Michael in the Garden crying, "Who me?" of Iago telling Othello, "I coulda sworn she was a whore," of Eichmann turning raised eyes on his judge and asking, "6,000,000?"

"Now, repeat after me, 'I,' and your name."

The candidate turned white and mumbled, "I, P-Pearson Causley."

"Louder," the Sergeant shouted gleefully. "Louder."

" 'Of free mind and body.' "

" 'Of free m-mind and b-b-body . . .' "

CHAPTER 4

❧ Schlemovitz takes America to heart and our heroes leave it.

Some two hundred miles south of Concord, two hundred miles laden with wicker baskets, hooked rugs, local produce, antiques, two hundred miles dying of textile mills, pipe-rack living, neighborliness, two hundred miles struggling in split-levels on ball bearings, from one to ten lanes, sounds, ways of looking at a blackguard, south two hundred miles lies the metropolis. And somewhere in one of the remotest sections of New York City beyond urban renewal and the end of the line, unmapped and impossible to reach by direct dialing, hangs the peeling sign of Schlemovitz's Sans Souci. A mausoleum harboring the remnants of a lifetime and smelling of old school supplies gone bad, a coffin stuffed with two Schlemovitzes, three stools, and a Hamilton Beach mixer, no cold steel and glass put-up job but a cluttered closet in which the owners had turned white along with the chocolate they sold, the Sans Souci had the look of a candy store that had been lived in. Days, nights, weekends, holidays, it was never closed, never but for an hour on May 1st when Mr. Schlemovitz, under the guise of Loyalty, turned the public away from his threshold for a brief period of private devotion to his radical past. Habit and a room in the rear, rather than a rapacious nature, had produced the S.O.D.P. (SCHLEMOVITZ OPEN DOOR POLICY), for in truth Mr. Schlemovitz was as untouched by the profit motive as a Trappist in his cell. If he was ambitious at all, if he carried a dream bagged on his back as lightly as one of Chagall's elderly fliers, it was for his son. The way some men want college presidents and dentists, more than anything else Schlemovitz wanted a labor organizer in the family, but being a free thinker, he could only pass the word along and keep his fingers crossed. Mrs. Schlemovitz, for her part, was ready to settle for the president of a dental college, though she held her tongue out of deference to her husband. Reduced to a worried look and body English in order to ease her son into the vocational pocket of her choice, Mrs. Schlemovitz played a waiting game. But the boy's appearances in the store had become so rare as to rank him with the whooping crane for out-and-out scarcity, and now he was about to go, perhaps forever, leaving them nothing but Sans Souci, which he had brought back at the end of his very first year in the Ivy League and they had promptly hung above their door in pride and wonder.

Standing in her customary place behind the small, antiquated one-spigot fountain, which held the same revered place in the refreshment industry that Spads and Fokkers occupied in aviation and was known familiarly in the trade as the last of the single seltzers, Mrs. Schlemovitz dispensed a chocolate malted to a glum little rat-faced girl wearing a tee shirt, shorts, and blue sneakers that had been cut off at the toes but seemed to have as many lives as a cat. Dressed à la mode for June, the rat-faced kid didn't seem to mind the cold at all as she strawed up her malted, although inside the gloomy Sans Souci there was really only one season and that one winter. Mrs. Schlemovitz, a tough old bird, wiry and keen on survival, wore heavy shoes, heavy socks, heavy underwear, heavy skirts, and heavy sweaters, the lot, all this insulation capped by a heavy apron strung around her neck, so that at the end of any given day it would be safe to say that her clothing probably took more out of her than the work. Her dark gray hair was pulled straight back and tied in a bun at the nape of her neck, and her thin face bore the scars of a youthful beauty. With the dry spots on her voluminous apron she wiped the counter, the Hamilton Beach and its chocolate spray, the metal straw container, her hands, and then casually turned to her husband and asked, "Well?"—as if a decision might be forthcoming.

Schlemovitz, who pondered everything as if it required a signature, turned the page of his newspaper and groaned. He sat on a low stool behind the cigar counter at the front of the store with the strained, preoccupied face peculiar to large, athletic men who have known and lived with constipation. A gray shirt buttoned to the neck, a brown cardigan sweater, a gleaming black suit that had once marked his intellectual aspirations but was still found to be serviceable, set the scene for a marvelous black felt, wide ribboned and upbrimmed, darkly awesome in its indoor authority, beneath which two tufts of white hair sprung out above his ears giving wings to his imagination. The cigarette that was always in his mouth and puffed from one end to the other, no hands, was like a thermometer that registered his emotional temperature, and just now Schlemovitz seemed to be reaching fever pitch. A burner incensed, he disappeared in an angry cloud of smoke, only the furious rattling of a newspaper indicating that he was still on the job. Beneath a trinity of cutouts tacked to the wall behind—Einstein in his sweatshirt, La Guardia at the comics, and (a lover of beauty) Man of War in the blue grass of retirement —Schlemovitz seethed.

"Gray hairs, and you never learn," he told himself passionately, but in such a quiet voice that he had to bend over to hear. "Idiot . . . you're a lover. You want to sit on a park bench with the world in your arms. HA! But what about the splinters? Believe me, Schlemovitz, it's a dung heap. Listen."

His wife, either sensing what was coming or feeling herself an intruder, turned away and opening a napkin filled it with a dozen chocolate-covered, long-stemmed cherries (sweets to the sweet) destined for foreign ports.

" 'Once more Julius Lunt has done the impossible,' " read the candy-store proprietor, squeezing the words like toothpaste out of the side of his mouth, his large face flushed with excitement.

" 'Lunt, well known in gangland as THE RED SHARK because of his weakness for red carnations, has again succeeded in putting one over on the big domes of the big town. This time playing a doctor, he cleverly swindled his way into the brand-new Lebanon Hospital. Badly understaffed, they let him remove a half-dozen appendixes, two gall bladders, and a kidney, before getting around to his ID. An administration official at the hospital commented, "Without question, one of the reasons for the high cost of medical care today is the shortage of trained doctors." When asked for a statement at her home where she is *still* convalescing, Miss Rita Gooseberry, one of his former patients, had this to say, "I'm glad it's out!" The SHARK is being held under maximum security pending trial for operating without a license.' "

The reader raised eyes pale beyond reason, crying, "Schlemovitz, where are we going?"

"Balls!" the rat-faced kid observed, and replacing the straw in her mouth sucked wind.

"You think that's all, Schlemovitz my friend. A piss in the ocean. Take off the rose-colored glasses and live. Listen.

" 'The DEPRAVED Monster Killer was nearly apprehended early today by a mounted policeman as he attacked his seventeenth victim. Again the object of his crime was a TEEN-AGE GIRL wearing an ankle bracelet. Mothers are urged to forbid their daughters to wear such ornaments until the FIEND is caught.

" 'Patrolman Doyle, who stumbled on the attempted CRIME at 2 A.M. while making his regular tour of duty on the upper West Side, was unable to identify the criminal because of the early morning hour. He reported that his suspicions were first aroused when he heard the CLANK of the tire CHAINS the MONSTER always uses to GARROTE his victims. Patrolman Doyle was unhurt in the encounter, but his horse, Pegasus, received a nasty GASH IN THE CHEST that might have been made with a fork. Now, in addition to checking automobile supply stores, bilingual policemen are pursuing this new development by keeping a close watch on all restaurants and luncheonettes in the predominantly PUERTO RICAN neighborhood.'

"Ha! There it is," fumed the speaker, smashing the picture of the wounded animal with the back of his hand. "Look inside the package, citizen. America has gift-wrapped your brains."

The rat-faced kid was not to be ignored. "Balls!" she repeated feelingly.

"It's getting late, Papa," Mrs. Schlemovitz gently advised her husband, while bending over and easing the wrapped cherries into a shopping bag that had been loaded as attentively as a time capsule.

"Remember the Alamo, Schlemovitz. Self-deception is for the weak. Look here . . .

" 'Preliminary reports from the Committee investigating the unfortunate collapse of the Ocean Street School, which luckily occurred on a Sunday and resulted in only one death, the janitor, Carl Manheim, sixty-two, indicate that the cement used contained over 82 per cent water. A spokesman for the company that did the work on the building, Fidelity Contruction, whose president, John McLeod, is nephew of the popular Senator, hotly denies the charge, accusing the school board of "politics, irresponsible innuendo, character assassination, muckraking, slander, calumny, ugly cynicism, and behavior unbecoming gentlemen." Mr. McLeod, however, said only that he is eager to be fair to all parties and has refused to comment prematurely, preferring to wait until the final report's more balanced picture is presented.' "

The reader rose in triumph over the still writhing carcass of his illusions. "Now do you believe me, meddler? Curb your dog. Keep off the grass. No trespassing. Don't feed the animals. Wrongs only. It's worse than even I thought, Schlemovitz. Robin Hood has been banned from the public libraries of a thousand Midwestern cities. Pack your trunk and get out before it's too late. . . . Forget your trunk, drop everything and run!"

Removing her apron, Mrs. Schlemovitz pulled her skinny self together in the store mirror angled to protect portable merchandise and pleaded, "Answer me, Papa, yes or no."

"The welcome mat is out. Our address is known. What else? Let the boy live his own life says Schlemovitz."

The rat-faced kid threw down her straw like a gauntlet. "Who you kidding? Red sharks! Like, didn't you ever make the 3-R scene, dad?"

Mrs. Schlemovitz abandoned her toilet and put her anger where it would do the most good. "Pay up, hoodlum, and get out in the sunshine."

"Don't push, Mrs. S," warned the rat-faced kid. Pulling up her shorts like a gun belt, she sauntered over to the magazine rack, withdrew a comic book, and waved it disrespectfully under the outraged nose of the proprietress. "I'm temporarily complicated," she admitted airily. "Cuff the lot."

An old sport, Mrs. Schlemovitz picked off the magazine like a line drive. "*Hot Love* is for cash only, Konikowski. Your father will hear of this."

A shadow passed over Miss Konikowski's heart. Thrown objects —shoes, plates, bottles, belts, TV dinners—marinated in her memory. Soberly she asked, "Don't you have any feelings? . . . What's the matter with you anyway? My father is a sick man."

"Look out for the young," moaned Schlemovitz with a dying fall, as he sank down on his stool. "Take care, the stink of old failure is blowing through the noses of the Boy Scouts of America. Let them be like peppermints, green under glass. Reflect, Woman, our children are our strength."

"Cash, Konikowski, and not another word."

At bay, the little girl tapped the commercially weaker vessel, but Schlemovitz was unavailable for consultation. He sat crushing his newspaper into a ball, reducing the world to lifesize, pursuing lost causes through the endless subterranean channels of yet, absent without leave, gone.

Trapped like a rat, sneering like Malvolio, Konikowski dug down and paid up.

"Call again, sweetheart," invited the proprietress, dropping the change into a cigar box, but Konikowski lingered in the hope of taking it out in merchandise. Mrs. Schlemovitz took up her shopping bag, ran her fingers lightly over the contents, and announced, "I'm ready, Papa."

Her husband coughed once, but there were no other symptoms.

Worried, Mrs. Schlemovitz appealed to a higher court. "He *needs* you, Papa. You saw the letter. Do you think I'm asking for myself?"

"The letter has been received and noted. Yet . . ."—and here the old man dropped the ball from his hands and straightened his back proudly—"Schlemovitz is *not* a chocolate bar. Send the package. Don't send me."

"What's wrong if he wants a little sweets?"

"Send the package, Woman, and get out of my eardrum."

"I only want to see that he's well with my own eyes. Is that being selfish . . . ? Answer me, Papa."

Schlemovitz paused to light another cigarette. "Sometimes," he said, "kissing is possible only at a distance. Send it."

"You don't remember how different it is over there. What will be when they see all of the beautiful little buttons on his shirt collars! —*anything* might happen. Please, Papa," begged Mrs. Schlemovitz, "just once before he leaves."

"Up, down, on both sides and in between, people are people, and that's the *ding an sich* of it. Don't worry, Lovely—he'll survive."

"But Papa!"

"My final word."

Mrs. Schlemovitz wrapped her arms about the shopping bag as if it had received some nameless injury and hid her face in its contents, but her husband was too old a campaigner to be taken in by the strategy of defeat. New tactics were called for, and so stiffening her resistance, the resourceful Mrs. Schlemovitz was preparing to adopt a scorched earth policy when she first smelled the smoke.

"Mr. Schlemovitz!" she called, her face swollen with fear. "Is that you?" But her husband, a man of his final word, puffed on, incommunicado.

Suddenly, a blaze of light shot up from the magazine rack, and even though Konikowski had expected something of her match, she was not unimpressed. Awed by the beauty of her anger, fascinated by its color and scope, mesmerized by its independent existence, the rat-faced artist lingered over her work innocent of the speed of the fuse. Konikowski stared unbelievingly as old, brittle, juiceless copies of *Popular Astronomy, Masses and Mainstream, Popular Mechanics, I. F. Stone's Weekly,* and the *Reader's Digest* exploded in the air, one after the other in quick succession, and humbled by the magnitude of her achievement, she neglected the flames snapping eagerly at her shorts like hungry puppies. Konikowski screamed. Her feet carried her in a meaningless circle. Her hands jerked. Her eyes blinked incessantly like a tilted doll. She tripped, stumbled, lurched, fell—crackling to the floor.

"HELP! HELP!" shrieked Mrs. Schlemovitz, and grabbing up her sealskin coat and hugging her shopping bag, she stood rooted to the spot, immobile, bemused, as if she had forgotten what came next. Her mouth, opening and closing, worked in spasms, moving with a terrific stillness, producing finally only a desperate and whispered, "help . . ."

There was something. Schlemovitz seemed to listen for a long time before identifying it as a human voice, a cry of distress. He got up and looked around and on every side he saw the flames of corruption. He was not surprised. Throwing his cigarette to the winds, Schlemovitz turned his back to the fire and shouted, "Every man for himself!" and ran, but it was impossible to reason with a lunatic. Wheeling about, the madman darted toward the flames. A Prometheus unbound, he plucked the coat from his wife, draped it over the burning child, rolled her up like a winter rug, tossed her on to his shoulder, clutched his wife by the back of her astonished neck, and, with Wagnerian sirens splashing about them, the blackened trio emerged from the burning building.

A cheer went up from the crowd that had quickly gathered on the other side of the street, and only determined policework held their enthusiasm in check.

"You're a hero," said a youthful doctor approvingly, and with his attendant threw the child into the waiting ambulance.

Schlemovitz blinked in the limelight. "An ass, an ass," he repeated disconsolately.

The doctor chalked it up to shock and reassured him, "Don't worry. She'll be all right."

"She should burn in hell over a low flame with a red-hot pepper up her hole!" cried Mrs. Schlemovitz bitterly. Startled to find that she had regained her tongue, she tried to do as well by her coat and yanked the sealskin out of the ambulance. She shook it, beat it, caressed it, but there was no sign of life, nothing. Its once dark sleek surface that had mirrored a world of young men in tight pants who spoke in clever foreign accents of Chopin and golden thighs was reduced to a few shriveled patches like some poorly tended lawn in late August, and the smell of death hovered over the land. Unable to catch her breath, Mrs. Schlemovitz sank down to the ground and wept in gasps.

Since coming to New York to do his internship, the doctor—a country boy with an antiseptic eye—had trained himself to look upon the most grotesque abominations clinically, but he was still tender enough to be threatened by unnatural parents. Monsters . . . they're monsters, he thought—even if it was a change-of-life baby. "You," he said curtly to the hero. "Let me see your hands."

With limp wrists, Schlemovitz extended the burnt offerings.

The doctor pounced upon them roughly and the gauze flew. "It'll be a while before you lay a hand on her again," he said with satisfaction, when the job was done. "Now, get out of my sight."

Mittened in white, the weary battler dropped down beside his wife on the pavement and placed his arm protectively around her shoulders. "Schlemovitz," he said softly, his great black hat weaving from side to side like some stray lobster pot drifting aimlessly over obscure and fathomless seas, "is this life possible for a human being? Answer me. No more stalling. Sixty years of waiting is not exactly putting the screws on. Out with it." Unable to reach his handkerchief, Schlemovitz wiped his nose with the back of a bandaged hand and, taking a deep breath, sighed. "You're right," he admitted, "it might be better."

"Mr. Schlemovitz!" came a muffled cry from somewhere in the crowd. "Excuse me . . . sorry . . . a thousand pardons, Madam. Mr. Schlemovitz!" A man wearing a striped seersucker suit with a red bow tie could be seen fighting his way through the ranks—

smiling radiantly. His round cherry cheeks bespoke a presumptuous state of health that was almost offensive.

"All right, Buddy Boy, that's far enough," an officer of the law said liltingly.

"Mr. Schlemovitz," the eager man called. "Moffitt's here. Don't you worry about one little thing. North America is with you."

"Another teensy step, friend," said the annoyed officer, bringing his nightstick crashing down into the calloused palm of his hand for emphasis, "just one more, and P–O–W!"

By way of introduction, Moffitt said, "North America and Beyond," and, completely unruffled, he presented his card.

The crowd drew near as the officer studied the message.

"There's no need to push, ladies and gentlemen. I have one for each of you. And remember this," Moffitt informed them, passing out cards to all within reaching distance. "When disaster strikes and life looks mean, North America is on the scene. Here you are sir, with my compliments."

Where she sat ash-covered in the desperate street amidst the serpent hoses, Mrs. Schlemovitz felt life quicken. She shook, quivered, and finally doubled up with laughter, chortling like a pirate.

Schlemovitz became alarmed. "Calm yourself, Woman," he soothed. "Private property has scorched your perspective."

"Did you hear what I heard, Mr. Schlemovitz?" she asked, giggling, and using her husband's shoulder as a banister pulled herself up. Standing over the doubting Thomas, she spun around three times in joy and wonder and ran off crying ecstatically, "North America is calling."

Joan of Arc also heard voices, Schlemovitz remembered, and her they *burned*. My God, he thought, her brains have flown the coop. "Come back, Lovely," he cried out in the wilderness, "come back."

But Mrs. Schlemovitz was deaf to reason. Her feet spurning the ground, her toes churning the air, she sped toward the crowd and with a breathtaking leap sank ten broken and unpolished nails deep into Moffitt's assured throat.

"The money!" she demanded, laughter and tears mingling in her mouth like a piquant sauce.

Mr. Moffitt paled, extricated himself, smiled wanly at suspicious bystanders and, taking Mrs. Schlemovitz by the arm a bit more firmly than good manners required, led her off to one side proclaiming, "Your loss is mine, little lady. Calm yourself. You have the perfect sympathy, unqualified and sustaining, of our entire organization."

Mrs. Schlemovitz wiped her eyes thankfully and recovering herself asked, "What does that come to in dollars?"

"Of course," said Moffitt. "I understand completely." He draped a consoling seersucker around the bony woman, creating for a moment a moving tableau of charity, but almost before anyone realized what was happening, he had pushed her out of sight behind one of the still pumping engines.

Shielded from prying eyes, Moffitt removed his arm. His full ruby lips drawn thin to a purple line, he squinted shrewdly at the bewildered woman. "You are doubtless aware, Madam," he began, his words sprawling over one another excitedly, "that North America and Beyond is eager to make *complete* restitution to you and yours pursuant to your policy with us against all direct loss incurred as a consequence of fire, wind, rain, hail, lightning, earthquake, meteors, and civil commotion. There are, however, certain minor considerations relevant to the provisions and stipulations of our agreement with you that must be adequately satisfied before payment can be made. Do you follow me?"

"You lousy welcher! Come quick, Mr. Schlemovitz," screamed the enraged policy holder, "big business is stealing the bread from our mouths."

"Shhhh, not so loud. Shhhh. You're upset, Madam."

"Mr. Schlemovitz!"

Moffitt slapped a pink hand over the woman's black mouth and raised a finger to his lips. "Shhhh." He shivered, looked both ways nervously, and whispered, "My God, I'm only trying to help you. Be reasonable. Just answer the following questions correctly and the money is yours. What could be fairer?"

As soon as she heard the word "money," Mrs. Schlemovitz gave up struggling.

"That's being sensible . . . fine . . . much better. Now let's get down to business. Are all of your premiums paid?"

"Naturally," said Mrs. Schlemovitz, and folded her arms confidently across her chest.

"Were any of the statements you made when applying for our protection calculated to deceive?"

"The truth, the whole truth, and nothing but . . ."

"Have you submitted a written report respecting the time, place, and circumstances of the occurrence, plus names and addresses of two or more witnesses not members of your immediate family?"

"Give me a pencil."

"Mrs. Schlemovitz! I'll have you know this is no joking matter. Please be responsive. Just a yes or no will be sufficient. Now"—Moffitt's eyes narrowed eliminating distractions—"was your alleged misfortune in any way related to an attack by military, naval, or air forces of a foreign power?"

". . . You should live so long."

"Admit it," commanded Moffitt, dropping his velvet glove, "you neglected the property producing innumerable fire hazards, didn't you?—You didn't run a *candy* store at all. It was nothing more than a front for inflammable materials, wasn't it?"

"Never!"

"Cleaning fluids, shoe polish, pencils, crepe paper, pornography . . ."

"Mr. Schlemovitz!"

From nowhere Schlemovitz appeared, his long face a cry of alarm. "Unhand her, Insurance Man, this is a sick woman."

"Mr. Schlemovitz," cried Moffitt, "thank God you've come. Your wife is completely unreasonable."

"Innocent until proven guilty. Are you all right, Lovely? This is still a free country run on democratic principles. What's to become of us? We'll plead insanity. You can't touch her. The woman has suffered. Don't let them frighten you, Lovely, a smart lawyer protects the poor."

"Mr. Schlemovitz," said Moffitt helplessly, "I don't understand.—If this is some kind of shakedown . . ."

"And exactly *what's* going on here?" the officer of the law asked as if he expected some improbable answer, and the curious pressed forward on his heels, clustering around to hear.

Schlemovitz turned blue, the pouches under his eyes inflating as his face fell away, his bandaged hands struggling clumsily to unbutton his shirt collar.

"Let me, Mr. Schlemovitz," said his wife gently, and undid the button. "You don't look well. Are you sick?"

"My hour is over, and what's to come is nothing more than a flush and a woosh."

"Step back there," directed the officer. "Give the old man air. Oh . . . "it's you again," he exclaimed, recognizing Moffitt's suspicious complexion. "Are you the troublemaker?"

"*He's* the one, all right," someone shouted, and the mood of the crowd became ugly.

"Look at those plucked eyebrows!" screamed a young woman with plucked eyebrows.

"Search his pockets," cried a Little Leaguer. "I bet he's got matches."

Fretting in immaculate white, a Good Humor salesman could stand it no longer. "What are we waiting for?" he challenged those around him. "Let's string him up."

The officer reached under his coat and fingered his thirty-eight. "Now hold on! Just hold on."

The besieged insurance man pulled out a neatly folded handkerchief and glumly wiped the perspiration from his upper lip. The thought of Mrs. Moffitt collecting his life insurance was not reassuring. "Mr. Schlemovitz . . . Mrs. Schlemovitz . . . My *poor* neighbors," he lamented, his voice cracking under the strain. "How tragic it is for me to discover that Fortune has crept up behind and dealt you this foul, unnatural, and most cruel blow in the stern. But God, in His infinite care, has seen your plight and North America is happy to do His bidding. Your check will be in the mail this very day. No," Moffitt cautioned, raising his hand and slowly edging off down the street, "don't thank me. Farewell, Schlemovitzes—God bless you!"

Shivering with excitement, Mrs. Schlemovitz embraced her husband. "We're rich, Mr. Schlemovitz. RICH!"

Standing with a funereal stiffness—his eyes glistening street lights on a rain-swept midnight pavement—the old man mumbled, "Impossible. Money without gainful employment is like a titless woman. Interesting to look at . . . but who needs it? Schlemovitz, where are we going?!"

Mrs. Schlemovitz knew, and there wasn't a minute to lose.

When the elderly couple arrived at the pier, they were immediately caught up in a huge crowd and thrust forward like packages on a conveyor belt. Facing what must have seemed the wrong direction, Schlemovitz pushed his hat down recklessly low over his eyes and with the doomed look of a man fated to spend his days struggling upward on a down escalator, he sailed smoothly along beneath the gay banners and pennants. Mrs. Schlemovitz, aided by the crowd, drove him onward, neatly juggling her coat and shopping bag while softly humming to herself snatches from Old World airs she had sung to her boy in the cradle. Speeding breathlessly along, she scanned the tourist-class horizon with dark, squinty, nervous eyes like a German U-boat commander in an American movie and, before long, a bloodcurdling grin slashed her face in two.

"Cooshkie!" she cried hysterically, yanking the struggling Schlemovitz out of the wheel of the sea. "Sweetheart, Cooshkie darling. It's me."

A tall, dark, gorgeous young man who was wearing a radiant blue blazer, orange ascot, and white yachting cap dangerously cocked fell down in exhaustion upon the stolen suitcase he was guarding and closed his eyes.

Mrs. Schlemovitz raced to the stricken youth, and dropping her burden at his feet, sang in his ear, "Little Cooshkie. What is it, sweet face? Are you sick, darling? Where does it hurt?" She locked the limp figure in her bony arms and rocked him back and forth to the rhythm of love, "Tell Momma/Momma/Momma."

The handsome young man calmly opened his eyes, blinked once

or twice, cleverly passed wind in silence, sighed pleasantly, mumbled finally, "Oh . . . hello there," and sank back into darkness.

"Schlemovitz, look, look at our Cooshila," the anguished mother wailed, as if their boy dangled by a shoelace above some abysmal gorge. "Quick, wrap him up and we'll take it home."

A hesitant step forward, a pause, and the old man said quietly, "Hello, boy." He looked his son over—window-shopping—and blew through his nose in approval. "Good! Sensible hat. Warm scarf. No nonsense. Good."

The young man raised his head. "Joe," he cried, his voice big in surprise, and jumped up. He stopped. The two looked at one another uncertainly. ". . . Who's minding the store?" he asked after a while.

Schlemovitz scowled, glanced off into the distance, and said nothing.

Hopping up and down on her toes, his wife, a luftwench, airborne in her thinness, gleefully recited, "No more sodas, no more straws, no more crooks in dirty drawers—We're free, Cooshkie, like sparrows. The Sansoochee is C.O.D." Mrs. Schlemovitz laughed insanely.

The tastily dressed youth looked to the old man for confirmation of the woman's condition.

Schlemovitz wearily held up his bandaged hands. "True," he admitted. "What was . . . is no more. No more the rich syrups that filled the air with their dizzying fragrance. No more the ringing echo of sun-drenched children at their gum. The print-stained fingers that untied a thousand daily newspapers—no more. No more. Schlemovitz's occupation's gone."

"Right!" the old woman cheered, refusing to play his game. "We're gillionaires," she calculated, rummaging frantically about in her shopping bag, and delirious with excitement added, "Maybe more. Have a cherry?"

The suave youth embraced the little old lady thankfully. "Mother!" he cried.

"Congratulations, green thumb, you lucked out that time."

Mrs. Schlemovitz felt a chill on her kidneys. She clutched her shopping bag, and nestling in her son's arms, sized up the fog horn as bearded, squint-eyed, hulking, frayed, double-breasted trouble. "We don't want any," she snapped.

"Mother," said the young man grandly, "allow me to introduce my friend and fellow graduate, Mr. Ivan Storch."

"Who?" she demanded.

"Any friend of D.C.'s is a friend of mine," said Storch, coming forward and shaking the old woman's reluctant hand until her kneecaps rattled. "Charmed, Mrs. Widdemore."

"*Schlemovitz* to you, cowboy," rasped the injured woman, and glancing up at her son incredulously asked, "*That's* a college boy?"

"Joe," the young man reached over and affectionately drew his father into the family circle. "I want you to meet Ivan Storch, B.A., one of the truly great minds of my generation. His senior thesis on the reinforcement of Negative Capability in quasi-Fascistic personality types is already a minor classic. Ivan, my father."

The bearded one rapped his heels together. "A pleasure, Herr Schlemovitz," he declared, and squeezed the lint out of the old man's bandages.

In the presence of pain and brilliance, the old man mourned his genes, but there was no room in his heart for envy. "Schlemovitz salutes you, Starch—But tell me," he whispered from under his hat, "how can you leave the sinking ship when the rats are at the wheel and mediocrity sits with a Bigelow on the floor? Tell me, has America stewed your prunes, too?"

Unconsciously slipping his hand wrist-deep into his jacket front, Storch cocked his head and gave the old man his good eye. "All the world is America, Monsieur Schlemovitz." He snickered with insight. ". . . All the world."

The old man mulled. His chest heaved as if something had gone down the wrong way. "A cigarette," he called inscrutably, and no sooner had his son popped one in his mouth and set it ablaze than Schlemovitz began to puff in earnest, exhaling great clouds of smoke that roiled about him in the troubled air. Lost in thought, he didn't seem to realize that he was smoking a perfumed Jezebel.

"Hey! Over here! Over here!" Widdemore was shouting at a gray-haired porter whose back belonged to the Fun Lane Route. "Is everything aboard?"

The porter—short, thick, unprimed, his shirt spread in a V-formation down to the navel revealing a petrified forest, and his pants a belted sack—approached dispiritedly. "What else you got?"

"Is everything aboard?" repeated the elegant young man pleasantly.

"Fine. Nice," the porter indulged him. "That too?" he groaned, and reached for the opulent suitcase near the young man's leg. It was made out of a material that resembled cashmere and the First-Class label on the handle showed that it belonged to the wealthy Miss Sidney Finch-Bradish, a charming young girl whom D.C. intended to know better before very long.

"No, no." Widdemore waved him off with a smile. "I'm minding it for a friend."

"O.K.," the porter said conclusively, and whipping out a rag, he mopped his face. "You mustofad stones in them bags. My back kills me like needles. I got a belt this thick." He spread his hands imaginatively. "You want to see?" By way of invitation, he opened the top of the sack to daylight. "Look."

Mrs. Schlemovitz didn't like the element. "Can we peek inside, Richard?" she asked primly, indicating the ship.

"No, I'm afraid not, Mother," Widdemore answered hurriedly, "against *Maritime Regulations* you know. Never do."

"This your mamma?" the waiting porter intervened. "She can go, sure. Go ahead, lady. It's O.K. Fine."

Widdemore addressed the porter and declared unashamedly, "I *like* you. You've done your work well and should be rewarded. Four BIG ones, if you please, Ivan."

Without a moment's hesitation, Storch pulled out a wallet swollen with promise and removed four crisp bills. Their absence was undetectable in the bulging leather.

"Wait!" blazed Schlemovitz, spitting shreds of tobacco from his lips like machine-gun bullets. "Put your money away, boy, and clear the air of temptation. Labor wants wages, not gifts for good behavior. If the system stinks take a deep breath but don't deboom a man's instrument." He turned and fixed the porter with a glittering eye. "Remember, you're a worker . . . the mind and heart of the country. Think!"

"Four BIG ones it is," Storch announced indifferently, strumming the money like a green ukulele.

"Did Eugene Debs uncouple Pullman cars so that you should have to crawl?" screamed Schlemovitz, beside himself. "Keep your hands in your pockets. . . . Hold on."

The porter looked from one to the other and shook his head in disbelief. "—You got a family, Mister?" he asked angrily, and grabbing up the money whizzed off.

Storch laughed understandingly in the porter's wake.

The ship's whistle sounded the vessel's imminent departure. "That means us, folks," Widdemore declared, yanking up the suitcase.

"Is this Sore Bun a good school?" Mrs. Schlemovitz attempted to cling to her son a bit longer.

Widdemore embraced the old lady. "The best," he said, and added sincerely, "but even with a scholarship it's expensive, Mother."

"Leave it to me," Mrs. Schlemovitz said with a twinkle. "Only write."

"Don't noodge, Woman. Give the boy the shopping bag and stop holding up his education."

Flustered, Mrs. Schlemovitz handed over the goods.

Widdemore, his hands full, regarded his father. It was apparent that any attempt to shake hands would be doomed to failure. "Good-bye, Joe," the young man said with a wink. "Good-bye."

Schlemovitz watched in silence as the two friends ran to the ship, and no sooner were they aboard than the gangplank was pulled away. As the great ocean liner moved out from the pier, snapping the coiled strands of confetti that linked it to the shore, the porter came rushing up to the weary and heartsore couple.

"You . . . you . . . you think I got a hole in the head?" he growled, and held out the money. "Who's the WISE GUY?"

Schlemovitz glanced down at one of the bills and studied it solemnly through heavy-lidded eyes.

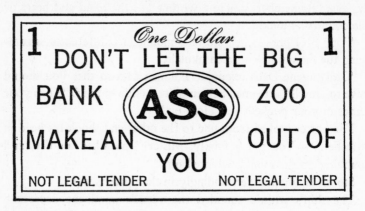

Turning his back on the porter and forgetting his wife in his excitement, the surprised old man walked off. "Schlemovitz," he told himself in confidence, "that Starch is nobody's fool. The boy was right."

CHAPTER 5

❧ Wooing Sidney.

It has been noted. Reciprocity plays a part in all human intercourse. This does not necessarily mean that the trade in any single relationship will appear equitable to the innocent bystander untutored in mutuality. In fact, to him it rarely seems so. Modern Science, however, has shown us that there are in man certain subtle and somewhat mysterious psychological forces at work forever jiggling the balance. Plainly there is more salt on the short end of the pretzel than has hitherto been suspected. That a sly young rogue should receive love in exchange for a heisted suitcase might seem perversely disproportionate to a Victorian mind, but to D.C., a child of his age, it was even-steven.

Sidney Finch-Bradish—a gentle, serious-minded subdeb and student of oriental philosophy—was convinced that her shipboard meeting with the beautiful stranger was karma. Her mother, on the other hand, wasn't so sure. A strange woman, she hovered possessively over D.C. like a lavatory attendant, never leaving the young couple alone for a minute. Even when she herself went to the bathroom she would remain on sentry duty by sitting with the light off and the door slightly ajar. It was during one of these interludes of relative privacy that Sidney had unburdened herself by explaining in a whisper the real reason for her trip, something that she had but darkly alluded to before. She was going away to forget injustice.

Sidney had been dismissed from the Dimity Field and Stream School of Virginia because of modern dancing. She had surprisingly firm views about the art form. Her attitude was that dancing should be more than just an athletic mishmash of wholeness, harmony, and radiance, and in her junior year at Dimity she had specialized in controversial dances with strong civil rights themes. Her favorite was one about a beautiful, impoverished, Negro sharecropper—played by a Dimity girl in symbolic black leotards —whom she taught to read, encouraged to vote, and climactically married in a whirlwind courtship of mutual consent and racial harmony. There had of course been academic repercussions, and so she was traveling.

Because of her mother's extraordinary vigilance, Sidney's academic suspension was the only intimacy D.C. had been able to share with her in the three days they had known one another, and he was becoming despondent. He lay listlessly on his bunk in his dinner jacket with no appetite, unable to concentrate on the novel he was reading. If Jay Gatsby had had a mother instead of a husband to deal with it might have sparked his interest but as it was he closed his eyes, covered his face with the book, and listened to Ivan thumping about on the floor.

Blooming like a rash, Ivan sprang up from his push-ups. "What's next?" he asked, kneading his triceps which were as big as coconuts.

"I suppose I'll have to shoot her," reasoned D.C. in a muffled voice.

"What's next," prodded Ivan, "before I lose my sweat?"

Grudgingly removing the novel from his face, D.C. picked up an opened pamphlet lying beside him entitled, *The Watusi Way: Physical Fitness for Survival*. The glossy cover showed two natives grinning diabolically over a fallen victim. "Chart III . . . Ferocity Level 5 . . . 350 runs in place." As Ivan jogged off, D.C. jeered lazily, *"Mens sana in corpore sano,"* and returned to his moping.

When Ivan had finished, he toweled off his glistening body,

wrung out his beard like a wet bathing suit, and humored his miserable friend. "Maybe the old lady wants you for herself," he suggested.

D.C. shrieked, whistled, laughed derisively, and then stopped in astonishment. "She *is* odd," he acknowledged.

Ivan grinned. Stepping out of his shabby undershorts and leaving them on the floor, he said, "I'm going to take a shower."

"Do you really think so?" asked D.C., fascinated by the idea. ". . . But she's so old."

"Is there a Schlemovitz under every Widdemore?" remarked Ivan cryptically. "Who knows?" And he disappeared into the bathroom.

D.C. placed his hands behind his head and smiled to himself. Since the pier he had been expecting something like this. "If Gatsby can turn out to be Gatz," he shouted in order to be heard above the shower, "why not Schlemovitz? Think of it this way. When Nature errs, man must act. If animals survive through protective coloration, why not appellative camouflage for human beings to smooth their comings and goings? Right?"

Ivan stuck his dripping head out of the bathroom door. "Did you say something?" he asked.

D.C. felt as badly used as his friend's discarded underwear. Resignedly he got up from the bunk and straightened his elegantly cut maroon dinner jacket in the mirror. "Nothing," he replied wearily. "I'll try again. Maybe we can just outrun the old bag."

"Courage, dreamer! See you in the lounge at eight," said Ivan, ducking back under the shower.

"Sure," agreed D.C., opening the cabin door. "Why not?"

Ivan soaped his pectorals. The tiny bar slipped from his hand, as elusive as a butterfly. He retrieved it, brooding on anonymity and Thomas Malthus. Bevy, covey, gaggle, gam, pack, pride, Widdemores—the world was a feral ark, each animal stuffed into its categorical bin and all scrambling. But with luck and some quick footwork there could be no plural large enough to hold a clever, unpredictable, bearded Storch. Ivan soaped his trapezius. What of

Indonesia, China, Japan, India, flesh-crammed and steaming with fertility? More than one born every second, 4000 every hour, 34,000,000 every year, annually four cities the size of New York with enough left over to fill Hoboken, Jersey City, and Paramus. Genitalia gone mad. The solution: contraception, abortion, infanticide, or, if all else failed, abstinence, but pending action he would not be caught in the crush. Ivan soaped his latissimus dorsi. At Allahabad—where the Jumna and the Ganges meet—the Hindu festival of Kumbh-Mela is held. Every twelfth year it is especially sacred, and pilgrims come from as far away as Karikal and Madras and Mysore and Trivandrum to throw themselves into the opaque waters in quest of the pearl. Four and one-half million people poised queasily on the narrow river flats like burnt sienna angels on the head of a pin. Their consolidated defecation alone sufficient in a single day to rival one of the lesser peaks of the Olympics. His testicles tingled at the thought. Ivan soaped his penis. The water poured down suffocatingly hot, but he made no effort to control it. Ingres' harem of Turkish bathers—boneless oriental women loose in their skins—surrounded him. Nameless bodies indifferent to the touch, they exuded the dense smell of enclosed sex that mingled with the incense. Unique, apart, his erection trumpeting his presence, his soap-capped maleness the call of the wild. But they looked on with only a casual interest. He moved his hips with a compelling intensity, undulating his cabled belly, flaunting his muscled thighs, a carnal whirlpool, a dancing David ecstatic in being, coiling, stretching, his sprung rhythm lost to time, glossolalia filling his mouth in shudders, he plastered the walls of the stall with his seed. "A few less to worry about," he congratulated himself as he watched the smoky semen slip down the drain.

The stenciled sign on the bulkhead read:

FIRST-CLASS ONLY!!!
ALL TOURIST-CLASS PASSENGERS WHO ATTEMPT TO GO BEYOND THIS POINT, LOOK ON THESE WORDS, YE LOWLY, AND DESPAIR.

Caveat to the general. D.C. ignored the message and knocked on a First-Class cabin door. It opened, revealing a tall, athletically built woman of about forty with bobbed blonde hair and a tanned, weather-beaten face. She was wearing tailored dungarees and a man's shirt, the top four buttons of which were undone. She was not wearing a bra. She was looking at him through the lens of a Zeiss four-power scope on Stith Streamline mounts attached to a .300 Weatherby Magnum. She was not smiling.

"My God, Mrs. Finch-Bradish, don't shoot!"

"Honest Abe! Boy Scout! Returner of Lost Suitcases! . . . You rat fuck, I've been waiting for you."

The perhaps anti-Semitic overtones of the salutation were not lost on D.C. "I'll come back later," he declared simply.

Mrs. Finch-Bradish giggled. "Honey, that's what I like about you. You've got nuts." She lowered her rifle and, grabbing him by the wrist, yanked him cleanly through the door. "Welcome!" she cried, slamming it closed behind him. Her enthusiasm was genuine.

There was another unsheathed rifle on the couch. Alarmed, D.C. quickly raised his tongue in self-defense. "I only came to ask Sidney if she wanted to take a walk on deck but she's probably tired and there's probably too much salt in the air and anyway I can see she's not here and you're busy so I'll just—"

"Silly boy," admonished Mrs. Finch-Bradish, calling attention to her décolletage by demurely closing the fourth button. "Come here."

D.C. looked toward the door hopelessly.

"Over *here*," she coaxed, laying her gun aside. "I want to show you something n-i-c-e." Sitting down on the couch, Mrs. Finch-Bradish lighted up a small cork-tipped cigar. She inhaled deeply, blew two perfect smoke rings, fluffed up the pillow beside her and inquired, "Whatsamatter, Lover, you got lead in your can?"

Spiritlessly, D.C. placed himself down next to her.

Without further ado, she exclaimed, "Hold this!" and leaned with abandon across the astonished young man's lap.

D.C.'s hands hovered incredulously over the smartly trim buttocks of Mrs. Finch-Bradish. "What?" he asked, the remnant of his composure gone.

Looking up, Mrs. Finch-Bradish giggled. "*This*, silly." She slapped a .375 Magnum into his waiting hands.

"But I don't believe in guns."

"Do I look like a missionary? Just shut your crack and hold it. *No*, not that way." Wrenching his hands from the stock where they were frozen in panic, she wrapped them around the barrel and jammed it into his navel. "Like so! Dig?"

D.C. had had enough. Impulsively he considered which karate blow to use, but his memory—tarnished by chivalry and youth—failed him and he could not recall those knocks that only maim. Stymied, burning like Sterno with a cool blue flame, he prepared for arbitration.

"Mrs. Finch-Bradish," he announced, with sublime hauteur, "for *shame!* Violence is for the weak. Crimes of passion are for the lower classes. Upright, whole of heart, undefiled by sin, man needs no Moorish javelin, neither bow, nor yet a quiver heavy with poisoned arrows—Mrs. Finch-Bradish!" he screamed, as the muzzle of the gun was rammed home once more, fairly taking his breath away.

"Call me Jen," she admonished, rubbing at the stock with an oil-soaked flannel and a businesslike air. Working at great speed in the face of a wiggling Widdemore, her hand was skimming quicksilver on the glistening wood. "Isn't this the goddamn most?" she said offhandedly. "Tiger Flame maple. *Wild* Tiger Flame maple."

For a time, D.C. tried to think of himself as holding a hank of yarn, but finally managing to dislodge the muzzle, he cried out with desperate levity, "You're mad, Mrs. Finch-Bradish. Mad!"

She held the gun up in admiration. "Here, take it."

D.C. thoughtlessly obeyed. Although keeping the weapon at arm's length, he was impressed in spite of himself by the wood's hepatic brilliance.

Mrs. Finch-Bradish moved closer and carelessly threw an arm about D.C.'s neck. "How about that!" she said, her voice husky with emotion. "When I was a kid all I had was an old man and an old lady who loved me, youth, money, and good looks. But *no* cachet . . . dig? In school the arty bastards put me down as an anachronism, a D.A.R. fink, and didn't even bother not to talk to me. If I had been a Eurasian, or a Jew, or black, or had a hump," she sighed, "it might have been different. After school, three husbands came and went like salesmen so wrapped up in their own product that they didn't even see me. I wore capes, died my hair black, spoke in odd accents, but nothing happened. Then one Thursday at the corner of 42nd and Fifth while waiting for the WALK signal, I saw hanging on the front of this newsstand my first copy of *Sports Afield*." There was a catch in Mrs. Finch-Bradish's voice as she added, "It changed my fuckin' life."

Easing the gun onto an end table, D.C. clutched his neck. "You're scratching me, Mrs. Finch-Bradish," he said in pained accusation.

Without removing her hand, the huntress stripped her ring finger of a diamond the size of the Kohinoor and dropped it casually to the floor. Having undressed her finger, she did not hesitate to disrobe the rest of her. Mrs. Finch-Bradish's sunburned face was a furnace of excitement. "I *love* to hunt," she revealed passionately, snatching off her shirt and running her tongue over her lips. "Any jerk can pull a trigger, but you've got to be nails to stalk,"—in one savage motion she upzipped her pants—"and I'm a stalker. After I dump Sidney in Sweden for her operation, I'm off to Tanganyika for eland, sable, and kudu. But I don't care a crap for trophies!" She giggled slyly, squirming out of her pants, and added, "The horns are for my husband. *Now*," Mrs. Finch-Bradish cried in anticipation, the sheen of her taut panties blinding the college graduate, "how would you like a little dik-dik?"

D.C. drew back in horror and disbelief. "A Swedish operation for Sidney!"

"You know . . ." winked Mrs. Finch-Bradish, a woman of the world.

"But that's not true! Sidney's not that kind of girl."

"Live and let live," observed the mother generously, "as long as I'm getting mine." And with that she threw her dynamic self headlong at the good-looking young man, toppling him like a reedy poplar.

As D.C. went down, he saw himself a Gulliver surrounded by countless nipple-sized women spelunking his cavities. There was relatively little danger in lying there seemingly helpless, but was it good form he wondered. They were so elderly.

"MOTHER! RICHARD!" cried Sidney incredulously, as she entered from the adjoining room and saw the turmoil on the couch. Her defenseless Peter Pan collar seemed to snuggle up in fright under a gaping jaw. "I don't believe it," she said, giving them the benefit of the doubt.

The spinning confusion of arms and legs gave the trapped couple the appearance of a modern Laocoön. Above the roaring melee came the POP! of champagne as Mrs. Finch-Bradish uncorked her pale left breast. At liberty, D.C. suddenly sat bolt upright. He wiped his mouth with the back of his hand and lowered his eyes to avoid those of the hurt young girl. His air was tragic. "Would you care to go for a walk, Sidney?" he asked dismally.

"I don't believe it," repeated Sidney, in a state of shock. "It's not true." She squirmed about agonizingly in her tiny blue sneakers, her dark bangs drooping.

D.C. couldn't bear being disliked. "Listen to me," he said firmly, taking hold of Sidney's hands.

"Don't touch me," screamed the offended teen-ager. "You're naked."

D.C. zipped up his fly. "Be reasonable, Sidney," he begged, "let me explain. Please."

Under no circumstances did Sidney wish to be unfair. After all, it was only circumstantial evidence. "I'm listening, Richard. But keep your distance."

Indifferent to her nakedness, Mrs. Finch-Bradish tucked her legs beneath her and squatted on the couch like a child about to be entertained. Her expression was one of indiscriminate bonhomie.

"Go ahead, Richard," urged Sidney impatiently. "I'm *waiting*."

D.C. had been so absorbed in getting a hearing for himself that he hadn't given much thought to what he would say. Unable to think of anything appropriate, he decided to change the subject and collapsed.

"Dear God!" keened Sidney, rushing to his crumpled body. "What is it, Richard?"

Wheezing grotesquely and shaking his head, D.C. explained, "I have the falling sickness."

"Oh no!" gasped Sidney, her eyes as round as rose windows.

"Oh *yes!*" he insisted truculently, and sitting up, added, "just like Alexander, Caesar, Dostoyevsky, Byron, William Pitt, and Mohammed," to make it sound official. With her interest in the East, D.C. was sure that Mohammed would go over big.

Granting him full clemency, Sidney rushed off to the bathroom for a wet rag. "If I had only known," she said compassionately, while tenderly bathing his brow. "You poor poor dear."

Mrs. Finch-Bradish's face burned ominously like an enemy campfire. "Back to your sandpile, hustler, before I lose my lunch on your kneecaps."

"Honestly, Mother," said Sidney, glaring at her, "sometimes you say the queerest things. You must be tired. Why don't you go inside and lie down?"

Mrs. Finch-Bradish laughed at the catty little bitch, but her eyes were incinerators. She crouched, leapt from the couch, and dropped down beside her pale child, foaming slightly at the corners of the mouth. "I'm wise," she snarled. "Buzz off."

Before D.C. could take any real pleasure in the proceedings, however, there was a knock at the door—a faint, distant sound, the careful note of a dependent.

"Who is it?" asked Sidney, her nerves as tense as thieves.

"It is your own Fideo, ladies. I have come for the beds."

"Oh, just a minute Fideo," called Sidney gaily, and then turning to her naked mother whispered, "*Now* will you go inside?"

Mrs. Finch-Bradish folded her arms. Her glance moved suspiciously back and forth from her daughter to the good-looking young man.

"Pl-e-e-ease, Mother," Sidney insisted, tears glazing her eyes satin, "you can't stay here like that. Not before a member of one of the underprivileged nations. For goodness' sake!"

In an attempt to force the older woman's hand, D.C. inched toward the cabin door and, unnoticed, unlocked it.

"Good evening, ladies." A dark little man with enormous white teeth entered, chuckling over the drawers of his past. He glanced at the unclothed Mrs. Finch-Bradish indifferently, his starched, white steward's jacket heightening the medical air. "Please, do not let me molest you, ladies and gentleman. In your country I have learned the lightning speed, to come and go like a fart. Look," he said laughing, and snatched a bed out from the wall, "already I am half-finished."

"Mother," sobbed Sidney miserably, "how could you!"

"Style!" exclaimed Mrs. Finch-Bradish and, by way of invitation, she wiggled her bottom unmercifully under the youth's trembling nose and walked off.

D.C.'s eyes clung to the departing figure like Band-Aids. Suddenly collecting himself, he pulled out his handkerchief and, taking Sidney around, tenderly dried her damp cheeks and then wet them with a thousand kisses. Sidney was not unresponsive and in the crash of bosoms the cabin rocked like a bridal bed and the sopping handkerchief spilled to the floor. Overcome by passion, D.C. dropped to his knees, scooped up Mrs. Finch-Bradish's diamond in his innocent hanky, and pocketing both, whispered into Sidney's love-sick ear, "Midnight . . . at the lifeboat station."

CHAPTER 6

🐚 Two sharpers pull it off.

In the crowded lounge, the ship's purser was acting as master of ceremonies for a costume contest. He stood behind a microphone and as a kimono-clad geisha came up with itsy-bitsy steps and her hands buried in her sleeves, he was saying, "Isn't that something?" and applauding. Unable to find his friend among the audience, D.C. sauntered across the makeshift stage, ruthlessly ignoring all of the women present by way of titillation and intrigue, and passed through to the bar beyond. His aloof progress was a conversation piece for quivering vaginas, a telegram that read TEAR UP YOUR LIBRARY CARDS AND LIVE. He often composed little impromptu dramas such as this among strangers.

Pushing open the glass door of the United Nations Bar, he entered to the march from "The Bridge on the River Kwai." He paused like royalty and lifted a critical eyebrow—an actor's dodge. Oblivious patrons whistled and stomped their feet in time to the piano as waiters in full military dress with the blue insignia of the United Nations Peace-Keeping Force moved crisply about the crowded room taking orders. Suspended from the ceiling were gay, multicolored balloons on which were written Korea, Katanga, Cyprus, the Gaza Strip, and the room, filled with noise and smoke, shook like a battlefield. No one seemed to notice him. D.C. reached for his pocket in self-defense. The feel of the jewel as he ran his fingertips over its polished multiple facets was calming. As he had always suspected, money did make a difference.

At the bar sat Ivan. He was listening with both ears to someone who looked like an undertaker. The man's enormous head was covered by a thin layer of hair parted down the middle with such geometric precision as to suggest a wig. He wore a black suit, the metallic knot of his tie screwed forever into his thin, academic neck. Bent forward, he was deep in conversation, a funereal intensity in his manner.

As D.C. came up, he overheard a voice quietly moving, persuasive without italics, elegant without ostentation: ". . . colitis and other bowel troubles, arteriosclerosis, prostate difficulties, nephritis, female diseases, T.B., neuroses of all kinds, spinal curvatures, deafness, blindness, headaches, tonsillitis, and yaws. There are, of course, others, but this will give you some idea of the scope of our operation."

D.C. laughed indulgently, but whoever the fraud was he was not a punster.

"Dr. Luckenback . . ."—Ivan got up smiling—"I'd like you to meet my traveling companion, Richard Widdemore."

"Very fine," said the doctor blandly, but when he tried to rise he found that his clubfoot was stuck. Absorbed in the conversation, he had unthinkingly wrapped it about one of the barstool legs forming a caduceus. Wrenching himself free, he lost his balance and lurched forward into D.C.'s wincing scrotum. But he did not remain there long.

"Luckenback, at your service. Specializing in nerve adjustment and colonic irrigation. How do you do."

"Are you all right?" asked D.C. with civility, smoothing his rumpled midsection.

Barely concealing his irritation, the doctor snapped, "Luckenback *is* health," and limped back to his stool.

There was an awesome economy in the single name. D.C. was chastened by thoughts of Homer, Bismarck, Einstein, and Manolete; yet Hildegarde was proof that there was more here than met the eye. He wondered what Ivan wanted with the impostor.

"But what do you offer against the germ theory and viral infection?" Ivan asked, picking up the conversation with his drink.

"Subluxations!" said Luckenback. His brown eyes damp with sincerity, his voice as rich as pumpernickel, the doctor explained, "The secret is current imbalance."

"What?" D.C. was uncertain if his ears could be trusted in the noisy room.

Turning to Ivan, Luckenback whispered dubiously, "Am I correct in assuming that we are all college graduates here?"

Ivan sipped and nodded.

"Very well," declared the reassured doctor, "then I needn't mince words. Today we know that *all* human ailments can be traced to two causes, either *too* much or *too* little. Take the two most common types of insanity: in melancholia, not enough current; in the wild, raving, uncontrollable maniac, too much. Fine, you say, but what about internal organs? A good point! Take the kidneys: diabetes, too much; Bright's disease, not enough. Bartender," cried the enthusiast, "a bottle of bourbon and a shot glass."

Ivan polished off his orangeade in a gulp and, wiping his beard, self-consciously inquired, "What about strabismus?"

Luckenback looked grave and made a convulsive chewing motion with his lips. At last he shook his head, placed a bone-white hand on the young man's shoulder, leaned forward and blurted, "VOM!"

Ivan brushed the spittle from his cheeks casually, so as not to offend the older man.

"Have a Tums," advised D.C. sympathetically.

"Mock on! mock on! Voltaire, Rousseau," Luckenback recited, eyeing the dandy like a grease stain on a new pair of pants. Turning away, he addressed the worthier youth. "Regardless of the gravity of the problem, our Vital Organs Massager is the answer. Where the medicals thrive on snips and cuts, we prefer to nudge and coax. Look here." He picked up the empty shot glass the bartender had placed before him and held it up to the light. "A system without current is like this glass, useful only in its potential. Watch, now, as the current begins to flow," he said, picking up the bottle of bourbon and tipping it in. "See how the glass takes on a new vitality. But should the current exceed the capacity of the system, then——look out." With that, he impulsively turned the bottle bottoms-up and torrents of bourbon spilled lavishly over the sides of the little glass, poured across the bar, and cascaded down, soaking his crotch in an amber flow.

"No matter, no matter," shouted Luckenback, scarcely acknowledging the puddle in his lap. "You see—a graphic example of the dangers of excess." Having proven his case, the doctor smugly returned the empty bottle to the bar. "But enough about me and my work. What are you two interesting young men doing on the high seas beyond the point of no return?"

"Biding our time," replied D.C. slyly, savoring his secret midnight assignation.

Luckenback was puzzled. He took advantage of the opportunity to squirm about on his seat with a reflective air while secretly rubbing his legs together in a drying process as slow as rust. "Oh . . . mmn . . . I think I see what you mean. But that's hardly possible. Traveling by ship provides such an ideal opportunity to do so much. Take me for instance. I spend most of my time working at my hobby—vegetable diseases. Have you ever stopped to think how many afflictions are suffered by the peas and beans of New Zealand?"

"Certainly," said Ivan, without expression. "Among the fungus diseases are collar rot, pea wilt, septoria blotch, and downy mildew."

D.C. shivered with delight. That would put the tin hat on the phony.

"Fungus!" snorted the doctor, his back to the wall. "Botanical quackery! Black magic! Nonsense! My research proves beyond question that the systemic problem is liquid imbalance—but there I go again taxing you with my special interests. Perhaps a more exciting way to pass the time might be found for this young man here," he suggested, indicating D.C. "I have it!" he cried, his heart big with holiday. "Why not a friendly game of cards?"

"Not me," demurred Ivan at once.

"A friendly game of cards," said D.C. in a milk-white voice

with blood-stained thoughts of single combat. Ignoring his friend's forbidding eye, he coolly accepted. "Why not, indeed?"

"Splendid," said Luckenback. He got up and limped to a nearby table. Unfolding a green baize cloth—the same material as that used to cover the gaming tables of Las Vegas and Monte Carlo—he set it before him. From his jacket pocket he removed a deck of cards. He broke the seal and thumbed through them familiarly. In his hands the cards came alive, spinning, twisting, flashing through the air with the awful precision of a flock of migrating geese and alighting as one. "Shall we begin, young man?"

Suddenly D.C. ached all over, his molars fire engines of despair.

"Excuse me," said Ivan, and abruptly left the table. He strolled to the bar and returned with a package the bartender had been keeping for him. "Happy birthday, Richard Courtney. Forgive the lack of gift wrapping."

The package sat in the middle of the table like an invoked spirit at a séance. D.C. studied it suspiciously. Not only did Ivan never give presents, but this one was eight months too early.

"A birthday!" declared Luckenback. "I had no idea that this was such a festive occasion. My deepest congratulations, young man."

Eager to count off someone else's years, a shriveled, blue-haired woman at the next table shouted to her companions, "It's his birthday. That good-looking boy over there."

The pianist, a social opportunist, interrupted a farrago of farandoles to spread "Happy Birthday" over the keyboard, his left hand weaving ever more intricate figures in accompaniment to the crescendo of enthusiasm as the barroom swung with wartime camaraderie.

D.C. smiled shyly and nodded his head in response to the applause, but his mind was a supermarket of fatal choices. Reaching out in slow-motion, he gingerly opened the bag. His nostrils flared and began to twitch uncontrollably. Overcome with emotion, he removed a long rectangular box with a message emblazoned on its cover which was as moving in its own way as the copulations of the gods in Hesiod. In blues and greens and whites and reds—a raging palette—the single word, MONOPOLY.

Now D.C. understood what Ivan had in mind. This was *their* game. They were past masters, having explored scientifically all of its permutations and combinations in the tower during the annual College blizzard when for a week they were snowed in. Working in tandem, they would negotiate, monopolize, wheel and deal, and build luxury apartments, plush skyscrapers on the choicest property, while reducing the sea-going charlatan to the tenements and stews of Baltic Avenue.

"Thank you, my friend," said D.C., brazening it out. "You'll play, of course."

Ivan sat down. "But only because it's your birthday," he said.

Opening the board and distributing the silver tokens—the racing car, the top hat, the battleship—D.C. handed the dice with sportsmanlike élan to the popeyed Luckenback, saying, "After you, cool doctor."

Luckenback's clubfoot thrashed about on the floor like a dying fish. "I note with heavy heart," he noted with heavy heart, "that we have before us a four-sided playing field and there are but three of us. Perhaps stud or seven-card draw would be more fitting to the size of our party and the droll occasion."

Ivan examined the rules. "It says nothing about symmetry," he reported, "but I like your logic." He pointed to the one conspicuously lone drinker in the room, a black man with a gray pompadour whose open wash-and-wear jacket revealed a golden Phi Beta Kappa key gleaming as if it could unlock a thousand doors. "I'll ask him to join us."

"You don't mean that dark citizen," Luckenback called after the departing Ivan, but too late.

When Ivan returned, he had with him lonely Enzo Castelli whose stiffness suggested the formality of death.

"Enzo Castelli! Hoorumphrrr!" spluttered the irate doctor, and raising his voice he informed D.C., "It's an alias."

"I'm certainly pleased to make the acquaintance of you gentlemen," said Enzo, forcing a smile. "It's not much fun traveling alone."

"I've seen his dangerous face on post office walls throughout Iowa. Something about sending sepia picture postcards to Caucasian women, wasn't it?" continued Luckenback slyly, trying to pin down his man.

"No, sir," Enzo gently corrected him. "I've never been west of Raccoon Creek, Pennsylvania."

"Or perhaps public exhibitionism in the parcel-post window of the main post office at Davenport? Ahhh . . . that's it! Look at him," he cried in satisfaction as the sweet-tempered Negro dropped his eyes to study the board. "It was in all the evening papers. He presented his member to the clerk for weighing and only ran off when that conscientious official refused to stamp it educational materials. We know you, Castelli!"

"I hate to say this now I'm here," admitted the embarrassed Enzo, "but I'm not so good at games. I guess I was always too busy to learn. You'll have to excuse me. I'm sorry."

"Nonsense," said Ivan brusquely. Staying the gray-haired man, he declared, "Mr. Castelli is a college graduate, too."

"Why yes." Enzo's black eyes turned luminous as he instinctively fondled his key. "Cornell '46."

"A likely story!" Luckenback was adamant. He folded his arms and fidgeted.

"Have a thimble, Mr. Castelli," invited D.C. warmly, handing over a token. "We've been looking for someone just like you who's never played before. Welcome."

Grinning, the black man relaxed in laughter, a remarkable, piercing sound as complicated as the ragged dreams of hysterical women. "My friends call me Enzo," he said, collecting himself.

D.C. held up a bloated bundle of saffron-colored five-hundred-dollar bills. "Who'll take care of the money?"

"Well, now . . ." Luckenback unfolded his arms and leaned forward in the line of duty.

"I'd be glad to help out," volunteered Enzo brightly, "if being a professional don't disqualify me." His flat nose wriggled up with pleasure.

"There's nothing like having a specialist," observed D.C., and he gave up the bankroll without a tremor.

Luckenback's flushed cheeks flamed over the scene like a sunset. "That man is no more a banker than I'm Dr. Palmer. Why he doesn't even look American to me. Test him. See if he can name who first played Charlie Chan . . . or the Green Hornet . . . or Uncle Don. He's a fraud."

"I guess you've got me there all right," admitted Enzo, shifting about uncomfortably. "But I recall my mother was always partial to Mr. Keene, Tracer of White Persons."

"That's good enough for me," said Ivan, smashing the table for emphasis.

"Fifteen hundred all around, Enzo," directed D.C. Removing his dinner jacket and his cuff links, he rolled up his dazzling piqué sleeves with precision and elegance. "We'll settle for a tenth."

"A fifth," cried Luckenback the gambler, his gorge risen, his Adam's apple striking out futilely in all directions. Frustrated and exhausted, he fell back in his chair heavily, and lifting resigned eyes heavenward, he crossed himself and moaned, "God's will be done."

After several hours there could be no doubt of the divine intention. Whereas Enzo and Luckenback had amassed great fortunes, the boys had fallen on evil days, victims of Income Tax, Luxury Tax, and Chance. Each time they turned an orange card it read, "Go Directly To Jail. Do Not Pass Go. Do Not Collect $200." Each time they threw the dice they landed on somebody else's Boardwalk or Park Place. Although Pope held partial evil to be universal good, Ivan, owner of a few shabby pieces of mortgaged real estate, refused to take the larger view and repeatedly called for new dice. D.C. sat glum and colorless, reduced to his last few hundred, and only frequent trips to the bar prevented the dust of ruin from settling on his fancy. Enzo, a monopolistic genius, shuffled his holdings in moneyed ease and, with an amused air, watched the white men arrive at his hotels. While ensconced behind his own rows of title deeds—a smorgasbord of color—Luckenback glared at him carnivorously.

"Marvin Gardens . . . how much?" he asked, in a grim, sullen voice that sounded like hammer blows in the now nearly deserted room.

Enzo brushed his dry chin with a neatly folded handkerchief and, closing his heavy eyelids, sighed helplessly. "I'd surely like to cooperate with you, Doc. . . ."

"Damn it! You've got no business in that part of town," warned Luckenback, red-faced and trembling. "And you"—he moved his great head around like heavy artillery—"shut up!"

In a dark corner of the room, a German shepherd with periscopic ears and eyes swollen with sleeplessness ululated still louder, a murderous wail exposing sorrow under the fur. Beside him was seated a square-jawed German, also with periscopic ears and eyes swollen with sleeplessness. The man's stubble face was a funeral wreath as he blindly devoured little crackers covered with caviar and liver paté.

Luckenback turned to Ivan in disgust. "I'd like to know what that animal is doing in the First-Class bar."

"Having a nightcap, I suppose," said D.C., yawning. Getting up from the table, he stretched and contemplated the men's room.

Ivan squinted into the distance. "It's Torwächter," he muttered. "Who?" asked D.C.

"And that must be Von Hippel. Poor man." Ivan picked up the dice and slapped them into Luckenback's palm. "Your play."

Enzo's face was an opera of emotion. "You don't say! I read about that dog in the ship's paper. He's *some* animal. Did you see where his master dedicated him to lick violence all over the world to make up for Hitler?"

D.C. glanced at the demoralized beast. "I guess America was too much for him."

"He bit off more than he could chew," agreed Ivan.

Enzo shook his head sympathetically. "What a shame after coming all them miles for that Monster Killer. But I thought he got sick drinking the water. You sure can't be too careful about your health when you travel," was his friendly advice to all.

The doctor was livid. "Luckenback *is* health," he crackled. "Don't tamper with my civil liberties, boy."

In his confusion, Enzo turned to D.C. "What did I say?" he asked pitifully.

"That's it," cried Luckenback, looking as if his drying underwear had stopped all circulation. Struggling to his feet, he threw the dice angrily at the table but missed and broke two champagne glasses behind the bar. "I know where I'm not wanted. Just give me my money and I'll go."

Ivan leaped up and thrust his beard into the doctor's pale-blue ear. "Steady, steady," he soothed, squeezing the man's heaving shoulders. "It's only the middle of the afternoon. You can't leave now."

Luckenback bit his lip and admitted, "I have a tendency to be sensitive. If I don't get paid soon I'll cry."

In the background Torwächter howled miserably.

"I guess it is sort of late," said Enzo, adding up his assets with innocent pleasure. "Maybe we can all play again tomorrow. I like this game."

"I'm with you, Enzo," seconded D.C., laughing heartily while quickly slipping into his jacket. "And we can settle all our little debts then."

Ivan consulted his chronometer by way of reconsideration. "True," he decided, "time has us by the short hairs."

"Four hundred and . . . sixty . . . two . . . dollars," Enzo cried, totaling up his astonishment. "My! My!" And then ashamed of his greediness, he said soberly, "You just can't beat sports for bringing ethnic groups together."

"Don't try to blend *me*, nigger," roared Luckenback, unleashing his anger like a mad dog. "I'm through with integration. Go integrate yourself. You don't even talk like a black man you . . . you . . . SHAMALON!"

Enzo turned white. Removing his Phi Beta Kappa key as if it were a pair of glasses, he rose up and sputtered, "See here! See here! See here!"

Silence. Torwächter, a surprised look on his face, observed events. Von Hippel watched too. The two men, their muscles rigid, their faces contorted into alarming shapes, stood nose to nose in a fearful tableau. Circling about, they raised and lowered their arms with dreadful care and growled ominously like old houses in the wind. On top of the bar sat Death picking his nose as the sleeping ship rolled on oblivious through the rainy night.

D.C., the first to see him, was worried. He had grown fond of Enzo, the kind of affection one might feel for a favorite toothbrush, and Luckenback appeared a booby trap of deception. Believing that desperate situations require desperate remedies, D.C. dropped to the table, snapped open a slim leatherette wallet of traveler's checks, whipped out his ballpoint, and in a frenzy of compassion so perfect that he failed to fill in the dates, repeatedly signed his name on the dotted line of one check after another.

Ivan's bad eye rolled about aimlessly in his head but his good one was riveted on the penmanship. He had never seen a nervous breakdown before. "You sonofabitch! Don't you know that the pen is mightier than the sword? Knock it off."

Ripping out the gold with both hands like a sun-mad prospector, D.C. dodged past Ivan and ran full-speed at the combatants, pushing them apart, and thrusting the checks into their clenched fists he shouted, "HODIE MIHI, CRAS TIBI!"

Enzo dropped his guard. Luckenback lurched backward in surprise, but with the presence of mind of a professional gambler, he counted the money as he went. In a Faustian attempt to trip the stumbling cripple, Ivan extended his leg. Somehow the doctor managed to hop over it. Torwächter snarled. The skipping clubfoot was an affront to his Aryan sensibility. Delighted that the animal was once more taking an active interest in life, Von Hippel snatched up a plate of leftover cucumbers sprinkled with dill and munched on them ravenously.

D.C. looked on all benevolently. He felt serene, harmonious, untroubled by petty thoughts, the great heart of mankind beating in a swaying triumphal chorus. He had saved a human life and it had only cost him nearly every penny they had. "My God," he observed with composure, walking peacefully in the direction of the men's room, "what have I done?"

Abruptly the snarling stopped. Torwächter lifted his nose and sampled the air, cocking his head quizzically. From his throat came a small eerie noise like a rusty scissor.

Von Hippel sent his chair flying and was on his feet. Although he did not salute, he stood rigidly at attention, his crew cut erect, his leather trench coat rumbling and flashing like a distant storm. "You speak, *Schöne*," said he to the dog. "*Was ist den los?*"

A booming crash against the outside bulkhead, a bloody scream, and Torwächter, his bark a blaring claxon, raced off striking sparks on the burnished linoleum. "I come! I come!" panted the illustrious detective in pursuit. As everyone ran out into the night, Luckenback pocketed his money and promised, "The healing science will serve. Depend on it." Briskly he walked off in the opposite direction toward the lounge, explaining to the bartender, "But first my neurocalometer and white jacket."

Outside the wind threw rain at the ship in handfuls and the footing was uncertain. Torwächter skidded, righted himself, and bolted off, leaving in his wake the hapless bipeds strewn over the glistening deck like water lilies. Halfway down the deck two figures grappled madly in the shadows. Von Hippel pushed himself up. "*Schöne*," he grunted, shaking the water out of his ears, "I come."

Alerted by the shouts, a dark shape shrouded in secrecy broke from the shadows and away, even before the dog could reach him.

"There he goes!" was the throbbing cry of the pursuers, but the fugitive, a gyroscopic wraith, moved with uncanny sure-footedness over the slick surface and disappeared forever down a gangway leading to the complex underworld of the luxury liner.

Bending down in the gloom, Ivan examined the trail. His subtle fingers detected perforations in the planks. "Track shoes," he informed D.C. without surprise. "Come on!"

But D.C. remained behind. Forgotten in the excitement was a small puddle of sobbing humanity. Dragging the victim up against a bulkhead and out of the full force of the rain, the drenched Samaritan paused to catch his breath. He reached for his handkerchief but then, thinking better of it, removed his tie. Blotting his own neck and hair, D.C. rolled up the narrow swatch and held it out to the broken creature at his feet. "You'd better dry yourself," he advised. "You don't want to catch cold."

The moaner looked up in delirium.

"Sidney!" The young man was shocked, unable to believe his eyes. "Here," he knelt down and removed the tire chains from around her neck. "Is that better?"

"O Richard! Richard! Richard! Richard!" gasped the hysterical girl, lashing her head back and forth against the bulkhead. "How could you be tardy for our first date?"

"Answer me, Sidney, are you all right?"

"Look at my dress," the distraught girl spread the skirt over her knees and fingered the splattered material. "What will Mother say? How will I explain? Where am I?"

"Sidney, listen to me," D.C. insisted, and grabbed the girl harshly. "Who was it? Did you see who it was?"

"Oh my God!" screamed the unhinged teen-ager in sudden realization, "I've been soiled."

"Sidney!" D.C. cracked her across the mouth and droplets of blood popped out between her front teeth. "For goodness' sake, pull yourself together. Now listen. Did he . . . are you . . . is anything missing?"

"It's gone, Richard," groaned Sidney, through her puffed lips. "Daddy gave it to me for my sweet sixteen and that monster snatched it. It had the darlingest little chain that cuddled around my ankle and was all gold and said, 'YOU ARE MY SUNSHINE,' and oh . . . oh . . . Richard!" she wailed, and threw herself on the young man's heaving shirt front.

Pressed against him, her young breasts were roasting chestnuts. The pungent smell of her damp untouched flesh swelled his imagination.

The unhappy girl blew her nose in his tie. "I must get back. Mother will be wondering what's become of me."

"Don't go, Sidney," implored D.C., his passionate lips moving over her bangs like a dryer. He fondled her wrists, elbows, the hem of her skirt. "God!" he cried with ecstasy, kissing her scalp. "You're such a wonderful person. We have so much in common."

"Richard! What are you doing? Please don't, Richard. Pl-e-e-ease." Though the girl doubled over, shortening her perimeter of provocation, her cheeks glowed in the dark like foxfire.

Forgetting his sick heart and pale blood, D.C., mad with desire, swore, "I respect you, Sidney," and watched his hand move cleverly through the folds of her wet garments, a digital Theseus maze-plunging. "I knew it!" he muttered in muffled triumph, his ardent fingers caressing her indisputable hymen. Facing in the general direction of Mrs. Finch-Bradish's stateroom, D.C. cried out righteously, "She's as pure as streptococcus. You lose, you lying fuck!"

"Wait, Richard. Think!" breathed the inflamed virgin, a young plant alive under his green thumb.

"Shhhh!" D. C. placed a finger to his lips as behind them a cabin light snapped on and murmuring voices were heard. Attracted by a familiar sound, he let go of Sidney, and crawling on all fours to the window, peered inside through a rift in the drawn blinds. There behind a table so burdened with loot that the legs bowed sat Dr. Luckenback, his jacket off and his hair awry, drinking and talking quietly over his treasure. The doctor's back obscured the other party whose laugh was muffled by the thick glass. Luckenback nodded in agreement. More laughter. The conspirators talked on together in a harmony of hushed tones, their voices occasionally rising only to fall again like tranquil dust, and as the doctor hobbled over to freshen his guest's drink with more ice, D.C. looked to see who his confederate was. Although the man's face was in shadows, his suit was wash and wear and he wore the golden key of Enzo Castelli.

CHAPTER 7

❦ In which Ivan eschews revenge
and delivers a memorable sermon
on true love, reassuring many
and reaping other rich returns.

Revenge was out of the question, degenerate, unsporting, emotionally wasteful, and difficult. Ivan, hashing over the night's events with his friend in their cabin, had nothing but respect for the wily bi-racial pincer that had snared them. If, however, in casting a wide net to recoup their losses, they happened by chance to enmesh the salt-and-pepper flammers, so much the better.

Since only two days remained before reaching Le Havre where they would doubtless be turned back as paupers, Ivan was inclined to Think Big and his plan was a bold one. He would take over the ship. With love. The success of the venture would depend on his knowledge of two things—the ship's Captain and human nature —and he was unassumingly confident of both. Of the two, however, the Captain had to be regarded as the more questionable quantity. Although he had only observed the man once at close quarters—a distinguished-looking officer who wore his sparkling white uniform as if he were promoting some particular brand of soap flakes—Ivan considered his conclusion inescapable. But it was hard to believe. Like all travelers on mass means of transportation who put their lives in another's hands, Ivan assumed the professional genius of his chauffeur and he was startled to discover that this man was unquestionably an enormous, brimful, thorough-going, out and out, utter ass. No one else seemed to notice. Apparently he had been picked for his job because of his stature and his ability to instill confidence, as is frequently the case with the leaders of primitive tribes and backward nations. All things to all men, the Captain of course was a potentially dangerous character, but Ivan suspected that he had a place in his heart for love.

Once the Captain had been won over, the rest of the ship would succumb in short order. But it would be necessary to advertise.

advertise (ăd′ vĕr·tīz; ăd′ vĕr·tīz′), v.t. [L. *ad* to + *sorbere* suck in.] To coerce slyly for personal aggrandizement.

Research had shown the young psychologist that in dealing with the human species an appeal to reason could only be regarded as the last absurd refuge of madness. However, stimulate anxiety and humanity fell into line like goose-steppers or lacquered curls. That little tickle in a throat neglected was triple pneumonia with unsightly complications. That spurned request for Heart Fund research money was the coronary kiss of death.

Freud said it. Anxious men are anxious about one thing. Standing shoulder to shoulder in the hard truth of white tile and hygiene, they secretly scan the sex like doomed comparison shoppers. What civilized man is easy with an ax in his hand or a bird that goes snick-snick-snick-snick-snick? But with women it's love. Fat women read in their newspapers that they are unworthy and give up, locking themselves away in their well-stocked Frigidaires. Thin women take off their falsies in sealed closets fearful of exposure, their bones rattling like hangers. And the rest, the rest sit with bullet-headed stolidity under hair dryers sweating it out. Through the waning, flesh-faded hours of the night, Ivan explained all this to his admiring friend.

D.C. let him go on and said nothing of the ritzy diamond in his pocket. Having taken the gem merely to try it on for size and test its therapeutic qualities—a temporary loan—he hesitated mentioning it to Ivan, who would undoubtedly insist on making the loan permanent. Yet it seemed to D.C. that Mrs. Finch-Bradish almost deserved to lose her diamond. She was a careless woman. It was just his luck that concerning her daughter she happened to be a reconnoitering Argus-eyed bloodhound. When several hours earlier he had walked the still virginal Sidney back to her cabin, he had been met at the door by her ungrateful mother, belching fire. Never again would he be allowed to see Sidney, for he had kept her up past her bedtime. "But I had to get these off her neck," D.C. had attempted to explain, jangling the tire chains futilely under the irate mother's nose. He would have argued the point further, but once again Mrs. Finch-Bradish was armed and presumably dangerous.

Perhaps he should tell Ivan after all. He was undecided. Guilty at not sharing his secret with his friend as well as of having squandered what Ivan liked to call their joint funds (even though most of the money really had been his own), D.C. compensated by throwing himself wholeheartedly into the preparations for re-plenishment. "Take my cape," he offered with enthusiasm, pulling it out of the narrow metal locker that served as a closet in their Tourist-Class cabin.

"Don't be silly," said Ivan, laughing. "What do I need that for?"

"Take it, take it," insisted D.C., and wrapped the cape around his friend. "This has to be done with style. Wow! Look at yourself in the mirror. It's great!"

Ivan considered the mental age of the Captain and wondered if perhaps a prop or two might not indeed be useful for what he had to do. Then, too, it seemed to make his friend so childishly happy. "All right," he gave in, "but that's all."

As D.C. went about selecting an outfit for himself, whistling gaily as he scavenged through his clothes, Ivan sat on the edge of his upper bunk, which had not been slept in all night, staring out of the porthole. The dawn was just coming up shedding a pale light on the still water and the rain clouds had auspiciously lifted.

Morning, and in the wheelhouse hurled aloft like the feverishly compact brain of a dinosaur, colored light bulbs flickered on and off across the humming panels. On large screens rising up out of immaculate steel cabinets, concentric light rings swelled to bursting and exploded in silence. A keen sailor with eagle eye and beak stood intently at the steering console. Above his head hung a star-strewn banner, sewn by the Captain's wife, on which she had crocheted in plum-colored wool, "GOD BLESS OUR HOME."

The outside door opened. As Ivan and D.C. burst in, a spick-and-span lieutenant looked up from the charts he was studying and scowled at their clothes, his bushy eyebrows fused malevolently. Although not tall, he was an impenetrable jungle in width and density.

"Get out!" he ordered. "*No* one is allowed up here when the Captain is on duty."

"We must speak with the Captain," said D.C. urgently, from behind dark glasses which he had insisted on wearing despite Ivan's objections. "When does he go off duty?"

"The Captain *never* rests," stated the Lieutenant in admiration. "Beat it."

Wearing a yoke-backed Byronic shirt, open at the neck, with dancing Caravaggio sleeves, D.C. waved his arms in alarm. "The safety of the ship is at stake!"

The officer stared at him, dumbfounded. "What are you, some kind of nut?"

Swirling his friend's Franco-green cape over his shoulder, Ivan stepped forward. "It's true, beloved. Be warned. My slide rule has parted the fat thighs of mystery. I have the figures. You're all in grave danger."

The Lieutenant weighed the beard in the balance. Under the combined thrust of anxiety and a low forehead, his eyes extruded from their sockets. "You've counted the lifeboats?" he asked in an incredulous whisper, a twisted smile on his face.

"Danger? Danger?" The Captain put in an appearance. A splendid man radiating the serene confidence of one invulnerable to nocturnal emissions, he confronted danger calmly, his long boot-brown face framed in silver. "What's this all about, Mellon?"

"Sorry to disturb you, sir. These passengers. They don't seem to know where they belong. They're confused. But it's nothing for you to worry about, Captain. I'll take care of everything. It won't happen again. Trust *me*, sir, it won't happen again."

"That's all right, Mellon. I'm never too busy to spare a moment for some of these people."

Ivan grasped the opportunity. "You are the Captain of this ship?" he demanded.

"Yes, I'm the Captain . . ."

"Good," said Ivan firmly. "We've come to help you."

". . . but it's really not that simple." There was longing in the bright eyes of the ship's senior officer. "I mean it would be very hard to say what my actual role is or even, for that matter, what I think my role is."

"I *see*," Ivan said darkly. "Very philosophic."

"Well," the Captain chuckled indulgently, "I'd say it's a little bit more complicated than that. You see, this is a tremendous thing and there are all sorts of people doing their share. Frankly, I like to think of myself as just one of the team."

"The team is in danger," said Ivan.

"We have the figures," added D.C.

"Let me throw them out, sir," urged the Lieutenant. "There's something fishy here."

The Captain was judicial. "We can't expect—after all there's no reason for everyone to dress the way we do, Mellon," he said mildly. "Believe me I'm aware there are people of evil intent even aboard our ship, but we know how to keep them in their place, don't we?"

"Yes sir, but—"

"Come with me, boys," was the Captain's courteous invitation. "Let me show you around."

Having lost their momentum, the boys followed vaguely, at a temporary loss as to how to crack the imperturbable mariner.

The Captain paused in front of the sloping wheelhouse windows, his face oiled by the morning sunlight. "To my mind that's one of the prettiest views anywhere." He remained mute before the plastic-blue horizon in a ceremony of admiration.

"What's this?" inquired D.C., changing the subject. He pointed to a rectangular box on the wall. Against a background of pins and tiny pieces of broken glass, a long, sharp, double-pronged instrument was suspended on a thin platinum wire.

"I wouldn't want to say exactly what that is," explained the Captain significantly as he studied the box. "I'm not suggesting that I've never thought about it because to tell the truth I'm genuinely interested in this sort of thing. But if I were you I wouldn't jump to any hasty conclusions. These are very complicated machines up here and we have experts—top people who really know their business on every one. Don't forget this ship flies the stars and stripes and our passengers want comfort. You're not going to fool the American people long, I'll tell you that."

"Speaking of animal gratification," said D.C. in an aggrieved tone, "did you know that one of your passengers was nearly throttled last night?"

"Throttled?"

"Strangled."

"Strangled! What class?" inquired the Captain.

"First," D.C. informed him indignantly.

"That *is* serious," acknowledged the Captain. "But that's why we—these are our suggestion boxes." He handed one to D.C. proudly. "I've given matters of this kind a good deal of thought and, on balance, we feel this is the best way to handle these situations. I don't mind telling you"—the Captain preened his silver locks and smiled—"that I've actually had a hand in all this. Here, let me show you—"

"Captain!" interrupted Ivan sternly, his beard crackling with static electricity. "We've come to alert you to danger and you show us boxes. Be sensible, man."

"What's this all about?" asked the Captain, revealing a trace of annoyance.

Glancing furtively over his shoulder to make certain that the Lieutenant was out of earshot, D.C. joined in. "There's not a minute to lose. Tell him."

Ivan's voice was hoarse and terrible when he asked, "Do you believe in religious freedom?"

The Captain was considerably relieved. "Well now," he began, with unshakable poise, "I couldn't make a definite statement one way or the other. There are a great number of—you have to take many factors into consideration. After all, when you are talking about this kind of thing you are talking the very—down at the very depths of conviction in the hearts of free men."

"The ship's calendar provides services for Catholics, Protestants, and Jews," said Ivan sharply. "Are you discriminating?"

"What about the separation of Church and State?" asked D.C.

"Men do not live by bread alone," advised Ivan.

"Rumor has it that our spiritual sovereignty is being surrendered. You forget," stormed D.C., flapping his sleeves joyously, "that we are a sleeping giant. Is this a one-god ship?"

Ivan stared hard at the Captain and shook his head. "Tut-tut-tut!" he went.

"I'm a Christian Constitutional Conservative," complained the Captain. "Someone is making all sorts of misrepresentations or misinterpretations of my position in this thing. I certainly believe in—there's no reason why anything that's found to be reasonable and proper shouldn't have equal time aboard this ship. What I mean is that until we can explore the whole situation I would be very careful in my moves."

Ivan had hoped that he meant something else. "Caution goeth before a fall," he cried pugnaciously, exasperated with the man.

"There's no time for that now, Captain," said D.C.

"You must be born again."

"Or changed—somehow."

"Life must be poured into your sterile veins," prescribed Ivan, "and the windows of your heart thrown open."

"Uncork your mind," pleaded D.C.

"Bare your soul."

"Unbutton your wallet."

"Smear your eyelashes with woodruff," inspired Ivan, "and let May into your backyard."

"You look sick."

"Be with us, beloved."

"Paralyzed."

"Take my hand."

"Limboized."

"Let freedom ring."

"Ding, Dong, Ding."

"The wrath of the tribulation is upon him," shouted Ivan ecstatically. "Burn your crutches, Ahab!"

"Now hold on here," demanded the harassed Captain loudly, asserting his authority. "Wait a minute." He clasped his hands behind his back to keep from biting his nails. "Just what are the basic issues in this thing? You seem to be getting at something that I don't—what do you have in mind exactly? Let me make this clear so there's absolutely no room for confusion," he said sternly. "If there's one thing I'm not afraid of saying it's I don't know."

In mystical turmoil, Ivan's vatic eye looked to the future. "Without love," he warned, his kinky lips barely parting, "this ship is doomed."

"I believe in love!" The Captain seemed definitely refreshed. "I don't mind going on the record—I've always believed in—there's no reason to shilly-shally about *that*."

"Then you have no objections," concluded Ivan calmly.

The Captain looked blank.

"Good!" exclaimed Ivan. "The Holy Tabernacle of the Latter Day Apostles of the Science of Love will congregate in the theater tomorrow morning at ten sharp."

"I've always tried to keep an open mind . . ." muttered the bemused trimmer.

"Do you have a ditto machine?" asked Ivan.

"A ditto machine!" The Captain was unmistakably daunted, his nerve failing him at last.

"Never mind. We'll find one ourselves. There's much to be done," declared Ivan solemnly, pulling his friend away. "We shall expect you a few minutes before the hour, Captain. Don't let anyone tell you that you're going to miss the rapture."

"Put money in your purse," cried D.C., flying out the door.

Tentatively, pain dogging his steps like a detective, the Captain made his way back to the wheelhouse windows and summed up the shabby world outside. He blew on the glass, rubbed languidly at the misty surface, smudged the view with good intentions. The sun darkened under his streaking fingers.

"Lieutenant," he called dreamily, doodling on the glass.

"Right here, sir. Captain, are you all right?"

"Lieutenant."

"Would you care for some nice hot bouillon, sir?"

"Lieutenant."

"That business about the lifeboats, sir, I can . . ."

"Oh, there you are Mellon," observed the Captain, hugging him affectionately. "My right arm."

The Lieutenant blushed in appreciation. "Thank you, sir," he said, and added, "sincerely."

Snapping open a case lined with tufted silk, the Captain took out a pair of half-glasses and placed them on the edge of his tanned nose. "Appeasement is counter-productive," he explained. "I mean—Damn it!" he snarled. "Are we going to let the kooks push us around? Bring me the ship's passenger list, Mellon."

A small ditto machine was located in the Information Office, which was squeezed economically between the public toilet and Juniors' Playland on B Deck. All that day D.C. and Ivan composed their flier and purpled their fingers with ink furiously cranking out hundreds of invitations. Through the night they rioted down the ship's passageways distributing their leaflets like moonstruck mailmen, giddy from lack of sleep. Back at their cabin, they dove huggermugger into their bunks, and D.C. laughed himself to sleep while Ivan, his eyes closed in contemplation, quietly mulled over his sermon for the following day and prayed for a full house.

In the morning, each still sluggish passenger stooped to the eye-opening news.

MEN! LADIES!

Are you unhappy?
Are you different from the vast majority?
Why are you *secretly* nibbling on sunflower seeds in obscurity
while others devour red meat on life's promenade deck?

Something is *SERIOUSLY* wrong.

LADIES!   Are your beds as silent as cold storage???????
MEN!   A stiff upper lip is not enough!!!!!

The Science of Love cordially invites you to attend our unique morning inspirational service where your life may be changed and your confidence restored. Thousands of ordinary miserable people have already been helped to unprecedented peace of mind and supreme emotional fulfillment. YOU may be next!

CONGREGATE FOR LOVE
10 A.M.

The Holy Tabernacle of the Latter Day Apostles
of the Science of Love

Cable address: "HOTSAP"

PROFESSOR Ivan Storch, B.A., at the auditorium lectern.

ADULTS *ONLY!*

By 10 A.M. the small auditorium was thick with anxiety, even the sloping aisles were preoccupied, but there was still no sign of the Captain. Fearful of exposure, worried teen-agers hid in the corners, slumping in disguise. Above their heads, streamers left over from Amateur Night covered the ceiling. Mrs. Finch-Bradish sat in the first row, buffing her riding boots with a twitching trigger finger. Behind the stage apron on the closed curtain, two naked women sat uncertainly in champagne glasses as the bubbles rose. Arcing upward in front of the lectern, the large fronds of a potted fern suggested the religious nature of the program. D.C.'s idea. Affable around dark glasses, he stood at the entrance collecting handkerchiefs like limp tickets. There was no room for sorrow in the Science of Love.

"Dr. Luckenback!" exclaimed D.C., at the presence of the lame healer. It was too good to be true. "What an unexpected pleasure."

The doctor blinked his contempt and said, "FUT!" A thoughtful man, he seemed to care nothing for the large stain that ringed the front of his pants like a black target.

"I thought you'd be too busy with your own experiments to join us."

With a touch of bravado in his limp, the doctor ambled to the door and looked in. "Where there's science, there's Luckenback. Any niggers?" he asked, scanning the full house, and, satisfied, remarked, "You've got a good thing here, college boy."

"I'm sorry, Doctor, but you'll have to leave your handkerchief at the door if you wish to enter the Holy Tabernacle."

"Handkerchief!" snarled the physician, turning his lips inside out. "Luckenback is Health!"

"But," the gatekeeper reminded him respectfully, "Storch is Love!" and resolutely barred the door.

Luckenback saw that it was no use. Reluctant to miss any opportunity that might be turned to account, he groused and coughed up two tattered pieces of Kleenex.

Unblocking the doorway with a happy step, D.C. whispered, "The service is about to begin. On tiptoe, Doctor, if you please."

D.C. closed the door like a vault. Making his way to the front of the auditorium, he climbed onto the stage. From behind the closed curtain, he dragged out a gargantuan prompt card and raised it aloft, his ankles shivering under the weight. He smiled painfully down at the audience, casual under his accomplishment, but his breathless words were barely audible as he announced, "The opening hymn will be sung allegretto senza sordino to the strains of 'Row, Row, Row Your Boat.' Will you all please rise quickly?"

Lighting up a cigar, Mrs. Finch-Bradish settled back to watch the appetizing young conductor. Although nearly everyone else was standing, there were a few curiosity seekers who scowled dimly in their seats. D.C. grunted and the voices burst forth like big animals from tiny cages, leaping, rolling, swelling in freedom, threatening the smooth bulkheads with crashing sound and loose rivets until the final stanza of wild exultation and joy—

> Love, Love, Love, you've come,
> Now I have a friend,
> Capriole, capriole, capriole, capriole,
> Funk is at an end.

There was an unsettling pause when D.C. staggered off leaving the stage bare. The singers dropped to their seats and looked expectantly to the wings, clearing their throats in anticipation. But nothing happened. After several minutes of the shared silence of homicidal elevators, the audience began to squirm—restless, edgy, goose pimples on the more impressionable. The stage was scanned for clues.

"What's that!" screamed a high-strung woman dressed in large buttons.

Rising up above the great blades of the potted fern like a shaggy coconut was the sacral face of Ivan Storch. The drama of his sudden appearance was heightened by his caped solemnity. Yet stepping into full view, he seemed to reject his theatrical past as if to emphasize that his unconventional entrance was but a homily on the lurking presence of love. He opened D.C.'s well-worn copy of the *Artis Amatoriae* and carefully turned the leaves until, finding his text, he closed the book on his index finger and said in a crunchy voice, "You are loved. *All* of you. Every single heart within the sound of my words is touched by sweetness from the source. Every single face within the sight of my face is warmed by radiance from the radiator. Today, my friends, HERE AND NOW, cresting smoothly above the sea-cold depths of loneliness, we are preaching *not* a religion, *not* a philosophy, but a way of life, a dynamic vision that pierces through to untapped reservoirs in the marrow of love.

"Stop burning dead leaves, beloved, and listen. Be vigilant! They are trying to take it away from you. You have been put into a black box by Twentieth-Century Fox and believe that everywhere beautiful people are marrying beautiful people in technicolor. You have been turned on by your radio and think that only tones as round as BB's ever become the wives of wealthy and titled Englishmen. You have looked for help to secular walls and been smitten with the news that happiness is impossible without good teeth. And what have you done? What have you *done*, you foolish virgins? You squeezed, you twisted, you creamed, you brushed, to witness your lovingness. Deceived you stooped to deception. Corrupted you sought to corrupt. Although knowing full well that you lacked the correct change, you stood brazenly at better bus stops in tight pants with exposed zippers waiting to be flushed out.

"Beloved, listen! I have here in my hand the diabolical utterances of the Antilove. Listen to the snares he has prepared for you. 'With names,' he says, 'you can soften shortcomings.' SHORTCOMINGS, beloved, listen! 'Let her be called swarthy, whose blood is blacker than Illyrian pitch; if cross-eyed, she is like Venus; call her slender whose thinness impairs her health; if short, call her trim; if stout, of full body; let its nearness to a virtue conceal a fault.' The Arch-Deceiver in his own voice, beloved, and you sipped the honeyed words of the sellers of pyrex glass as if they were unbreakable.

"Dear Hearts, believe me, romantic love is death, a grotesque conspiracy with its headquarters in the beauty parlors of America. The Holy Tabernacle of the Latter Day Apostles of the Science of Love is *life*—tingling natural unadulterated joy. Our calling, our mission, our crusade is consecrated to ACCURATE love. True lovers love truly, exaggerating nothing, extenuating nothing, appraising all like an exquisite jeweler. For beauty lies not in the vision, but in its exactitude. There is no loveliness in fabulous light. I know you and I tell you that I love you *for what you are*.

"Look to your Bible, my friends, and learn. See Joseph, son of Jacob, brother of Reuben, and Simeon, and Levi, and Judah, and Issachar, and Zebulun, etc., Joseph, a prosperous man, an overseer on a great plantation, the date king of the Nile, confronted by a poor, lonely woman who asks for his companionship. In her need she is beautiful, but his mind is so warped getting and spending that for him *accuracy* is impossible. Love is staring Joseph in the face, a PATRIARCH mind you, and what does he do? I'll tell you what he does. He bolts for the crops leaving her nothing but ill will and a few secondhand clothes. My friends, if Joseph came a cropper, you know that the Science of Love is no easy test tube.

"Hear me, beloved. Where Joseph slipped you will caper. Our hand-holding fellowship of micrometic lovers is ringing the globe. All denominations are coming into the fold. The message is fizzing worldwide like Coca-Cola. PRAISE LOVE! They say I'm excited. Yes, I'm excited! The good work is being done, and I'm excited. Just before coming out here to speak to you this morning I received a message from one of our workers in the field. Yes, a message, beloved, here in the middle of the ocean Jonahed in a steel maw. PRAISE SCIENCE! It was from Sheila. Let me tell you about this girl. Golden Sheila not too many years ago was running barefoot through the South winning spelling bees, a brilliant kid frisking in the sun. They gave her prizes. Bubble gum, protractors, pencil cases, the complete works of Shakespeare in one volume with footnotes. Hardback! But so subtile is the Antilove that even the Bard has been duped, and she believed. Goggle-eyed, innocent Sheila read the amorous tales of Rosalind and Orlando, Perdita and Florizel, Miranda and Ferdinand, Juliet and Romeo, and she believed. Love at first sight was being preached in a *school prize* and, YES, of course, she did believe. I ask you, how is accuracy possible under such conditions! Leaving home, this deluded speller with nymphomaniacal single-mindedness sought love in every eye, and when we found her stretched out in one of our larger Northern cities tagged an Abandoned Snow-Bird by the police, she had a torn retina and no focus. But now, PRAISE LOVE, Sheila is one of us, calling a heart a heart, spreading the meticulous word among the outcasts of society throughout the Mato Grosso in a hut-to-hut clean-up. My friends, I *know* that jungle. That jungle is the international refuse dump of romance, THICK with unrequited lovers of all nationalities, and Sheila is saving them for our side. PRAISE SCIENCE! This is *dangerous* work, beloved. The trees are heavy with bows and arrows. Vultures hover in the air, piranha boil the sea, and on the ground the fatal linoleum of coral, cascavel, and anaconda. But this means nothing to Sheila. She writes that her problem is the blood-sucking flies. These flies are as large as lemons and as tricky as blackmail. Up till now they have been impossible to destroy. D.D.T. is an aphrodisiac to them, flypaper a brown trampoline. Old age only makes them more nasty and irritable.

"I'm going to let you in on a secret, friends. Although always smiling as she makes her rounds, Sheila is not well. Our little lover is barely kept alive by constant transfusions. She's in *trouble*. But Sheila has a plan, visionary in scope, simple in design. Oh honey, listen! Those flies are dealing with loving science now and we've got them by the short cilia. Together, somehow, *regardless* of the personal sacrifice, we're all going to raise the money, money to saturate that jungle with raw blood in open containers and glut those greedy bastards to death. PRAISE LOVE, Sheila, help is on the way!

"Y-E-S-S-S, I'm excited. The hour of temptation is at hand and WHOOOEEEEE I'm excited. We're going to be saved. Yes I know we're going to be delivered from the nightmare of illusion. FREE at last! No more disguises. No more skulking behind popcorn under pancake makeup at spectator sports. From now on, the players are *you.* Show your pimples, beloved, with a majestic scorn for risk and danger. Let them be loved scientifically. Uncringe! The autograph books are on the way.

"And while your pens are out, dear hearts, don't forget Sheila. Hardly a day goes by that some miserable soul isn't saved by her efforts. Any little offering will be blessed. That same fifty dollars you give will be returned to you a hundredfold in ecstatic peace of mind and rapturous glands. Grieve no more! As my assistant passes among you distributing handkerchiefs, turn each one into a container of joy. Think of your generous gift as a green infusion of tax-deductible love. Remember, dear ones, plenitude is nature's law. Don't be unnatural. Lay your hands on them, love, set these people free. Liberate them! I take dominion over their sorrow. I command it to go. LEAVE! Those with their hands on their pocketbooks, their checkbooks, their bank books, bless them, love, bless them. Bless the older folks with their stocks and bonds and give them social security, and the young marrieds with their wedding gifts. Bless every one of them, love, TOUCH THEM ALL. Amen, honey, you are loved!"

"A-MEN! ! !" the audience thundered in response. As the collection was taken up, pulsing women were seen to remove their earrings and necklaces and strong men drop their wads. Wallets, gems, watches, and cuff links were thrown in with a Dionysian frenzy. Every aisle was turned into a fiduciary fire brigade passing the brimming sacks from hand to hand down to the front where they were placed lovingly on the floor before the lectern.

As D.C. approached the row in which Mrs. Finch-Bradish was sitting, he asked somewhat apprehensively, "Where's Sidney?"

The huntress bristled. "She's not old enough to see this kind of stuff. What *cojones!*" she cried, and mockingly emptied her pockets of a seventeen-jewel compass, two halozone tablets, and a travel-size tube of vaginal jelly.

The young man accepted her offering and turned his back. Removing Mrs. Finch-Bradish's diamond ring from his pocket, he generously tossed it in the handkerchief and leaped to the stage mumbling, "Bless you, Mother."

The myriad little white bundles bulging with opulence pyramided upward, several tumbling to Ivan's feet. But he still wasn't satisfied. Without taking a step, he kneeled down pensively and hefted the swag. His powerful hands made light work of it and as he straightened up he was scowling. His eye swept the audience like a searchlight and settled on Luckenback, fixing him in its ruthless glare. Ivan did not mince words. "We are nine hundred and ninety-nine dollars and sixty-three cents short of our goal," he rumbled.

D.C. called out firmly, "Love is waiting, Doctor."

Everyone looked to see what was what and the doctor was pinned down in a crossfire of stares. Folding his arms casually across his chest, Luckenback cased the exits.

"Beloved," growled Ivan, riveting his man, "that Mato Grosso is no sanitary napkin and someone in this auditorium hasn't done his share."

Squirming about uncomfortably on the cache of lumpy hankies that he had craftily managed to divert in transit, Luckenback yawned, playing for time.

Ivan's face twitched and his words were smothered in heartburn. "We've told you once, and we'll tell you twice. Someone in this good gathering is curbing his natural tendencies, skimping on Sheila, holding out on love. There is one among us posing as a reverend man of science who has been revealed. Unmasked! Exposed as a pierced boil on the postern of progress. And he's going to burn. Oh, that man is going to F-F-F-F-R-R-Y."

The audience made angry noises.

"But wait," cried Ivan, throwing up his hands. "Hold on. Even now, at this eleventh hour, it's not too late. I ask you, dreamer, will you stop abusing yourself within the privacy of your own imagination and come to us? There is yet a little time."

"*Satis verborum*," shouted D.C. "Praise *quid pro quo*."

With a tentative nudge, a sweet young woman in the uniform of a Girl Scout troop leader who was sitting beside Luckenback introduced herself and, cupping her hands over her mouth, hurriedly whispered, "Psssst. Excuse me, sir, but I think he's talking about *you*. Did you hear him, sir?"

"I heard him, Madam," responded the doctor, somewhat testily, clambering to his feet. "Fuck him!"

The confused woman gasped. "I beg your pardon," she said, clutching her empty pocketbook.

A born pedagogue, the doctor held his middle finger stiffly aloft and made a series of violent thrusting gestures. "You know," he explained, with patient urbanity.

Luckenback had hoped to escape in the ensuing confusion. But seated directly behind him, an outraged dowager with adamantine dentures piped up, "Heathen, curb your tongue!" and banging her oxfords down smartly on the back of his seat, she snapped it up like a giant paddle catching the exposed doctor off balance, overcoming his inertia, and emptying him and all he possessed into the next row like a cornucopia. He was fleeced in a trice and his donation rushed to the front.

"Bless you, Doctor," intoned Ivan, turning the other cheek. "To him who gives shall be given. But in the future bear in mind that he gives twice who gives quickly."

Stripped down to his stained undershorts, Luckenback clawed his way to the aisle and got up, wobbling like a punctured tire. He looked about him wildly, drooling, twitching, gnashing his teeth, and said, ". . . ARGH . . . FLEH . . . BICBICBIC."

Those standing nearby removed themselves.

The tormented man raised his fists. "I'll be revenged on the whole pack of you," he screamed, smashing both hands into a bulkhead.

"Good God, look out!" someone yelled.

A hanging extinguisher loosened by the concussion toppled from its rack, covering the doctor with instant foam.

The audience was convulsed. HAW-HAW-HO-HO-HA-HA-HE-HE-HEEEEEEEE. Rocking back and forth in their seats, they giggled, howled, wept, shrieked, and fell helplessly over one another like Chiclets.

The doctor wiped his eyes and peered out. Even people with incurable diseases were laughing at him.

"White trash," he spluttered, and turning, moved carefully up the aisle and out of the auditorium like a snow-covered Volkswagen.

Some time later when the laughter finally began to subside, D.C. rapped on the lectern for order and announced, "Please rise for our closing hymnsing." Now the entire membership was up and as satisfied as if they had just put away a Lucullan spread. Even skeptical monotones were standing and warming their note in anticipation. But as D.C. raised his hand, Ivan caught it and mumbled, "Wait." Coming down the aisle with a full bag in his arms was the ship's senior officer. Ivan's cup ranneth over.

"Hold on, here," commanded the Captain indignantly, coming to the stage and gently setting down his burden. "As your Captain I have something to say about these people. This is important, so if you don't mind I'd prefer to read it. I have a statement here somewhere that I stuck in my pocket. Just a minute."

As the Captain searched through his white suit, D.C. puzzled over his gift. There was something oddly familiar about the merchandise.

"Quiet, please," requested the Captain, snooding the hairy multitude. Unfolding a paper, he put on his glasses. "It has come to our attention than an organization calling itself 'The Holy Tabernacle of the Latter Day Apostles of the Science of Love' is conducting spiritual exercises aboard this ship. The management of the Fun Lane, ever vigilant in protecting the rights and pleasures of its passengers, has investigated this body, and it is our considered judgment that the bona fide operation of said body is open to the gravest dubiety." Thrusting the bellicose document back into his pocket, the Captain confronted an uneasy Ivan. "In short, sir, it is our view—that is, we feel the time has come —hang it, man, they didn't even *know* you at HOTSAP!"

"Of course not," bickered Ivan in defense. "Scientific love has no place for the cult of personality."

"Right! One hundred per cent! You said it!" D.C. smiled confidently at the hushed audience.

The Captain waved the explanation away. "I don't know anything about that. And if there's one thing I'm not afraid of saying it's I don't know. But what about the bomb?"

"Bomb?"

"BOMB?"

Both boys appeared nonplused.

"Don't try to trick me. Lieutenant Mellon found that bag there in the hold with your luggage. It was propped up against a hot-water pipe that you might say was supposed to act as some kind of slow fuse. To my mind, we've got an open and—you don't have a leg—it all looks pretty black."

Ivan scoffed and held the fused mass up for the audience's inspection. "Explosive plastic is normally produced in slabs about eight inches long, two inches wide, and one inch thick. Not in ten-pound globs. It is light brown in color and not burnt umber. Its characteristic smell is that of marzipan and not chocolate. Clearly, Captain, you are mistaken."

"Why he knows all about the thing! You must be one of those mad Bakuninites."

"You're overwrought, Captain."

"Frankly, I suspected something like this. But real Americans always give the other fellow a fair—the benefit of the—equal time. Maybe to a fault . . . but that's our way, the democratic thing. But when we finally make up our minds, *look out!* Isn't that so, folks?"

The auditorium rumbled deadly.

Plunging his fingers into the amorphous mass as if it were nubile flesh, D.C. extracted a red button. "Cherry, Captain?"

Laughter bounced irreverently off the proceedings.

"Please," appealed the Captain to the audience, "listen to me.

[103]

Please. Something is all mixed up here. I don't for a minute believe that any master debaters—we're not going to let great appearance of sincerity or anything else—THEY'RE MILKING YOU!"

The hall suffered a paroxysm of silence, which was broken almost immediately by angry shouts from the audience.

"So what?"

"Close your hatch, Hornblower!"

"It's only money."

"We're loved! Muckraker, fend for yourself!"

In the front row Mrs. Finch-Bradish threw her head back and stretched exotically. "Natch," she sneered and added complacently, "everyone wants to be in the in-crowd."

There was a hurt expression on the Captain's face. "I just thought you should know. That's all."

"As long as you're here, sir," said D.C. suavely, "would you care to join us in the closing hymnsing?"

Stiffening, the Captain contemplated his whiteness—shoes, socks, pants, shirt, jacket—all white and all bearing the hidden stamp of his employers. Removing his white-braided officer's hat as if to symbolize that for the nonce he was no longer representing official company policy, he placed it smartly under his arm and said softly, "Maybe just this once. I always did like these religious things."

Ivan opened his arms wide in sympathy. "Welcome, my Captain!"

CHAPTER 8

News from home and elsewhere.

Despite his new assets, Ivan failed to make a hit with the French customs officials at Le Havre. It was hard to tell whether it was his rambling eye, his concealing beard, or his unpressed exterior, but they immediately pigeonholed him as a craggy irregular and detained him for further questioning.

While they fluoroscoped his friend's ditty bag, clean-cut D.C., who had passed muster with flying colors and his pockets heavy with contraband jewelry, caught sight of Sidney coming toward him through the crowd. Her small face was radiant and her big brown eyes were shining like egg rolls. He sped blissfully toward her and then pulled up short, his blood running cold. Mrs. Finch-Bradish had appeared out of nowhere. Sidney had only enough time to cry, "American Express—" before she was yanked unceremoniously away. Beleed and calmed, D.C. watched helplessly as the mother and daughter breezed through customs and, outside, got into a waiting limousine that whizzed them away in the direction of Paris.

It took some time for Ivan finally to convince the skeptical officials that his intentions were honorable, and since they could pin nothing specific on him, they reluctantly let him into the Old

World. When the boys got off the train in Paris after what seemed to D.C. an interminable ride, he insisted on going to the American Express office at once. Ivan, however, refused to do anything before they had converted the jewelry to cash, which they did effortlessly, if at less than market value, two blocks from the Gare St. Lazare at a run-down, no-questions-asked pawn shop called the "Francs-Vite," owned by a gloomy man with a solid green face and a solid gold toothpick. After that, their next stop was American Express where they found no trace of Sidney, but several letters from other people.

THE BEIGE TOWERS

Dearest Cooshkie

There is still no word from you—not even a tiny postcard—every day I go downstairs in my new housecoat and fill the empty mailbox with tears—but I suppose that you are very busy getting settled at your new school and have no time to write to your mother who loves you—not even a postcard—I realize that a mother can be nervous in her love some time and will not worry too much if we don't hear from you so often but write every day—I am losing my appetite over your health—the least you could do is send a postcard.

At home everything is the same—we are now rich and happy in our new apartment which is classy—very—when you come home I will take you on a tour of it and when I say a *tour* I am serious because you can get lost in this place without help—you will see it only in the movies especially technicolor—our first day the old neighbors made us a nice housewarming and it was really something— Moffitt from the insurance company came and was very sentimental —he couldn't keep back his tears—then your crazy aunt gave us a song and everybody applauded her—it was really something!

Mr. Schlemovitz only sits around the house and mopes—I am trying to find a hobby for him other than painting—yesterday I saw some pictures hanging in the street and one artist had a naked woman out in the open for small children to see—I don't know where he got the nerve to show a thing like that in a residential neighborhood—it didn't even look like a woman—it looked like a monster with no clothes. Do you think he would be interested in tropical fish?

As for me I have just had my ears pierced scientifically—I feel like a gypsy and have bought a whole new outfit to match—there is a fine lady in the house here much older than me who takes dancing lessons at the ethical culture twice a week—she says it's good exercise

—who knows—you wouldn't believe it but in Warsaw when I was a girl my friends called me Little Fairy Steps.

Wait a minute Mr. Schlemovitz wants to say a few words—when will you be coming home? Don't study too hard—keep well my dear one only write—love and xxxxxxxxxx.

Your grieving MOTHER

This is your father, boy. HELP! I am being held captive by the American dream.

Best wishes,
MR. SCHLEMOVITZ

DEPARTMENT   STATE

PASSPORT DIVISION

Dear European Traveler:

You are a representative of the United States of America on foreign soil. Always remember this. As a citizen of the richest and most powerful country on earth, you will naturally be approached by European nationals eager to make your acquaintance. They will want to know about the democratic organization of our government, our free system of public education, and the high standard of living we enjoy. If you tell them the truth, they will say either that you are a boaster or a liar. Our advice to you is to tell them nothing. Since even a friendly smile can be misconstrued, we suggest that whenever possible you avoid such contacts. In the event that somehow you have no choice (e.g., German beer halls, Turkish wrestling matches, French rest rooms, Italian streets), it might be wise to convey the idea without fanfare that you are hopelessly retarded. This, of course, is optional.

Furthermore, you are doubtless aware of your government's efforts to improve its posture regarding balance of payments. In the last few months the situation has deteriorated dramatically, and we are urging all Americans abroad to "Think Cheap." Tourists on cruise ships in the Mediterranean have literally been throwing our money away to native divers. This must stop! Bear in mind that these sun-bronzed athletes are proud but simple children who would jump at anything to exhibit themselves in a pair of skimpy trunks. If you must throw something, toss peach pits, life preservers, used Kleenex, and cracked Ping-Pong balls. Economies can also be effected by staying clear of deadly foreign lettuce. This vegetable, fertilized with God knows what, has not been sufficiently abused—it is a hotbed of coccidioido-mycosis, blastomycosis, brucellosis, Q fever, and glanders. In my youth, I myself once recklessly ordered a mixed salad in a Sicilian café, and to this day the sight of any green leafy growth can shake my confidence. I mention this only by way of pointing out that your interests and your country's are one. Let me assure you that your determined efforts at thrift will be matched by your government, frugal for frugal. I am free to say that the Secretary of Defense has recently ordered SAC commanders around the globe to begin a five-year phase out of liquid soap dispensers. In addition, at every single one of our European embassies we have already taken steps to elim-inate immediately all superfluous furniture, lighting fixtures, and per-sonnel, and this is only the beginning. You can help. Be tight. "Think Cheap."

As you well know, your passport is not a right and not a privilege, but a gift. Use it wisely. There are certain rotten countries that you are absolutely forbidden to visit and these are stamped clearly on your passport; so they should present no problem. The other European nations fall into what we here at State call the twilight zone of acceptability. Although we are not prepared to take stronger measures against them at this time, most of them have a history of political instability and moral turpitude.

Unless you are in the military, we recommend that you make your stay abroad as brief as possible.

Enjoy yourself and please, for God's sake, be careful.

Your Secretary

Little America

You Bastards!

How I envy you. When I saw the two of you walk out the door at the induction center, I felt as if my balls had just dropped off. What was it like getting on the ship without me? It's funny, but I don't even know where my ticket is anymore. It doesn't matter.

In Basic, they wanted to make a murderer out of me, but I told the lieutenant I wasn't angry at anyone. By and large, I like people. He didn't care for that. So for the next three days he used me as an ashtray, dropping live ashes into my pockets and starting a million little fires. My uniform seemed to be smoking all the time and I was driven nearly out of my mind beating down the flames. It got so that I couldn't bear the smell of burning material any longer and the next time we went out for bayonet practice and the lieutenant told us that it helps to scream when you hit the dummy, I followed his advice. Raising my bayonet high and howling, I ran hard at the stuffed figure but close up it looked so real that I couldn't bring myself to do it. So instead, I screamed and just cut my own wrists. Although he was a complete shit and I was glad that I didn't have to spend more than four days with him, the lieutenant was right about the screaming.

After that I thought they'd let me go, but each time I try suicide they only move me to another base. I've been to three already. Now, finally, I guess they've given up and have decided to bury me alive. Out of sight, out of mind (or vice versa). I'm lying here on a cot in a subterranean Quonset hut fifteen feet under the South Pole listening to my head shrink. They say there's a terrible storm outside and no trees. The truth is everybody in this place hates me. They're worried that I'm a professional dier. What a joke! That I could be professional at anything.

I don't suppose I'll ever get to see Paris now.

P.

P.S. I expected more . . . somehow.

Rue de Luxembourg 29
June 22nd

My Dear Pratt,

The Paris of my youth and the world's is no more, and I am leaving for home as soon as I can pack my things and make the necessary arrangements. Take my advice and for God's sake go home; you are doomed to disenchantment. Your young friend, I fear, is a creature of exhaustible sensibility and, *tu verras*, he will desert you as the City has betrayed me.

Paris has become Modernity writ small, drained of all subtlety and leering at the age like some ancient courtesan wearing culottes. Her once Momic wit—a splendid science and a deadly art—has degenerated into mere posturing, graceless theatricality, bombast, and one looks in vain for a living style. For a man of feeling it is difficult to breathe in a milieu where automobiles choke the streets like madmen.

I suppose that one must learn to live with America, for America is the present and there is no escape. But it is hard. I keep turning over in my mind the happy trip to Madrid and our shared laughter

[109]

at the Museo del Siglo XIX, where all of the paintings on the walls seemed still-born, pale copies of the shimmering Renoirs, Monets, and Pissarros we knew so well, and now (*quel dommage!*) this second-hand existence has come to Paris and to me. Imitation dulls the senses, and the tired *ambiance* of the galleries and theater is little more than a repeating decimal. One must look elsewhere for life.

And so, despite the risk, I am going home to confront the vulgarity of America and seek in its vital matrix the complex imagination of our time. I shall always remember how we two strolled the eloquent boulevards or sat contentedly in the fringed sunlight of fluttering awnings to watch the spectacle of the world. But—my dear, dear friend—the world has moved on, and so must I. Adieu. . . .

Henry

"Who's Henry?" inquired Ivan, moving out of the way of a spirited co-ed group that had just come in out of the rain strumming guitars and singing. They wore gibbous parkas and knapsacks that reeked of the open road.

D.C. watched them pass, looking longingly for Sidney among the girls, but they all were marsupial blondes from California. He had expected to find at least a note from her in the mail telling where she would be in Paris, and there had been nothing. Sidney was not the kind of girl to break a promise. He was convinced that her jealous mother was holding her incommunicado like the man in the iron mask. Dejectedly, he went over and sat down on his luggage beside Ivan.

"A friend of yours?" asked Ivan, inquiring about Henry again.

"Oh . . . I don't know," replied D.C. indifferently, and glanced at the forgotten letter in his hand. The paper was yellowed with age and it looked as if it had lain around the American Express mail room for years. "I guess they gave it to me by mistake." If they could make one mistake they might have made two. He hurried back to the crowded counter and insisted that the lady in charge check again to see if there wasn't something else for Widdemore that she had missed.

The piqued clerk flipped disdainfully through the W's. "*Noth-*

ing," she said definitively, and put the letters back in their cubby-hole.

She was lying, of course, but there was nothing more that D.C. could do. He returned morosely to his friend.

"Come on," declared Ivan, adverse to crowds, "let's get out of here and find a place to stay." He noticed that his friend still held the misdelivered letter. "I thought you went to return it."

"I will not," snapped D.C. maliciously.

Ivan understood. "Come on. As soon as we get settled I'll help you find her," he offered, mildly amused at his friend's latest manic-depressive passion.

"That woman isn't going to get compost from me," D.C. continued angrily. Jamming the letter back into its envelope, he resealed it and taking out his pen, furiously re-addressed it to Little America. Although spiteful in its orgin, it was in the last analysis an act of kindness. Pearson would see that he wasn't missing a damn thing.

CHAPTER 9

The arrival and departure of the jealous M. Blefuscu, an old-world confidence man, briefly interrupted by another person not much expected.

According to D.C. who read the society columns of newspapers the way other young men his age read the sports pages, there was really only *one* hotel in Paris. For those who desired tone, who longed for patinaed splendor reckless of the cost, who craved service personalized beyond the most extravagant whim of narcissism, there was only the internationally famous, chic, elegant, noble, terrific, clean, *Résidence Ancienne des Quatre-Belles-Reines et Monsieur Freppel*. It was located in the Marais on the rue des Bossus, a quiet side street of small old houses tilting with age, where its weathered façade barely hinted at the glories within. Radiating out from the main reception hall like a silent carousel were public rooms crammed with rare antiques and so vast that foaming horses might gallop blindly over the subtlety of endless oriental carpets. Everywhere there was the smell of old leather. Although almost metallic in their sheen, grand pianos, priceless instruments topped by unopened scores, glowed softly in the rich shadows of obscure corners. On the walls hung the classically composed authentic work of Batolinni, Zuccarelli, and Vizantini the Younger—paintings polished with a dark brown tranquility. Above, designed by Cayré, great chandeliers draped in crystal pendants dazzled space by night and day. Whole squadrons of Marie Antoinette's gliding cherubs fluted the hushed rooms and heavy velvet drapes from the Third Republic fell fold on fold like collapsed parachutes. There was even said to be an interior rose garden with a waterfall spilling over white marble chips and giant travertine pillars surmounted by Corinthian capitals that supported an overlooking gallery, but only guests who had been coming for many years knew its exact location in the hotel.

It was to this remarkable establishment that D.C. brought his amused friend after leaving the proletarian American Express, and they were immediately swathed in luxury by six grown men marching in shameless cadence, all of whom wore the short jacket with braided front and stiff collar of the eighteenth-century Hussar. The suite of rooms the boys occupied was gay with rococo wallpaper in pastel shades depicting garlanded ladies and gentlemen at blindman's buff. On a wide mantelpiece above the fireplace the three graces danced before a gilded clock that whirled them about to the quarter hour. The high lacunared ceiling, French doors, Empire sofas, and silver candelabra, but perhaps most of all the sprawling Sybaritic beds on which mattresses swelled upward like soufflés, suggested past glories and a scale of self-indulgence undreamed of in countries with planned economies.

D.C. felt that he had come home. Thanks to the Science of Love he was *actually* staying at the "Freppel." POOR BOY MAKES GOOD AND FITS IN! He had to pinch himself. Although some individuals are dwarfed and exposed by architectural grandeur, there are others who blossom. The tall, handsome youth was touched by a princely air in his new environment, his jet hair taking on a subdued aristocratic luster and the blatant whites of his dark eyes muted with royal blue. Contentment reigned in his ennobled bosom and all of his little neuroses seemed to melt away. However, no sooner was he at peace with himself than his very tranquility became a source of disquietude. He wanted to preserve this halcyon state of mind at all costs, but what would happen on the day the money gave out? As he had suspected, the only thing that he could count on from his doting mother was letters. If he didn't find Sidney and marry her instantly, he might well end up a neurotic post-graduate all his impoverished life. Overnight D.C. had become a conservative.

Disregarding the inclement weather, he immediately plunged back into the wet streets of Paris dragging his friend after him, and for two weeks the boys searched on both sides of the Seine for the wealthy and elusive teen-ager. At each hotel they visited, D.C. would describe the mother and daughter, fearing that Mrs. Finch-Bradish might be using an alias to keep his treasure in hiding, but wherever they went it was always the same. No one had seen the American ladies. Downcast, he would leave a few francs with the desk clerk, informing him where he could be reached in the event that they turned up, and reentering the street, cross off another listing in his *Guide Bleu.* By the time all of the *grand luxe* five and plain *luxe* four-star hotels had been ticked off, Ivan's patience had run out. He had something more important to attend to than a misplaced teen-ager. But D.C. doggedly went on alone through the O.K. three stars and, desperate, even looked in on one unlisted hovel in a questionable alley just off the Quai Voltaire where it was rumored Clyde Beatty had once stayed. But Mrs. Finch-Bradish was not slumming. After several more days of fruitless searching, D.C. returned to the hotel feeling glum, cheated, surly, and as pinched as an empty toothpaste tube. There no longer seemed to be any reason to go out. Sealed up comfortably in his luxurious suite, he forgot time, sleeping in fits, waking in starts, and now and then mumbling on the tender hearts of artichokes despondently.

Once on his own, Ivan paid a visit to the Sorbonne. It was brief. Everywhere he looked there was a depressing adherence to the past and even the newest buildings resembled monuments. The formality and self-importance of the concierge of his college, who presented his letter to him as if knowing that it contained dollars, made him wince. After opening the envelope and satisfying himself that his orphan's scholarship (which he now saw as a meager amount compared to what ingenuity had collected for him on the boat) had not been tampered with, Ivan washed his hands of the cheap, Francophilic snob, Thaddeus Tick, and walked out. He had no more use for French education.

It continued to rain on and off in the city for the next two weeks and Ivan, curious to see what the capital of France had to offer as long as he was there, soaked himself in damp statues and local color without enthusiasm. Nothing was unexpected, and by the end of the month when the sky had finally cleared he could see that Paris was dying of history. It was a city in which everything seemed to have already been done by the dead. Ivan didn't care for it at all, but he had no intention of taking the easy way out. He would not quit Europe quite yet. Somehow he would turn the decadent Old World once again into a launching pad to the American Dream. This time, however, the Mayflower would carry only *one* passenger. Ivan returned to the hotel to consider his next move.

During the days that followed, he ascetically combined exercise with meditation and, in the process, subtly struck back at the antiquated decor. In his ribbed white undershirt and old striped shorts that ballooned down to his knees, he stomped from room to room lifting lamps, curling chairs, pressing desks, moving beds, and straining isometrically against the ancient, unyielding walls. His face, oriental in its flatness, seemed uninvolved in the odd noises that burst forth from his beard like assassins as he prepared to confront life.

In an age of specialization, he had chosen to specialize in himself rather than one of the more constrictive fragmented disciplines. He was a realist in a world larded with hypocritical bullshit and worse, and life was too short to waste it in indignation. If he wanted power it was not to correct abuses *or* commit them, nor was it to indulge himself mindlessly in the decor of the hotel at the top. The political nature of man could not explain *his* craving. Power was the ultimate reality of the twentieth century, a goal that was in itself of undeniable value in an era of debased currency, and, for Ivan, to wield power was to define himself as invulnerable. He would have it.

A plan was required. Ivan was well-trained and thorough, patient too—unwieldy details were small children to be coaxed into place—and now his ultimate goal was once more firmly in view. For money was not enough. Surprisingly, the new wealth only made him more deliberate and calculating. While his friend slept on submerged in his newly purchased monogrammed silk, Ivan sat cross-legged and alone on the carpet crackling over possibilities, and as he considered the paths open to a young man of means, there was an explosive knock at the door.

Ivan sprang to the knob, but whether his purpose was to bar the door or open it was unclear. On his toes, his calves bulging with veins, he moved his ear up and down sounding the door like a physician. All was lurking silence on the other side. In his underwear, Ivan was not indifferent to opportunity, only cautious, and waiting for the extreme moment when the visitor would be uncertain whether to knock again or leave, he suddenly threw open the door.

The small, sad man who stood there blinked several times in the breeze, wiggled his drooping mustache, and gave no indication that he was aware of any impropriety in Ivan's costume. As for his own dress, it was quite correct, trim as a thimble, but there was pathos in his tiny bow tie. Although conservative in appearance, he smelled like a wedding and his tousled hair suggested hidden depths. In his delicate hand he carried a large black portmanteau. He introduced himself with restraint—M. Blefuscu—and, eyes downcast, he entered the suite confidently, as if his reputation had preceded him. Ivan said nothing, biding his time.

The unsmiling visitor looked up carelessly as D.C. came into the room exhausted from sleep, applying cold compresses. He was wearing a Paisley silk dressing gown of cornflower blue, on the breast pocket a heraldic lion rampant, the collar and sash trimmed in gold thread. M. Blefuscu averted his glance, perhaps tact, perhaps disdaining to utter his name twice, and tears filled his eyes as he spoke glumly of the business of art in contemporary France. On second thought, Ivan was sorry that he had let the little man in. Like all salesmen, now that he had begun there was no stopping him.

The government had destroyed everything—everything—persecuting creative talent in its École des Beaux-Arts, encouraging mediocrity in its official salons, and what the government had not desecrated was consigned to oblivion by public indifference.

In America there was taste, curiosity, and the means to satisfy them through enlightened tax policies. In France there was only apathy and the *force de frappe*. Dealers priced paintings for quick turnover regardless of their quality as if they were strawberries. How was it possible for an art lover to endure in such an *ambiance*? At great personal sacrifice, he had closed his world-renowned gallery in order to seek out and encourage the Manets and Braques of the new generation. Darting through Paris, he scoured the left bank, the right bank, the Metro, the Tour St. Jacques, in search of greatness, going without meals, ruining his health, the blackness of the city gathering under his fingernails like storm clouds. Until one day a friend advised him to visit the nearby studio of a young painter who had only recently returned from America. This man was working in a new style, a style he called "Capitalist Realism." Blefuscu went and found genius—as spicy as pickles, as quick as drumsticks—under wraps and behind locked doors. Under the same wraps he also found his wife. (His friend's discretion was legendary.) The trumpet joy of discovery, the cock-strut of success, lasted only a minute, for the ill-starred young artist died on the spot under mysterious circumstances. As always, the world was not ready for genius.

D.C. removed his compresses and, sitting up, observed the visitor's shoes, eel-black and as thin as wafers, the tips honed to dagger points, the leather heels suspiciously worn. Although Blefuscu was no Othello, D.C. felt that his footwear verified at least one part of his story. They were unmistakably the shoes of a jealous homicidal maniac. The impressionable American wondered if the little man was selling protection. Lighting up a long Swiss Sullana, he casually inquired the name of the painter.

M. Blefuscu was satisfied to let the dead bury the dead. It was enough to say that the loss of the young painter had been a tragedy for art without raking over cold coals. But one man's loss is another's income. From the dead man's easel, M. Blefuscu, damp with emotion, had removed a final canvas and since that day he had dedicated his life to placing it in the glad hands of appreciation. With that, he then solemnly unpacked his portmanteau. The huge room was still except for the critical noise of Ivan's toes wriggling morosely on the carpet.

The painting was propped up on the mantelpiece, a folio-size canvas framed in pitted olive. M. Blefuscu's small face glowed as he skipped idly about the furniture with silent pockets. The picture would speak for itself.

It was a brilliant canvas, filled exclusively with primary colors that spiraled off the surface like a meringue. There was a large divan in the foreground covered with the stars and stripes and tricolor side by side. On top of this was the reclining figure of a healthy young woman with curls, her thick, wide-spread legs pushing lustily against the picture plane. She smiled slyly and in each hand held a large white tit, the red nipples popping up out of the canvas like hydrants. A toy poodle played mischievously with her toes. Behind the woman's back, the Smith Brothers in profile and wearing oversized derbies that hid their ears, clasped hands in solemn agreement.

A curious optical feature of the painting was that if one moved even slightly while viewing it, the woman appeared to lean forward, wink, nod, beckon, and roll about on the flags making wild sucking motions with her mouth. When asked about this by Ivan, M. Blefuscu stamped both feet in irritation. He seemed to be considering whether he had made a mistake in coming. All he cared to say was that the work went under the title of *L'Entente Cordiale*.

Although he disliked the past, Ivan was not ignorant of it. He assumed that he and his friend had been fingered by the front desk as *nouveaux riches*. His strong teeth flashed in the yellow underbrush like jeweled spears and his slow laughter swelled and swirled about the room like a dozen French horns setting all the dangling crystal in motion. He clapped his hands together—a rifle shot—and taking up the visitor's portmanteau by its handles, he tore the heart out of it, smiling. M. Blefuscu bled from every pore as the black stringy remnants fell to the carpet. Before strolling off to continue his training for survival, Ivan pointed to the American flag in the painting and mentioned that the Entente Cordiale was between France and *England*, but D.C. was laughing so hard that he failed to hear the year.

His tormentor having exited, the dapper little man fretted and sweated, French dribbling from his lips, large pools forming in his armpits. He wrung his hands and blew his nose in an effort to hold back the tears. His handkerchief was as filled with holes as a winter road. He pleaded his imperfect English, a poor night's sleep, marital difficulties, and citing artistic license explained the difference between history and art.

D.C. took another cigarette, got up, and examined the painting more closely. He pursed his shapely lips as if a fugleman to a brigade of buglers and imagined himself Bernard Berenson. It wasn't the first time. He frequently saw himself contemplating Aristotle contemplating the bust of Homer, wagging his head and announcing, "But not clever enough!" until the museum directors, contemplating their investment, dragged him away. It was plain to his trained eyes that Blefuscu was handling hot merchandise. The impasto had been lifted from Hatofsky, the couch from Oldenburg, the tits from Wesselmann, and the hats from the heads of Kosta Alex. A beautiful youthful rage bloomed on his smooth cheeks, anger not so much at the attempt as at the implied assumption of susceptibility. He dismissed calling the gendarmerie as crude admission of failure. D.C. considered the long, dead ash at the tip of his cigarette. Blefuscu's complexion was an identical hue. At the sight of the sad eyes of the dealer, his pale blue ears, his birdlike shoulders, the young man, temporarily unburdened of vanity, felt his irritation evaporate, leaving only a gray residue of weary discomfort. With tired arms he drew back the long drapes and threw open the great shutters—sunlight slicing the room in two. It was still summer outside. Below, on the rue des Bossus, silent couples moved through the afternoon heat as if it were a web. Across the sunbaked, cobbled street was a tiny park and there under an umbrageous chestnut tree a diapered baby with a white bonnet slept motionless in its carriage like a mounted fish. A red ball bounced out of an open door front and dropped into the gutter. Though D.C. waited, no one came after it. As he stood there watching, he wondered if he would ever see Sidney again. There was something about the clean kid that piqued his appetite—her youth, her sincerity, her affection, her innocence, her big blue eyes, her tiny blue sneakers, her putative annual compensation.

And all the while the distraught Blefuscu held forth on history and art. The title meant nothing absolutely, a convenience, Braille for the blind. Critics, teachers, and curators felt insecure without it. But for a man of taste, of knowledgeability, of temperament, it was irrelevant, to be forgotten, wasn't that so? In reality there was only the painting itself and nothing else. The balanced compositon, classically serene, a monument to the triumph of reason. The deep space, as profound as an old man's gaze. The conception of color, of course symbolic. But, truly, the artist's master stroke, to seize upon humble imagery for his epic statement. The hats, the beards, the little black dog—so insignificant and yet . . . perfect! Wasn't that so?

D.C. vowed that somehow he would find her and she would not get away a second time.

But for a man of blood, of inclination, of twinkle, even this, *bien sûr*, even this was perhaps irrelevant, to be forgotten. For such a rare spirit there was only the model herself.

At last Blefuscu had his man. As D.C. watched in amazement, the little art dealer opened the door and led in from the hallway the curly-headed, healthy young woman of the painting whom he introduced with some misgivings as Madame Blefuscu. Yanking her hand from out of her husband's grasp, Madame Blefuscu took in the room like an auctioneer, smacking her lips with pleasure. A simple creature, she owned the things she looked on and her looks went everywhere. M. Blefuscu pointed to the bed and bore his cross in silence as his wife sullenly began removing her clothes. Piece by piece the fragrant garments dropped to the carpet, but there were no heroics. Madame Blefuscu might have been alone. Climbing on the bed, she rubbed up against the smooth sheet like a cat in the sun, her naked fingers idling over the creases in the cambric, her hairy armpits alive with secrets. She stretched, she squirmed, she wriggled, she closed her eyes and sighed, and, in general, made herself at home.

D.C. had to acknowledge that M. Blefuscu was clearly an inspired traveling salesman. With his hands stuffed in the pockets of his dressing gown like Noel Coward, he bent over the healthy young woman in appraisal. He sniffed. She smelled of Europe. Madame Blefuscu opened sunken amber eyes and looked up at him with a languid gaze of dazzling vagueness but made no attempt to say anything. Picking up one of her emerald-green stockings as sheer as a dragonfly's wing, D.C. bunched it up into a rag and wiped the woman around. Satisfied, he went swiftly to a large armoire and took his personal checkbook from the pocket of his hanging jacket. The time had come to discuss price.

M. Blefuscu, holding the painting fondly in his arms, made a clean breast of it. *La grêle avait gâté ses vignes:* his business had gone bankrupt, his wife had gone to the devil, and his father had gone out of his mind speaking only German, a language he didn't know. All that stood between the little dealer in art and common objects was this masterpiece. *L'Entente Cordiale* was to be sacrificed for four figures. To the right party, three and change.

On the bed, Madame Blefuscu ran her hands blindly, restlessly, over her pink body—her thighs, her stomach, her collar bone—and one corner of her mouth smiled welcome. Although under the jealous eye of her husband, she seemed to be working independently. D.C. thought it over while untying his dressing gown. The price was high, but considering that the artist had died mysteriously, worth every penny. He was about to mount the bed when Blefuscu slipped a pen into his hand. There was no time to bargain. It was a sad moment, and big black tears of frustration splattered the washable blue ink as he filled in the blanks, but Blefuscu was too quick for him. Grabbing the check, he sprinkled it with talcum and, walking to the door, blew the powder off in a white cloud of satisfaction. Momentarily forsaken, Madame Blefuscu propped herself up on her elbows, shook out her bosom, lifted one knee coyly, bared her teeth, smiled like an incinerator, and coooooooed at the attractive young man. Having made his bed, D.C. decided to lie in it.

But suddenly people of all sorts poured in from the hallway flooding the young man's stream of consciousness. Covering himself with his robe, D.C. smarted as Blefuscu arranged the group into a living tableau entitled "L'Entente Cordiale"—including flags. A trio of musicians was stationed at the window—two violins and an accordion—their instruments at the ready and their minds swollen with sixteenth notes. A corps of chambermaids in felt slippers and tan smocks who had somehow entered during the confusion was pushed back into the hallway. Then the art dealer, a Stanislavsky for details, adjusted the derbies, smoothed the flags, stepped back and, twirling his fingers through the wilderness of his hair, scowled. Opening the door a crack, he whistled, and a small black poodle padded in, hopped up on the bed, and sported mischievously with the naked woman's twiddling toes. Blefuscu looked things over like a man threading a needle, approved of what he saw, told D.C. to take as long as he wanted, and tiptoed to the nearest chair.

D.C.'s heart was as drenched with poison as Rappaccini's daughter. Blefuscu had sold him a bill of goods and it was all perfectly legal. He couldn't even be turned in for pimping because regardless of his wife's inclinations he had no intention of sharing her with anyone. The unscrupulous salesman must have known that as an American he was accustomed to privacy and had cunningly created a psychological situation in restraint of trade. D.C.'s unhappiness became outrage for M. Blefuscu was not a straight shooter. Girding up his bare loins, D.C. was determined to overlook the spectators and consummate the deal right under the nose of the green-eyed monster. And when the trio struck up "J'ai Dansé Avec l'Amour" all his ardor returned in heaps, and he could hardly control himself. Thoughts of mad immortal passions—of Heloise and Abelard, of Pyramus and Thisbe, of David and Goliath —doomed lovers all, covered his mind like wallpaper. The music framed lonely, secret, daring vigils on empty moonlit beaches stippled with sea spray in never-to-be-repeated patterns of loveliness, and Madame Blefuscu stirred the pot. She yearned, she burned, she squirmed, and seemed to be urging him on like a teammate in a relay race. The sweetness of her dimpled knees electrified his tendencies. The shyness of her closed eyes charred his marshmallow. There were only the two of them now—Huck Finn and Mary Jane—about to gorge themselves on corn flakes from the same bowl. As D.C. sprinted toward love like a shower of sparks from a rising rocket, M. Blefuscu crooked his little finger and the trio changed its tune, blazing forth with the triumphant opening notes of the French National Anthem.

Something was wrong. Madame Blefuscu's eyelids snapped open like underground silos. Her eyes bulged with atrocities—slivers of steel wool in the eardrum, nasal enemas, genital mayhem, Chinese drips—and as she rose up she seemed to be seized by the spirit of the Resistance. It was evident that M. Blefuscu knew his wife's little weaknesses. Taking a boxer's stance, she gripped the yapping dog by his hind legs and struck out repeatedly at the astonished young man, indifferent to the musical beat. In her curious derangement, she addressed him as Bôche.

Although taken by surprise, the dazed lover did manage after several bars to smash her in the chest—a lightning jab—but to no avail. Madame Blefuscu was a hard woman without illusions. She struck back viciously, heaving the writhing animal at his head and methodically following up with a series of arcing bolo punches to the kidneys. She was going strong and was far ahead on points when the music stopped and she fell tearfully into her opponent's arms. Her chest heaved in search of air and the flanges of her nose flushed red. The lipstick that she wore—"Barely Peach" or "Scarcely Plum"—so delicious only a few minutes earlier, had dried up and flaked off in the struggle. There was a large raspberry mark where she had been hit, four of the nails on her right hand were chipped, and she was wet all over. Yet even close up and grubby, she strangely excited the imagination. She was so muscular. Lifting her up, D.C. held her sweating body in his bruised arms and blew on it as if cooling soup. He was still busy blowing when Sidney arrived.

"RICHARD!!!!!"

The Smith Brothers turned full face to see what was up, draping their beards over the bed's padded headboard. At the sight of the teen-ager's bloodless cheeks and delicate bone structure, the musicians hugged their instruments. The fey creature in the doorway wore a ghastly expression, only the cloudy whites of her eyes showing, and if not for the doorpost to which she clung, she might have fallen. In the stunned silence that followed, D.C. feared he was losing his panache. He wanted to say something pleasant, crack a joke, tidy up the room, don his robe, inflate his cheeks and make ambiguous plopping sounds, but nothing happened. It was the frozen moment of a Grecian urn. D.C. wheezed, shuddered, and felt severe shooting pains in his rectum. The social burden of Madame Blefuscu had become unbearable. Stumbling casually over to the armoire, he was unable to find a plastic bag in which to hang her, so he briskly tucked the body away in the bottom like a pile of rumpled shirts. The closed door muffled her tormented cries. Although the rattling closet fought desperately to be airborne, D.C. wedged his bare back against it and assumed an expression wise, tolerant, patient, scrupulous, lofty, and imperturbable as he struggled to hold down the lid. Had Sidney remained to see it, she would have undoubtedly approved.

The embattled young man took a calm second look at the empty doorway, and his nose began to bleed apocalyptically. Sweeping out of the room, along the hall, down the great staircase, and from one deserted public room to the next, he covered a good deal of the hotel with blood. But there wasn't a teen-ager in sight. Suffering acute deprivation, he stood dazed and grief-stricken in the empty dining room among the ghostly tablecloths. "Sidney," he moaned inconsolably. There was a weird noise from the kitchen. All was not lost! Racing in, he confronted a mountainous refrigerator with double doors. He drew back, breathless, blood-splattered, red and white like a barber's pole, and slowly pressed down on the handles. A loud click and the doors swung wide. It was filled with mushrooms. D.C. screamed in confusion, his long fingers white and trembling in the arctic air, and from behind the machine came an answering, eerie, high-pitched echo. Springing to the rear, he detected a derby pressing up against the keyboard of a whining accordion. It was M. Blefuscu and his gang wedged together like mosaic tile. In order to avoid him, they had ducked behind the refrigerator while trying to make good their escape. Blefuscu was not in the least repentant despite his incriminating position. In a crabby voice, he demanded to know at once the whereabouts of his wife whom he had assumed was in the departing crowd. D.C. bolted.

Sidney was not to be found in the hotel. She had come and gone like a timid joke. If not for the blue sneaker that he discovered on the newel post at the top of the great staircase, D.C. might have believed that it had all been a grim *cauchemar*. As he walked toward his suite, turning the little item over in his hands, he wondered whether it had been left as accusation or invitaton. The inside was still warm to the touch, and he allowed his hand to nestle in the spongy dark tingling with the sweet pain of proximity. It was wonderful to be alive: it hurt so. A woman flurried past him with her head buried in an orange parasol, and yanking out his hand, he tried to appear nonchalant, to behave as if nothing had happened. Suddenly D.C. beat at his forehead. Trained in symbolism, he had overlooked the essential fact about the sneaker. With only one, Sidney would naturally be slowed up in making her way through Paris—the hot, viscous Tarmac of summer would cling to her exposed cotton sock like melted cheese. He ran for his clothes.

But the door was locked, bolted, chained, inexorably closed, dumb to negotiation. D.C.'s knuckles were soon flayed with beating, his voice cracked with pleading, his nose drained with bleeding. He sank down to his knees, faint, and peered in through the keyhole. There was much to be seen for it was an antique lock with a large opening and his pursuit was gradually forgotten. His dark eyebrows brushed softly up and down against the golden doorknob.

A porter appeared. He wore a sky-blue uniform with a mandarin collar, and wielding the hose of a roaring vacuum as lightly as an artist's brush—a dab here, a touch there—he skipped about the bloodstained hall. When he came to D.C., he stopped the machine, pursed his lips at the red streaks, and took out a wicked-looking attachment, chromium-plated and bristling with bristles. The machine screamed like a high speed drill as he scoured the naked surfaces. Turning it off once more, he shook his head in dissatisfaction, and removed a large muslin rag from his patch pocket. He twirled it about gracefully between his hands until it was as hard as a blackjack and sent it snapping through the air at the immobile low object. He paused. Again he shook his head. From behind the door came squeals, giggles, grunts, pants, moans, groans, oohs, and aaaaaaga-ga-ga-gaaahs. The porter reared back and kicked D.C. in the can, freeing the keyhole at last.

Sprawled out on the carpet coughing, the tall young man raised his head and looked back at the kneeling porter whose wild eye was now glued to the opening. Although disguised there could be no doubt. It was the cunning Blefuscu. His face was so twisted up that it was almost unrecognizable. All together, Blefuscu moaned, raved, sang snatches of "La Marseillaise" falsetto, and prayed feverishly, holy water drizzling from his lips. There was a pungent smell of gas in the air. The weakness of the little man was unforgivable, unmanly, un-American. Filled with pity and disgust, D.C. took him roughly by the heels and jerked him away from the door where he was attached like a lamprey to a salmon, his eye making a crisp uncoupling sound as it left the keyhole. D.C. promptly resumed his place and, intent on the action, he heard nothing of the dealer's sickening offers to buy back his wife at a professional discount.

Blefuscu returned the check to his pocket and took a final glance at the locked door through smeared lenses. Inside, in the market place of the New World his wife was being ravaged by the bearded *peau rouge* and he had been paid in full. He picked up the hose of his vacuum and stood very still for a time. His body had produced waste faster than his heart could carry it away. As he started off dragging the dead machine behind him, its casters locked, and it bumped and bounced and jiggled all the way down the hall.

CHAPTER 10

✣ Introducing a French widow, a German Americanophile, and the mysterious pock-marked stranger, with some remarks on the past that should not be overlooked.

"*Je ne suis pas une sirène,*" said a heavy-faced woman, as the engine of the auto at the curb barked and sputtered futilely. "*Comment puis-je parler avec tant de vacarme?*" Oppressed, she sipped her sweet vermouth in silence.

Her quiet companion who wore a large straw hat squinted out at the great sunburst of chromium. She cleared her throat. "*N'est-ce pas la voiture de Madame d'Allégret?*"

A convoy of white-starred American military trucks rumbled by, snorting and farting noxious gases.

"*Eux, aussi!*" cried the heavy-faced woman when the trucks had passed. She pressed her lips together and looked about as if she intended to lodge a complaint with the *patron*.

Her companion tasted her anisette and coughed several times. She cleared her throat. "*C'est la voiture de Madame d'Allégret, n'est-ce pas?*"

"*Oui, oui. Bien sûr.*" The heavy-faced woman was still distracted by the noise of the failing engine.

"*Elle a une belle ligne,*" her companion mused. "*Une femme remarquable, l'Allégret.*"

"*Elle a vieilli,*" said the heavy-faced woman, her voice magnified by the sudden silence of the engine. She glanced uncomfortably at the nearby tables and then ran her hand over her neck. "*C'est ici que cela se voit. Même une perruque ne peut cacher cela.*"

Her companion removed her hands from the table and hid them in her lap.

"*Vrai, elle a souffert,*" the heavy-faced woman continued. "*Toute sa famille. . . . Elle est devenue une drôle d'excentrique. Vous avez entendu parler de ses soirées?*"

The woman in the straw hat watched Madame d'Allégret's chauffeur get out of the car and lift the hood. Removing a handkerchief from her straw handbag, she wiped her lips. "*Vous savez, je bave terriblement depuis mon embolie.*"

The heavy-faced woman smiled painfully, took a sip of her drink and asked, "*Quand partez-vous pour la campagne?*"

From where he sat at the next table drinking his coffee, Ivan studied the car. It was a long black 1936 Duesenberg with a touring body and wire wheels. It could still probably move from rest to 100 mph in twenty-one seconds. There was very likely a cocktail bar, a picnic table, sheepskin rugs, and fittings of engraved silver in the rear, and perhaps even brocaded seats and ebony woodwork with ivory inlays. It was as American as Thorstein Veblen. Ivan had never owned a car of any kind and had never cared to, but the Duesenberg was so big that it could not be overlooked. It appealed strongly to some atavistic part of his nature for it stretched before him like power incarnate, a new frontier so vast that only possession could make it real. There were approximately thirty feet between where he sat and the glittering object. The problem, as Ivan saw it, was to bridge the gap with impunity.

Across the table from him, unshaven D.C. moped over a blue totem with white laces.

"We did what we could," said Ivan by way of consolation. "We'll find her. What we need is a good car to step up the pace. Don't you think so?"

D.C. stirred. "We should never have checked out of the 'Freppel,'" he said bitterly. "What if she comes back?"

"I left a forwarding address."

"I doubt it," grumbled D.C. suspiciously. "Anyway they've probably lost it."

Ivan *had* left a forwarding address. Upon learning of his friend's folly with Blefuscu, he had insisted that they get out of the hotel at once and shrewdly left a bum steer at the front desk in the event the traveling salesman returned. His word doubted, Ivan wearied of appeasement. When he spoke again his voice had nothing to do with his patient expression. "If you hadn't written that check, I wouldn't have had to stop payment on it. We might still be at the goddamn hotel. First on the ship and now this! Take my advice, Weak Link, and stop rattling the Great Chain."

D.C. closed his eyes and seemed to doze for a minute. Finally he said, "You didn't answer the door, Ivan."

"I was busy."

"Too busy to answer the knock of a friend in need? A fellow traveler? A brother?" D.C.'s anger bubbled up like tar. He slammed down the sneaker on the table top and his thin-stemmed wine glass shivered. "You stink!"

Ivan grinned. "You'll be all right," he said. Seeing Madame d'Allégret's chauffeur go off in search of help, he signaled for the waiter. "Damn it, if we only had a car we could find her in half the time."

D.C. considered this. He thrust the sneaker into his pants' top like a pirate's pistol and, jaunty in despair, remarked, "Have you ever thought of buying one?"

Ivan paid the check and got up. "Frankly," he answered, "no," and strode toward the Duesenberg as if he had two sets of keys in his pocket.

As Ivan tinkered under the hood crossing wires, D.C. walked solemnly around the car, running his hand over its long chassis, its gleaming headlamps, its yellow fog lights, its rain-jacketed spare tire mounted on the front fender, its hot and fragrant bumpers. The sight of his plaid madras jacket shimmering on the dark surface of the door panel excited him strangely. All at once his gloom vanished. This was the vehicle in which to find Sidney. To find her in any other way would be not to find her at all, a travesty, *infra dig*. Behind the wheel of such a car failure was impossible, or, at least, irrelevant. For evening driving he would wear the white silk scarf of the Lafayette Escadrille. D.C. came around to where his friend worked with the cagey fingers of a demolition expert to show that he was not disinterested.

"All right." Ivan placed both hands on the fender and scanned the polished engine. "Start it up."

Sliding in behind the wheel, D.C. faced a brilliant field of instruments and dials, and like Adam gave each a name so that all might live in harmony. His sense of mastery was absolute as suddenly thousands of aristocratic revolutions per minute sprang up under his white buck. Checking a reckless impulse to wave at the pock-marked tough who watched narrowly from across the street, D.C. gripped the wheel and sang out, "The joy, the triumph, the delight, the madness!/ The boundless, overflowing bursting gladness,/ The vaporous exultation not to be confined!/ Ha! Ha!"

Ivan slammed the hood closed and jumped in, his beard dancing, his eyes twinkling with pleasure. "Beat it," he growled.

D.C. reached for the gearshift.

"*Merci*, gentlemen," said the dashboard carefully, with just a hint of ennui. "These days one rarely comes upon anyone who remembers the past. I am in your debt."

There was momentary confusion in the front seat. The radio had not been turned on, the matted floor was unsullied by foreign particles, the glove compartment was free of both midgets and ventriloquists posing as midgets. Adjusting quickly, D.C. seemed cheered by the thought of a talking dashboard. Ivan directed his friend's attention to the rear and groped for words.

Stretched out on the seat like a white effigy on a sarcophagus was a slender, elegant woman holding a silver speaking tube. Her hands were covered by white net gloves and her face by a hat designed to resemble a space helmet. Only a lock of gray hair was visible. If not for that, she might have been a starlet in mufti.

"I'm sorry," struck up the moody dashboard behind them, "but the heat makes conversation impossible. Besides . . . who would believe it?" The woman's arm came out like lazy tongs, a pincered card at the end. "Do come tonight and perhaps we can chat. I like Americans. They're so *sympathique*."

The embossed card said only "ALLEGRET," as if she were a well-known restaurant. The boys put their heads together and while D.C. argued the insignificance of the penalty for kidnapping old aristocrats in Republican France, the door beside Ivan opened and there stood the chauffeur, wide-mouthed, fang-toothed, an exquisite clarity in the projection of his frontal lobe. Behind him a mechanic in coveralls.

"Glad to have been of service," said Ivan hoarsely, as he leaped to the sidewalk.

Reluctantly, D.C. moved out from behind the wheel. "You might have said thank you, you know. We did get it started."

"*Merde*," said the sneering chauffeur, and drove off.

It was not difficult to learn the Duesenberg's address for apparently everyone in Paris knew Allégret. It seemed as if they could hardly walk a block in any direction without having someone rush up to them eager to pass along some little anecdote about the woman. How she had suffered a tragic loss, how she always wore black, how in her youth she had swum the English Channel both ways ungreased, how after studying the shawm for only three days she had become a concert performer on the rebec touring all principal cities, how in the Vatican gardens when Pope John had disclosed his blighted monkshood she had remarked "Pacem in Terris," how she had written the sketchy first draft of her Rabelaisian critique of the *Roman de la Rose* while in an Iron Maiden at Auschwitz, how she always wore white. Although sometimes the stories were about duchesses, princesses, and movie stars, not one was without merit. All, however, were time consuming, and it was not until late that night that the two young men arrived at what they took to be the eccentric residence of Madame d'Allégret.

A great deal of shrubbery surrounded the house and the smell of night-blooming jasmine filled the air. There were few lights on the block, few sounds. Above, the stars stood out like sails. Although they had been told that Madame d'Allégret lived next to the Cimetière du Montparnasse, this house was so close that it might have been considered an annex, and no doubt tear-stained mourners occasionally dropped wreaths on her doorstep in their bewilderment. There was nothing on the doorstep now but a hastily scrawled chalk message barely visible which read: *"N'Importez Pas Du Vin Étranger."* In the darkness, the house itself seemed to have been bombed out. Dangling wires, exposed pipes, fallen timbers, broken glass, rubble.

Tripping over a rusty playpen, Ivan whirled about, on guard, fearless. He saw nothing outrageous, nothing to equal the dark house before him. Lifting the playpen out of the path, he heaved it into the cemetery, narrowly missing a man who had been watching them from behind a tombstone. Ivan wiped his hands and knocked on the door. While waiting for someone to answer his friend's knock, D.C. wondered why the pock-marked hoodlum was trailing them. A definite criminal type—ectomorphic with a Roman nose, cavernous parietal fissure, and no chin. It was not impossible that this was the police.

No one was home. As Ivan had suspected, their informants weren't to be trusted. Madame d'Allégret's house was not on the south side of the cemetery at all but rather on the broad Boulevard Edgar Quinet which bordered it on the north. The house itself was a seventeenth-century baroque mansion, a small-scale Hôtel de Ville carved out of warm, rose-tinted stone that had only recently been cleaned. D.C. ran eagerly up the stairs to the arched doorway and banged on the splendid brass knocker. This was more like it. The white-capped maid who promptly opened the door was a forbidding middle-aged woman with a small gold cross around her neck. She received her mistress's card from Ivan as if nothing could possibly surprise her and leading the boys through the tastefully decorated foyer to a large oaken door, she went about her business. The party was being held downstairs in the Rumpus Room.

D.C. threw open the door and stopped short. The stairs were dark, but far below, like something viewed through the wrong end of a telescope, he could make out a dab of light. Shouts, laughter, gay badinage, and the woeful siren of Bessie Smith echoed up the stairs. Ivan led the way down and gradually the noise became louder and the light more reassuring.

"Hello!" shouted D.C., nervously bringing up the rear. "Anyone down there?"

From below, a friendly English voice called out above the din, "Hail Native Language, that by sinews weak didst move my first endeavoring tongue to speak and mads't imperfect words with childish trips, half unpronounced, slide through my infant lips."

D.C. concluded that it was safe to proceed. At the bottom of the stairs, in the depths of Paris—far from the rising middle class—beneath underground cables, air raid shelters, and radioactive refuse, a party was going on. The Englishman, who seemed to be functioning as host, greeted them warmly. "Unmuffle, thou blabbing eastern scouts!" On his head he wore a snug calotte of Moroccan leather and his feet were wrapped in something that resembled green Harvard book bags. Heedless of the revelry behind his back, he puffed soulfully on a meerschaum with his eyelids closed. D.C. wondered if he had been underground so long that he had suffered the blind fate of unfathomable fish and early Greek bronze sculpture. "You may call me Milton," he said, as if there were other possibilities.

"John?" quipped D.C.

"Milton," puffed the piper. "Milton Milton. I happen to be an expatriate poet, author of sonnets, odes, villanelles, virelays, pastorals, pastoral elegies, elegiac rondels, vers de société, and currently completing an epic zeugma. What are you?"

"It's an interesting question," said D.C. enthusiastically. "It's worth asking."

Ivan looked about the candlelit room and inquired, "Is Madame d'Allégret on the premises?"

Milton Milton admitted that it *was* an interesting question and released a very sweet cloud of smoke. "Yes," he said, "thank God for my poetry," and relapsed into a calm stupor.

Ivan and D.C. squeezed past him into the atmospheric room, as jammed with merrymakers as a gypsy's cave. It was an underground discothèque. From the transistor radio, Fats Waller leered out at the seductively gowned ladies hopping about in the center of the floor with straight-backed gentlemen in formal wear who appeared to be pale White Russian princes, light green Italian dukes, and the last of the colorless Hapsburgs. A considerable amount of good-natured intramural pinching was going on but no one seemed to mind in the general hilarity. Forming a ring about the dancers and filling the corners of the Rumpus Room were groups of thoughtful young people looking for answers. Hypodermic needles gleamed in the candlelight like truth. Eubodal, pantapon, dicodid, diosane, dolophine—all of the modern wonderworking drugs were in use. An old-fashioned teen-age couple wearing earrings smoked hand-rolled cigarillos dipped in laudanum. Psychedeliacs swallowed, peyoteers munched. Junk was sniffed, smoked, eaten, injected in veins, muscles, skin, rubbed on raw spots, and inserted in rectal suppositories. In every nook and cranny, the room was a beehive of activity. Although Ivan regarded it as wasted energy, he was pleased to see that there was a little life left in Paris after all.

D.C. felt a tug at his sleeve. He tugged back. A pretty German girl with a pale, impassive face and Bavarian eye makeup was offering him a sip from her flask of paregoric. "I like you," she said, breathing fire. "You are American, yes?"

"Why yes!" D.C. was elated, and taking the silver flask from her hand, he toasted his new friend. The swastika he explained away as war surplus.

The girl's face suddenly went lumpy. "But I like so many men," she muttered, wrinkling his crease. "You are American, yes?"

"Maybe yes, maybe no," D.C. equivocated, fascinated by this complex creature.

Ivan considered her rabid interest in Americans as unnatural. "Take care," he warned, slipping away into the crowd in search of their hostess, "she's juicy."

D.C. didn't realize that his friend was referring to the paregoric. For inside her striped polo shirt the German girl looked very juicy indeed. Her hair was black raspberry, her lips tomato, her breasts orange, and her behind a vegetable cocktail. This girl was just full of juice.

Eyes downcast, she placed her hand to her cheek and touched her little finger to half-opened lips. "I have lost something," was what she said and they were the saddest words that D.C. had ever heard.

He took her hand and smiled like St. Valentine. "Lucky girl. I'm a finder. Uncanceled stamps, wallets, cracks in reservoirs, telephone numbers not listed in the yellow pages, lost tribes. The most elusive. Look" —he impulsively pulled out Sidney's sneaker— "even when I'm not trying. It's uncanny." The sight of the little blue sneaker in his hand came as somewhat of a shock to D.C. and, his braggadocio ruffled, he quickly put it away. "Please," he begged, "let me help you. What is it you've lost?"

"My father. On the Western front."

"Your worries are over."

"Every night," she continued, overcome by nostalgia, "behind the blackout curtains he would take out a fresh copy of *Mein Kampf* and shoot it. He hated Jews. Christ, Freud, Hitler, it made no difference to him. He was a democrat, a real American who went West."

Although the Schlemovitzes loathed Germans, their child carried few scars. To Widdemore, history was a series of water-tight chambers that had nothing to do with one another.

"Where was he last seen?" asked D.C. gravely, his face sharing her problem.

"Here and there. An arm in Munster, a tooth in Rauffach, an ear in Hattstatt."

"Leprosy?" A tremor, sharp yet subtle, shook the handsome young man in the neighborhood of exotic infectious disease.

"Technology," replied the girl, and laughed and laughed. "It's just as well. He could never stand being in one place. *Er war ein lustige Dudelsackpfeifer.* The dirty old man." Her finger returned to her lips pensively. "But what about the little ones?"

"Are they lost, too?" D.C. was put out. This kid had psycho-logical problems. She couldn't hold on to anything. But when the German girl began snapping her fingers and grinding her teeth in time to Louis Armstrong's trumpet, he relented and acknowl-edged that by all means they should be considered. Nervously he drained off the rest of the paregoric.

"Professor Schnitzer loved nature," she told him, wriggling like Salomé. "He would take his cane and lead us out into the woods to gather nuts and mushrooms and wild berries. I held hands with my friend Eva. She was a good student and had a wrist watch. We were always the first to fill our brown bags, even sooner than the boys. One day I heard a plane and ran, and the Professor, whose ears were hairy and no longer sharp, thought I was sick. He caught me hiding on my knees behind a rock and began loosening my clothes. Whenever a girl in the class was sick he would loosen her clothes. I pointed to the plane's American star but it was too late. After the explosion, his cane stuck out of his scalp like an aerial." She tossed her head and grinned slyly. "The dirty old man."

"And the others?" D.C. held his breath.

"I saw only three, Otto, Golo, and Bodo—the maniacs—hanging like leaves from an oak tree."

"You poor kid." D.C. patted her knuckles consolingly. "You must hate us."

"The past is for old ladies. My stepfather is an American general." She looked up at him, her eyes like faucets, one hot one cold. "Give me a kiss."

D.C. was relieved that there wasn't a hostile bone in her body. He held her snug and their paregoric-sweetened lips met and clung together, fierce mouth-to-mouth resuscitation, hot drama in the round. Upon his return, D.C. saw that they were not unobserved. Dodging about on the dance floor with a woman in ostrich feathers and open-back shoes, the lithe pock-marked gangster was rapping his metal taps defiantly. Tat-tat-a-tat, he twirled her in, tat-tat-a-tat, and out and about, as quick as a cat, as grim as an ax, and watched her with folded arms as she spun on and on hysterically. He had cunningly followed them from the south side of the cemetery. What was he after? On the back of his tight Glen plaid suit D.C. imagined that he saw the word "TREMBLE" written in bold black studs. He rubbed his eyes and looked again but Pock Mark was gone, his wedge-shaped head popping up unexpectedly all around the room like a groundhog.

"What is the matter?" the girl asked, pulling herself away from him. "You don't like me?"

Before D.C. could reassure her, something fell on the floor

between them. It was Pock Mark, the cutthroat, sitting inconspicuously with his nose in a bottle of airplane glue.

D.C. pulled his flat belly out of harm's way and began to sweat. BIG DROPS. Suddenly, the sweeping unpleasantness of his predicament descended on him with crushing force. This was the German girl's bloodthirsty boyfriend and Ivan was nowhere in the immediate vicinity. Not since he first looked down and saw his own nose out there like a stranger was he so overwhelmed with his mortality.

"You're making a mistake," he told her, his voice jarringly nasal. "You're too good for me. My blood is tainted."

"Bah!" She stuck out her luscious lower lip.

"Believe me," declared D.C., riled up by her cynicism. "Have you ever heard of Billy the Kid, Spoon-Meat Jensen, Iron Duke Diddle, or Big Jim Cockolovitch?"

"Come?" said the German girl.

D.C. paused, in doubt, and when he spoke there was mingled pain and pride in his choked-up throat. "Have you," he asked, "have you ever heard of The Immaculate Cooler?"

She said, "Bah," but it was evident that this time she was not at all sure.

"My brother," he revealed tenderly. "Public Enemy No. 6. He murdered exclusively in the New England area and never left a clue. The papers called him the cleanest criminal between Scranton and Bellows Falls. But one day he slipped up and dropped Dad, a candy baron, into a vat of butter crunch. As soon as the first shipment went on sale, the Pure Food and Drugs people had him."

"You *are* American!" She leaned forward and squeezed him in delight. Under the tent of their arms, Pock Mark looked up sourly.

"You mustn't," yelped D.C., frantically pushing her away. "We were identical twins. One egg, two yolks. Think of the Corsican Brothers, the James Brothers, the Brothers Karamazov. My ontogeny is checkered with doubtful chromosomes. Something might snap at any moment and the families of a dozen cops would be turned into widows and orphans. I can't be trusted.

We looked alike, talked alike, dressed alike, we were so much alike that even Mom still calls me Irwin."

"What *is* your name?" she wanted to know.

"Irwin," said D.C., "but sometimes I think I'm capable of anything." His story had sounded so convincing that Irwin was carried away. Without warning he jumped back, bounced up and down on the balls of his feet, and swung his arms about in a deadly circle. "Don't think I don't see you down there," he cried dangerously. "What do you want anyway?"

The pock-marked sniffer raised his nose like a pitted steel blade. He stood up, his thin face an expressionless parchment with no message. On the radio a moody rendition of "Celray Stalks at Midnight" with violins and cream cheese. He went for his pocket, a silver shaft glinted in his claw, a click, and D.C.'s arms fell, his arches fell, his testicles cannon balls on gossamer threads.

"God help you!" shouted D.C. bravely. "One false move and I'm dead."

The Pock Mark paid no attention but merely clipped his nails as if he were Horowitz about to sit down at a Steinway. He put away the clipper and about-faced to the German girl. He felt her all over like a chicken.

She giggled. "You're an American, yes?"

Ignoring her, he about-faced to the young man. "*Fashtaist mame loshen?*" he asked, confidentially.

The little Jew left in D.C. moaned. "Man," he said, his youthful spirits returning and his face rock, "are you trying to make a fool of me?"

Jerking his thumb at the German girl, the pock-marked villain whispered out of the side of his mouth, "No sweat, kid. You will," and tripped to the dance floor where his partner was still spinning like a top.

CHAPTER 11

Showing that fair exchange is no robbery.

Madame d'Allégret did not come to the Rumpus Room that night. Of course there were rumors. Ivan went through them like a giant thresher and came out with intriguing shredded wheat. The owner of the Duesenberg began to seem more relevant to his future than the car itself, for ostensibly she had friends in high places on both sides of the Atlantic. But Ivan was not one to rely on gossip in matters of consequence and so the following day he paid a visit to the hushed reading room of the Bibliothèque Nationale in order to thumb through a copy of *Who's Who in France*. According to the editors' entry, she was a woman, fifty-two years old, who had been born in Paris, attended the Institut Normal Catholique Adelina-Desir and Académie Julian, and consecrated her life to the assemblage movement in sculpture. Her works were owned by museums in Orléans, Dijon, Bayonne, and the Université de Montreal in Canada. For her construction *Sodome et Gomorrhe* she received the Prix Arp. Her relations included Pous de Lauzières (cabinet minister), Simon DuBos Caravelle (cabinet minister), Emile Martin-Deslias (cabinet minister), and Armand Schlumberger (*inspecteur des contributions indirectes*). Ivan wasn't certain what Schlumberger did but he appeared to be performing useful labor, and the credentials of the other three were impeccable. Madame's husband Coup, the former ambassador to Turkey, was a national hero who had been killed during the war and each of her nine children had died in one tragic accident after another. Since the death of her last child, she was devoting herself full time to her sculpture. Her spare time she gave over to the writing of her memoirs (one volume of which had already been published under the title *L'Angoisse*) and the church. She was a member of the Académie Française, the Action Catholique Générale Féminine, and the Comité des Amis de Marcel Proust du Soroptimist Club.

Rereading her dossier, Ivan concluded that such a woman unquestionably required pity and understanding and, in return, who knew what interesting doors might be opened to a young man of promise. Full of compassion, he spent his days keeping the house on the Boulevard Edgar Quinet under close surveillance from the cemetery across the street. He was determined not to miss his opportunity, but after five days of watching the front door, he was still waiting for Allégret.

Meanwhile D.C. had written off his pock-marked oppressor as either a live-wire recruiting officer for the Irgun Zvi Lumi or an anti-German Jewish figment of his imagination, and together with Lilo (for that was the name of the German girl), he honeymooned among the monuments of the Cimetière du Montparnasse. There is nothing quite like sleeping out of doors under the stars when one is young and as yet untouched by arthritis and brittle bones, and D.C. and Lilo were in blissfully high spirits. They rumpled hair, tickled ears, told jokes, held hands, rubbed lips, and exchanged their secret scars like rings. Never a dull moment. After the appetizers, they set up housekeeping in earnest at the granite gravestone of Barbezieux (1846–1939) whose posthumous advice to the young couple was "*Cueillez, cueillez votre jeunesse mais ne trouble mon repos—je dors.*"

If there was a snake in the garden it was asparagus. With D.C.'s money, Lilo would shop all morning and return in triumph from the marketplace with bread, cheese, and long, thick, succulent, phallic asparagus, as white as Moby Dick, wrapped in old copies of *Le Monde*. It was always asparagus—and raw. As far as D.C. could make out, in her mind the asparagus seemed to be all tangled up with larger issues like restitution for war crimes and German-American relations, and there was even a ritual in getting them down. It was crazy, but girls were like that. She would fluff up the dry, brown pine needles and he would lie on them and she would hand him the damp *Le Monde* and he would read the jumble of type faces and she would place the tip of the vegetable lovingly between his even teeth and he would humor her and munch and crunch and smile and read. *"REGLE-MENTS DE COMPTES A O.K. CORRAL"* (chomp). *"Les Vraies Chemises—ARROW"* (chomp-chomp). *"Le retour du féticheur: une autre teen-ager Américaine morte"* (chomp-chomp-chomp). She was positively radiant as asparagus were torn to shreds and ground to glob. D.C. couldn't see that it hurt anything, and aside from this mosquito in the blue sky of their love, all was perfection.

In the evenings, Ivan and D.C. with Lilo in tow would return to Madame d'Allégret's mansion for her nightly party. These soirées had acquired such a vogue among the advanced, the eccentric, and the jaded that they went on regardless of the hostess' absence. To those who knew Madame d'Allégret well, her scarcity was but another indication that she was an original. Upon descending to the Rumpus Room, Ivan would move off to one side of the crowded floor and take up his tenacious vigil leaning against one of the damp brick walls that had been scarred by age and underground moisture, while D.C. and Lilo spun about in the thick of it to "Blue Reefer Blues." Night after night the music on the radio was interrupted. Urgent bulletins were being received from panicky announcers screaming DOOM! DOOM! DOOM! The world was being occupied by hostile forces— earth monsters and spatial nogoodniks. King Kong was loose in Latin America and U.S. Marines carrying atomic crossbows were stabilizing the situation. American interests were safe! Unidentified Flying Objects had contaminated Eastern Europe with capitalistic scrofula and Soviet tanks laden with doctors, nurses, and the Moiseyev dancers were innoculating all counterrevolutionaries.

Russian interests were safe! The Abominable Snow Man was clumping around in Tibet and Chinese volunteers armed with rice patties were attacking in human waves. Chinese interests were safe! But the gay old revelers had heard it all before and the serious young weren't interested, so the dancing and drugging went on uninterrupted in the snuggery. Skid-Dat-De-Dat!

There were rats down there in that three-hundred-year-old basement, large ones—so large that they might have had human names like John or Henry or Old Ben. Their hair was beaver brown, as long as the mane of a Shetland pony, and their tails snapped in the air like circus whips. Now and then an older lady would shriek thrillingly upon seeing one, for they had much in common with champion prizefighters, being excitingly nasty and extremely fit. But they were not often seen, for they were incredibly quick and furtive in their ways.

One evening when Johnny Dodds and his Chicago Foot-warmers were "Doin' the Voom Voom," the music and festive babble were drowned out by what sounded like someone violently shaking out a large rubber sheet. A great shadow fell across the room, circled swiftly about, and streaked for a corner where two young men in lederhosen were stretched out on straw pallets. A wild squealing and screeching and thrashing about shook the corner and dust flew like buckshot. "C'est Talleyrand!" cried several patriotic dancers, and they put more zing in their Voom Voom. When the battle was over, a speckled falcon, a magnificent bloodstained bird with the hunched shoulders and blank eye of a gynecologist, seized the rat in its talons and spreading its fringed wings rose effortlessly like the sun.

"It is impossible, Haushofer," said one pair of lederhosen to the other. "For in the very act of explaining myself to you I become another. The truth is it is all lies. *Nicht wahr?*"

Haushofer, his hands clasped behind his head, seemed to be sleeping.

Elsewhere there was much excitement. As Ivan mingled with the bustling crowd he kept hearing people say, "If Talleyrand comes, can *she* be far behind?" Madame d'Allégret apparently valued the bird highly, a present from her dead husband. Some said that it had been his great passion in life, others spoke of his feather allergy, but all agreed on Allégret's devotion to the medieval creature. Yet that night she still did not appear.

Ivan took his disappointment stoically and returned to his observation post in the cemetery with a cool heart. If not today, tomorrow. He stretched out on the ground, tranquil, and closed his eyes. The brown, double-breasted revolutionary suit he had worn since the beginning of the trip seemed at home here in the cemetery among the monuments. It shined like oilcloth. Spiders nested in his beard and grasshoppers skipped in and out of his pockets. At peace with the living and the dead, Ivan waited confidently for the dawn.

East of Eden, events were taking another turn. Chez Barbezieux the honeymoon was over. As day inexorably followed day, the lovers were no longer marching in lock step. Little disagreements appeared piecemeal like debris from a gutted submarine rising lazily to the surface. They began when D.C. first suggested peas and carrots. It wasn't that he didn't care for asparagus, that he didn't recognize their significance in the ultimate scheme of things, but the solemn oath he had sworn to his blind, invalid, widowed, worry-wart of a mother that he would eat a balanced diet had to be considered. Lilo waited until he had finished his little story, like a nurse with a wayward child, and then rammed the vegetable home with sadistic relish. His pique peaking, D.C. openly accused her of squash, eggplant, and kohlrabi.

Lilo kissed him patiently on both cheeks. She patted his hair back. Twitting the buttons on his shirt collar, she snickered and called him "decadent." She mocked his neatness, the constant brushing of his clothes, the tapered lucite comb he carried like a dagger in his sock. She found fault with his bearded Russian friend who never spoke to her and who had the crooked eyes of a child molester. She poked the blue sneaker he carried about with him and called it his little weakness. She was as hard as a helmet.

D.C. could no longer lie to himself. No matter how he had wanted to believe the contrary, asparagus was finally not a recognized aphrodisiac. He saw that she was only using him to satisfy some kink in her computer. Concentrating, he imagined her with no chin and their love affair was through. He cut off her shopping allowance, but she used her own money and, a resourceful girl, found bargains. Though her marketing expeditions now took longer, she never returned empty-handed. First there were bruised asparagus, then thin, then mottled, and in the fall, he knew, there would be canned. He would never last. Already he was as gaunt as a refugee, while she grew fat on air.

"We're through, finished, kaput," he screamed matter-of-factly one day, and clammed up in the face of the hated vegetable.

Lilo seemed surprised and hurt. The tiny creases in her forehead were filled with remorse as she explained that the only French vegetable she knew was *asperges*. She promised him that she would do better tomorrow. She swore on the heads of her dead father and grandfather (also killed by Americans), and two distant relatives from Säarbrucken who had been wholesale butchers that she would make it up to him. D.C. listened to her whining, sniveling apology with aloof distrust. She hugged him like a tight pair of pants and swabbed out his mouth with her tongue. Her hands stroked him this way and that and she called him her "*Schöne Auster*." She locked her knees around his legs and brushed her flagrant self across his chest like a whiskbroom. D.C. had to admit that in her own way the girl was definitely suffering.

He forgave her everything and it was something to see. Right in the middle of a working day when all of Paris was turning a buck these happy two were turning the other cheek. In their mad frenzy they toppled headstones, uprooted perennials, lapped each other in gobs of love. Orderly funeral processions were routed; abandoned coffins piled up on the path. The ground quaked as they bubbled and steamed like active volcanos under the clear blue sky. O Love! O Ecstasy! All day and all night they continued to bury the ax. About five o'clock in the morning when even the stars were fading, D.C. felt that she had been sufficiently forgiven. Lilo, however, was a Puritan in her guilt. Her anxiety would not let him sleep.

"*Ich bin schlecht. Ich bin unwürdig,*" she chanted, pounding him awake.

"All right, all right," he grouched. "Horsepiss! All right." D.C. roused himself and pardoned her once more.

But no sooner had she been absolved, given the extremest unction he was capable of under the circumstances, then she was at him again, slapping him lustily on the back and crying, "*Ich bin schlecht. Ich bin unwürdig.*"

D.C. shook himself like a fallen fighter and sat up. Lint lined the roof of his mouth. His eyes looked as if they had been lying at the bottom of a heavily chlorinated pool for several days. Horripilation afflicted the balls of his feet, thrombotic wastes glutted his groin. In that darkness before the dawn when fresh birds hop and skip and comb their wings in anticipation of the new day, D.C. crawled blindly toward his neatly folded trousers.

When he awoke time and Lilo had both marched on. Although he tried to sit up, his legs seemed to have become detached during the night. The steady diet of asparagus had taken its toll. The thought of orange juice, pure orange juice, spotless, pulpless, pitless orange juice, caused a loud buzzing in his ears and even the prospect of a continental breakfast produced a painful hum. He craned his neck about for a sign and found one under the letterhead of Barbezieux written in eyebrow pencil. "Schatz Irwin. Wait here. Today you will feast." He admired her penmanship—the gymnasium twirl—but the possibility that it might not mean food made him giddy and he sprang up like a hunted animal.

Too late. There she was rushing toward him, threading her way through the tombstones, waving gleefully with both hands, a song in her heart. She seemed so fleet, so incredibly well rested. There was nothing edible in sight, and here, bearing down on him, was the Olympic champion of love all aglow. His one hope was that the food was being delivered.

"Hi, there," he called, putting Barbezieux between them and trying to start a jolly conversation.

"They come for you, Irwin." She was breathless. "I ran to be the first."

"Hi, there!" He gave her a delicious smile and, looking up, nodded affably at the sky. "It certainly is. I love stationary high-pressure systems, don't you?"

"Irwin, *listen*. The games are over. They want you, but *I* am first." There was a nasty determination in her voice.

"Believe me, I'd love to," he said sympathetically. "Nothing would give me more pleasure. But I have a dental appointment for an impacted crevice." He hooked his pinkies into his mouth and spread his lips wide. "OOK. Eee or orelf."

"Do you hear that, Irwin? Those are sirens. They are almost here."

Sure enough there were sirens, rising and falling, wailing and flailing, profane decibels in the sacred grove.

"That's funny," he was mildly perplexed. "Those *are* sirens, aren't they? What do you suppose they can be doing here?"

"You are *blossgestelt*, Irwin. They will put you in and throw away the key. Ha!" she gloated. "Did you think you could pick my flower like a love-crazed gardener and not be punished?"

D.C.'s heart sank. He had been enticed and snared by a raving anti-American deviate. "I only did a little weeding," he piped, defensively.

"The French are gentlemen. *Gentlemen*, Irwin!" She was insanely happy. "They will know what to do with you. They will hang you up by your asparagus and make medical experiments. Irwin!" she screamed. "You have violated my air space and you will pay and pay and pay."

"I will?" He looked sick, haggard, woebegone, and devoid of zest. Preventive medicine made him ill. "But I've never had an operation in my life. Not even tonsils. Not even plantar's warts." He smiled wistfully, paled, and plummeted to earth behind the tombstone.

"You will not escape by tricks, Irwin. They are here."

Sirens screaming, bells tinkling, horns going agooooga-agooooo-ga, two mad peddlers in blue and white police uniforms sped down the cemetery path hunched over their handlebars. Their bicycle chains were circular saws, whirring about with such speed that they seemed motionless. Slamming on their brakes, they jumped from the saddles and, either to relieve the excitement or assert their authority, they blew their whistles shrilly in all directions.

"*Voilà!*" said helpful Lilo. "*There* is your rapist. To the guillotine!"

D.C. stood up, a victim of malnutrition, slave to every passing breeze. In the distance he could already hear the rackety wheels of the tumbrel that was coming for him. His only hope lay in the truth. He explained how he and the other honor students of the Union Theological Seminary had been on a Cook's Tour of the glorious, sublime, and world-famous French Romanesque cathedrals when he was suddenly stricken by amnesia while praying— but the veteran gendarmes paid no attention to him. They gaped at Lilo, slapping one another on the back and leering like the Elders at Susannah. Her orchidaceous underthings (peeping out from the bottom of her skirt and the top of her waistband) were being introduced in evidence. "I think you should know," muttered D.C., faltering, "that at home I've signed petitions against capital punishment."

The gendarmes spruced up their uniforms and drew closer to Lilo. Moved by her detailed account of voluptuous ravishment, they removed their hats in sympathy and tribute. Only once did they glance at D.C. with interest, and that was when she disclosed the Byzantine design of his strange, insatiable appetite.

"And over here," Lilo was saying, immensely pleased with herself as she pointed to the headstone, "here you may see how I baited the trap by appealing to his weakness. Well, gentlemen," she concluded, "*there* is your rapist. Take him away!"

The grizzled gendarmes looked at one another in tremulous disbelief. Swallowing their disillusionment, they rammed their hats back on and, stepping forward grimly, seized Lilo for defacing private monuments.

"Take your hands off me you dirty old men. Help, Irwin, help!" she shouted, struggling as they each took an elbow and hoisted her into the air.

Exhausted, D.C. limply waved good-bye.

"Irwin!" she screeched, as they laid her across the handlebars and tied her down. "I thought you were an American, Irwin, but you're nothing but a damned Jew. You *verrotteter* rapist!"

"My name is Richard," D. C. told himself, his heart dead ashes like a burned out synagogue. "*Gute Fahrt.*"

Young plants mend quickly and D.C.'s recovery was swift—eighty-four seconds to be exact. No sooner had the gendarmes' rear reflector buttons disappeared down the path than he was back telling Ivan of his nine-day orgy and how he had had the German girl eating out of his hand. Together they had scaled the heights, step by step, orgasm by orgasm, until in one enormous paregoric-scented fit of churning, shrieking, clawing, absolute ecstasy she had thrown her belly to the moon and died of a broken neck.

It was evident that D.C. had been victimized. Ivan regarded failure in any endeavor as a sentimental luxury and an intellectual disgrace. From his observation post, he had noted the policemen carrying off the struggling Lilo. He was not envious.

As D.C. put back his lost weight in the days that followed, there were increasingly more magnificent tales of glittering copulations involving outrageous orifices, heartwarming innovations, record-breaking stamina, and thrilling, never-to-be-forgotten, hard-hitting, wild, moving, ACTION! Although these descriptions were somewhat theatrical, Ivan joined in the laughter. "I will not be dehumanized," he told himself. "Not yet."

When not reminiscing, D.C. spent most of his time at the shop of a French-English custom tailor by the name of Rothschild who wore a boutonnière and charged accordingly. Rothschild's business boomed but the man himself languished, for he was one of those unfortunate artists with a talent unequal to his imagination. He had a bony, blue-shadowed face and heavy-lidded eyes, and standing glumly behind his customers within the shop's three-mirror complex, he would lament full-face and in profile—"Another failure by Rothschild!" His customers liked his sense of humor as much as his suits and everyone called him "Rothie." The dream of his life was to fashion clothes in keeping with the buyer's profession, civilian uniforms for easy identification and psychological security. Firemen would wear blazers, lawyers would wear briefs, and composers would wear fugal suits in four parts. It was a utopian plan far ahead of its time. When informed that D.C. was an American heir, Rothschild, dreamer of the impossible, Copernicus of the clothing industry, imagined a garment that would be one huge, glorious cul-de-sac. But failing once again to realize his vision, to square his dream with reality, he dressed D.C. in white like a bride and returned to his cutting room to groan over his tape measure. On the remarkable night in late summer when Madame d'Allégret finally appeared, D.C., suited in shining virgin white, was dressed for the occasion.

At first the evening seemed like so many others they had spent underground. There was the music, the laughter, the shuffling of dancing feet, the squish-squish of syringes. And then the exciting flutter of distant wings. Talleyrand was airborne, his great wings slapping the air vigorously like wet clothes against a washboard. The deadly hunter in quest of his prey. Under the long, baronial liquor table, a drunken rat that had been gnawing on a shot glass looked up, its mouth covered with glass splinters, and belched defiantly. Talleyrand's eyes popped out of his head like telescopes, and, enraged, he clawed the air. His beak was a grappling hook and every keyed-up feather on his body signaled danger as he reared back and stooped, swooping under the liquor table with itching talons. Suddenly, there was an explosion, shouts, heavy breathing from guests with enlarged adenoids, and the magnificent Talleyrand cried out in pain. The rat's head had been blown off as clean as a whistle. For a stunned moment, the frustrated bird sniffed forlornly around and moped over the rat's carcass with his wings in his pockets. He was terribly upset. It was as if a lodge brother had passed away. He turned and looked in the direction from which the shot had come and seeing the glint of a gun barrel, he seemed to go out of his mind. His eyes became mean little peas. Screaming one barbaric yawp after another, he took off like a pursuit plane and bore down on the enemy. A second shot rang out and fierce, gallant, supple, haughty Talleyrand, the great-hearted warrior, the noble victor of a thousand mortal strifes, was just another fricasseed fowl.

"Mad as a hatter," said Mrs. Finch-Bradish carelessly, and

ejected the spent cartridge from its chamber. She wore a pith helmet and camouflaged Army fatigues with hand smocking.

"You have killed Talleyrand!" An elderly dancer was shaken up. "You have murdered l'Allégret's glorious bird! You have destroyed grandeur! Lunatic! May your menopause be filled with flashes."

"The law of the jungle," responded the lady hunter, snapping on the safety catch of her gun. "More sang-frwa!"

D.C. came over to the scene of the commotion in his heraldic white suit and people looking for a leader gathered around him as if he were Mahatma Gandhi. When he saw who it was his mind disintegrated and his expression became vapidly childlike.

"Is it really you, Mrs. Finch-Bradish?" he asked, with a touching timidity. "Is it really you?"

"In the flesh," said Mrs. Finch-Bradish. She opened the top of her fatigues and urged, "Feel."

"But what about Africa? Your safari? The snows of Kilimanjaro?"

"It's drafty down here. Cut the crap. Are you going to feel or not?"

D.C. touched her with the shy tip of his index finer. "It *is* you!" he announced, and buttoned her up quickly. "Where's Sidney?"

"I've been tracking the lousy little creep since she gave me the slip in the Tuileries two months ago." Mrs. Finch-Bradish banged the butt of her rifle down on his toes. "Live and let live," she advised.

Wincing, D.C. removed the blue sneaker from his belt. "But this belongs to her," he argued, plaintively. "She can't walk all over Europe with a bare foot. She'll get calluses."

"Forget it. Where she is they love calluses."

"You know!" exclaimed the excited young man.

"Everything," said Mrs. Finch-Bradish, smugly. "She's taken up the veil."

D.C.'s face went black. "Saudi Arabia? A harem?"

"No! Spain. A nun." She laughed like a hyena. Releasing the safety catch on her rifle, she took Sidney's sneaker from his hand, tossed it up like a skeet, and neatly drilled eight new eyelets.

"Now that you're free, how would you like to come with me to the dark continent, Whitey?"

D.C. was overwhelmed with remorse. He had driven Sidney to a nunnery. Somehow he would drive her out. But Mrs. Finch-Bradish was not above massaging the truth. He would test her story by masterful indirection, cunning strategems, daring thrusts, and dirty pool. He wrapped himself around her arm like a lie detector and smiled deceitfully. As they walked out of the limelight, he began subtly by asking, "Which continent is the dark one?"

"Don't try to pump me, Whitey, or it's all off."

Taking out a match, D.C. lighted Mrs. Finch-Bradish's cork-tipped cigar like a tired waiter anxious to clean up and go home.

From the congealed darkness at the far side of the dance floor, a cry went up. It swelled and reverberated poignantly above the music.

"Hillo, ho, ho, boy! Come, bird, come. Ho! Ho! Ho! HO! HO!!!"

Ivan, who had been examining the dead bird, instantly recognized the disembodied voice of Madame d'Allégret, and bursting through the dancing couples, he plunged into the shadows. His hour had come at last!

"Have you seen my Talleyrand?" inquired an obscure figure.

Ivan chose his words carefully. "There's been an accident," he explained.

"Accident," she repeated, a catch in her voice.

"I'm afraid," he revealed sadly, "that your bird is dead."

There was a long silence, and then, quietly, "I see." And saying no more, she turned and walked off down the narrow winding brick tunnel that led away from the Rumpus Room to the other side of the house.

Now that she had finally appeared, Ivan was not about to lose Madame d'Allégret. He followed after her at a discreet distance, his footsteps echoing on the stone floor. At the end of the tunnel there was a well-lighted, carpeted staircase that led upstairs and near the foot of the stairway, a door. She opened it and went in, leaving the door ajar behind her.

Madame d'Allégret was so absorbed that she didn't seem to realize that he had followed her. Ivan approached the door cautiously and hesitated on the threshold, gauging the situation.

"Come in," she invited, and wearily sank down into a small canvas-back chair without bothering to see who it was.

Ivan stepped through the doorway. Shyness had never been a problem for him. Although the room was not large, it struck him as barren. The floor, walls, and ceiling were white, nubbly white, and the only furniture was a bed, a large wardrobe, a round night table, and a hatrack—an exiguous set the color of straw. Ivan judged that the hatrack had been the bird's perch for its rigid arms were covered with all sorts of nicks and scratches. The walls were empty except for a gilded, machine-made crucifix that had been ground down to the essentials. Beneath it on the night table, a tall votive candle was burning. Given the simplicity of the furniture and the room's location in the house, it probably belonged to the maid, but to Ivan its starkness suggested a monastic cell.

Madame d'Allégret was holding the falcon's doll-like hood in her hands and gazing down at it dreamily. There was a tiny orange plume at the top and it rippled uneasily in the dank air. She sat motionless, not even thinking about not thinking so to speak, as still as a shrine. Her taffeta gown, lush swirls of rich avocado green, made no sound. In the candlelight her narrow face was all angles and mystery, and her long straight black tresses, precisely streaked with gray, extended to the small of her back. An elegant woman, and despite the gray hair, Ivan could scarcely believe that *Who's Who in France* had been right about her birthday.

Laying the dead falcon's hood aside on the bed, she folded her hands composedly in her perfumed lap, fluttered her delicate lilac-tinted lids, and looked up. "Ah, it's you." Madame d'Allégret did not seem surprised in the least. Her voice was that of the confessional. "Once again you have turned up unannounced to assist me. What would one do without friends?"

Ivan stood motionless like a duck hunter.

"Talleyrand dead," she continued philosophically. "He was a

bird for all seasons. It would appear that La Rochefoucauld was right. Life does squeeze one like a lemon."

She bore her sorrow as if she were a queen. In fact, she didn't seem to be broken up at all. More thoughtful than unhappy. Even so, Ivan didn't care to risk adding to her burden by mentioning that his examination of the bird had revealed that *he* was not a bird for all seasons. *She* was. "If there's anything I can do," he offered generously.

"Talleyrand gone. Another link broken. Dying, it seems, is to lose the past bit by bit."

"A remarkable bird," Ivan commiserated.

Rousing herself, Madame d'Allégret spoke with quiet determination. "I'll have him cremated. That way at least I shall always have his ashes. I'll keep them beside those of my husband and children."

"Were there many?" Ivan inquired gently, as if he didn't already know.

"Who would believe it?" she replied, and crossed herself.

"Children are hard to keep track of," he conceded. "And nowadays there are so many loopholes for them to fall through. You mustn't blame yourself."

Madame d'Allégret looked up at him dubiously. Ivan feared that he had overstated his case and, with a touch of discomfort, added, "What I mean is accidents happen."

She glanced down at her hands, her bare neck as shapely as a Botticelli. She appeared to be amused by his good intentions.

"You've been through hell!" cried Ivan passionately, hoping to worm his way back into her confidence.

Madame d'Allégret gave him a slow, gap-toothed smile. "Americans are always kind. What do you do?"

"I travel."

"A pilgrim. My late husband, the Ambassador, was also a rolling stone." She sighed. "That was his way. He would go anywhere for a medal. It finally cost him his life." Madame d'Allégret rose, and stepping majestically to the wardrobe, she opened one of its two doors. "Come over here."

Ivan looked in at a jumble of dolls, stamp albums, old hats, deflated balls, hand-wound electromagnets, and peeling artificial flowers.

"I keep them down here to remind me of my children. But what do you think of this?" She indicated a shelf piled high with small leather cases. "Each one represents an act of statesmanship or heroism that turned the world on its head in amazement." She opened a case at random. "You see?"

Having had the foresight to investigate her husband's background while at the Bibliothèque Nationale, Ivan happily recognized it immediately. "The Liverpool Shipwreck and Humane Society's Marine Medal," he said in admiration. "Plus gold bars!"

"And this?"

"The Thiha Bala Tazeit of Burma."

"You know your medals," commented Madame d'Allégret wryly. She snapped open another case and pushed it toward him.

Perplexed, his tongue shackled by ignorance, Ivan nibbled on his beard in silence.

Madame d'Allégret was curious which of her husband's medals it was that had stumped him. Looking into the case, she blushed ever so slightly. "Forgive me," she said in an undertone. "I myself have won a ribbon or two . . . but this one is obsolete."

"Could it be the French Medal for Civilian Wounded?" ventured Ivan.

"No," she corrected. "It is the Turkish Order of Chastity . . . my first." She looked at the five-pointed star thoughtfully and closed the case. "Long ago my husband was attached to the Embassy at Ankara. We had just been married a week and he was a proud man. With him it was a question of honor, and the Turkish government could do no less. Even then he was eager to make his mark. A few years later he helped me to my second decoration, the Médaille de la Famille Française . . . he was a devout Catholic and practiced the rhythm method night and day."

"A man like that should have lived forever," swore Ivan.

"That was his intention," revealed Madame d'Allégret ironically. "Who knows how far he might have gone with it if not for his *metallumphilia*? He had a will of iron."

"There were giants in the earth in those days," he said hoarsely. Madame d'Allégret looked at him.

Ivan didn't seem to be able to help himself. He felt certain that sympathy was not the answer, yet like a cipher in a totalitarian state, he didn't quite know how to alter things. It was a novel experience for him and he loathed it.

"My husband knew shorthand," Madame d'Allégret confided, ignoring his remark. "It happened on a secret intelligence mission for the Allies during the last war. No doubt you've heard of the events that occurred on July 20, 1944, at the 'Wolfsschanze' in East Prussia. When Colonel Von Stauffenberg left his bomb under the conference table, Hitler escaped with only a few scratches, but Stenographer Berger squirted all over the walls like a grapefruit. After that," she spoke with great calm, "after that the medals were all posthumous. A year later, with the fall of Germany, his body was returned to me in a sealed envelope."

Ivan stroked his beard pensively. "You must be very proud of him," was his only comment.

"For a young man," remarked Madame d'Allégret coolly, "you're *very* understanding. It's kind of you, but there's no necessity to pity me. Fortunately, I have been able to turn my life into art and thereby master it. You see?" She opened the second wardrobe door. "Tell me, what is your impression?" she asked.

The hint of eagerness he detected in her voice convinced Ivan that flattery here would not be wasted. "An unusual piece." He congratulated her on the monstrosity. "I like it."

Inside, a little old lady with a shawl sat knitting in a rocking chair. Her head was a large Mason jar. On the front of the jar was pasted the photograph of an apple-cheeked young girl, and within, a calcimined skull. She wore a necklace of smaller bottles containing dust and ashes and the whole assemblage smelled of sour peccavi.

"A self-portrait. But it still requires work," explained Madame d'Allégret. "The ashes of Talleyrand will go here." She pointed to an empty bottle in the chain about the old lady's neck.

Ivan leaned forward for a better look. "You've caught something," he agreed, squinting into the closet. "It does you justice."

Madame d'Allégret smiled her gap-toothed smile. "All in all," she judged, "you are a most curious young gentleman. There is about you *une gravité sublime* that reminds me of my eighth child." She tapped nostalgically on the eighth bottle of the necklace. "Jean-Paul."

Ivan disliked having himself compared to anyone, and maternal comparisons he regarded as most offensive. Nevertheless, in this instance he gritted his teeth, and without the slightest objection, he allowed himself to be given a familial reference point.

"A queer boy," she admitted candidly, and closed the wardrobe door on the stale aroma. "I had a strange dream of him recently."

"I'd like to hear about it," said Ivan. Family secrets! At last he felt he was gaining the upper hand.

"It happened at night."

"Go on."

"My husband and I had just come out of the theater. It was our first evening out in some time for I had been busy nursing Jean-Paul. Apparently the poor child had been ill with a severe case of chicken pox and by watching him closely I had prevented him from scarring himself. You know how children can't resist picking the scabs."

"So I've heard. Go on."

"Outside the theater the night was soft and the sky was thick with stars, so we decided to walk home. As we left the theater crowds and made our way down the narrow deserted streets past the closed shops, my husband put his arm around me, and pushing me up against the side of a building, he began to make love to me. He seemed to think that I delighted in having my ear lobes massaged and seized them immediately. At first, I was annoyed and told him that he was hopelessly depraved, but seeing that there was no one near, I laughed at him and started to sway a little. Suddenly, however, he pulled away from me and stared at the nearby doorway of a shuttered bakery shop where there was something crouching in the corner. Startled, I screamed and covered my mouth. A light went on upstairs and the baker, an old man wearing an undershirt, cleared the ledge of two wine bottles and slammed closed his window. Darting out from the doorway, a frightened mouse—snow-white and pink-eyed—ran mechanically back and forth on tip toes. My husband picked up a stick lying on the pavement and struck out at the mouse repeatedly, but each time it eluded him. Unable to restrain myself, I wrenched the stick from his hand and smashed the little beast to oblivion in a frenzy of hatred. I can't describe to you the sweetness of the relief I felt when it flopped over on its back. Then, it seems, I reached into my handbag for an apple to quiet my nerves. But no sooner was the mouse flattened out than its hips began to grow, to swell, to flare out as if they were flying buttresses and its belly rose up huge and trembled with life like a pregnant woman. It had turned into one of the great rats we have down here. I struck one blow after another with all my strength, and it set its body rigidly for death. Its stiffness reminded me of Jean-Paul at the shoe store when the salesman would tell him to stand up to test the fit of his new shoes and how he would place his hands tightly at his sides, and as I brought my stick down on the animal's face, it smiled. Although I couldn't bring myself to strike the two new front teeth that Jean-Paul was so proud of, I continued beating it over the head with a sinking heart."

Ivan, who had begun pacing up and down the room as she spoke, came to a halt in front of Madame d'Allégret. "And you say I remind you of him?" Ivan was dauntless in pursuing the relationship, willing to take any risk.

She laughed amiably, and opening a bottom drawer in the wardrobe beneath her husband's medals, Madame d'Allégret withdrew a beaded pocketbook. She stepped across the room to the night table, removed her wallet, and carelessly tossed her bag on the bed. "Look here," she said, finding the photograph she wanted and holding it near the candle.

Ivan came up behind her.

"This picture was taken on a holiday at Deauville when Jean-Paul was thirteen. As you can see he was not terribly photogenic. But it is in the broad, flat forehead and the area about the eyes that I find a similarity. Do you see what I mean?"

Ivan took the wallet from her cold hands. The boy's head was enlarged as if he had suffered from hydrocephalus during his lifetime. "Definitely," he gladly humored her. "An uncanny re-semblance." As he leafed through the other photographs in her wallet, he remarked, "Husband . . . children . . . falcon . . . all you love caught up in a rush of breakneck dying. Dear lady, no wonder everyone in Paris speaks of your courage."

Madame d'Allégret raised her eyebrows. "I should think it's none of their business," she observed with some disgust.

"You're quite right, of course," he put in hastily. It seemed to Ivan as he returned the wallet that she was a distressingly unpre-dictable woman.

"Courage is stupidly irrelevant," she continued irritably. "Once a year I make a two-week retreat to this room, as I have just done, and that seems to be quite enough for me. I have my art and my faith. Despite the nonsense that you may have heard to the con-trary, it is not difficult to become reconciled to other people's dying. One's own death is another matter."

Ivan bowed from the shoulders, an instrument of precision. "You are a model of Christian renunciation," he said ambiguously, hoping that she would take it in any way that seemed a com-pliment to her.

"One tries," she responded with mock humility.

Emboldened, Ivan cunningly pried into the family. "Your rela-tives must be a great comfort to you," he supposed.

"I never see them anymore. They don't seem to approve of the way I live."

"Never?" said Ivan dismally. Sickened by the thought of the time he had wasted in waiting for this woman without viable connections, he sat down heavily on the bed. Somehow he had slipped up.

"Frankly," she confided, "I find them rather stuffy. They're all Gaullists. Could you imagine one of *them* at my parties?" She laughed.

Ivan felt short-changed. He didn't care for the feeling. "May I ask you a blunt question before leaving?"

"Please," she invited, pleasantly. "Americans are always frank."

"Then tell me," he inquired out of curiosity, "do you really *like* parties?"

Struck by his amusing question, the elegant Madame d'Allégret walked to the canvas-back chair, sat down, and toyed with the folds of her dress. She twisted toward him, a Skopaic curve, and giving him the engaging grin of a dental cripple, she said, "Why yes, I think so. I find them a diversion."

"And what about your husband? Your children?"

Madame d'Allégret laughed cheerfully. "I don't seem to be able to get terribly excited about that. They're gone and that's that. I try to hold on to what I can."

"I suppose that's wise," agreed Ivan, getting up to go.

"I think so," she said. "Just a minute," she called after Ivan, stopping him at the door.

"I've got to be going," he explained impatiently. "My friend's waiting for me."

"I understand," Madame d'Allégret said compassionately, pleased to be turning the emotional tables on him. "But *before* you go," she spoke in a calm voice, "would you please be good enough to return the set of car keys that you took from my purse?"

Ivan looked at her blankly.

"Don't bore me with denials," she advised him. "I *know* you have them. It happens that I heard you take them when my back was turned."

"That's right," admitted Ivan brazenly. He had earned the Duesenberg by indulging this crank and he had no intention of giving it up simply because she chanced to have caught him in the act. With the keys in his possession, he could always claim that she had loaned the car to him.

It was rare that Madame d'Allégret was angry and even now she couldn't decide whether she was more upset or amused by the gall of the young American. "I don't believe you understand. That car has great sentimental value for me. Do put the keys back where you found them."

"Don't make me laugh," he snickered. "Nothing could have sentimental value for *you*."

Madame d'Allégret's taffeta gown rustled as she leaned forward and thrust out her hand. "The keys!" she insisted stonily.

Her face was as rigid as the arms of the hatrack and suddenly seemed to be covered with an equal number of nicks and scratches. Ivan felt that now that the aging process had begun in earnest, she would grow old very quickly. In any event, she was in no condition to drive. "*Ciaou!*" he called breezily and left.

Madame d'Allégret clutched the arms of her chair and the backs of her slim hands were blue with rage. She would go upstairs and call the police and they would stop the car before it had gone two blocks. The car. . . . Her anger deserted her and was replaced by some deeper feeling such as she had never known before. She was overwhelmed by a stifling sense of loss. All at once she felt very old, very spent, and very human. She couldn't bear to remain in that room another minute. Raising herself from the chair, she blew out the candle, shut the door, and started up the stairs. As she ascended, she began to laugh softly to herself. It seemed to Madame d'Allégret that the irony of her emotional life was truly amazing. In ruthlessly stealing her car, a senseless machine, he had succeeded in affecting her more deeply than she had been moved by the loss of her entire family. She felt that she had been stretched, expanded, breached, that she had plumbed strange and exquisite depths full of unimaginable treasure and was all the richer for the experience. As an artist, she prized the new resonance. He wasn't really a very good thief at all, leaving more than he stole.

Hurrying from the back of the house, she arrived at the front door just in time to catch a glimpse of the two Americans as the Duesenberg thundered out of the driveway and zoomed off down the Boulevard. At that hour of the morning the street was nearly deserted and she was able to follow the rear lights of the car for quite a way before they were swallowed up by the darkness. She looked up at the sky. Already there was a hint of autumn in the air. After standing out on the front steps for a while in her thin gown, she realized that she was chilled and stepped back into the house. "A most extraordinary young man," she thought, as she sadly closed the door behind her.

CHAPTER 12

🐍 A note from Sidney and other correspondence.

Basement, The Pentagon

Dear Pals,

Disregard my last letter. I've never been happier. It's just taken me longer to adjust than some of the other guys. I see now that my attitude was all wrong and I was going about things ass-backwards. Don't worry, I haven't turned into some kind of flag-waving, psalm-singing, nut booster, but frankly there are things to be said for the military life that I never imagined, and constructive criticism is always welcomed.

One thing I've learned these last few months is that you've got to give and take to survive in this world. I always thought that "compromise" was a dirty word but really it's "rigidity" that kills you. Youthful idealism, finally, is too mythological for real people.

You're going to find this hard to believe but I haven't met a single person in this whole building who likes war. Honest! Is there anyone in his right mind who wants to murder healthy men, women, and children? After all, these guys aren't crank amateurs, they're *pros*. All they care about is protecting democracy throughout the world, and if *they* don't do the job, who will? It's a responsibility.

And don't believe what you hear about the Army's indifference to individual strengths and weaknesses. Although it did take them a little time, they even sent a special counselor to see me under the ice cap. When he heard that I was a pre-med, he gave me some special tests, told my commanding officer that I was needed elsewhere, and had me shipped right off to Washington. I still can't bear wearing a uniform, but there are thinking types down here and the work (more or less in my field) is kind of fun. I'm now attached to CBR IN THE BASEMENT and though it's terribly hush-hush, I can tell you that every one of these weapons will provide a more humane means of guaranteeing peace.

What's the use? Who can hide secrets from old buddies? But keep the following under your hats when talking to strange, beautiful, deep-clefted women with foreign accents and no underwear. We've got something here that makes mustard --- seem less dangerous than a clogged john at a bean bake. It's in the nerve --- series of Tabun, Sarin, and Soman, and it's so new that it doesn't even have a name yet. The guys in the lab call it "Zyrian" because it's the last word, but that's not yet official. The stuff has no color, no odor, no taste, is completely undetectable, cheap, painless, and can penetrate anything—brick, steel, Kotex, concrete—in lethal quantities. It's an anticholinesterase agent and acts almost instantaneously. Even lungs that have been breathing in and out all their lives forget to take the next breath. What a tranquilizer!

The people who object to this kind of weapon just don't understand. They think that toxic agents are mysterious, sinister, evil, because they're invisible, but then so are bullets. Believe me, to know them is to love them. They cause less suffering and permanent wear and tear than any other form of warfare. Zyrian will probably save thousands of lives, hundreds of thousands, in any engagement and on both sides, but uninformed types have always resisted the new. Think of the hard knocks taken by Galileo, the Salon des Refusés, and Dr. Ehrlich's Magic Bullet! It's enough to make you wonder about the human race. You'd have supposed by now that sensible people would realize that they can't continue shitting on progress indefinitely without fouling their own nests.

The moral issues in this case are as clear as consommé. Zyrian is so effective that it would be not only wrong, but unthinkable not to use it in the event. The chief of the lab told all of us that at the International Convention for the Pacific Settlement of International Disputes in 1899 an agreement was reached banning --- warfare, but fortunately we never signed it. The United States delegate made our position clear when he said, "I represent a people that is animated by a lively desire to make warfare humane." And you can bet your ass that every one of the guys down here in the basement is doing his bit to help. I know this sounds practically religious and you'll probably laugh, but honestly it's a good feeling to be a part of something bigger than yourself and doing work that counts on a winning team.

People like me here. They seem to think I'm doing a good job. It may be that I'm becoming a leader of men. Whatever it is, I no longer stutter and have put on twenty-three pounds. I hope you jokers are getting along among all those strangers. As for me, it's see America first!

Over and out,
Corporal Causley, A.B.D.*

* Always Breathe Deeply (our motto)
P.S. Do you happen to know anyone in Paris by the name of Henry?

THE EXCLUSIVE

GOLDEN UNICORN

ON LAKE ONEKO·I·HA·HA

All Recognized Sports
Olympic Pool (two filters)
Lectures on the Floating World
Ice Skating
Two Indoor Ski Slopes
  (chair lift)
BIG NAMES
Three Bands (unusual instru-
  ments)
The UNICORN Symphony
  Herschel Poliokoff, Dir.
Traditional Cuisine
Sauna
Bagnio
Kiddie Kastle Kandy Bar
Tweener Program
Superteen Frolic Room
Two Championship Golf
  Courses
Eight Autoclaves
Six Sistrums
Three Stopcocks

Cooshkila de Momis

I thought your father should have a change so I brought him to the country for his first vacation in forty-three years—he needed it. This hotel is a palace—twice a day they come round with a blue light to sanitize the sheets. Who knew such places existed? My eyes are being opened wide like hampers—when I think of the years I wasted over egg creams and spilled milk I could cry—work is the opium of the people—but don't tell Schlemovitz.

Since we arrived last month I have already played many recognized sports and eaten a lot of traditional cuisine which is good—very. Also I have finally taken the plunge and am learning modern dances from the social director S. Fish who doesn't have the slightest trace of an accent although he

Two Undershot Water Wheels
Tiled Roofs
Stairs
Windows
Numerous Walls
Fluoridated Water in every
room
FREE Sachets

has been through a great deal—even if he didn't say a word you could tell he was a brain surgeon in Europe because he washes his hands after every lesson—now he is completely Americanized. Someone told me that his wife lives with a Nazi rocketman among the Arabs but he says only that she doesn't care for the dampness of the country. He is a fine person that any woman could trust—his long wavy hair makes him look graceful and close up he smells like a Whitman Sampler covered with brilliantine. And dance? He is so light on his feet that he could waltz on the water—to see him glide around a room in his narrow pants is such a treat that grown women break out in rashes—the girl in the commissary tells me that this has been going on all summer and they have run out of cornstarch—but even though his feet spin like dredels there is sadness in S. Fish. How can he show me the countryside if he is ashamed of his car? This is a sensitive artist but if I play my cards right it's not impossible that I can bring a little green into both our lives—God willing.

Schlemovitz is becoming more difficult every day—he spends all of his time down by the pool inflaming the teen-agers with songs of protest against the hotel—somewhere he has learned to play the guitar—the only time I see him any more is when he comes back to the room for me to give him his diabetes injection and even then he refuses to speak to me. The management is laughing now because he sings of working conditions and minimum wages to the children but I think together they are planning to burn down the hotel and free the slaves—who knows what wild things go on under his hat?

At home everything is the same—the new apartment is beautiful like a mink coat filled with all modern appliances and we love it. I am expecting a crowded mail box there when we return so don't fail me—the last time we heard from you was at the dock. I will try to write more often but don't count on it because S. Fish demands so much—anyway a smart boy like you will be coming home before I turn around.

Unknown to Schlemovitz under scotch tape I am enclosing every single penny in my purse (37¢) for incidentals—use it in good health.

Your sunkist MOTHER

Sweet Richard,
Somehow you must find the strength to forget me as I have forgotten you. Believe me when I say that there is no longer any bitter-

ness in my heart for you, but please, I beg of you, don't try to follow me down here to Zaragoza. Be content to know that I am happy at last. Here among the simple nuns at the Convento de la Sagrada Familia (Calvo Sotelo 26) I am never alone.

Hail and farewell.

Pasionately,
Sidney

v.h. 3-5 Monday through Friday

CHAPTER 13

An incident at the border.

Paris, Chartres, Tours, Poitiers, Angoulême, Bordeaux, Bayonne, Hendaye—the Grand National Road to Spain, a broad concourse rolling over gentle hills, through green valleys, and past the faded splendor of stately castles, cathedrals, and chateaux, is thronged with peeing transients in all seasons of the year. In winter their little jets of steam puff up everywhere, soon to be followed by spring's expansive freedom spraying itself over the awakening landscape, and, before long, summer's sultry, languorous flows are succeeded by the autumnal nip and tuck, and another year has come and gone on the G.N.R. Those citizens in their Citroens, Peugeots, and Renaults who haven't pulled off onto the shoulder of the highway to salute the respective seasons, are forever clogging the road like refugees fleeing from an invading army and racing for their lives.

One early autumn morning under clear skies, turning leaves, falling chestnuts, and the threat of a convent-initiated Sidney as bald as a hub cap, the two boys sped over the newly washed streets of Paris and out of town, joining up with the caravan inexorably moving South. D.C., his gray tweed traveling jacket caped over his shoulders and sporting a green felt Tyrolean hat with a small cerise feather tucked neatly away in the band, wheeled the stately Duesenberg to the head of the pack heedless of life and limb, and there the giant car glided effortlessly, hurtling forward, its happy pistons innocent of friction.

Seated in the roomy front seat beside his dashing friend, Ivan, his seedy togs set off dramatically by the car's deep-cushioned class, considered the great historians of the past. His reading of them had convinced him that destinations were easier then, but now in a world of live people, it was no laughing matter. What was Zaragoza to him or he to Zaragoza? Other travelers who had made their mark went, like the old and venerable Jekutiel of Viggasolo, to the Holy Land, or, like the proud Abd Er Rahman of Cordoba and the questionable blood, to Mecca, but he, Ivan Storch, American, honor graduate and twentieth-century Odysseus impelled by internal combustion and prospects, was bound for the remote capital of Aragon, a city uncluttered with fortune hunters. It appealed to his sense of the fitness of things. The beaten track was not going to be beaten by Storch . . . and so Zaragoza, of course Zaragoza, famous only for the fanatical Palafox, the Inquisition, and thousands of women named Pilar. Zaragoza, Augsburg, Sevastopol—the glory of Augustus. But, typically, even its name was a corruption. Zaragoza, brown city of the plateau, blasted by flies and surrounded by winds. *El cierzo es el novio de Zaragoza.* Zaragoza, city of the big cockroach. Zaragoza, the town that asked the question, "Why?" Zaragoza, its very name was synonymous with drab. The Castilian lisp twice in one word! Ivan, who loved a challenge, was confident that the difficulties would be almost insurmountable.

To D.C., Zaragoza was Sidney and Sidney was love. He would save her in the nick, return home over the waters, eliminate the charlatan S. Fish, claim his inheritance, and they would be married in a gala affair attended by multiple foreign heads of state, Nobel Prize winners, and Hymen and his merry rout. The prothalamion would be written by the Library of Congress, incidental music supplied by Shirley and her Magic Violin. The wedding itself a civil service performed by the supreme justice of the Supreme Court and chronicled in the society columns of America with

[167]

pictures of the smiling, handsome couple in the back seat of their limousine gaily singing the "Liebestod" from *Tristan und Isolde*.

RICHARD COURTNEY WIDDEMORE MARRIES UNEXPECTEDLY

In a gala affair attended by multiple foreign heads of state, Nobel Prize winners, and Hymen and his merry rout, one of America's most eligible bachelors, Richard Courtney Widdemore, was married early this afternoon. The alfresco ceremony was performed by the Chief Justice of the Supreme Court high atop the Empire State Building on the exclusive Observation Deck.

The bridegroom wore a white linen suit designed by Rothschild and black patent leather pumps. His shirt of ivory peau de soie displayed a cascade of Brussels lace ruffles down the front. He carried a blue sneaker in his right hand.

The bridegroom's mother, the noted eccentric dancer Schlemovitz who performs to the accompaniment of her husband's guitar, was on tour, and thus, unfortunately, his parents were unable to attend the ceremony.

An alumnus of the Quick Quill Country Day School, the bridegroom graduated last year from The College where he was elected to Phi Beta Kappa in his junior year. He was a member of the Cosmopolitan Club, the Boston Teas of 1773, and the secret senior society, Radix. He also attended the Sorbonne where he studied art history with M. Blefuscu.

Ivan Storch was the best man.

The bride was the former Sidney Finch-Bradish. Her mother, Mrs. Finch-Bradish of Park Avenue and Nairobi, is the well-known huntress. After an extended honeymoon sojourn in his mother-in-law's safe deposit box, Mr. Widdemore plans to become a patron of the arts.

D.C. felt his heart swell up like a haggis. Only a few months out in the world and already he was on the verge of being totally absorbed by well-to-do, non-sectarian, melting-pot love. Life was good. And even if they should arrive too late at the Convento de la Sagrada Familia, he could still stimulate her scalp with olive oil when no one was looking and hope for the best.

As the day waned, D.C.'s excitement translated itself into daring swoops around curves, cars, whole cities, and stray wildlife regardless of international road signs and the pendulum swing of Ivan's sleeping bulk. It was just outside the little town of Pétignac that it began to drizzle. Trial and error moved the windshield wipers at last, and D.C., once more on top of the mechanism, settled back tight-lipped against the sumptuous upholstery and lit up a long Turkish Rami with one hand like a gunfighter. Despite the darkening sky, despite the random flashes of lightning pricking the landscape, D.C. would not yield to the elements. He recklessly pushed the Duesenberg forward as if engaged in some ingenious backbreaking drama of his own making. Heroism was not dead! Head high, his face set in determination, he might have been Achilles at Troy, Nelson at Trafalgar, or Cooper at High Noon. His spirits bubbled as the cozy Duesenberg roared along past inclement Montlieu and Cavignac. As he approached the gray outskirts of Bordeaux, D.C. quietly sang a ballad to himself.

> I'm not worthy of your love
> I don't deserve your heart
> I can't believe that you want me
> My breath is slightly tart.

But before he could get into the chorus, he slammed his foot down on the brake, the floorboard, and the accelerator in quick succession. Up ahead, two stranded figures stood in dim outline in the middle of the road waving frantically. They were trying to flag the car down, but D.C., unable to stop in time on the wet pavement, spun the wheel with all his might. The Duesenberg swerved in a long tortuous screaming skid, kicking up a tremendous shower. On the road the two drenched men ran amuk. Ivan bolted up, wide awake. "Luckenback and Castelli," he observed, and stretching, added negligently, "You missed."

Pulling the car out of its spin, D.C. curbed his speed and drove on. Numb. His lips were as white as his teeth. In the excitement, he had bitten clean through the cigarette in his mouth. "Well, well," he said. Attempting to laugh, he succeeded only in covering the dashboard with shreds of tobacco. "Well, well," he repeated. "Well, well, well." He seemed for the moment unwilling to try anything more complicated.

"Are you O.K.?" asked Ivan.

"Never better."

"Good." Ivan reached over and snuffed out the fiery ash that was burning through his friend's knee. "On to Zaragoza," he cried, and brushed off his hands on the upholstery. "But no more tricks."

After driving on in silence for a while, D.C. said, "I thought we'd seen the last of those crooks."

"Chance," remarked Ivan, as he scanned the lighted streets of Bordeaux.

D.C. stopped the car for a traffic light and turned. "You don't think they're following us, do you?"

"Why?"

"Oh, I don't know," replied D.C., evasively, and started the car in motion again. "Maybe revenge. Who knows?"

"Revenge?" Ivan looked at the driver's romantic profile in scornful disbelief. Slouching back down on the seat, he stretched out his legs contentedly and smiled as if tickled by the absurdity of the idea. "Revenge," he chuckled softly to himself, and closed his eyes and yawned. "How primitive." Falling asleep, he did not wake up again until they had arrived at the border.

Although it was well past midnight and quiet at the border, the small cluster of stores that catered to tourists still showed lights, but they seemed to be pasted in the windows like signs and gave the buildings an unreal, two-dimensional quality. D.C. pulled up in front of a money-changing establishment, and when the two boys got out—leg weary, crumpled, and chilled by the night air—it was still lightly drizzling. The moody muttering sounds from the nearby river that they would have to cross into Spain were those of a slumbering geriatrics ward. Over the deserted streets the wind blew fitfully.

As soon as they entered his store, the elderly money changer looked up from the book he was reading and smiled at the door. He wore thick glasses behind which his shapeless eyes swam idly about with no hope of actually seeing anything. Ivan produced three French bank notes and laid them before him on the counter, informing the man that he wished to exchange them for pesetas. The money changer groped for the bills, and picking them up, he stretched them one at a time across his lenses like colored filters.

"A nasty night," he said pleasantly, and smiling, he placed the money down and smoothed it out on the counter top. "Would you prefer small pesetas, large pesetas, or very large pesetas?" he asked.

"Mix it up," said Ivan, with an indifferent gesture.

"Very good." The money changer bent down and from somewhere beneath the counter he began pulling out great stacks of multicolored Spanish money neatly tied with string, until finally the entire counter was covered with a spectrum of bills. Straightening up, his knee joints cracking and his face red with exertion, the elderly man drew a deep breath in pain and disgustedly threw one last bundle onto the pile. "*Espagne!*" he cursed, and spit on the floor.

"A favorable rate of exchange," said Ivan to D.C., and tossed him a bundle. "Help yourself."

Stuffing the currency away as best they could, the boys bid *au revoir* to the wistfully smiling money changer and left with distended pockets.

They stood outside in the shelter of the doorway, darkly intimate, and laughed at their inflationary lumpiness. One hundred yards away, bathed in light and gleaming like an invitation, was the bridge to Spain. A whole country lay waiting for them on the other side—helpless. Excitement ran high.

Recalling that in school some types crossed themselves before swimming meets and examinations, D.C. reasoned that before Spain a little prayer would not be out of order. "The world is my oyster," he recited, "I shall not want. It maketh—" He stopped abruptly and pointed in horror at their mud-splattered car. "Sweet Jesus," he cried, "what the hell is going on there?"

Crouched and shielded by the automobile's left rear tire, a gray-faced woman bundled up in sexless anonymity knelt brazenly with her pants down as if putting a period at the end of the Grand National Road. Her drizzle-dampened hair fringed her face like cold noodles.

"*Madame,*" shouted D.C., running up to her and frankly staring, "*qu'est-ce que vous faites?*"

She replied that she was peeing.

[171]

Exasperated, D.C. turned to his friend for support, but Ivan only shrugged and stood mutely gathering rain in his beard.

"*Mais, c'est une Duesenberg,*" complained D.C. "*Je proteste cette comédie.*"

"*Est-ce française?*" inquired the woman, interested.

"*Mais non!*" D.C. stroked the muddy fender and explained to her as if she were a prospective buyer, "*C'est une classique américaine.*"

"*Une classique américaine?*" Pulling up her pants, the bemused woman swept the car in a single incredulous glance and shuffled off, mumbling, "*Tout est possible.*"

"Forget it," said Ivan, as his friend yelled terrible, womb-withering, belly-blistering, ass-biting oaths after the woman. "Come on." Ivan opened the car door and got in out of the rain. He lowered his window and shouted, "Come on! Haven't you read Muñoz-Grandes' *Diary of a Spanish Nun?* Once they give up the white veil of the novice and take on the black veil and solemn vows, they stitch their vulvas like stuffed chickens. Hurry!"

D.C. quit his ranting and got in. "Keep her privates private," he sulked, and the car leaped forward exactly one hundred yards and screeched to a halt beside a small wooden guardhouse.

D.C. raced the engine and blew the horn, but no one came out. The single heat-steamed window opposite him rattled. It opened a crack and a languorous, impeccably white glove appeared like spectral dry goods and wafted them on their way. The Duesenberg roared off. When they were halfway across the wooden bridge, the structure began to shimmy-moan-shimmy, shake, rattle, and roll under the weight of the car. At last . . . Spain.

In the middle of the road a border guard stood motionless. He was wrapped in a rain-soaked, khaki-colored, woolen army blanket and wore a three-cornered hat that held water like a cistern, the added load forcing the headgear down low on his forehead so that only 180° of eyeball were visible. Two fingers appeared from beneath his blanket ordering them over to the *aduana*—a box of a custom house covered with red clay tiles. Flattened up against the stucco side of the building were three blanketed soldiers bedded down vertically for the night. D.C. drew up in front of them.

The sopping guard came over and tapped on D.C.'s window. "*Muy buenas, señores,*" he saluted, the rich memory of smoked fish clinging to his words. "*Por favor, vengan Vds. acá.*" He wanted them to go inside the custom house.

"We're pressed for time," D.C. argued, getting out.

"*Por favor.*" He led the way.

At the entrance to the building, Ivan looked back and there were the three soldiers swarming all over the Duesenberg, opening and closing doors, lifting seats, peering under floor mats, tapping the chassis with an instrument resembling a divining rod, and probing the silver speaking tube to its roots. He had never seen a police state in action before.

The office was damp and gloomy, the scarred beams of the ceiling hanging so low that D.C. had to stoop in order to follow the guard across to the desk. Seated behind it in an overcoat buttoned up to the neck, his face partially hidden by a small bronze lamp, was a man holding a tweezers. A stamp album was open in front of him.

"*El jefe,*" the guard whispered to the tourists, and departed. The puddle that had collected where he had been standing trickled away across the uneven floor.

Without waiting to be asked, D.C. threw his passport across the desk. "I suppose that's what you want," he said, "but would you please step on it? We've got to make Zaragoza before it's too late."

The Chief looked up from his album and revealed a dark triangular face with a chin that curved out like a scimitar. As he observed his visitors, his mouth seemed faintly amused but there was melodrama in his black eyes.

"Time is money, eh?" he lightly chided them, and flipped through the pages of D.C.'s passport. Glancing up at Ivan, he asked, "And yours?"

Ivan handed it to him and, with no unseemly haste, he picked up a rubber stamp, put it down, took another, examined it under the light, spit on it, flourished it in the manner of a descending glider, and made his mark in each of the books.

"Fine." D. C. reached out, prodding him for the documents.

"Here in Spain," the Chief went on quietly, shuffling their passports, "we have an expression. *Poco a poco se va lejos.* Roughly translated, it says simply that it is better to walk to Madrid than run to Zaragoza." His eyes sparkled mischievously. "Now that we understand one another, let us proceed. Do you have anything to declare?"

"Nothing," replied D.C. sullenly.

Ivan pulled him back into the shadows to hide his bulging pockets, but the young lover refused to be held in check.

"Not a damn thing," he repeated, thrusting himself under the Chief's nose. "Now can we go?"

The room rang with the grim sound of rifles being cocked. D.C. looked about in surprise. Hugging the dark walls were muffled soldiers who hovered sinisterly in the background as if painted by Goya. He had gotten too close.

With an artful wave of his hand, the Chief placed his guards at ease. "You Americans," he began, clearly pleased with his opportunity to discuss the national character, "always hurry, hurry, hurry, rush, rush, rush. I see it in your corners." Turning the pages of his album, he pushed it toward his visitors and pointed with the tweezers. "'In Memory and in Honor of the Mothers of America.' A moving tribute. Good design. Good color. Excellent paper. And all for three cents. But . . ." —he tapped his tweezers in annoyance—"hasty perforations. They chew up your corners like mad dogs. Why do you do such things?"

D.C., his face red, suppressed rage chafing his skin, looked longingly at his friend. Ivan gave the Chief an unctuous smile of cringing submission. "It won't happen again, sir. We're a very young nation."

Patronized! And by Americans! The man behind the desk closed his stamp album and, placing it out of harm's way, he studied the boys shrewdly. When he spoke his voice was subtly corrugated with sly innuendo. "You are driving, I presume? May I see your Green Card, gentlemen?"

The man wanted a *green* card. Light green or dark green? D.C., who loved cards, knew that they were baptized by function and not hue. Why his entire life story could be summed up in cards like diary entries—better than Pepys, better than Evelyn, more richly quixotic than the Marquis de Sade. There were birth announcements, flash cards, birthday cards, bar mitzvah cards, playing cards, New Year's cards, credit cards, Valentines, get-well-quickees, soon there would be frosty wedding cards, and finally, at round-up time, the starkly formal condolence. A green card? It could only be a trap.

"Ivan . . ." The premonition of a condolence card affected D.C.'s wind. "Ivan . . . Our green card . . . *Please*."

In self-defense, Ivan ducked into his wallet and, coming forward, he placed a card down on top of a thick bundle of green pesetas.

The Chief yanked open a drawer and exhibiting the deft scoop of a croupier, he raked in the money. Plop-Whisk-Slam! A single blink and it would all have gone unseen. Then squinting at the card under the light, he nodded his head several times and returned it to Ivan. "It seems that you've made a mistake," he informed him patiently, still courteous, still willing to make allowances. "The card I wish is much greener."

No longer floundering, D.C. threw down his Blue Cross Membership and another sumptuous stack of bills. "What do you know about that! I had it all the time," he announced, and heaved an enormous sigh of relief.

The money might have been wormy wood chips or unsightly dandruff the way the Chief swept it out of sight. "Wrong again," he said sadly, and tossed the card back. Confronted with human fallibility, he was practically a Schweitzer. "I understand," he continued, his tone sickeningly benevolent. "Take your time. *Mas despacio*. I am interested in seeing only the International Motor Insurance Card. A bright green document, yes? What could be simpler? Your color is still a shade off."

Ivan opened all of the buttons on his double-breasted jacket and began throwing out odds and ends like a man in a burning house. Toothpicks, movie stubs, handkerchief, a packet of sugar from the boat, a wedge of cellophane-wrapped Brie, the letter from Pearson, a squash ball that he was in the habit of squeezing from time to time in moments of unusual tension. Thumping his money-laden pockets as if he expected them to boom like empty oil drums, Ivan seemed confounded. "Very odd," he said mystified. "We'd better check the car," was his decision, and had he not shoved his friend so unexpectedly toward the door that he cracked his head on a low-hanging beam, they might have made good their escape.

"Stop!" ordered the Chief, jumping up from his seat.

"I stopped," D.C. was quick to point out, although in a dazed condition.

"Stay where you are."

"What?"

"Quiet!"

"You're shouting," said D.C., and spitefully covered his ears.

Ivan, who had been held in suspended animation by the accident, reconsidered the exit. It was now securely corked. Soldiers were jammed in the doorway so tightly that their rifles clicked against one another like knitting needles. He pinched the end of his broad nose, muting his frustration, and returned to face the music.

"Did I forget something?" Ivan asked slyly.

"Please." The Chief raised a hand for silence. He leaned forward, the brass buttons on his overcoat twinkling in the lamplight, and sifted through the debris with which Ivan had littered his desk. "So," he said. "So."

"What is it?" D.C. came up behind his friend and gazed down at the officer.

"I don't know," muttered Ivan, uncertainly.

"What?"

Ivan turned back and standing on tiptoe he pushed his rambling beard into his friend's mouth. "Shut up," he growled.

"Right," hollered D.C., angrily.

"Quiet," demanded the Chief. He snatched up his album and quickly thumbed through the pages. "Ah!" he exclaimed. "*Maravillosa*." Tearing off the canceled Statue of Liberty from Pearson's envelope, he placed it tenderly on the page where it belonged, and slammed down the cover. Gloating, he cheerfully stroked the album, holding the stage in silence like a big-name star. Then gathering up Ivan's possessions, he dashed spryly around to the front of the desk and dumped them into the arms of the surprised tourist.

"Your papers are quite in order, gentlemen. I might go so far as to say neat as a pin. Spain bids you welcome," he declared, "and extends to you and yours bonds of fraternal cordiality," and saying this he urged them out into the bleak night.

When they reached the Duesenberg, the smug Chief, attentive to the point of depravity, held open the door for the young men, assisted them in like invalids, and prayed that God would be their co-pilot, as the soldiers looked on nervously from a respectful distance and tried without success to attract his attention. They watched their leader with purple, trembling, and waterlogged lips. Taking out a stub of chalk, he scrawled a cabalistic mark full of elegant twists and turns across the car's windshield, approving the Americans for entry. "*Adios*," he called, stepping back from the revving engine and lifting his hand, knuckles out, in farewell.

D.C. waved back and erased the chalk mark with his windshield wipers. "Screw you," he hummed, smiling conspicuously at the Chief. "Hold tight, little Sidney, we're slapping leather."

"Move it," snarled Ivan. "He's coming back."

"I can't," D.C. whined helplessly. "I'll squash him. I can't."

Ivan averted his eyes in contempt and sneered at his friend's morbid sensitivity.

"A moment, gentlemen, if you please," called the Chief, somewhat testily. "Let us have forms, forms, measured forms." This time he selected the long hood for his mark, but it was so thoroughly pimpled with rain drops that the tiny piece of chalk in his hand immediately disintegrated into a white sludge. Cursing, the Chief turned on his men. "*Hombres*," he bellowed, "*una tiza. Prisa! Prisa!*"

Like benchwarmers hailed by their coach, the three soldiers threw off their blankets and came running, their rifles in one hand, their chalk in the other. The chief looked at their wrinkled and baggy uniforms with loathing. That these men were in any way associated with him was such a repugnant fact of life that he seemed barely able to keep down his supper, let alone bring himself to take their proffered chalk. While he hesitated, the boldest of the three, whose teeth were long and yellow like pencils, whispered something in a voice that slunk and groveled. Tearing the soldier's chalk away from him as if he were removing his epaulets, the Chief ordered him to the rear of the Duesenberg with a flick of his pinky.

"Please." He motioned to D.C. to shut off the car's engine. "A formality," he said, in response to D.C.'s scowling impatience, and opened the door. "Rumor has it that your trunk is locked. In my capacity, I must know the contents of every foreign container entering Spain. Would you be so kind?"

"Stay dry, chicken," taunted Ivan, slumping down in his seat.

Muttering all the way, D.C. dragged himself to the rear of the car, and after fumbling with Madame d'Allégret's keys, he found one that turned in the lock. More than that he refused to do.

"¡Abrelo!" The Chief commanded his man to open it.

The bold soldier raced up. Lifting the top of the trunk, he gawked, flinched, and fell back in astonishment tripping over his own boots and firing his rifle willy-nilly into the mud.

Wondering what the excitement was all about, the two onlookers went to see for themselves. Inside the trunk were hand grenades, lugars, Thompson submachine guns, bazookas, land mines, Molotov cocktails, blowguns, and boomerangs—the forgotten toy arsenal of Madame d'Allégret's army of dead children.

"What's up?" inquired Ivan, who came running as soon as he heard the shots.

"Look," D.C. showed him the trunk, and then seeing the frightened soldier trembling on the rim of despair, he began to laugh uncontrollably.

Regardless of his personal views, the Chief did not enjoy seeing his man publicly ridiculed. He lowered, glowered, and stamped his hands together summoning the rank and file with a haughty flamenco barrage.

"Enemies of the State," he shouted, "you are surrounded!"

Ivan squinted into the night but saw only two cowering blankets.

"What a joker," gasped D.C. between laughs, irresistibly tickled by the solitary soldier's quaking rifle.

Humiliated, the Chief's neck swelled up like a trumpet player as he screamed for his men. His shrill cry ransacked the custom house, shook the cobwebs, and brought down a squadron of sleepy-eyed soldiers. They encircled the two boys and poked their rifle nozzles deep into their flesh to suggest efficiency.

"Hands up," cried the Chief, triumphantly.

"But they're only toys," said Ivan.

"Made in Japan," said D.C.

"Forward march!" said the Chief.

CHAPTER 14

❧ Operation Fecaldip.

The cramped prison cell was a tropical fish tank—all shapes, sizes, colors weaving in and out in an undulant submarine ravel. Bodies twisted themselves into grotesque jigsaw patterns covering every inch of available space and leaving vacant only a three-foot-wide hole in the middle of the floor above which a cloud of green flies buzzed uninhibitedly, blind drunk on the rising stench. Two time-charred women, their heads covered by black shawls, stood gazing out of the cell's lone window at the endless Duesenberg parked across the dusty street. Attempting to get a better look, one of them forgetfully took hold of the bars and they came off in her fingers. Embarrassed, she hurriedly pushed them back into place as the guard who sat outside under the window shouted some indifferent obscenity. Although long ago the bars had rotted out of their steel frame, they were maintained for their symbolic value, and rather than make costly repairs, the authorities had introduced the sentry as an economy measure.

Directly beneath the frayed black skirts of the old women and hemmed in by hot flesh, D.C. and Ivan bunched together in the thin air current that dribbled through the window like a puny wretch. The wall behind their backs was covered with Ivan's tables, diagrams, formulas, in addition to his meticulous scoring of forty days set off in tidy stacks of five. D.C., who had by now reconciled himself to wigging a bald teen-ager, sat looking out morosely from under the narrow brim of his Tyrolean at a fight between two cutthroats that spurted and raged like a hot spring.

"She's got *some* jelly beans," acknowledged Ivan, regarding the almost infinite chest that had led to hostilities as if it were a tricky experiment that had somehow been brought off.

"Disgusting," said D.C. professionally, and followed the sweep of her hair with furtive and love-sick eyes.

"*Pace,*" called a pale young priest, piping sweetly from outside the barred door.

The battle ceased with an implausible abruptness, and the cell became as still as a tree stump.

The priest glanced at the short, moon-faced guard beside him who had advised against disturbing the animals before their lunch. His expression was charitable. "*Pace,*" he repeated gently to the prisoners, and smiled. He wore dark glasses and a pleated black skirt, and he had come all the way from San Sebastian in order to hear their confessions and to love and comfort them in their affliction. When he had explained all this, he beamed and asked, "Who then will be first?"

Before anyone could move, the chesty woman had rushed up to the bars, tramping casually over bodies like Christ on the water. "Take me," she insisted, and jerking her skirt up to her eyebrows added, "if you're man enough."

At this, the prisoners unleashed a wild barrage of catcalls, lewd gestures, and piercing whistles.

A brute of a man wearing a worker's red scarf knotted about his neck stood up. "Fuck off!" he boomed at the celibate. "We don't want any."

The pale priest grew paler, the blood draining out of his ears, his nose, even his clerical collar looked whiter, and his Adam's apple stuck out like a jetty at low tide.

"*Hambre, hambre, hambre,*" chanted the cell, roaring gruesomely for its meal.

"*¡Silencio!*" blustered the guard, and as he led the forlorn bedraggled priest shuffling away, he was moved to say, "Maybe later. Maybe after food. You try again. O.K.?"

Shortly thereafter, the guard returned alone with the single daily meal provided by the state for its prisoners. The food—a soupy, smoking, bubbly mixture on top of which floated lumps of meat gleaming like cats' eyes—was in a huge dented container that resembled a garbage pail.

"Stand back," grunted the guard, setting down the food and opening the barred door. Quickly he pushed the container inside, slopping some of the mixture onto the floor in his haste to slam the door. But once this was done, he did not leave, for ever since the two Americans had arrived, something odd had been going on, something that in all his years at the jail, in all his years of dealing with *malos,* he had never before seen. Among these prisoners there were murderers, impatient men who, unable to work out their problems, had cut them up into small pieces, and yet for the last two weeks even these waited—assassins as docile as housewives at a check-out counter. He could not explain it.

"Go ahead," he enticed them. "It's good. It has meat in it. Big chunks. *Meat.*"

A stringy old rag bag and bone man sprang forward with the leap of a rabid jack rabbit. "Meat!" he cried feverishly, making frantic dipping motions with his rusty tin cup. But before he was close enough to the pot to actually dip in, he was plucked out of the air like a line drive by the prisoner who wore the red scarf and hurled rattling against the wall. "Away, you greedy little turd," clucked the brute. "Wait your turn."

The guard tried to intervene, but no one paid any attention to him. They were watching the two Americans who whispered together oblivious of the sharp interest of their fellow prisoners.

Under the strain of prolonged waiting, there were as usual a few weak vessels that cracked and turned raging eyes on the scar-faced gypsy. Seated cross-legged and dark-skinned on the floor, his patent-leather sideburns extending almost to his lips, the gypsy spent his impassive days slowly peeling succulent apples, oranges, and grapes with a nail file so finely sharpened that it could shave the leg of a pismire. The source of his supply of fresh fruit was a woman. Since his arrest, she had sat fixedly outside in the middle of the road nursing her infant child despite the sporadic attempts of the police to drive her off. Somehow during the night she managed to elude the guard and pass blood red oranges and ripe passionfruit through the bars to her waiting lover. As the gypsy concentrated on his carving, intent on producing the longest continuous peel in all of Spain, two prisoners rushed him from opposite directions, their mouths slavering like one-way kamikazes. Just when it looked as if he were about to be overwhelmed by the surprise attack, when his assailants were so close to his head that they might have been hats, he whipped his nail file around and, without a word, severed their Achilles' tendons. They each gave a bitter little cry and hobbled off, and the gypsy peeled and peeled.

Ivan stopped whispering to D.C. and picked up his tin cup. "Now let's have some lunch," he invited, as if a board meeting had just been concluded.

D.C. eagerly approved of the idea, but then he saw the dented pot and remembered, and his stomach shriveled up to the size of a dead bug.

"What's the matter?" asked Ivan.

"You go," said D.C., hanging back. "I'm full."

"You can't sing on an empty stomach," Ivan reasoned with him in a low voice. "You need your strength."

"I'm strong," insisted D.C. loudly.

Ivan glanced at the watching guard. "You're not only eating for you," he hissed under his breath, "you're eating for *us*."

"What are you whispering about?" yelled D.C. angrily. "He doesn't understand a word. I'll be ready when the time comes. Just leave me alone. You eat. Go ahead. Run along. Swill it up. Eat, eat, eat. Eat yourself into a muscle-bound coma."

"Malnutritic delirium," judged Ivan, and wrapping his hand around his friend's arm like a tourniquet, he led him to the pot.

The guard stared in disbelief as the prisoners parted like the Red Sea to make way for the Americans. A miracle. A timeless moment. No one breathed. Oily pimples came and went unnoticed. But no sooner had the two young men filled their cups and sat down again than the spell splintered like a rotten plank and the great bubbling pot was swarmed over by wailing, foul-mouthed, and kicking humanity. Puzzled, the guard inclined his nose over a chubby index finger and wandered vaguely off.

As the prisoners looted the pot, the ragged wreck who had earlier been pushed aside crawled painfully across to Ivan and D.C., his shin bones streaking the floor.

"*Excelentísimos señores*," he began, nearly losing consciousness for a moment at the sight of Ivan licking his fingers. "Gentlemen. You see he talk your dictionary. She is hungry. She is great hungry. Help! He is here for years. No one know how long. She fight with you at Lerida. You know?"

Ivan stopped licking and studied him in cold silence.

Mistaking the bearded Amercian's behavior for encouragement, the old man became excited, slapping his knees and clapping his hands, his thin face as blue as an icicle. Tears filled his eyes. He smiled. The language was exhausting him.

"Hungry. Yes? Lincoln Brigade. Yes? Beans, beans, make you fill your jeans. O.K.?"

Ivan put down his cup. "You again. I never saw you before in my life," he said coolly. "No work, no eat."

The old man decided to risk everything. "*Viva la quinze brigada*," he implored.

"Forget it," snapped Ivan. "I wasn't even born then. Poor bastard," he informed him solemnly, "you've been left behind like a moth-eaten codpiece. Today, no work, no eat. From each according to his ability, to each according to his production. That's capitalism, Darwin, and the N.A.M. The way of the world. There's no place in modern society for an underachiever. Face up to it, you're a full-time dropout."

"*Si me quieres escribir, ya sabes mi paradero*," sang the frantic old soldier, trying desperately to drum up some *esprit de corps*. "*En el frente de gondeza, primera linea . . .*"

"Here," offered D.C., extending his cup. "Take mine. I'm not hungry."

Stunned by the suddenness of the offer, the old man gurgled emotionally and mucus plugged his system. His bare stone-cold toes wriggled up, his lymph glands trembled, and then came tears of gratitude that splashed down his cheeks in waves.

"Scram," growled Ivan, and he knocked the cup out of D.C.'s hand.

As the liquid flew past his gaping mouth, the old man seemed to go into convulsions. His thin chest rattled like a shade covering an open window. He stared at Ivan with his lips opening and closing as if he were searching for words. Suddenly, he squeezed out one short, undistinguished, lackluster bark muted by saliva and jumped for the food, but three other prisoners had already lapped it up.

"You didn't have to do that," protested D.C. "The poor guy is sick."

"His brother's keeper."

"That's right. You're damn right," shouted D.C., loud with self-righteousness.

"Keepers are for animals. Let him be a man . . . if he can."

"But the guy is *sick*," D.C. stubbornly insisted. "He needs help."

"Do you know," explained Ivan, taking the larger view, "that when an Eskimo gets so old that he can't get it up anymore he goes off by himself to freeze to death."

"That's Lawrence," cracked D.C., dryly.

"No," corrected Ivan. "That's life." He consulted his watch. "Time," he called, and smashed the stone floor with his fist four times as if he were striking the hour.

Hugging his long legs, D.C. ignored him and sulked in a den of strangers, far from amber waves of grain, the Rose Bowl Queen, Transcendentalism, McIntosh apples, and a couple of newly minted Schlemovitzes.

The green flies that hovered over the opening in the floor began to swarm together excitedly, and the next moment they had shot apart in all directions diving for the walls. In response to Ivan's signal, a huge oozing eggplant rose ominously out of the hole and scanned the premises. Satisfied, it popped up into the cell with arms and legs, a refugee from a public school pageant on nutrition. Before long, another had appeared, and then another, and yet one more. They poured out of the trim little hole one after the other, like soiled clowns from a circus car. When they were all out, seven tired but happy shit-covered men and women stood in line waiting for their pay envelopes, their broad smiles unmistakably visible beneath the ordure.

Ivan stood up and eagerly demanded to know, "How far?"

The foreman of the group made his dripping way to the wall and planted a brown smudge on Ivan's diagram.

"Good," said Ivan, studying his drawing. His face glowed with a hard and gemlike flame of satisfaction. "Very good."

They were ahead of schedule. Forty days earlier when he had first proposed Operation Fecaldip, his friend had compared the difficulty of the project to bridging the Brahmaputra at flood stage with defective toothpicks. Right then Ivan knew that he had something he could sink his teeth into. They would tunnel their way to freedom under the wall with only tin cups and muscle and pluck. Careful planning had eliminated most of the problems and motivation was kept at a fever-pitch by Ivan's:

1. Clear statement of their shared objective
2. Personal interest in employee's welfare
3. Emphasis on the pleasure and security to be derived from repetitive labor
4. Stacks and stacks of pesetas.

In fact the prisoners were making so much money behind bars that after a week their employer discovered that they had lost sight of freedom and settled for overtime, producing a long irrelevant hole that snaked like a maze or a Chinese dragon on New Year's. Sweeping changes were made to an anarchic chorus of D.C.'s hoots, snickers, and scoffs. In place of MER (Maximum Efficiency Ratio for individual workers), Ivan substituted GIP (Group Incentive Plan), a bonus program based on combined output and American Know-how. As soon as total performance rather than time determined the pay scale the tunnel unwrinkled. D.C. conceded grudgingly that it was a brilliant idea. Group rapport became spectacular. Never better. Anyone found wandering off tangentially with his tin cup was never found again. And now they were even ahead of schedule. In only a few more hours they would be surfacing under the Duesenberg's full gas tank, but these hours would be the most dangerous of all. According to Ivan's plan, the tunnel, once it cleared the prison walls, was to run directly under the guard posted at the window. There was no alternative. The digging would have to be quick and silent. A picked crew was assembled for the final thrust composed of skilled men under sixty inches tall with strong family attachments who enjoyed a good joke and could see in the dark. Music would both cut down on fatigue and be a blasting mat to muffle the operation. As soon as the befouled miners had been paid off and dispersed, everything was in readiness for the Great Adventure. Seven shrimps lined up on the lip of the abyss like seven Toulouse-Lautrecs contemplating coitus and waited for final instructions. Ivan circled them in review and shook each dwarfish hand soberly but without squeezing lest he endanger their digging fingers.

D.C., the apostate, looked on with unconcealed amusement. "Fellows in arms," he mocked in a bassoon voice ceremoniously pompous, "and my most loving friends, bruised underneath the yoke of tyranny, thus far into the bowels of the land have we marched on without impediment—"

"Eat it!" commanded Ivan, sizzling and glaringly grim.

Believing that the order was for them, the seven shrimps without further ado flung themselves head first into the void.

Exeunt omnes. It was impossible to call them back and there were so many little things that he had wanted to say. Ivan sensed an evil omen. Chance had faked out reason and produced a quick score. Although inauspiciously, the Great Adventure had begun.

Ivan remained motionless, waiting, listening, his eyes shut and his ear cocked over the hole. The cell held its breath. Nothing happened for a while and then . . . and then . . . the raw sound of scraping tin cups went off like a burglar alarm.

Ivan's eyes shot open and he flushed with embarrassment. Although he had not anticipated a completely soundless operation, this was ridiculous. His picked men, his little band of choice nimble spirits had turned out to be all clutz and gorilla. As he turned to D.C., he nevertheless appeared confident, but the color of his face was worried.

"Sing," he said bluntly.

Drawing his jacket about him, D.C. reluctantly pushed through to the barred window and looked out. The napping guard stirred, mumbled, stirred again uneasily brushing flies from his sun-drenched face and fell back into his dream. "Anything in particular?" he asked Ivan, trying to be accommodating.

"Sing, dammit, sing!" fumed Ivan, briefly drowning out the racket below. "And loud."

D.C. had a sweet voice. He had kept it free of vibrato, adenitis, and other rococo embellishments. But it had been even better when he was younger for then he had had such purity of tone that at his bar mitzvah the rabbi, a waxen elder who was ordinarily as spontaneous as a chest of drawers, had lifted him into the air with hugs and kisses crying, "An angel with a golden horn!" For several weeks after that he regularly drank a solution of sugar in water and dreamed of the big time.

As he sang, his voice rose heavenward thin and clear, its spirituality heightened by lack of food, and the rapt prisoners clung to each impossible note like a bannister. Even the gypsy stopped peeling and listened.

> When you were small, alone and blue,
> Who was watching over you?
> Who steered you straight when you went wrong?
> Who had a smile, a kiss, a song?
> But now she's ninety-two and blue,
> A-wanting just a word from you.

> Less toil for Mother
> Don't let her get old.
> Less toil for Mother
> Protect her from mold.

> Less sweat for Mama
> Keep her armpits pure.
> If she gets cancer,
> You don't have a cure.

Less angst for Mommy
Make her mind serene,
For once she's twisted
It's all sour cream.

More love for your Mom
Revere her fair sex.
She's Queen of your heart.
You're Oedipus Rex.

"*Otra vez.*" The sleeping guard was no longer sleeping. He had been awakened by the music and stood looking in through the bars with tears streaming down his pock-marked cheeks. "American," he blubbered, "sing it again."

D.C. was staggered. "Pock Mark! What are *you* doing here?" he demanded to know.

"*Otra vez,*" said the guard, and blew his nose.

D.C. bent toward the bars. "I'll take a ham and cheese," he whispered urgently, "and light on the mustard."

"*¿Como?*" the guard frowned and put away his handkerchief. "Is this an American song *and dance*?" he asked with sarcasm.

"What do you mean you gave me my chance?"

"Quiet," snapped the guard losing his temper, "or I come in there."

"Fair! You call this fair? You're persecuting me."

"*¡Bastante!* You through."

"Only by birth," shouted D.C., seriously overwrought. "I'm a changed man now. I'm an American."

The guard's baggy uniform stiffened like wet rags left out overnight as he raised his rifle with malicious deliberateness and pushed it through the bars. "You through," he cried resolutely.

Ivan, who all along had been trying to silence his friend by means of black looks and bloody gestures, saw forty days of creeping plot about to be uncovered. Shouldering D.C. aside, he tossed a bundle of bills that were almost the size of newspapers through the bars. They landed heavily at the guard's feet and kicked up a cloud of yellow dust. "I won't insult Integrity by bargaining. Take it all."

Throwing down his rifle, the guard opened his coarse, khaki-colored jacket and stuffed the loot inside. In his haste to button up, he began too high, and with still several buttons left to go he ran out of holes. His jacket pressed in on his chest like a cast-iron pot, but he was too busy to notice as he retrieved his gun and dusted it off. Straightening up as best he could, the hunched soldier pitched back and forth on his heels in search of his center of gravity, smiling generously all the while. "*Olvidemos lo pasado*," he announced, offering pardon in a thick voice. "The heart of man is a mystery."

"You devil. Your mind is like quicksilver," admired Ivan, and the lines went out of his face.

"Your friend sings all the notes," replied the guard, returning the compliment. He hummed memorable bits and pieces of D.C.'s melody, blinked his eyes as if warding off gnats, and smiled tearfully in the gay lemon sunlight before the ground suddenly opened beneath his boots and he was swallowed up in one gulp.

D.C., tense with hunger, cried, "Don Giovanni," but Ivan knew better. His soft one-eyed gaze was calm with resignation as he looked out on the struggling hole. "Of course," he shrugged, "cheap foreign labor. It's a blot on the industrial horizon." Ivan began to bang his tin cup against the bars and continued to bellow treason until his strange behavior attracted a squad of armed guards. He indicated the hole and they surrounded it like a khaki fence. At a safe distance, their squad leader pranced about thrashing the heavens with his sword. "Jesus," he prayed, "keep them safe from harm." The soldiers promptly fired a million bullets point-blank into the black hole killing everything in sight.

When it was all over, the squad leader counted his men. "Thank God," he breathed, and using his sleeve he wiped the imagined blood from his clean Toledo blade. Dismissing his soldiers, he about-faced and turned to the prisoner Ivan. "I make no promises!" he shouted angrily. "Nothing. Do you hear?" Abruptly, he turned his back and hurried away as if he had already said too much.

Shortly thereafter the American consul resident in the town appeared at the gates of the prison. In Spain it is a poor community indeed that cannot afford to have its own representative of the United States of America and even those rare villages that lack churches and military barracks do not want for an American consul. Occasionally some of these men, as a consequence of their long stays in remote outposts, adopt foreign ways and grow slow and shaggy, but this was not the case with the consul Quivers. The only change—a perverse one—that living abroad had wrought in him was that he now chewed gum (which he hated) with an overcompensating, aggressive, damn-your-eyes crank of his patriotic jaws. He was a broad-shouldered man whose face was as long and narrow as an ironing board, and while he chewed and paced back and forth before the gates waiting for the fumbling sentry to open the locks, he exuded the restless energy of a caged animal.

"An outrage! Why wasn't I notified sooner?" he seethed, and before the sentry could get out of his way he had burst through the half-open gate and was inside the cramped, insignificant prison office shouting accusations. The officer in charge heard him out in silence and guardedly acceded to his request. After the proper papers had been filled out, the prisoners under guard would be allowed to accompany him to City Hall for an interview with his friend the *alcalde*. The consul signed the forms, paid for the tax stamps that were affixed to them, and snapped his gum viciously as the boys were brought out, blinking in the light like afternoon moviegoers.

"Terrible," said Quivers, when he saw their condition. "You haven't heard the last of this," he promised and, patrolled by fixed bayonets, they left.

All the way to the City Hall, D.C. would not be still. Thin, shrill, and jumpy from lack of sleep, he kept explaining with guilty elaboration the circumstances of their imprisonment as if the consul were attorney for the prosecution rather than the defense. Quivers stopped chewing and listened, his lips set in a narrow line, and when they arrived at the steps of the gaudy municipal building he threw back his head in contempt.

"Nonsense . . . vague rumors. They haven't a leg to stand on and they know it. We'll have you out of this in no time."

"I hope you're right," remarked Ivan, skeptically.

"Of course I'm right! Your worries are over. Come on." Racing up the stairs two at a time, the consul suddenly stopped, turned, and ran breathlessly back to the prisoners with his mouth open. "Did they make you sign any papers? Depositions? Anything?"

D.C. seemed to recall something.

"Nothing," replied Ivan, cutting him short.

"Good, good. That simplifies things." Then grabbing his unhappy clients by the elbows, he pushed them up the stairs exhorting them all the way. "Chin up! Don't worry! Remember you're Americans! You could smile you know. If they see those faces they'll bury you. Come on. Here we go."

In the main office there was a great deal of noise and confusion. Uniformed messengers ran up and down like relay teams. Telephones rang continuously. Before the reception desk, troubled people were gathered in small, nervous groups talking animatedly among themselves. An old man with high cheekbones and a beret leaned against one of the room's marble pillars reading a newspaper out loud. "*¡Dios mio!*" he shouted raucously, the paper rattling in his skeletal hands. "*Diez y nueve chicas. ¡Que raro!*" But no one seemed to care.

"Don't worry. I know my way around here," the consul reassured his countrymen as they passed through the crowd to the main desk. "What's new in the States?"

"Electron microscopic studies on the developmental cycle of mycoplasma laidlawii," Ivan volunteered at once, forgetting his predicament.

"Typical!" the consul said with disgust. He rested the palms of his hands on the desk and scanned the horizon with a hard, nautical eye, but still no one noticed their presence. Three rows of typists clicked away intensely at their machines. "Typical. Sssss," he hissed, trying to get the attention of the brown-haired girl nearest them, but her eyes never lifted from her work.

"Wait, wait, wait. It's always the same," he cried out in exasperation. "Well, we'll just have to wait. What's new in the States?"

Ivan refused to answer.

"Is there a place to eat here," inquired D.C., looking about. "I haven't eaten anything in weeks."

"First things first," insisted Quivers, dogmatically. He fidgeted about in a small space—chewing, twisting, turning. "Aha!" he finally announced.

Ivan and D.C. looked up. Coming toward them was a square lady with a large mouth.

"Remember," the consul nudged them with last minute instructions, "let me do the talking."

"Can I help you gentlemen?" the woman inquired briskly, her manner an official document.

"Naturally. I'm Quivers from America. We want to see the Mayor at once."

"Do you have an appointment?"

"An appointment!" The consul appeared outraged. "Don't you understand this is urgent? An emergency. *Urgencia.* We must talk to the Mayor *now.*"

"Impossible," the woman snapped back.

"What do you mean *impossible?*"

"The Mayor is out of town. He won't be back for a week."

Though incredulous, the consul had lived in Spain long enough to recognize futility, so cutting his losses he advanced on another front. "Then what about the Assistant Mayor?"

"Out of the question. His calendar is black with appointments."

The consul sputtered and fumed and his hand swept down his face in one long slide of frustration.

No longer able to keep silent, D.C. stepped aside to reveal the bayonets at his back and pleaded, "Don't let them take me away. I'm being tortured. They're shrinking me. Look at my wrists, they're as thin as candlewicks. My poor mother hasn't seen me for months and she's an invalid with a ruptured spleen and no one to look after her. I beg you as a woman and a secretary, isn't there someone we can talk to?"

"Right," said the consul delightedly, failing to note the young man's breach of tactics. "Someone else in authority. Right!"

"W-e-l-l," considered the woman, her eye traveling from the

cold impersonality of the bayonets to the good-looking prisoner with the feather in his hat. "Perhaps our Señor Fratero will be able to help you. May I have your names?"

The consul produced his card in seconds.

"Beautiful," D.C. called after her as she walked off.

"Right," echoed Quivers with satisfaction. "Now we're getting somewhere. It's not the Mayor, but it's a start. I know Fratero and he can be of use to us. In Spain these things are done differently. Just leave it to me. From now on, leave everything to me."

When Señor Fratero appeared he was a surprise. Both Ivan and D.C. had expected someone much larger, but in fact he was a small package neatly wrapped. He wore a tightly fitted jacket with narrow lapels, and his hair, combed straight back, gleamed like a black cloche made of plastic. Resting lightly on the bridge of his well-shaped nose were rimless glasses with tiny pink-tinted square lenses that gave him the appearance of a child peering out at the world from a doll's house.

As the gentleman shuffled over to them, Quivers leaped toward him with an outstretched hand. "Fratero. It's good to see you again, *amigo mio*. How goes it?"

"As well as can be expected in this life," Señor Fratero responded, wearily. "And you?"

"You know. Still running, as always." He laughed at himself and drew the two young men into the ambience of affability. "Let me introduce—"

"A moment." Señor Fratero raised five diminutive fingers. "Please. Let's sit down. My feet are destroying me."

The four men, followed possessively by the heavy-footed guards, made their way to a relatively quiet corner of the hall and seated themselves behind a pillar.

"Ah! That's better," said Señor Fratero with feeling, his feet lying before him like debris. "Now, you were saying."

"My countrymen, Storch and Widdemore."

"Ah, yes." Fratero acknowledged the names, but it was clear that they meant nothing to him.

"Currently innocent victims of a ridiculous misunderstanding that, I'm happy to say, casts doubt on no man's integrity."

"Ah, yes," sighed Fratero, but instead of extending a hand, he bent over and rubbed the heel of his right foot.

"Anything wrong?" asked Quivers.

"I fear these shoes are too small after all."

"New?"

"They arrived in the mail this morning. Perhaps it was foolishness. Do you think so? It's the first time I've ever done anything quite like this."

The consul leaned down and stroked the black leather admiringly. "Fine shoes. You could go anywhere in shoes like that."

Fratero's face brightened. "They're from England, of course. Where else could you get this style and workmanship? Incomparable! There's nothing like it within five hundred kilometers of here. Did you notice how expertly this welt is stitched? Look here." He ran his fingers lightly along the juncture of the sole and the upper part of the shoe.

"I congratulate you. They're a pleasure for the eye. But have you ever visited the great factories of Nashua, New Hampshire?"

Fratero's face drooped perceptibly.

"No question," the consul compromised. "You can't beat the English for homecrafts and small goods. It goes without saying."

Fratero's eyes passed over Ivan's scuffed and disreputably brown shoes like a sentence. Gripping the consul's arm, he pitched his voice to exclude the prisoners. "Don't think I was so silly that I didn't take into consideration the difference between their lasts and those of my country. Oh no! Nothing so foolish. My planning was thorough even to the leather laces. As you can see, from heel to toe the unity of conception is complete. But . . ." he faltered, "but somehow they don't fit."

"Of course you could stretch them," the consul placated. "First-rate shoes often require small adjustments. It's a sign of their quality. Why not?"

"Yes," Fratero allowed, dispiritedly. "I suppose so. But that's not at all the idea. It isn't as if I had a sudden urge, some queer whim that had to be satisfied, and sent for them on impulse. If only that were the case. You see, the truth of the matter is that I've been preparing for these shoes all my life."

"A good job. They're splendid."

Unable to control himself any longer, D.C. leaned over and blurted out, "I'm innocent."

"Oh?" Fratero appeared put out at the interruption.

Quivers regarded the young man sourly and then turning to the dapper official, he added, "I've never seen their equal. All your life, you say?"

Señor Fratero was silent for a moment and seemed to be weighing something in his mind. "I'll tell you about it," he whispered confidentially. "Have you ever wanted anything so much that your whole life was merely a means to that end, some perfect object, no matter how trivial, that could give meaning to all the rest and on which you set your heart?"

"Interesting. Very interesting," pondered the consul.

"In my case it was these shoes. Nothing was left to chance, absolutely nothing. I gathered together photographs, descriptions, abstracts, made countless scale drawings incorporating those features that seemed to me essential for what I had in mind, and then threw them out and made others, always refining and improving in order to achieve the perfection I desired. A thousand samples of leather must have passed through my hands and each one was examined for strength, texture, durability, and suppleness, and rated accordingly. My files on these studies alone fill *three* metal cabinets."

"You're a marvel. What energy!"

"Mind you," Fratero was becoming excited, "I told no one of my work. It wasn't that there was any particular necessity for secrecy in the matter. In fact several times, especially at the beginning, I considered discussing my research with friends. But as I progressed and learned more about the scope and intricacy of my subject, it became increasingly more difficult to hope for understanding. And by then I had discovered that an artist can only work his way free of the prison of his obsession alone and in silence. Do you think *La Maja Desnuda* was done while Goya sat joking with his friends in a café? Ridiculous!"

The consul was wide-eyed. "I've never thought of it that way. Right. You've got a point."

"It's only now, with the achieved results before us, that I can again bring myself to speak of my work." Fratero's face darkened as if it had suddenly gone behind a cloud, and he rubbed morosely at the heel of his left foot. "I can't understand it," he mumbled to himself. "Could it be these socks?"

"Look at me." D.C. raised his hat to give Fratero a better view. "I'm thin, but without bitterness. Do I look like a revolutionary?"

"Yes, yes," Fratero indulged him. "That's very good." He stood up unexpectedly and addressed the consul. "I'm sorry, but I really must go. We're quite busy just now. Most unusual. Good-bye."

As Señor Fratero shuffled off wincing in his new shoes, Ivan shouted after him, "Wait!" There's no other answer, he told himself, visibly annoyed at not having realized it sooner.

Fratero turned morosely. "Yes?"

"There's no other answer," said Ivan, his voice riddled with conviction. "You're in the clear. It's *them*. They've muffed the job."

Quivers was beside himself. "Marvelous!" he applauded, losing his gum in the excitement. "Send them back."

Fratero considered the impossible, his head bowed, his hands knotted behind his back. "Do you honestly think so?" he asked in a subdued voice. "They were made in England, you know."

"Beyond a doubt," Ivan assured him. "Like us, you've been had by obscure forces."

"Naturally the possibility occurred to me," Fratero explained to the jubilant consul, "but it seemed so remote."

"Congratulations!" cried Quivers gleefully.

Señor Fratero seemed dazed by the swift turn of events, but he refused to be rushed. He just stood there shifting about uncomfortably in his shoes, not saying anything, putting the pieces together for himself. After a while, he motioned the consul aside. "Even in Eden there were weeds," he informed him. "Man is not a perfect machine."

"Right," said the consul diplomatically.

As the two men continued to talk, the noise in the hall grew louder. There was an argument going on. A hurrying messenger had collided with a woman on crutches in the purple shadows of the unlit hall. Shouts. Lights flickered on—small dirty globes that resembled limes hanging from the walls. Señor Fratero and the consul ignored the disturbance and slowly walked off together arm-in-arm, as thick as thieves, enjoying each other's company. Gloating like successful marriage brokers, Ivan and D.C. watched them go.

CHAPTER 15

🌿 Death late in the afternoon.

As the dawn came up over the Duesenberg's glowing dashboard, D.C. could see above the olive trees, beyond the night-frosted hills, the legendary city of Pamplona rising in the distance like a popover. At first it seemed chocolate brown. But as they came closer and the sun rose in the sky, the color of the buildings faded—first to burnt sienna, then butterscotch, and finally, up close, camel's hair. At that early hour the streets were deserted except for five men wearing black corduroy suits who walked doggedly down the middle of the road in single file pushing garbage pails on wheels. D.C. swung wide to avoid hitting them and drove on to the plaza in the center of town where he stopped the car in front of the Hotel Béla and slumped over the wheel.

Although Señor Fratero had insisted on their remaining at least one more day as his personal guests in order to rest and recover from the ordeal they had suffered, D.C. felt that they had imposed on local hospitality long enough. He wanted nothing more from that miserable community than absence. Desperate to get to Zaragoza and Sidney, he had persuaded Ivan that they should leave at once. But now after having driven all night he could go no farther.

The indefatigable Ivan was annoyed. Once on the road, he didn't care to stop short of their destination, and so he spoke forebodingly of Sidney and the ravages of time. Pamplona reminded him of the prison cell they had just left, and he was anxious to get on to the capital of Aragon. He suggested that D.C. try fresh air, another cigarette, a crumb of Brie he found in his pocket, but seeing his friend's eyes as red as poppies, Ivan recognized that he had no choice and got out. "But only a cat nap," he grudged, as D.C. dragged himself punch-drunk into the hotel.

The Béla was a sullen, two-story building without airs, its lobby little more than a broom closet. Although there were newer and grander hotels in the city, it was evident that when a bullfighter came to fight in Pamplona he came to the Béla. All of the great ones had stayed there and, in departing, they had left their autographed pictures on the walls as proof. D.C. slumped against the plaster, looking through glassy eyes at the Persian lamb hats and floral capes of the picturesque *matadors* while Ivan rang the silver desk bell summoning help.

"We have nothing." The man who appeared wore a maroon bathrobe, one sleeve filled with flesh and the other air. He was not at all interested in conversation. Ivan hit the bell in anger and demanded to see the manager.

"I am Béla," he declared stolidly, and shook his head. "Nothing."

"I see," said Ivan, not believing a word of it. "Is there another hotel nearby?"

"The same." Béla was growing impatient waiting for him to go.

"I see." Ivan drew out his wallet and opened it like a telephone book. "It would only be for a few hours," he pointed out, clarifying the situation in a friendly, intimate, I-Thou sort of way.

"Out!" cried Béla. His eyes short-circuited and a perfectly round puff of black smoke shot from his mouth.

Not wanting to go away empty-handed, Ivan removed a folded paper cup from his wallet. "Could you fill this up with water?" he inquired. "My friend isn't feeling well."

Béla became very still, terrifically still, like a man sleeping in the same bed as a bishop. "What friend?" he wanted to know.

Ivan looked for D.C. and found that he had slipped out of sight.

Luckily he had not gone far. Somehow he had unobtrusively fallen to the floor where he lay sleeping in a tangled heap of arms and legs, a sly, mocking smile on his lips. Ivan yanked him to his feet and extracted the framed photograph of a bullfighter that he had clutched in his arms. "This is yours," he admitted, brazenly. "We've got nothing to hide."

Béla stuffed his empty sleeve in his pocket and came out from behind the desk to claim his property. He did not like Ivan and so he did not look at him as he took the picture, but the tall American who coveted it was another matter. Touching him, Béla said only *"Buen hombre,"* but it was enough.

D.C., whose eyes had been sealed in peace and dignity, awoke with a start to find Béla's unfamiliar palm on his chest. "Take your hand off me!" he shouted thoughtlessly and, as a final thrust, added, "Greaser."

Béla smiled in embarrassment as if they shared a guilty little secret, an innocent weakness for anonymous charity or women with straight pubic hair. He tapped the photograph that he had inserted in the front of his bathrobe. "For one with *afición,*" he swore, ex cathedra, "there is always room in my hotel."

"With bath," yawned D.C., and stumbled toward the stairway.

There was scarcely an American left who did not love bulls and bull fighting, but it was rare to come upon one who truly possessed The Feel. Béla watched him go protectively, his face spiritual like a stained glass window.

"Is it safe to leave our car out front?" Ivan was taking no chances.

"You need not worry," Béla promised, tolerating him only because of his friend. "Rest in peace."

But Ivan did not go. He distrusted Béla and Béla's sudden affection for his friend and made his suspicions known by questioning glances and impudent scowls.

"Señor," said Béla grandly, *"this* is Pamplona. Once capital of the kingdom of Navarra. When your country had only barefoot savages, the rulers of the earth lived here. In this city poetry, art, science, and the Church are all at home. Do you think you are in a jungle? Brush your teeth and go to sleep."

Ivan considered this outburst without comment and strode purposefully out of the hotel. In a minute he was back toting the Duesenberg's battery.

At the top of the stairs Ivan located their room, where he found his friend snoring comfortably on the floor. It was only by inches that D.C. had fallen short of the bed, but nevertheless it was a clean miss. Although he too was tired, so tired that he simply threw off all of his clothes and fell naked across the damp cotton bedspread without first bothering to remove it, Ivan did not rest well in the Hotel Béla. He had hardly fallen asleep when he dreamed that there was a knock on the door and a chambermaid came in. Seeing his bare flesh, she shrieked, apologized, and ran out slamming the door behind her. Soon there was a second knock. Again the door opened. The chambermaid had returned with two friends. At first they just stood in the doorway screaming their heads off. Afterward they apologized and giggled and gaped for several minutes in dumb admiration before banging the door closed. Unrefreshed, Ivan opened his eyes.

The heavy wooden *persianas* shut out all light, so it was impossible to tell how long he had actually been asleep. Outside in the street he could hear shots and commotion, but the room was as cold and still as an abandoned mine. Calling for D.C., he received no answer. Ivan groped about on the night table and switched on the lamp. Except for his scattered clothes, the floor was immaculate. D.C. was gone and on the bureau, where he had left the battery, only a black smudge remained.

Gathering up his wrinkled and misshapen clothing, Ivan got dressed quickly and hurried downstairs. In the tiny lobby crowded with international merrymakers he found Béla.

"Your friend said to say that he will be at the Plaza del Castillo," Béla informed him coldly, fulfilling his obligation.

Relieved, Ivan asked, "What's all this?" shouting to be heard above the din.

"*This,*" exclaimed Béla, astonished at his ignorance, "is San Benedicto."

"I thought your festival was the San Fermin in June."

The hotel owner scoffed. "Do you think a city such as Pamplona has but one *feria?* We fight up to the first day of winter. There are people all over the world who want to come to us. After the Fermin, there are the *corridas* of San Clemente, San Fernando, San Francisco, and San Bernardino. This year Benedicto is last, but next year who knows? We will *never* run out of saints," he declared proudly as if speaking of some natural resource like tin or water power, and with a withering formal bow he turned away to embrace a friend.

What had sounded like shots in the room were firecrackers in the street and as Ivan made his way through the crowded city, they were exploding everywhere. The men would light them from their cigarettes and watch the flaring wicks burn down until the very last second before flinging them high into the air. Four-fingered hands were not unusual. He hadn't cared for Pamplona empty, and now that the streets, the plazas, the cafés, were spilling over with dancing and singing humanity, he loathed it. Young girls in short skirts and high heels, their hair teased into beehives and coronas, ran into him with their arms linked followed by uniformed cadets making obscene noises through their teeth. Ivan pushed through them and moved on, his elbows protruding like spikes.

The thronged Plaza del Castillo, surrounded by an arcade, was strung with lights, and yellow and red streamers fluttered from the lampposts in the afternoon sun. By the fountain at the center, a grinning man with one ear played an accordion that could barely be heard. As Ivan searched for his friend among the revelers, someone shouted in his ear, "Hurray for wine! Hurray for the foreigners!" Without stopping, Ivan checked his pockets to make sure nothing was missing.

Although the Duesenberg was large, it was completely encircled and hidden by the admiring masses, and Ivan had gone around the plaza several times before he finally located it. The car was parked in front of one of the cafés, but D.C. was not to be seen at any of its outside tables. Using his large shoulders, Ivan forced his way through the door. It was dark and humid inside as he squeezed through the noise and laughter. At the far end of the bar was D.C., drinking expertly from a lofted wineskin and surrounded by a group of cheering Spaniards who counted off the seconds in unison. He was dressed like a bullfighter, wearing a green *traje de luces*, and his black hair was knotted into a tiny pigtail at the back. When he dropped the empty wineskin, gasping for breath, they whistled their approval and an unbelievably beautiful girl reached up and kissed him hard with blood-crazed enthusiasm.

Disgusted, Ivan pushed into the middle of the happy mob and tapped his friend on the shoulder. "It's getting late," he said nastily. "Let's blow."

D.C. was overjoyed to see him and introduced his girlfriend. Her name was Butternut Cliveden. She was an English model who had come to Spain for the bullfighters. Butternut gave Ivan a radiant smile. "Don't be a bloody ass," she laughed, and squeezed D.C. ardently around the waist.

"Now!" insisted Ivan, and waited with his arms folded across his chest.

Taking up the gauntlet, Butternut threw her arms around D.C. and kissed him again, a tantalizingly violent, lip-smacking, triple-tongued, deeply resolved labial conspiracy. D.C. languidly raised his lids. Even close up with her eyes fused cycloptically together above the bridge of her nose she was gorgeous.

"There's no reason why we all can't be friends," he said with a brave little smile. "Let's discuss this sensibly over something to eat."

The three of them walked to an occupied table which was instantly cleared out for the *torero Americano*. D.C.'s Spanish friends held the chairs back for them to be seated. Then from the harried waiter his friends quickly obtained clean table linen, silverware, and glasses, and with their own hands reset the table for their *amigo* after first having hurried the waiter back into the kitchen with special instructions.

Butternut was thrilled and laughed excitedly. D.C. was pleased and laughed excitedly. Ivan, who sat between them at the square table, looked on noncommittally like a judge at a tennis match.

"*Tres platos del mar*," announced the returning waiter with impressive swagger and beamed as he placed each of the splendid dishes onto the table. "*Complimentos de la casa*."

D.C smiled up at the hovering Spaniards in appreciation and lifted a small, delicately colored, pink-tinted clam to his mouth. Everyone standing around the table fell silent. As the clam was sucked out of its shell, the waiter bent forward and froze in space. D.C. saw no reason to hurry. He was enjoying himself, and he chewed for a long time in sober deliberation before swallowing. "¡*Bueno!*" he concluded, and gave the waiter a blazing and epiphanic smile of utter acceptance.

The cheers boomed out like church bells and the color returned to the waiter's face as he was deluged with embraces and led off in triumph.

Butternut reached across the table and caught the *torero's* hand. "You're beautiful!" she said, in a voice turbulent with sexual unrest.

"Clean clothes make all the difference," D.C. informed Ivan, lightly twitting the sloven. He removed an orange mussel from its black shell and raising it to his lips cried out joyously, "Isn't this fantastic?"

It seemed to Ivan that he was suggesting more than the mollusk. While his strong teeth tore through baked sharkskin, Ivan warily scrutinized the celebrity with a piercing scowl.

"Absolutely beautiful," sighed Butternut, and having withdrawn one foot from its suede boot, she sank down in her chair in order to run her toes over the *torero's* ankle.

"We were planning to see the bullfights this afternoon," D.C. told Ivan. He took off his shoe and furtively slouched down beneath the table. "Why don't you join us?"

Ticklish Butternut giggled and straightened up. "He'd be bored," she threw out carelessly, while pulling down her bulky turtle-neck sweater. It was yellow, the color of merriment and affability.

"What about your girlfriend in Zaragoza?" inquired Ivan, his great molars grinding the sharkskin into paste.

Annoyed and embarrassed, D.C. dismissed the question. "Let's just forget about that. O.K.?"

"Why not?" agreed the indifferent Ivan, grinding and grinding. "She's *your* friend."

"Will you drop it already!" screamed D.C., his style crimped.

"What's with you anyway? You're like a Puritan elephant. Do me a favor and forget Zaragoza. We're in Pamplona now, damn it. *Carpe diem*." He looked over and smiled sheepishly at Butternut whose heavily made-up eyes were like unfurnished rooms. "He's got this great sense of humor," D.C. offered by way of explanation. "Dead pan, you know? He never cracks. Look at him."

At the sight of the glowering Ivan, Butternut and D.C. both broke down and burst into laughter. "Seriously . . ." D.C. wrapped his arm fondly about Ivan's thick neck and tried to catch his breath. "Seriously," he collected himself and said, "seriously, he's brilliant. He's got it all figured out. The whole bit. But like all geniuses he's way ahead of his time. Frankly," he continued, without a trace of humor, "you can't believe a word he says."

"Who cares?" murmured Butternut, her mind on other things. From within the ring of saffron-colored rice on her plate in which were heaped such submarine delicacies as mussels, clams, squid, crab, shrimp, slugs, whelks, cuttlefish, and limpets, she plucked a small gray eel, as fresh as spearmint, and fed it to her *torero*.

"Marvelous!" cried D.C., and leaning across the table he deposited a fluffy white shrimp between her lips.

Butternut flushed with pleasure and lovingly dropped one of her snails down his gullet, even as she in turn received a slug in the teeth. They paused and looked at one another and there was an instant shock of recognition. Suddenly they began to eat in earnest. Eye to eye and hand to mouth, they stuffed one another with a growing and feverish rage, their arms churning cyclonically as they licked their platters clean.

To Ivan it was all painfully clear. He had always known that women loved to feed D.C., but he had never fully realized the size of his friend's appetite. If D.C. tossed bricks through Howard Johnson's picture windows at the satchel-assed, non-sectarian hostesses in their basic black, his missiles were finally only air mail reservations for a table on the inside. His warped Platonic image was up for adoption by America. He wanted in because once a Schlemovitz always a Schlemovitz. Ivan spit a wad of sharkskin paté onto the white tablecloth. He had nothing but nausea for weakness. Wiping the corners of his mouth with his whiskers, he rose and announced, "I'll be waiting for you back at the hotel." But the two gluttons were so full of each other that they never saw him go.

In Spain the one event that can be depended upon to begin on schedule is the *corrida* and it was fast approaching fight time when D.C. and Butternut got up to leave the now nearly deserted café. He stood tall, elegant, seemingly at ease in his constrictive pants, and she clung to his suit like embroidery. The one-eared accordionist was still playing his heart out by the plashing fountain, but the crowds had dwindled and only a handful of predatory die-hards remained salivating about the Duesenberg. Rather than drive after having sat all afternoon in the café with their swollen organs scrunched up, D.C. and Butternut preferred to cool off by walking the two blocks to the bullring, but they had barely gotten started when a hysterical mob of puffing and leaping Spaniards, their eyes darting out of their heads like wounded horses in a tapestry, entered the Plaza del Castillo pursued by large bulls. Somehow the animals had made a mistake on their way to the Plaza de Toros and turned down the wrong block. Bellowing with rage, they rumbled on with heads lowered and monster horns. The accordionist's fingers froze on the keyboard and without thinking he leaped into the fountain drenching his bellows. Everywhere people hung. From flagpoles, from awnings, from lamp-posts. The less agile spread-eagled themselves flat against the sides of buildings and prayed. These were among the first to be trampled, for the bulls, discovering that they had entered a cul-de-sac, swung wide around the fountain—their horns gouging giant hunks from the walls—and raced out of the plaza the way they had come, driving all before them.

When only the occasional moans of a victim could be heard sounding the all clear, D.C. crept out from his hiding place beneath the Duesenberg and pulled Butternut after him. She seemed angry. Brushing herself off, she refused to say what was wrong until finally, after repeated requests, she accused the *torero* point-blank of cowardice.

D.C. gave her an ugly look but quickly relented. "Silly girl," he gently chided her. "The *corrida* is one thing, the street another. Can't you see I don't have my red cape?"

Butternut had to admit that this was true.

"*Well*, then," declared D.C., having made his point, "don't blemish the reputation with hearsay." Not giving her a second glance, he crooked his elbow ever so slightly and Butternut hooked up, once more physically excited by her intimacy with the ballsy *torero*.

Despite their delay, it was exactly four o'clock as they entered the stadium, but unaccountably the bulls had not yet arrived. The stands were packed and restless. The President of the Association sulked in his box, not speaking to anyone, his sealed jaws as ponderous as bank vaults. From where they sat wedged in on cushions in the first row, D.C. and Butternut could look down into the passageway between the cement stands and the wooden *barrera* and watch the bullfighters' nervous managers and assistants scuttle about yelling at one another. A carbine-armed *guardia* leaned over the weathered *barrera* and smoked placidly in the sun, dropping long ashes onto the ice-smooth arena sand.

Butternut didn't mind waiting. She was eager to learn about everything and D.C. gave her answers. Her eyes glittered in the sunlight like the spinning wheels of roller skates when he spoke of danger. If the bullfighter failed to place his *espada* in exactly the right portion of the animal's huge neck, if he were off even by half an inch, the sword would strike bone and spring back, flying into the air. Once he had seen a bad *matador* miss six times and one by one wipe out an entire family in the first row.

Butternut frowned and said, "He behaved badly, didn't he?"

"Damned badly."

She clutched his arm. "I'd give anything to see *you* in the ring, love."

"Perhaps someday," he said vaguely.

She squeezed harder and promised him "anything."

D.C. laughed easily and kissed her, confident that later on some sort of an exchange could be worked out.

High up in his box, the President was on his feet and the fanfaronade of trumpets boasted of the arrival of the bulls. Two costumed riders in doublet and hose galloped straight across the arena and after doffing their feathered caps in the President's direction, they peeled off to right and left and quickly exited. Next came the *matadors*, each at the head of his own team of *banderilleros* and *picadors*, all moving heavily like racing cars being pushed to the starting line.

"My God!" squealed Butternut, "they're gorgeous. Look at that posture."

"So-so," muttered D.C., with professional reserve.

As the *toreros* left the arena, the pent-up excitement of the crowd broke loose and they emptied their lungs in anticipation. San Benedicto, the last *corrida* of the year, was about to begin.

The first bull to appear was a small one. He bounded recklessly into the sunlight and then pulled himself up short, distrustful of the vacant arena, taking it all in with shifty eyes, the head high and the tail flicking. His horns were not large but looked mean like ice picks. When he suddenly made his move, he accelerated so quickly that he was little more than a blur to the people in the stands and they whistled in amazement. In seconds he had struck three of the target-painted *burladeros*, the wooden shields guarding the openings in the *barrera*, and stopped cat-quick, innocent of the past, his flanks barely swelling. The crowd roared and fell silent, bloated with expectation.

"Here comes Manolo," whispered D.C. "He's a great old-timer. They say he's held together by stitches."

Butternut looked and saw a gaunt, regal figure walk stiff-leggedly into the arena.

"Watch his footwork," advised D.C.

The *matador* stopped and casually unfurled his bloodstained cape. At the other end of the ring, the bull watched him with interest, almost as if he had paid admission and was sitting in the stands. Manolo wagged his cape and called to the animal in a pinched, reedy voice. Apparently to get a better look, the bull trotted forward a few feet, his slow movement marked by an odd, playful, rolling gait, and came to a halt. "*Venga toro*," cried Manolo. Calm, cold, implacable, he glared deadly at the stagnant beast, and vice versa. Once more he shook out the red garment. Irritated, the bull shot forward, horns thrusting and hooves spinning like bicycle peddles.

"Forget the cape," D.C. shouted. "Watch his feet."

As the distance closed between racing beast and stationary bullfighter, Butternut, fascinated, saw the experienced feet of Manolo lightly pat the ground. They began to move faster and faster, tapping the very same square of earth, sending up an urgent tattoo. Then the pivot. He rose up on the balls of his feet, stiffened his ankles and perched on his toes. The points of his shoes spinning smoothly, his feet seemed to leave the ground. His feet now actually in the air making a breathtaking rainbow arc of instant suspension, his inverted soles hanging like a tableau in space. And then the crunch. The bullfighter's stitched seams had opened, and as mangled Manolo heaped up on the ground, the crowd gasped.

Butternut couldn't sit still. "I didn't realize it was like *that*," she kept repeating, squealing in her astonishment. "The poor man! He was like a bird. So graceful. His feet seemed to be trying to tell me something all the time."

"You're learning." D.C. patted her approvingly on the abdomen for several minutes.

There were loud boos. Astride his horse, a *picador* had come out into the ring, his feet cased in heavy wooden stirrups and the blindered animal sandwiched between thick mats to protect him from the bull's horns. The next *matador* was not permitted to engage his own bull until he had removed Manolo's, and the wealthy and shrewd Del Monte was taking no chances. Before deigning to put in an appearance himself, he had dispatched his *picador* to weaken the speedy beast, and the crowd didn't care for this at all. Neither did the bull, for he attacked at once, coming at the horse like a fusillade of buckshot and peppering him from all sides. Although the bedeviled animal managed to keep his feet, the *picador* was able to get in only a few unworthy jabs with his lance before the hoots of the onlookers drove him hangdog from the ring in shame.

Del Monte refused to look at the man. He was grossly upset. His chiseled nose which had earlier resembled a statue in a formal garden was now brown and pasty like peanut butter. The crowd was chanting his name in unison, hallooing Del Monte, demanding Del Monte, but Del Monte ignored them. He summoned his *banderillero* to him and the two men squatted down in secret session. After some hurried whispered instructions concerning sportsmanship, they stood up and looked at one another in full agreement, their expressions mirror images of stealth, intrigue, slyness, depravity, and psychopathic cunning. Together they studied the bull. He was gadding about the empty arena with just a trace of swagger and fidgeted until he came to rest looking idly up at the far stands, his back turned.

"Death to the black bull!" screamed the maniacal Del Monte, and shoved his co-worker out onto the field.

The *banderillero* nimbly zig-zagged his way through seven pillows and a small head of lettuce thrown from the seething stands and loped across the ring. The knife-tipped *banderillas* that he held in each hand might have been a child's festively adorned ski poles, and raising them high over his head, he accosted the bull's backside like a thief in the night. Just as he was about to plant them deep into the beast's flesh to humble the brute, he was distressed to note that one of the bull's great, round, storm-black, and pitiless eyes had rolled back and was unmistakably glaring at him in contempt. He lost his stride. But the downward stroke had already begun and he could not stop it any more than one can stop the flowing juice of an electric chair once the fatal switch has been thrown. The bull watched, never moving, as the off-balance *banderillero* brought his weapons down, the flashing knife points hissing through the air, and plunged them agonizingly into his own thighs. Snorting derisively, the bull trotted off. The crowd roared with laughter. In great pain, the *banderillero* hobbled from the ring, the festooned harpoons that protruded from his thighs bobbing gaily as he went.

Del Monte was humiliated. Driven by vanity, he forgot his money, his two Lincoln Continentals, his three mistresses, and his four snack bars called respectively The California, The Florida, The White House, and The Harlem, and raced onto the field of honor. Something spectacular was required to redeem him, to still the outraged masses. Snapping his cape furiously, Del Monte leaped to his knees and waited without fear. The bull saw him and charged, speeding through the outstretched cape like a turnstile.

"¡Olé!" shouted the crowd in one voice.

"¡Olé!" shouted Butternut, trying to get the hang of it.

Del Monte never looked better. As he sprang about on his knees like an eccentric dancer to face the bull once more, people were saying *this* was the old Del Monte, the great one, before the women and the big cars.

The *matador* had barely readied himself for the bull's next charge when the tricky beast was upon him again in a cloud of dust and a hearty thump-thump shiver. As the particles settled, there was Del Monte, still on his knees, still holding his cape which had been fringed by the bull's keen horns, still at the ready, grim, alert, masterful.

"¡Olé!" cheered the ravished crowd, "¡Olé!"

For the first time the bull seemed winded. He looked about in confusion. His tongue hung out and a thin white string of saliva appeared tied to his lips.

Del Monte was tremendous. A glorious, foolhardy paraplegic. With reckless daring, he kept his knees, depriving himself of escape, and called to the animal, taunting him with his mastery.

"I love that man," cried Butternut, outside of herself and palpitating. "He's mad! Oh, he's mad!"

"A cheap showman," grumbled D.C. "Even I could do better."

Butternut hugged him. "Jealous?"

"Nonsense," he scoffed. "See what I mean? There he goes. Always playing to the grandstand."

In the ring, Del Monte had torn off the shredded and dangling portions of his cape, spurning all offers of a new one from the sidelines, and what he now held out to the bull was a remnant the size of a doily. He shuffled forward a few inches on his knees and flaunted it in the animal's face, wary but confident.

The bull's anger burned through the haze fuddling his brain and, visually zeroing in on the *matador*, he licked his lips and attacked. Del Monte was a bastion of certitude. He held his ground. He extended his abbreviated cape at arm's length. He stirred it. He waggled it. He flapped it. He shook it convulsively and pointed, but the bull paid no attention to the miserable rag and bore down on Del Monte himself, irrevocably, like a steaming battleship on a dinky canoe.

Although Butternut did not cry when they carried Del Monte from the ring on a stretcher, some women did. However, he was not dead and, fortunately, because his legs had been tucked beneath his body they were unscathed. But the great Del Monte would never again play the violin.

The afternoon was rapidly becoming a nightmare. If nothing happened to change the course of events, the *corrida* of San Benedicto, which should have been the splendid culmination of the entire season, would set Spanish bullfighting back a century. Local merchants in the stands foresaw ruin. Even such world-famous cemeteries as Arlington and the catacombs of Rome did not attract big spenders. Six whole bulls remained to be knocked off and only the young, the willful, the rash Pacolito stood between Pamplona and disaster. The odds were staggering.

Always controversial, Pacolito immediately strode to a position beneath the President's box and removing his hat requested permission to eliminate the bull without further delay. He stood there looking up, his large choleric nose surmounting his childish face like a toucan's bill, and waited for a decision while the President paced it out. On the one hand the timing of the request was premature, dubious, unorthodox. On the other, if by some freak of nature he were to get in a lucky blow he might just kill the beast. Turning a deaf ear to the furious crowd, the President signaled his approval and the trumpets sounded.

Bullfighting purists were up in arms, clamoring, jostling one another, and puffing out their cheeks in rage. Pillows battered the ring like hailstones. Everywhere fans were on their feet, pushing and shoving. D.C. felt himself being squeezed from behind as two foreign bodies came forward and sandwiched him in, trapping his arms at his sides in such a manner that he fleetingly had the impression that he was about to be taken for a ride. Torpedoed in Spain! Laughing at his fancy, he looked around and the smile dribbled down his face like wet paint.

"You!" he gagged, ashen-faced, lily-livered, for he was being held in confidence by the revengeful Dr. Luckenback and his sneaky sidekick Enzo Castelli.

"A happy coincidence," remarked the doctor. "I feared that we had seen the last of you, but Europe is a small continent. I see that you're now a bull thrower."

Enzo Castelli giggled and said, "That surely is a good one, Doctor."

"Very fine. It's a pleasure to see the initiative of our young men on foreign soil. What do you call yourself?"

Gazing at the dumb bullfighter sympathetically, Enzo Castelli observed, "I do believe that cat's got his tongue."

"Speak up, son," encouraged Luckenback. "Don't hide your light under a lethargic system."

"I really don't know about such things," said Enzo, with engaging modesty, "but he looks like EL AG-SEE-DENT-EE to me." Enzo's weird laughter caused D.C. to shiver as if in the final stages of some fatal disease.

"I've warned you about that laugh, Castelli. Not yet." Luckenback gave D.C. a reassuring grimace. "By the way," he asked blandly, "is your clever friend in attendance?"

Pinioned like St. Sebastian, D.C. shook his head morosely. "I . . . he . . . you . . ." He caught his breath, cleared his throat, and unexpectedly began to wail, "Butternut! Butternut!"

"Quiet," threatened Luckenback, and thrusting his hand into his pocket, he jabbed something sharp into the victim's ribs.

D.C. looked down and saw that he was impaled on a ballpoint pen, the tip of which had made a jagged hole in the doctor's suit. "Butternut!" he cried fearlessly.

Luckenback hastily smoothed over his rent pocket. "A graphic lesson, young man," he lectured. "There's no substitute for quality."

"I see!" exclaimed Butternut, mistaking the summons. She was intent on the *matador* who had just refused the little red *muleta* and was taking only one thin sword into the ring with which to defend himself. "Oh, I see! That superb nose! He can do it. You can do it, Pacolito."

"Butternut!" screamed D.C.

The lovely girl tore herself away from the spectacle and was surprised to see her friend jammed between two total strangers. "What are you doing way over there?" she inquired, with some annoyance.

D.C. was barely able to wag his tongue for now they were putting the squeeze on him in earnest. Unable to sound the alarm, he conciliated by identifying the sharpers as fellow Americans.

Luckenback wet his thumbs and ran them down the center of his head, sprucing up the incision that parted his hair. "I happen to be a doctor, young woman," he revealed, introducing himself, "so permit me to say that you have remarkably dainty hips. I may be able to help you. Have you ever been troubled by low cramps?"

"Charmed," said Butternut, icily. She turned with more favor to the gray-haired Enzo. "I understand," she said, trying to make conversation, "I understand that you've been in bondage over there for four hundred years."

"Yes ma'm."

"They're afraid of your extraordinary virility."

"Yes ma'm."

"I bet you know a trick or two," she bantered slyly, suppressing a smile.

"Yes ma'm," was his sweet rejoinder.

All at once Butternut seemed conscience stricken. "Racially speaking," she said, and lowered her eyes, "you don't hate me, do you?"

"Hate you?" Enzo gave her an incredulous look. He was offended. "I'm an educated nigger, ma'm. Cornell '46. Look here." And as flirtatious Butternut bent her earnest white face over his Phi Beta Kappa key, Enzo Castelli laughed his laugh.

"Not yet," warned Luckenback. "Not—" He glanced up at the stands as though they were following him.

The crowd that had been screaming and mocking the attendants while they cleared the arena of cushions had become paralyzed by the appearance of the unequipped, harebrained, suicidal *matador*. They loomed up in tiered rows of silence as if painted there by Giotto. The bull now looked rested, calm, as fresh as a daisy.

The same could not be said for the bullfighter. Pacolito's brains seemed to be on fire. It meant nothing to him that there had been no mastery of the animal, no domination, no squaring of the beast before the *muleta*, no *muleta*. Unlike other *matadors*, his method was not to control the bull, but to overwhelm him. Pacolito rushed awkwardly across the ring, bounding along, a stubborn, graceless ruffian. From the opposite direction came the bull, gathering momentum as he swept over the ground. They galloped toward one another like medieval knights in a jousting tournament, drawing nearer and nearer, bodies straining forward, weapons poised, each bent on depriving the opposition of his seat. The people in the stands watched horror-stricken as head on they came together in the middle of the arena. For a time, they seemed to be enveloped in flames, and there were some who smelled burning rubber. When it was finally possible to judge what had happened, one great exclamation of wonder rose into the air like a thousand balloons released at the same instant. There on the ground were Pacolito and the bull so wrapped up in each other that they might have been lovers, their legs twitching anticly, both breathless, both dead.

The attendants ran out and separated them. Fearing that among the *aficionados* in the stands there might be some hotheads who would attempt to mutilate the corpse, they hurried the unconventional Pacolito into final obscurity. As his remains passed directly beneath her, Butternut was heard to remark in tribute, "There was nothing middle class about him. He didn't know the meaning of the word 'compromise.' " Except for the bewitching tyro, however, no one else had a decent thing to say about the late human. The late bull was another matter. The attendants hitched him up to a splendidly matched team of thick-shanked work horses wearing golden bridles and platinum bits, and with funereal pomp he was given a *vuelta* about the ring while the bereaved audience paid him their solemn last respects, magnanimously honoring *el toro bravo*.

Preferring men to other animals, Butternut was not happy with the conclusion of this *corrida*. It was not like any of the imported American films that she had seen on the subject. She leaned across Castelli and reached for her own *matador*, tightening the knot on his ritually narrow tie by way of preparation. "The bulls," she said, accusingly, "they're having it all their own way, don't you know?"

"We can't win them all," D.C. allowed, in a sickeningly ineffectual tone.

"Pacolito must not have died in vain!"

D.C.'s blue eyes made quick nervous darts between his two captors. "Well," he said brightly to Butternut, "time to be scooting along."

"You've got to get in there and do something," cried the overwrought beauty, her voice so penetrating that many people turned away from the ceremony to see what was going on. "You must," she demanded, and her small, high-fashion breasts heaved with emotion. "You can't let down on the dead. Or on me. Or your friends here."

"Don't be silly," D.C. dismissed her. Outstanding lateral vision told him that the two faces closing in on him from either side were grindstones. "It's ridiculous," he laughed shrilly. "Anyone can't just go out there. I'm not even on the program."

Luckenback shook his head with massive solemnity. "She's right, son," he said quietly, "we're counting on you to even the score. Show the spicks the way we do it back home. Get in there and KILL," he urged. "For America!"

"For integrated sports," cackled Enzo, gleefully.

Butternut kissed him and nipped his ear. "For me," she whispered.

D.C. stood there as if he were stuffed. Saying nothing, seeing nothing, he silently turned blue like an iceberg at twilight. "Someone . . ." he faltered, his voice barely audible but resembling his father's in an uncanny way, "someone give me a cigarette."

But while his guards groped for their smokes, D.C. took advantage of the opportunity and hopped up on the little cement wall in front of him where he perched, teetering over the alley below. "Stand back!" he warned them. "I'll jump."

"Be careful!" cried Butternut, alarmed.

"Get down, sir," snarled Luckenback under his breath, but

seeing that the entire stadium was watching, he changed his tune. "Ladies and gentlemen," he addressed the crowd, and thrust a finger in D.C.'s direction. "This supple young warrior from across the sea has come to lend you assistance. I give you the pride of America. The fruit of the loom. The pick of the pack—"

"The end of the line," quipped Enzo, and tangled, skirling, and demented laughter poured from his black heart.

"Now!" thundered Luckenback. "Now!"

With a deft nudge, Enzo toppled the weaving *matador* from the wall and he fell backward, tumbling down into the alley where a group of waiting handlers caught him in their strong arms and whisked him into the arena, a red cape tucked under his chin like a napkin.

Alone and tottering in the waning sunlight, D.C. tried to get his bearings. His legs wobbled in maritime. From where he stood, the enclosed ring seemed ridiculously small and there wasn't a decent hiding place anywhere. Police barred all the exits. Although in a state of shock, he had the presence of mind to fold up his cape into a tiny bundle and tuck it under his arm out of sight lest he rile the bull needlessly. As a child of the city, he was cheered by the thought that if he didn't move an animal would never attack him, and perhaps if he remained very still it would not even appear. He was dimly aware that the people in the stands had begun shouting and heaving things in his direction. Somehow he had blundered into a convention of storm troopers. Their cries were harsh, ursine, fanatical, and transparently truculent. Glancing around, he could see the blatant mass hysteria, the waving handkerchiefs, the warm, kindly (it would not be excessive to say even affectionate) faces. D.C. took a second look to make sure and broke out in a cold sweat. They were his friends, his allies. He gathered that on the basis of what they had heard from Luckenback they had gotten the imperfect impression that he was a Fulbright *matador* who had been sent over by the President of the United States to atone for his most recent political blunder of describing the heroic explorations of the Spanish Siglo de Oro as the worst sort of colonial imperialism. Gifts showered down on him like apple blossoms. Total strangers were presenting him with their hats, ties, shirts, and socks in an epidemic of international good will. Frankly, he had not expected such acceptance.

With a burst of confidence, D.C. picked a wine-skin out of the debris and took a richly satisfying swig. If he had been accepted before, he was loved now, and all over the huge stadium grown men were wiping their eyes and throwing kisses. The audience and the actor were made for each other. D.C. waved back with Papal restraint, but as the cheers swelled about him he grinned in embarrassment and clasped his hands above his head in victory. He *was* a *matador*. They saw it. There wasn't a bull going that could stop him. A flip of the cape, a zip of the blade, and it was all over. He was the greatest. As he listened to their acclaim, D.C. was gratified to learn that the suit he wore was his.

An attendant appeared in the center of the ring while the *matador* was still taking his bows. He carried a sign. D.C. noted that it said 510 kg., the weight of his first bull. For one brought up on pounds, the metric system was a stupid inconvenience, but alert to the fact that it was based on units of ten, he divided and came out with a miserable, shrunken specimen of fifty-one pounds. D.C. was satisfied that he could handle the beast.

But from the very first moment the bull appeared it was apparent that somewhere along the line there had been a trifling mathematical slip-up. Rather than weighing in at half a hundred-weight, the brute was closer to half a ton. Even at a distance he looked as huge and unreliable as a Trojan horse. The ground shivered under his stone hooves and he moved with such ponderous authority that the stands became hushed and submissive. A green uniformed *guardia* who had draped himself over the wooden *barrera* picked his nose as he watched the advancing bull. D.C. sidled over and stood unobtrusively beside him. He would not give in to fear. The closer the bull came, the more there was of him. His horns were as wide as wings and as thick as railroad ties. Running at full-tilt, he struck one of the *burladeros* head on and reduced it to powder.

"There is nothing to fear but fear itself," D.C. explained to the listless *guardia*.

The bull backed off and surveyed the damage. As a warm-up, he seemed to consider the results acceptable. Turning his head, he focused his steamy eyes on the *matador* and pawed the turf sending shock waves pulsating through the young man's urinary canal.

D.C. gazed at the beast unflinchingly and whispered, "The coward dies a thousand deaths, a brave man dies but once."

Enraged, the bull started for the bullfighter as if he intended to staple him to the wall. From the stands came the demonic laughter of Enzo Castelli egging him on. D.C. felt his heart swelling, stretching his chest so that it could no longer contain it, racing along and growing bigger every second like the charging bull. All at once he realized that bullfighting was not a part of the American tradition and his face hardened with a determination beyond language, beyond resolve, at the outer limits of sanity. This was no time for pacifism. In a lightning move, he swiped the *guardia*'s carbine, and bracing himself like a G-man, he blasted away at the lunging beast, mowing him down, and proceeded to empty the gun into his writhing carcass.

The onlookers sat immobilized in their seats. High above the stadium, festive pennants could be heard gently flapping.

"OH, NO!" moaned Butternut, and covered her face with her hands.

Startled, D.C. let the useless carbine slip from his fingers as he looked up.

"You sneak!" screamed Luckenback, livid with disappointment. "I'm through playing with a cheater. Short of the formalities, consider yourself dead. Just stay where you are," he ordered, as he struggled to lift his clubfoot over the wall. "Don't move a—"

Before he could say another word, however, several *aficionados* who believed him implicated in the crime had jumped up and seized the doctor, dragging him kicking from the wall, and the last that was seen of him was his clubfoot fluttering about in a melancholy and detached way.

The crowd, suddenly released, cascaded down from the stands like a waterfall, wave upon wave flooding the arena and spilling over one another in their eagerness to lay hands on the murderer.

D.C. watched them come with soaked armpits and misgivings. Rather than search for Butternut among the throng, he decided to wait for her elsewhere. In the midst of the confusion, he somehow managed to break out of the stadium and into the clear, but when he glanced over his shoulder, there was the raging, thumping, lunatic mob only half a step behind and gaining. D.C. flew like a tornado. He raced blindly through the narrow streets of Pamplona, wheezing asthmatically, his face turning black and his bloodshot heart swelling to such enormous proportions that the added weight was slowing him down. If he could only find the Plaza del Castillo. If he could only reach the café where the Duesenberg was parked before it was too late. If he could only take the next breath. . . .

CHAPTER 16

🎵 Ivan's successful entry into
Zaragoza, following a short
introductory passage on the
Napoleonic siege of that city,
putting events in perspective.

The historic siege of Zaragoza was begun in 1808 when Napoleon, hearing vague reports of revolt against his authority, dispatched Marshal Lefebvre-Desnöettes to subdue the populace. Although childishly simple, the Marshal was a stern disciplinarian and marched his small army of four thousand men the 176 kilometers from Pamplona to Zaragoza in record time. His prompt arrival, however, was his only significant achievement in the campaign. The xenophobic Spanish garrison under the command of the courageous, bold, dashing, and fanatical General Palafox proved more quarrelsome than expected, inflicting heavy losses on the French, who were forced to huddle outside the city gates waiting for reinforcements. The Marshal walked among his wounded men inconsolable. With the arrival of new troops came new commanders, following one another in quick succession like lemmings. After Lefebvre-Desnöettes there was Verdier who was replaced by Moncey and Mortier who were succeeded by Junot who was relieved by Lannes. Until the appearance of Lannes, it seemed to make little difference which Marshal was in charge of the opposition, for Palafox, with bullheaded tenacity, refused to budge. But Lannes, employing a new strategy, cleverly substituted artillery fire and mining for infantry assaults and on February 20, 1809, after months of bloody siege, the resistance of Zaragoza was finally broken. Ivan hoped to invade the city without so much fuss.

Although he traveled the same route taken by Lefebvre-Desnöettes through the towns of Tafalla, Arguedas, and Tudela, Ivan proceeded more cautiously. He had never driven before. He sat on the very edge of his seat and squinted out at the road, his nose streaking the windshield, his fingers locked about the steering wheel in a death grip as the Duesenberg imperceptibly crept forward one meter at a time. To judge by his progress, the Locomotives on Highways Act of 1861 which laid down a maximum speed limit of four miles per hour might still have been in effect. The sleek, powerful Duesenberg was passed by honking cars, thundering trucks, motorcycles, tractors, donkey carts, and one brazenly pregnant middle-aged woman wearing high heels on a bicycle. Occasionally he would overtake an elderly pedestrian with one leg carrying a shapeless, elephantine bundle on his back, but sometimes he would even fall behind the handicapped. The strain on Ivan was enormous, and upon entering dusty villages in which the populace often enjoyed walking along beside the car for a hundred yards or so and chatting, he would swear and roar at them tensely to get out of his way.

It was simply one crisis after another and Ivan was debating whether to forfeit the unique Duesenberg for the proletarian train when he saw that his path was blocked. A long, flat-bed U.S. Army trailer hauling shrouded, lumpy merchandise stenciled with "DANGER" and the letters "HB" as if to fool the natives into believing that it contained some huge, irregular cough drop, had stopped in the middle of the road, its red lights flashing. Ivan slammed on the brakes. Never having passed anything with wheels, he thought it best to wait his turn. The trailer was surrounded by an escort of six jeeps—three fore, three aft—crowded with teen-age GI's in full battle gear and armed to the teeth. A gangly second lieutenant wearing a holster strapped to his waist had gotten out of the halted lead vehicle and was talking with great good humor to a trio of hitchhikers who stood by the side of the road. They were plainly all Americans. Unable to induce the hitchhikers to join him, the Lieutenant glanced down the line of stalled vehicles and his eye fell on the Duesenberg. He motioned to the civilians to stay where they were and stepped over to where Ivan sat impatiently strangling the steering wheel.

"What's up?" asked Ivan, his self-control turning his knuckles white.

"I'll be damned," cried the loose soldier, a Southerner, and slapped the roof of the car affectionately. "Seems like I'm seeing only friendly faces today. Where you from, sir?"

Ivan looked him in the eye and said, "Georgia."

"Get out," said the Lieutenant and nearly doubled up with laughter. He shook his head in admiration. "That's cool. Say!" He leaned through the window and looked around. "This ain't no pig pen you got here. Sir, how would you like a little company?"

"Not much," Ivan informed him.

"Well, you see," confided the officer, not taking offense, "there's a few of our people waiting on a lift to Zaragoza. I offered to carry them, but they say they don't want to hold up the national defense which to my way of thinking is damn thoughtful. I sort of feel bound to do something for thoughtful folks like that, you understand sir?"

"All right," agreed Ivan. "But get that junk out of my way."

"Yes *sir*," snapped the delighted Lieutenant. "I knew you was from Georgia the minute I saw you."

Scampering back to the hitchhikers, the Lieutenant explained the situation, smiled, shook hands, climbed back into his jeep, and the entire convoy slowly got under way. As his two lady companions watched, the large man with whom they were traveling raised his Homburg in enthusiastic farewell and remained uncovered until the last U.S. Army vehicle had passed, his balding head a phrenological document of sincerity.

The man's name was Ambrose Winkie and sitting beside Ivan —fat, red-faced, and baggy-eyed—he held nothing back. He explained candidly that he was on a special assignment for INTRA, the Senate Committee on International Trade. He was destined for Zaragoza in order to set up a base of operations in that commercially neglected area and to establish a liaison with local business interests. He was smoothing the way for American investment in the form of a fifteen-man economic mission that was to follow in a month. He had been associated with governmental agencies in one capacity or another all his life. He loved the work. He admired the people. He appreciated a good cigar.

"Have one," he offered. "It's not a Corona but I don't believe in ostentation. Give me a good Gold Label Crystal any day. Same size and a fine middle-income smoke right down to the end. Senator Greene put me on to them after the Cuba business. Be my guest."

"I never smoke," said Ivan, grimly trying to keep the car's wheels on the road.

Mr. Winkie was sorry about this indifference to pleasure, but he could certainly see the merit of such an attitude in a young man. He, too, had read the Surgeon General's report on the relationship of tobacco to cancer, but he was frankly too weak to change his habits at this stage of the game. He admired Ivan's strength of character. He recognized his own limitations.

Ivan, despite his preoccupation, was amused by Winkie but something was troubling him. "What happened to your car?" he asked out of curiosity.

Ambrose Winkie chuckling looked like someone's well-upholstered, indulgent uncle. "As I say, I've been in the government business all my life. It's not easy to hold on year after year, but win or lose if you play a clean game your team isn't going to have many penalties called against it, now is it? That's why I don't have a car. You see, once you step on foreign soil a car means junket and junket means that you're not playing it square. Fly on an Air Force jet and it's junket. Hitch a ride in a jeep—junket. Take along two attractive secretaries—" He turned to the back seat and smiled at his companions who leaned forward simultaneously and chucked him under the chin, each having one to herself. "I've learned from men a whole lot smarter than I am," Winkie continued, "that there's a right way and a wrong way to do everything. That's why I pay the girls right out of my own pocket."

Ivan glanced at the girls in the rear-view mirror. They were both about forty, thin, sharp-nosed, their faces covered with congealed powder. One wore thick-lensed glasses, the other a red headache band to shorten a forehead that reared up monolithically and resembled the Great Wall of China. Although they might have been whizzes at dictation, their polished fingernails were far too long for typing. Whatever he was paying them, Winkie could not possibly be getting his money's worth.

Mr. Winkie hunched forward. "Say!" He pointed with pleasure to a sleek black and white bird that stood dourly at the roadside watching them creep by. "The common European *nuttalli* or magpie. I expected we'd be seeing a number of them before very long. They're thieves and chatterers and related to the jays. I must say," Winkie chuckled at the stern-looking bird, "he's a brassy customer."

"*Pica*," said Ivan.

"Pardon me?" Mr. Winkie turned to him inquisitively.

"*Pica*," repeated Ivan with a trace of irritation. "The European genotype is *pica*; the American is *nuttalli*."

Ambrose Winkie looked at the young man in amazement. "You're *exactly* right. Of course. *Nuttalli* and *hudsonia* are the American branches of the family." Mr. Winkie was terribly impressed. "I can't tell you how pleased I am to discover another bird fancier."

"Nature interests me only as a phenomenon," Ivan declared contemptuously. "I hate birds."

Mr. Winkie laughed heartily at this. Replacing his cigar, he puffed away on it in serious meditation. "Life," he began, "life's too short." He considered the statement, took another puff, and went on ruefully, "No one should make a mistake about magpies. I just don't have enough time to devote to them. But someday," he brightened, and squinted as if he were trying to see something on the horizon, "someday, when I retire, I'm going to give myself full time to birds."

Ivan didn't seem to think much of the idea, but he made no comment.

Ambrose Winkie put his head back, closed his eyes, and puffed. "Full time," he hummed lyrically.

As the trip wore on the road seemed an endless conveyor belt and Ivan, though still in superb physical condition, might well have abandoned the Duesenberg if it had not been for Mr. Winkie. With characteristic perversity, Ivan enjoyed Ambrose Winkie. With characteristic realism, he saw possibilities in him.

In a curious way Winkie helped to take the strain out of the driving. He was full of surprise, delight, and wonder, and everything reminded him of a story. The sullen shepherds in their sheepskins and furs prompted him to an erotic pastoral, whispered so as not to offend the ladies. An old truck that had been piled too high with oranges and overturned on a curve resulted in a whispered erotic melodrama. The stumps of clipped grape plants in neat rows like cloves in a ham led to a whispered erotic menu. Everything sparked his imagination.

It was when Mr. Winkie spoke of his acquaintances in Washington, however, that he was most eloquent, and Ivan contrived to draw him out on the subject. Now the muffled voice was gone. Now the hot cheeks and the dirty smirk sank like a stone beneath the unblemished face of innocence. As the awesome, monumental figures he had encountered in the capital of the world loomed up in his imagination, Winkie's words rang out in barefaced admiration. He spoke glowingly of such men as INTRA's Senators Spingle, Motts, and Kravitz, known and loved throughout the Free World. They were already legends in their own time, brilliant statesmen, powerhouses. They were history in the making and he, who did little more than sharpen their pencils, so to speak, had been privileged to know them and to look on and see it all happen first hand. An incredible experience!

Mr. Winkie was lavish in his praise. But the one individual for whom he reserved his most fervent encomiums was the current Chairman of INTRA, and his direct superior, Senator Marston Pettidrooper. He worshiped the man. It was Pettidrooper this, and Pettidrooper that, and nothing seemed to be beyond Pettidrooper's powers. Problems that brought others to their knees, he would struggle with through the night like Jacob and the Angel and in the morning limp into the committee room with the solution tucked away in his attaché case. The man had an amazing character. Anecdotes of his probity, sagacity, courage, and good will had been recorded dozens of times—historical facts. And though it was not generally known, Winkie confided that the Senator was something of an authority on the belted kingfisher of the lower Connecticut River Valley. All America could sleep peacefully knowing that down in Washington there was a man like Marston Pettidrooper helping to run the show.

"I see that you've led a rich life," reflected Ivan, "surrounded by great men at the red hot center."

"*Sizzling* center," Winkie gently corrected him. "Yes, you're quite right. I have been allowed to hug the walls in the corridors of power, so to speak."

"You've been very lucky. Someday I hope to do something like that."

"Naturally," said Winkie, beaming on the young man with a paternal fondness. "I quite understand."

Winkie liked the boy. Definitely! He initially had had some doubts about the beard, but now he viewed it charitably as an excess of youth. Although Ivan wasn't very talkative, there was a quiet, almost epigrammatic strength in him. That he didn't smoke suggested impressive will power. His caution was exemplary in an age of reckless speed and mass death on the highway. And he knew his birds.

"The United States," said Mr. Winkie, breaking the silence, "is a big country." He considered the statement. There was a visionary look in his eyes. "It should be suitably represented. In my opinion it simply does not look right to have such a small exploratory delegation. I believe, Ivan, that a fine young man like you could help me stand for America. If you're interested"— he chose his words carefully, not wanting to force the boy's hand —"I want to offer you a place, a small place, a beginning in government."

Ivan pulled the car off the road and stopped. He looked at Mr. Winkie gratefully with his good eye. "It's a wonderful opportunity," he said.

"The salary would be insignificant," warned Mr. Winkie.

"Experience is its own reward."

"Quite true," approved the older man. "Have you had that very long?" In attempting to be casual about the beard, he had only succeeded in making it sound like a disease. Mr. Winkie's face looked as if he had just removed it from a pot of boiling water. "I mean," he lowered his eyes uncomfortably, "doesn't so much hair below the nose . . . doesn't it interfere . . . get in your way?" He was growing increasingly sorry that he had brought up the subject.

Ivan assured him that it didn't.

"Oh . . ."

"It's not at all an antisocial beard," Ivan continued reassuringly. "It's a *social* beard."

"Oh!" Mr. Winkie was considerably cheered.

"My models were Lincoln, Grant, Hayes, Garfield, and Benjamin Harrison."

"But . . ." Mr. Winkie's lips quivered in alarm, "but they were *presidents*."

"Yes, I know."

"But *presidents!* I mean it's all well and good to have an ideal image on which you pattern your life, but to imitate a *president*. . . . It could be dangerous. They're different than you and I."

Ivan released the emergency brake. "Yes," he agreed, easing the car back on the road. "They have more votes."

"That goes without saying. They're politicians. Elected officials." Mr. Winkie earnestly studied Ivan's profile. "No, what I'm getting at is that Lincoln's beard may not fit *your* face. Bear in mind that these are unique men with unique qualifications. They have, for example, firm convictions, yet are sufficiently flexible to appeal to the majority. They are healthy, but not to such an excessive degree that sick voters are made to feel inferior. They are of course intelligent, though not offensively so. They are, in short, wonders of proportion, masters of the middle way who somehow have managed to strike a remarkable balance between unpopular extremes." Throwing his arm over the back of the seat, Mr. Winkie shifted his bulk and leaned secretively toward Ivan. "The current consensus in Washington is that a beard is political suicide. I think you'll find the standards less rigorous as an appointed official. I've always been . . ." he gave a small involuntary titter and frowned. Mr. Winkie removed his hand from the rear of the car where it was being fondled by twenty adoring digits. "I've always been quite content myself. Keep your whiskers, Ivan," he said gently, "and live."

Ivan stared out the windshield and gravely nodded his head in agreement. "I'll try to make you proud of me, Mr. Winkie," he promised.

The girls burst out with congratulations and clapped their hands in glee.

"Call me Ambrose," suggested Mr. Winkie affectionately.

"Ambrose."

"That's all I ask." Winkie was overjoyed. "That's all I ask. Let's just shake on that."

"Later," said Ivan.

The young man's reluctance to remove his hand from the wheel only confirmed Mr. Winkie's high opinion of him and before the journey was over they had struck up quite a pretty friendship.

That a United States commission was sending an emissary to his untouched city Ivan regarded as an ominous, if inevitable, straw in the wind, but he was genuinely dismayed to find that other Americans had also discovered remote Zaragoza. Thousands. An entire SAC base. It was only after he had been there several days, and with considerable relief, that he satisfied himself that the populace had not been tampered with. In fact, the airmen had hardly anything at all to do with the Spanish citizenry. For the most part they remained on the outskirts of town holed up in their base, Little America, a luxurious enclave as self-contained as an egg. On those rare occasions when they ventured into the city, it was only to come together again in civilian clothes in order to drink innocently in the dark at the bittersweet sign of "The Beachcomber" or "The Garden of Allah." Zaragoza had not yet been corrupted. Ivan welcomed the opportunity.

In anticipating an uningratiating city, Ivan had not fully pre-

pared himself for Zaragoza. It was as hard as a nut and as relent-
less as Yahweh. Even the newest buildings looked prematurely
old. They rose in confusion, embarrassed, their Venetian blinds
hanging shamefaced outside the windows, their balconies sagging.
All over the city, workers crouched indifferently in the middle
of the streets removing cobblestones. Hour after hour, with un-
believable patience and short picks, they cleaned the cobbles,
scraping them down, stacking them up, and then, replacing them,
moved on. Almost every street corner had its blind or mutilated
hawker of lottery tickets. They shouted "¡*Para hoy!*" in sudden,
calloused voices. The wind pushed people around, whipped up
unrest, and sent schoolboys scrambling, their tight, short pants
gathered in the anal cleft, their mouths scarved, their legs like
scarlet fever.

But whatever Zaragoza was, it had no illusions about itself.
Unlike Pamplona, here there was no affectation, no pretense at
being the biggest or the best. It was the brownest, but no one
boasted. Ivan appreciated the authenticity of the city. Though
it was cold, he enjoyed walking about the empty streets in the
early morning brightness, before the clatter and the buzz, when
only the flat bell of a streetcar named Casablanca could be heard
clunking moodily in passing.

As soon as Mr. Winkie discovered his young assistant's habit
of prework strolling, he asked to join him under the guise of
physical fitness. Ivan had no objections. Never having had a son
of his own, Winkie felt a growing affection for the young man.
He liked his company. He took pleasure in showing him the city.
Together they visited the Aljaferia, home of the Spanish Inquisition, and looked at the names of the tormented victims
scratched out on the dungeon walls. Arm in arm they entered
the gargantuan Basilica del Virgen del Pilar—its cupolas burning
in the sun like golden pagodas—in order to view the small, worn
statue of the Virgin within its gloomy vastness. Standing with
his hat in his hand, Mr. Winkie was thrilled. He put his arm around
Ivan.

"A vision of her," he whispered excitedly, his breath visible in the cold interior, "and thousands of people from all walks of life joined forces to produce all of this. It boggles the mind."

Ivan stared at the statue. It was propped up on a six-foot jasper column, and both statue and column had been eroded by more than 250 years of adoring, feverish, hot-lipped, acidic kisses from the faithful. To Ivan it was only another example of the dangers of love.

He consulted his watch and said, "I think it's time we got down to business, Ambrose."

Mr. Winkie looked his last on the Virgin, sighed, and turned to Ivan with a smile. "Ambitious boy," he said approvingly, moved by the sanctified ground to a confession, "I've come to rely on you more and more."

"Don't let it bother you," Ivan reassured him as he started toward the cathedral door. "I can take it."

CHAPTER 17

🦎 Words with the shammes.

D.C. was thin-skinned and a bleeder. As day after day he trudged the road to Zaragoza, painful recurring thoughts of the treatment he had suffered at the hands of the Pamplona mob caused the tiny, hairlike capillaries in his nose, which were particularly sensitive to hostility, to swell and pop, and a flood of red and white corpuscles drenched his bruises and dampened his scabs. He was forced to stop repeatedly to wash his face in the irrigation ditches along the way in order to make himself presentable to traffic. But traffic wasn't interested. Everything passed him by except for one toothless farmer in a dog cart smelling of chicken shit. The effluvium was tolerable but the animal was a rickety mongrel, weak on hills, and D.C. was called upon again and again to get out and push them up even the gentlest of slopes. Soon disenchanted, he abruptly took leave of the farmer. They parted company halfway up a back-breaking hill, without fanfare, going in opposite directions. As his cart slipped backward down the hill gathering momentum, the farmer sat placidly holding the reins and seemed reconciled to the fact that his journey would take a little longer.

Although winded and bloodstained, D.C. plodded on alone.

Pamplona had broken his watch, taken his money, and dimmed what it left of his suit of lights, but miraculously no one had touched Sidney's visiting hours. Clutching her crumpled letter in his hand with its promise of a New Deal, he at length dragged himself up to the Zaragoza city line and stumbled into town.

The day was cold, damp, gray, and over the majestic spires of the Basilica del Virgen del Pilar hung an impenetrable cloud as ominous as the Reformation. D.C. barely noticed. The excitement of his arrival, the anticipation of great expectations, drove him along like a sailboat in a high wind. His spirit soared, racing through the center of the city in search of Calvo Sotelo, darting from street corners, vaulting trolley tracks, and plunging through crowds, while his body limped hurriedly behind. He soon pooped out and paused to catch his breath in front of a *pastelería*. The store window was lighted against the darkness of the day and sweet with cakes and pies and tarts and chocolates nestled in red and yellow cellophane. D.C. peered in, tantalized by a long, succulent jelly roll sprinkled with flakes of confectioners' sugar. Without pockets, his penniless hands shivered in the chill gloom. There was only one lone salesgirl inside the store, a pale, thin-faced, shapeless nonentity with glasses wearing a white smock, and the good-looking young man tapped gently on the window to attract her attention. She looked up. His hair was blood-matted on his forehead, his tattered suit stained with the dust of the road, his face mauled and streaked and pinched by hunger. He beckoned to her, flashing his smile, the old smile, the smile that made a thousand chicks. She jumped. Her left eye began to twitch uncontrollably. Though alarmed, she moved slowly, irresistibly toward him like a log approaching a buzz saw. There was a pleading look in his dark eyes which seemed to hold her spellbound. Once more he flashed the old smile, and bending his head against the glass pointed to the jelly roll. While he wasn't looking, she snapped the lights in the window off and trembling barred the door.

The jelly roll was still there but faded, out of focus, its musical comedy colors banished by documentary grays. D.C.'s knees buckled in bewilderment. Leaning his cheek against the cold window for support, he wondered if he were dying. Ever since leaving Pamplona he had noticed the alteration in his health. There had been dizzy spells on the road and once he had actually fallen. It was not like him. He had always been an upright, despite what he had told Sidney under provocation. Hunger, he knew, had weakened him but that could not completely explain his condition. Why had Gandhi never been dizzy? In all of the books that he had read on the great man, there was not one mention of vertigo. He tried to think of himself as fasting for India.

There was a sharp pain in his chest. Someone was pulling at him. A boy who looked about ten by American standards (but was probably much older) was tugging at one of the shreds that dangled from his body like maypole streamers. Lightheaded, D.C. wondered if he had been sent from the jelly roll to patch things up for there was a message in his hand. D.C. opened the crumpled letter. It was from Sidney. He was surprised how quickly she had learned he was in town. Reading the letter he was disabused.

" *Gracias.*" He thanked the boy for retrieving his property and in a low state of mind dismissed him. But when he looked again the boy was still there. "*¡No tengo dinero!*" shouted D.C., short-tempered in his disappointment, and angrily waved him off.

The boy stood his ground, his scarred shins quivering in the wind. He was dressed shabbily in someone else's torn maroon sweater which he wore inside out. The sweater hung so low on his thighs that it was impossible to tell whether he was wearing any pants. He remained motionless, saying nothing, his big black anxious eyes gazing fondly on the invalid.

It dawned on D.C. that the boy wasn't hanging around for a tip at all, and he became seriously upset. This kid was actually worried about him. Oppressed by his symptoms, he wondered if he should see a doctor. Maybe it was his heart after all.

"*¿Conozces un medico?*" he asked, in considerable agitation.

The mute boy nodded wholeheartedly and taking D.C. by the arm he led him off. As they walked along, the boy kept glancing back anxiously at the limp cargo he held in tow and tried to speed up the pace as if he feared that they might not arrive in time. He took ingenious short cuts through lots, side streets, alleys, and approaching a high iron fence topped with spikes he motioned enthusiastically toward the building behind it, a turreted black stone heap reeking of sepsis. The sign over the gate said, "ZARA-GOZA FACULTAD DE MEDICINA." D.C., weakened by his efforts to keep up, read *Through Me Is The Way To The City Of Woe*, and fainted.

When he came to, the boy was hovering over him with glittering eyes looking for his pulse. D.C. mumbled something and he jumped back in surprise as if caught with his hand in the cash register. Sitting down against the fence a short distance away from D.C., he folded his arms, said nothing, and patiently waited.

For someone who had always taken pleasure in the sovereignty of his body, the thought that alien forces were in control was particularly painful to D.C. Enemy agents were running riot on the inside and he didn't even know where to begin to look. He placed his hand on his heart. Nothing rheumatic there. He stuck out his tongue. Normal—at least the tip, which was all he could see. And yet he was not feeling well at all. Seated on the cold pavement, he watched the sick being brought in awkwardly like rusty weathercocks, and as people filed through the gate two by two and filed out one by one he noted a slight improvement in his condition.

An approaching funeral procession caught his eye. It moved majestically up the avenue, heavy with self-importance, squashing the cobblestones under its load of grief. The hearse at the head of it was a 1938 Dodge sedan whose rear end had been removed and replaced by a black wooden superstructure crawling with Seraphim, Cherubim, Thrones, Dominions, Virtues, Powers, and Principalities. Strung out behind the hearse in dead march were the mourners on bicycles, their headlights on, their wheels wobbling for balance at the crawl. As the Dodge came abreast of the hospital, two loud reports exploded from its exhaust pipe. The hearse jumped forward, gathering speed as it rolled away, and veered down a side street backfiring furiously and whistling like a bomb. Taken by surprise, the mourners bent their backs to catch up with it and spun around the corner and out of sight.

D.C. was definitely on the mend. The sight of the passing hearse had speeded his recovery. He sat up straight, flexed his muscles, and told the kid to beat it. But the boy only moved away a few inches and stared at him with those big prune eyes of his full of unrequited love. There was nothing new in this to D.C., for his entire life the fruit of Mrs. Schlemovitz's loins had been the victim of unstinting devotion. Unable to eliminate his admirer, D.C. suppressed him and bent his mind on recuperation and Sidney.

Tearing up the avenue once more from the same direction came the mourning cyclists in hot pursuit. They had made a full circle. But the will-o-the-wisp hearse was nowhere in evidence. When the last of the peddlers had zipped by, D.C. saw the hood of the Dodge nose out of the same side street that it had entered. The driver looked slyly both ways and then gunning his engine until it belched fire, he roared across the avenue, through the gates, and tossed out his anchor at the back door of the hospital.

Leaving the motor idling consumptively, he rushed to the rear of the hearse, let down the tailgate, and began to struggle with the coffin. Two young men in white coats came out and helped him unload it. One of them raised the lid, releasing a small cloud of trapped flies, and after some hurried haggling over the contents, money changed hands. Hefting the stiff between them, the young men hustled their purchase out of sight, while the driver weighted the coffin with garbage from a nearby can, nailed down the lid, and shoved the box back beneath the Dodge's angelic canopy— as good as new.

D.C. winced. The hearseman was a ghoul, a body embezzler making a quick, cadaverous peseta en route to the graveyard. The white coats were unquestionably medical students, their brains soaked in formaldehyde and twisted by machine-scored examinations. He loathed them all. Shivering, D.C. began to shout at the little waiting Samaritan until in confusion the child agreed to swear that he would never become a doctor. But even as the overwrought invalid ranted in his fit, he watched dumbfounded as the cringing boy assumed the shape of a vulture, his eyes black beads, his silence predatory. D.C.'s cheeks went up in flame and he sprang to his feet in perfect health, totally rehabilitated. Rocking back and forth on his heels, he gazed down at the frightened animal and laughed hysterically. "Not yet!" he screamed, "HA! HA!"—and wheeling around, bolted in front of the open gate and away, narrowly missing being hit by the departing hearse which fired hydrocarbons like black bullets as it thundered off to rejoin the procession.

There were two Calvo Sotelos. One was a broad avenue crammed with high heels, baby carriages, barking dogs, and *supermercados* selling Campbell's soup from gourmet counters to the upper middle class. The other—Calvo Sotelo of the low numbers —was a small muddy appendix strewn with abandoned building materials and hemmed in by newly built, deserted tenements. It was to this one that D.C. was directed. He ran most of the way, and if not for a madwoman who seized him by the throat and shook her shopping bag full of misshapen carrots wildly in his face when he refused to sell her a lottery ticket, would have arrived much sooner. Aware of the rigidity of the Church, D.C. prayed that he was still in time for visiting hours as he hurried nervously into the grim alley.

26 Calvo Sotelo was situated between two empty cement carcasses. It was a boarded-up building hunched down behind a tall wooden fence with a number of small signs posted on it announcing that the property was condemned. The large signs advertised *Los Hermanos Marx Van Oeste* playing at the Palafox as entertainment suitable for the whole family. Upset, D.C. reexamined Sidney's letter, but there was no mistake. He had come to the right address. With a sinking heart, he knocked on the door that had been cut in the fence, but after several minutes of waiting under a leaden sky while the wind whistled through his rags, he knew it was hopeless. The Convento de la Sagrada Familia had folded its tent and taken Sidney with it.

The nervous energy that had kept him going now deserted him and D.C. sagged like a broken couch. He would have to look elsewhere for Sidney. But where? Trying to decide on his next move, he slumped, physically exhausted, against the door and fell through. The mud on the other side cushioned his fall. Picking himself up and wiping himself around, he slogged across what had once been a garden and came to the house. A tag hanging from the doorknob warned trespassers of prosecution. D.C. was crestfallen for he had hoped it was Sidney's forwarding address. With a growing conviction that the lovesick nun would never have gone without leaving him some little clue to her whereabouts, he rapped on the door and getting no answer recklessly tried to force it open, but the door refused to budge. He circled the building looking for an opening. There was none. It was sealed as tight as a submarine. Collapsing on the front step, D.C. dropped his head into his mud-streaked hands and sadly hummed the College "Fight Song" while making faces at the world. This was not the first time since leaving Pamplona that he missed his friend of brilliance and audacity. Unable to crack the building on his own, he had just resolved to check in at the local American Express for news when he heard the door behind him opening. D.C. hummed Fight! Fight! Fight! and got up.

The door stood wide open, not a soul in sight, and inside it was as black as deep water. Clearing his throat, he called out, "*¿Es esto el Convento de la Sagrada Familia?*" in a voice that was cheery, warm, innocent, maternally tender, and chock full of good intentions.

"*Sholom*," whispered someone from behind the door.

A few startled seconds flew by while D.C. wondered if it were a trap. "What," he asked, slippery like a cornered cockroach, "are *you* doing in there?"

"You're in hiding out there, I'm in hiding in here," the voice shot back. "Same difference. *Sholom*."

Not knowing what to make of this gnomic reply, D.C. kept his mouth shut and snapped a worldly sneer on the corners.

"In or out, sweetheart? I don't have all day."

D.C. hesitated. "Are you the watchman?"

"Who else would be hanging around a dump like this?"

"A question isn't an answer," insisted D.C., cagey. "I asked if you were the watchman."

"I'm not Princess Grace," cracked the darkness wryly. "In or out?"

D.C. snickered and, convinced that whoever he was he was harmless, ventured through the door. No sooner had he stepped inside than it was slammed shut, locked and bolted behind him, and he was in total darkness. Someone close by, smelling of rotting mushrooms and low-grade olive oil, was making an odd crunching sound as if chewing on matzoh. Nauseous and giddy, D.C. shrank back.

"You've got a nice little place here," he said, and fumbled for the lock.

"Right this way." An iron hand clamped itself around his upper arm and yanked him forward.

"Really, I can only stay a minute."

"Watch your step," cautioned the voice. "We've got big holes."

D.C. hopped up on his toes and, prodded, moved along gingerly as if crossing a mine field. His guide, a night-tripping fairy, seemed to be able to see in the dark. Passing swiftly through what must have been a hallway, he opened a door and they entered a long, rectangular chapel lined with pews on either side. At the far end was a niche that had no doubt once contained a crucifix but now held a velvet ark, wine red and fringed with gold, surrounded by flickering Yahrzeit candles. The room was cold but serene like a tranquilizer. Spellbound, D.C.'s soul pulled up a chair.

Pleased with the effect, his host leaned smugly against a pew and chewed his matzoh. "What do you think?" he asked.

D.C. gagged and clutched his head with both hands as if it had just been kicked in. "Son of a bitch! Son of a bitch! I'm wiped out! I'm dying!"

"It has the same effect on everyone," admitted his guide with quiet satisfaction. "Who expects to see something like this right under Franco's nose? But watch your language," he advised, coming over and ramming a brown fedora down over D.C.'s head, fingers, and ears. "This is a house of worship."

"Pock Mark!" D.C. choked up, suffocating, pulling out his hands and pointing wildly at the watchman's face, "Pock Mark!"

"I'm a Jew," confessed the hurt watchman, "but there are limits. I'm not a man of stone, you know."

"Pock Mark!"

The watchman ran his fingertips over his fiery cheeks. "A few holes. Big deal. I thought you Yankees didn't judge a man by the condition of his skin."

"Why are you following me? You've been on my trail all the way from Paris. What are you after?"

"Who's following? You knocked, I answered."

D.C. saw that he was dealing with a clever operator. He wiped his mouth and asked coolly, "What do you want from me?" But before the watchman could respond, he lost control and screamed, "You're not a watchman at all!"

"Did I say I was?"

"You hinted."

"A white lie. Who tells the truth 100 per cent? Do I look like an imbecile?"

D.C. looked. Since he had last seen him outside the prison window, Pock Mark had become barrel-chested, broad-shouldered, with the red-hot face of a zealot. Life seemed to be shooting out of him in all directions stretching his hands and feet, which now were enormous. His hips protruded and in his tight plaid mackinaw he resembled a camouflaged highboy.

"You've put on a little weight," said D.C., remembering him as being more on the stringy, aesthetic side.

"Enough! I invite you, a *landsman,* into the Temple Beth RaM BaM and right away you insult me before the ark, a total stranger. Watch your step, sweetheart, you're having words with the shammes."

It was all a bad dream. Unprotected against the chill, D.C. couldn't stop his teeth from rattling any more than he could stop taunting his persecutor. "Why don't you go back to Israel," he clicked, "and leave me alone?"

"Why should I?" demanded the offended shammes. "I was born here. *You* go to Israel."

"I'm an American. My name is Widdemore."

"So I'm a Spaniard. My name is Lopez."

D.C. gave him a look, a laugh, a hoot.

"Since Nebuchadnezzar!" roared Lopez, angered by the young man's skepticism. "From my family tree hang the greatest shammosim in the history of Spain. In Granada, in Seville, in Cordoba. If there was a synagogue, there was a Lopez lighting the candles. Do I have to tell you that the world-renowned shammes of Toledo who had a steel cross shoved up his ass in the pogrom of 1405 was Samuel Leví Lopez, a relative? Do I have to tell you that when the Inquisition was rounding up Jews right and left and closing all synagogues in Zaragoza, the one man they could never catch was Isaac ben Itzach Lopez, revered by Jews the world over as the Phantom Shammes? And when Los Reyes Catolicos"—he took out a handkerchief and spit in it— "when they forced our people to convert or be driven into the sea like herrings, the Lopez family went underground like guerrillas. We gave up our synagogue, but we've been hiding out in Zaragoza since the fifteenth century waiting for an opportunity like this to get back our own. They've changed the locks but I still have the old keys. See." He pulled out a large ring of bent and blackened keys and held them up. "Israel is for the Israelis," sneered Lopez, returning the keys carefully to his pockets. "I'm a Jew."

"If you're really a Jew," said D.C. suspiciously, "Why the tam-o'-shanter?"

"I should wear a *yarmulka* in Spain? What kind of lunatic do you take me for?"

An irreproachable argument. Stiffening his jaw to cut down on the dental hubbub, D.C. lowered his voice and drew out his ace in the hole. "Then why are you eating matzoh out of season? Tell me that," he insisted, tightening his net. "Why?"

Lopez lifted a sheet of matzoh to his mouth and fed it in like paper in a typewriter. Between crunches, he smacked his lips and said mildly, "I like it."

D.C.'s jaw dropped, an unbalanced washing machine full of clanking teeth. This shammes was a real shammes—as bright as a Menorah, as slippery as a seal. Everything he said was true. It was too much for the tired traveler.

"Got you," cried Lopez, scooping him up before he hit the floor. With one hand he cleaned off a pew and gently set the young man down. D.C.'s fingers were purple with the cold and the shammes rubbed life back into them as tenderly as if they belonged to Rubinstein. "You're in no condition," he observed, taking out a silk prayer shawl and wrapping it around the victim's neck. "You look like you've been through a mangler. Are you poor but honest or a wealthy eccentric?"

D.C. rubbed the foreign stubble that had collected on his chin while traveling and tried to remember who he was. He glanced about aimlessly, opened his mouth and sneezed.

"*Gesundheit!* Save your strength," advised Lopez.

"I seem to be doing a lot of falling lately," murmured D.C., depressed.

"Food." Lopez nodded, sympathetically. "That's what you need. Something to eat. I'll be right back." He disappeared and returned with a large metal strongbox that he placed down on the bench beside his worn guest.

D.C. stared at the box, puzzled.

"Matzoh," revealed Lopez, opening the heavy lid. "Preserves the freshness. Keeps it crispy. Have some."

D.C. gobbled down the unleavened bread.

"Crispy?"

"Very."

"Have some more," invited the pleased shammes, and with a nice delicacy he walked off allowing his guest to eat in peace. He went and stood beside the ark. "Some place, eh?" he called. He pointed to the stone ceiling which was covered with an intricate Moorish filigree barely visible in the shadows. "That's all that's left of the old glory, but you can imagine. After they kicked us out it was a home for unwed mothers, a barracks, a house of prostitution, an avant-garde theater, and a convent. But now the property has been reclaimed by its rightful owners." Lopez leaned forward and kissed the ark. "Once a synagogue, always a synagogue."

Feeling stronger, D.C. helped himself to another piece of matzoh and mentioned the signs posted on the fence outside announcing the building's imminent destruction.

"Nothing to *schvitz* over," Lopez reassured him. "In Spain that's like a ninety-nine-year lease. Besides," he started to walk back and forth excitedly with his hands in his pockets, "they've changed their plans. Originally the idea was for the government to doll up this alley and bring in the gypsies from the caves by the river. Social reform! A model project! Planned with American computers like a Swiss watch. They threw in hundreds of workmen, spent millions of pesetas, and as soon as the first new buildings were up they rushed down to the river and brought back a dozen families. When the gypsies came, the nuns left."

Reminded of his quest, D.C. stopped chewing. "Where did they go?" he interrupted.

"Who?" asked the pock-marked shammes, glaring at him in annoyance.

"The nuns," he said eagerly.

"Who cares? *Goyim*. They were here, they left. I don't believe in all this ecumenical garbage." Lopez resumed his pacing. "As I was saying, they moved in a dozen families. Everything new, everything clean. Electric lights, bathrooms, windows—the whole bit. In the morning comes the Mayor, distinguished guests, photographers, and when they knock on the door to inquire how the downtrodden and oppressed enjoy the lap of luxury, no one is home. They stand around with egg on their faces, yell at one another like yentas, and while the cameras wait for exposures, run to the river where they find the miserable gypsies griping, goofing off, and whistling their dirty hearts out. Back to society they drag them. Someone slips three bills to the king who turns to his people and says, "You can't go home again." Just in case, the police drop a few sticks of dynamite in the caves to play it safe. The next day the Mayor and his party return with big smiles and flash bulbs popping to do the job right, but the whole place is a vacancy. Dead like the moon. And the lighting fixtures, the water taps, the sinks, the toilet bowls—gone, all gone in the night without even a thank you. But more important," cried Lopez, swallowing hard with blood in his mouth, "when they went my congregation went with them." He stopped and sighed. "Those gypsies were one of the lost tribes," he explained, "and now they're lost again."

"I'm sorry to hear that," said the interested young man. "And you really don't have a congregation?"

"It gets a little lonely."

"You mean you run a synagogue that no one comes to?" His voice rose incredulously.

"I can tell you that today attendance has picked up 100 per

cent," the shammes reported with satisfaction. "Have another piece of matzoh."

D.C. wolfed it down nervously.

"O Lord," shouted the shammes with his eyes closed, "how beautiful upon the mountains are the feet of him that bringeth good tidings, how joyous the return of the lost sheep, how inscrutable are your ways."

D.C. choked on a mouthful of crumbs. "I've"—he started to get up—"I've got to—"

"Nonsense!" Lopez pinned him down with one hand. "In your condition? You won't last a minute out there in the diaspora."

"But I'm feeling better."

"A temporary delusion. If I let you go now it would be murder."

"But—But—But—"

"You see! A relapse. Don't get excited." Lopez sat down beside his agitated visitor and said soothingly. "Let's exchange a few quiet words. I enjoy your opinions. I've never heard a better conversationalist. Believe me it's nice to have someone around who speaks your language. I don't mind telling you that for me, a shammes who likes to mingle, this synagogue is a hardship post, but it comes with the territory so what can I do? If I were a Job it would be different. That man had a genius for suffering. But me, I'm just an average, C plus, run-of-the-mill complainer."

"Why don't you leave?" taunted D.C. "There's no reason for you to hang around here. You're useless. You don't even have a congregation. Go out and enjoy yourself. Live it up."

"Leave the synagogue?" The shammes' bushy eyebrows flew up under his tam-o'-shanter in astonishment. "Widdeman," he said, pityingly, "I believe you've taken a turn for the worst. Compose yourself. I may be mediocre in the misery department when compared with the greats, but I'm still a Jew. A Buddhist has his karma, a Christnik his vicarious atonement, but what Jew takes the easy way out? A Jew suffers. It's a sign of his humanity. Besides," he continued, and rubbed his hands together with pleasure, "it seems that I now have a new congregation. Small in number, but choice."

D.C., his nerves shot, reached for the matzoh. But the strongbox was empty. He peered inside and there on the metal bottom looking up at him was an orthodox member of the congregation with crumbs on his face and ashes in his heart. D.C.'s lips shuddered as if he were praying. Suddenly he grabbed Lopez by the mackinaw. "I've given up suffering," he howled. "I'm an American. A winner!"

The shammes appraised his visitor thoughtfully and then brushed his hands away. "It's curable," he informed him, rising. "You've got a good appetite. Hold on and I'll get you some more."

The minute the shammes turned his back the Winner threw off his hat, his prayer shawl, and was on his feet. Cautiously, soundlessly, he tiptoed out of the candlelit chapel into the black hallway and, like the gypsies before him, stole away through the darkness.

CHAPTER 18

A letter forwarded from Paris filled with low spirits.

Dear Buddies,

This isn't an easy letter for me to write and I can't quite believe it yet. It's all happened so fast. Last week out of the blue the Chief called me into his office and gave me my notice. The Army doesn't want me any more. They're replacing three of us down here with WEINSTEIN II, a visual computer, as part of some kind of new economy drive. I was told that I don't have enough seniority but that's a lot of hot air because they're keeping on Dimitri Mendeleyev who's only a Pfc., and I'm a corporal. I can't figure out what they've got against me. The Chief always used to say such nice things about my work.

I guess you know I'm not sorry to go but I've made so many friends here and all. I don't exactly know what I'm going to do now. You see my father died last month. If I didn't know better I'd say he did it on purpose to spite me, almost as if he foresaw that this was going to happen. He was a hard man. I suppose there's no point in going on to medical school now. I just can't figure out what I really want any more. I mean there are so many different things to do on the outside it's hard to decide on something like this right off the top of your head.

I was thinking maybe if I could find my old ticket I'd come visit you guys for a while in Paris, that is if it's all right with you. Just to give me some time to think things over. But on the other hand, I don't know, it seems so far away. I'll have to think about it. I'm sure going to miss the whipped potatoes and everything.

At least I hope things are all right with you.

Ex-Corporal Causley, H.D.*

* Honorable Discharge

CHAPTER 19

✍ Giving Ambrose the birds.

"The reputation of our country is at stake," declared Ambrose Winkie, surveying their large suite of rooms at the Grand Hotel with qualified satisfaction. "America, like the cedar waxwing, must always look good." Although personally nonaggressive, Winkie was a pregnant tiger when it came to protecting the image of the United States abroad. Three times he had had them moved out of what he regarded as inferior accommodations and the manager himself was called in to handle the situation before Winkie was finally content that American interests had been safeguarded. And at a fair price. The Zaragoza offices of INTRA's trade delegation were spacious and carpeted, with shoeshine rags in the bathrooms and Myrurgia in the air. All rooms faced the front of the hotel. But the view was trolley cars, the furniture ornately uncomfortable, and the toilet tissue one-ply, paper-bag brown. Yet it was the best that the city had to offer and Winkie could do no more for his country.

Ivan attempted to take up the slack. During their first week of operation when local businessmen interested in American goods, money, or markets overflowed their suite and stood three deep in the hall, the indefatigable young man worked tirelessly into the night, conducting interviews, evaluating prospects, assuming more and more authority while Ambrose, unencumbered in the inner office, gave light dictation to his secretaries. And even now that the flood had become a trickle, Ivan still remained at his desk long hours in the hope of lending a helping hand to one and all. Seated across from him with red eyes and pale gums, Señor Montemar appeared to be in need of assistance.

"In my heart," groaned Montemar, wringing his hands, "in my heart, Señor, I know that your movies are better than ever before. But I have not seen this with my own eyes. My customers have not seen this. For years in my theaters I have had *los hermanos* Marx, *los hermanos* Ritz, Charló, and El Buster, and always the audience they laughed, they cried, they tore their hair. But now my customers are tired. They don't laugh, they don't cry, they don't tear their hair. Señor," he rubbed his hands restlessly over his thighs in acute distress, "Señor," he whimpered, "they don't come."

Ivan, who had been taking notes like an analyst, looked up and shook his head. "I can't help you," he said flatly. "Go on."

"Don't say that," implored Señor Montemar. "Up on the screen my business is dying in front of my eyes. Don't say that. You are the last chance. In your magazines I have read about the new movies, the great movies that are being made by your country, but we have seen only *Pato Donald and the Singing Nuns!* Our censors look at each title like a cyst and remove it. But I must have them. I MUST!"

"There's nothing I can—"

"Stop!" cried Montemar, putting his fingers in his ears. He was a handsome man in his well-cut blue serge suit (natural shoulders, two vents), and if not for his cosmic overbite might have been a big movie star himself. "Get me them," he commanded in torment, reckless of the consequences, "and whatever the cost I will pay it."

Ivan scratched at the edge of his beard thoughtfully. "It won't be easy."

Ecstatic, Señor Montemar leaned over and taking up the young executive's free hand patted it ardently, pressed it to his cheek, and blessed him.

"You'll pay through the nose, of course."

"Anything, anything."

"A pretty penny. In advance."

"Please, Señor." The excited movie-house owner went for his wallet and removed a cellophane-covered photograph of a blonde Hollywood starlet naked from the toes up. "Can you," he asked with reverence, "can you get me one of these?"

"Difficult to say," judged Ivan, squinting at the picture. "It might be arranged. But you understand without clothes they're more expensive."

"I'll pay, I'll pay," he shouted jubilantly. "How much?"

Ivan jotted down a column of numbers, methodically added them up, and then with a lazy stroke crossed out his total. "Let's just say," he cocked his head in Señor Montemar's direction like a robin eyeing a worm, "that you'll fork over what the traffic will bear."

"Is that good?" inquired the Spaniard, puzzled by the expression.

"That depends," replied Ivan candidly. "For me, yes. For you, so-so."

Señor Montemar's protruding teeth smiled on involuntarily. "I have heard that you drive a hard bargain," he disclosed, his face purple with determination as he handed over his wallet. "I would not have come, Señor, if I were not a desperate man."

"One does what one can," said Ivan modestly, after counting the money.

"But what is to be done?" Montemar clutched Ivan's wrist and spoke in earnest. "What is to be done about the censor?"

"It's a problem," conceded Ivan with some discomfort.

"Yes, yes. And—?"

"I've considered it."

"Yes, you've considered it. And—?"

"Sticky."

Montemar's red eyes seemed to be bleeding and the veins in his forehead tumefied and became as exposed and vulnerable as his teeth. "Steeky?" he echoed lamely.

"Sticky. But," Ivan informed him cheerfully, "I think I've licked it." He showed Señor Montemar the paper he had been writing on. "You see, it's merely a matter of successfully merchandising the product. 'Hot Pants' we'll call *The Breath Of Summer*, 'The Nymph with the Golden Crack' will become *The Midas Touch*, and 'Call Girls of Tenerife' we'll change to *The Miracle of The Bells*. American movies for the whole family at popular prices. You'll pack them in."

"*EL MILAGRO DE LAS CAMPANAS!*" cried the captivated Montemar, rapturously. "Even the Pope himself would not object to such a title. I'll pack them in."

"It's likely."

"Señor!" Montemar pressed his benefactor's hand and pinched his cheeks. "You've saved my life. How can I thank you enough?"

"Cash," replied Ivan without hesitation, and led the happy soul to the door. "Your second payment will be due tomorrow morning at nine. *Hasta mañana*."

In his desk Ivan kept a small loose-leaf notebook which contained a cryptic record of his assets designed to resemble the index for a study of famous fellowships. A scholarly job. All groups alphabetically arranged and "ff." to indicate continuing payment. Among the names listed were those of the members of the Manhattan Project, the Scriblerus Club, the Pre-Raphaelite Brotherhood, the Seven Blocks of Granite, the Vienna School of Psychoanalysis, and the Titus Oates Plot. The numbers beside each entry were high but might have passed for page references in any work the size of *The Pharmacopoeia of the United States of America*. The system itself was simple: the first three letters of the code name were identical with that of the subscriber. Accordingly in the section reserved for the *Poetry* gang, Señor Montemar was entered alphabetically as Monroe, Harriet, preceding Pound, Ez—a SAC lieutenant colonel who had been passed over for promotion and on whom one night at the Beachcomber Ivan had unloaded the Duesenberg as instant therapy for his shrunken ego.

The notebook recorded a small fortune. Since the arrival of INTRA's avant-garde in Zaragoza, Ivan (free-lancing) had made promises, sold rights, and contracted to supply everything from blue movies to Nazi helmets in mint condition for the kiddies. But his most popular item was one of his own creation that he called "Sponge Gel," a secret chemical composition so absorbent that not only could it suck out the juice of an orange through the skin, but the pits as well. Morticians loved it. Sprinkled over a corpse like camphor it made all other forms of embalming obsolete, and Ivan granted five exclusive franchises in this field alone. Although he had performed a curettage on their pockets, sacked them like Troy, Ivan felt that in exchange he had given each of his customers something to live for, a new horizon, and he would have been completely happy in solving their little difficulties if not for the sickening adoration of Ambrose Winkie.

"You're driving yourself too hard, Ivan," he was always cautioning his young assistant. "I feel as if I'm to blame. If anything happened to you I'd never forgive myself. Are you getting enough sleep?"

Winkie's years of experience in government had never proved more painful to him than when he was obliged to refuse Ivan the use of the Grand Hotel as a bedroom. But there could be no hint of personal comfort at federal expense. For this reason, he had located the dingiest pension in town—a building down near the river that sagged heavy with cockroaches and mephitic air—where he cut corners by sharing a single black room with his secretaries while Ivan dwelt below with three diseased hens and a scaly rooster in the *portero*'s mucopurulent office. Every night Winkie would shuttle back and forth between the girls and Ivan to make certain that his young friend was comfortable. Every night he would bring along some small, inexpensive present—a WELCOME TO ZARAGOZA pennant for his wall, a salami-shaped pillow for his head—to cozy up his quarters. And every night he would find Ivan sleeping soundly on his cot, the pennant torn down and the pillow thrown in a corner and covered with roosting chickens.

A growing paternal concern for Ivan's welfare subtly affected Winkie's sinuses and mental tranquility, but his peace of mind was completely shattered by the sudden and inexplicable lapse of local interest in American trade. "I don't understand it," he moaned, as he entered Ivan's office shortly after Señor Montemar had left. He looked terrible. His round face which had previously been bloated with optimism now hung in folds like a theater curtain. "It's beyond reason. For one entire week they beat down the doors to get in here and now all we have are a few timid knocks." He dropped heavily into a monolithic wing chair, clasped his hands on top of the ledger in his lap, and turning in bewilderment to his assistant asked, "What does it mean, Ivan? What's gone wrong?"

Ivan reached for a copy of the *Heraldo de Aragon* that had been forgotten by Señor Montemar. "No reason for alarm, Ambrose," he said casually, while spreading the newspaper before him. "Psychologists call this a temporary plateau."

"Temporary." Winkie took heart. "But how can we be sure it's only temporary?"

Ivan hunted through the paper until he came upon the sort of article he was looking for and read. "'*ANARQUISTA AMERICANO ASESINA VIGÉSIMA VICTIMA.*'" He passed the article across to his superior. "That could explain it. We're dealing with the Latin temperament here. Sensitive people. But these things blow over."

Embarrassed by his ignorance of Spanish, Winkie looked at the pictures for a while and then hurriedly hid the newspaper away in his chair. "They *are* a sensitive people," he acknowledged. "That's why I'm worried, Ivan. Maybe we've unthinkingly done something to offend them."

"I doubt it," said Ivan, hoarsely, dismissing the subject. "Where are the ladies?"

"Shopping," replied Winkie, tapping nervously on his ledger. "Maybe," he continued to fret, "we could do something nice to regain their confidence."

Getting up, Ivan calmly turned his back and walked to the window where taking hold of the strap that controlled the heavy *persianas* he sent them crashing up and down with one hand.

"What do you think, Ivan?" Winkie called anxiously over the noise.

"Ambrose—" He let go of the strap and faced the melancholy Winkie whose bald head broke down the light like a prism. "Have you lost faith in my judgment?" he asked in a hurt voice. "Don't you trust me anymore, Ambrose?"

"I don't know what's the matter with me," groaned Winkie, dropping his eyes guiltily. "I've been so jumpy lately. You mustn't take it personally, Ivan. Good heavens, what would I do without you?"

"A hypothetical question. Don't think about it," he advised. "You're already on edge."

Winkie was so touched by the youth's loyalty that it was several minutes before he could allow himself to speak. "I knew you'd stand by me," he whispered gratefully. "And I'm sure"—he cleared the huskiness from his voice—"I'm convinced that you're right about its being only temporary. But you see every day that we're here it costs the taxpayers money. Isn't there something," he pleaded, "anything we can do to speed the return of the business community?"

Ivan began to pace about the room as if Mr. Winkie were treading on his toes every step of the way. He had had enough of the soggy meddler. "So you want a catalyst," he observed saturninely.

"That's it! A catalyst, Ivan. That's what we need." Elated, Winkie watched the young man stride about and waited on tenterhooks for more information.

Soon alighting on his desk, Ivan sat cross-legged, glanced down introspectively at his untied shoelaces, and with a quiet solemnity that lent added weight to his words said, "I suggest a joy bee."

Straining on the edge of his chair, Winkie appeared nonplused.

"A blast," explained Ivan. "A volcanic go-go-go."

Ambrose blanched. "A reception?" he inquired disconsolately.

"To show the burghers we're friendly. We'll invite everyone who counts and let nature take its course."

"But that costs money, Ivan. A great deal of money."

"Naturally there will be some bills." Ivan looked away from the nit-picker in disgust. "A small price to pay for the prompt elimination of a temporary plateau."

Winkie sagged. Caught between the disapproval of this young man he so greatly admired and the perils of an inflated expense account, he sank ever lower, his rainbow scalp slipping down the back of the wing chair like a sunset. He fondled his ledger poignantly. It was bound in black with cream-colored tips and spine and it contained a scrupulous itemized account of the frugality of the Zaragoza mission. From the beginning in Washington, Winkie's niggardliness had endeared him to his superiors. Never once had he been guilty of an omission. Even while enjoying his secretaries it was not uncommon for him to get up out of bed in order to note down some trifling expense, to correct some minor irregularity. Aware of his weakness for the ladies, Winkie safeguarded his private life by keeping an impeccable ledger filled with all sorts of fantastic economies, and the prospect of recording a large sum for entertainment cramped his colon.

"Haste—" (Ambrose clutching the ledger to his belly.) "Haste—" (Ambrose squirming about on his fatty tissue and breathing in and out) "makes waste." Ambrose was dissatisfied. He had wanted to take a stronger position. "Maybe something can be arranged, Ivan. Let me sleep on it. Is that all right? Ivan? All right?"

The following morning Ivan, an early riser, was shaken out of his cot by Ambrose Winkie. "Oh, it's you," he grouched, and keeping the pressure on went back to sleep.

Winkie knelt down beside the cot and in a quavering voice confessed, "I'm sure you're right, Ivan. You mustn't think I don't appreciate your advice."

Relenting, Ivan opened his good eye. "You look terrible," he observed.

"I couldn't sleep a wink," admitted Winkie, buttoning the neck of his silk, pin-striped pajamas. He dried his temples and sighed with relief. "I feel better now. I'll make up the guest list this very morning."

Tossing aside his blanket, Ivan, who slept fully clothed in order to insulate himself against the bed bugs, got up and put on his tie in silence.

"I don't see anything wrong with a *small* gathering," continued Ambrose, still placating although distracted by the *portero's* malignant rooster. "I'm certain Washington will understand." Suddenly he scrambled onto the cot and raised his feet as the scaly basilisk strutted over breathing contagion and greedily eyed his toes like giant corn kernels.

"Suit yourself," said Ivan, indifferently.

"What do you mean?" asked Ambrose, startled by the young man's tone but not daring to take his eyes off the deranged cock.

Buttoning his double-breasted mass of twisted wrinkle, Ivan replied, "I've practically washed my hands of the whole affair," and, as if to dramatize his apathy, he brought his right foot back and casually place-kicked the rooster through the door.

"You're joking." Liberated, Ambrose jumped up and grabbed the deserter as he was about to leave. "Just when your country is counting on you to make our balance of trade something that we can all be proud of you're throwing in the whistle. I didn't think you were a quitter, son."

Ivan hesitated on the threshold.

"I need you," whimpered Ambrose shamelessly, and dried his nose on his pajama sleeve.

Folding his arms, Ivan demanded, "Who makes up the guest list?"

"I had no idea!" cried Ambrose. He laughed through his tears at his brilliant protegé's charming touch of youthful vanity and patted his buttons with affection. "It was only that I didn't think it fair to ask you to carry the whole load. You've done so much already. But go to it. Handle everything. It's your baby. Only remember that time is running short. You'll have to hurry."

"The invitations went out last night," revealed Ivan flatly.

Unable to believe his ears, Ambrose gaped at the young man in amazement. "Last night?"

"A select group of notables."

Winkie's clenched face slowly opened up like a sunflower into a blooming smile of recognition. "I should have known," he said finally, hating himself for the harsh thoughts he had harbored. Never for a moment had Ivan intended to drop his oar. It was not easy for Ambrose to master his tender feelings. "What would I do without you, faithful boy?"

Shrugging off the compliment, Ivan brusquely announced, "It's almost time for our walk. Are you coming?"

With a parting squeeze of Ivan's hand, Ambrose, overflowing with emotion, rushed rhapsodically up the stairs for his pants.

It was going to be a surprise party. Despite his mounting curiosity in the days that followed, Ambrose could not bring himself to question Ivan for fear of suggesting a lack of confidence, and his independent assistant told him nothing. For some reason all of Ambrose's anxiety focused on Ivan's clothing. Every evening upon returning to their pension, he would hurry downstairs with a bundle of clothes over his arm and sticking his head into the *portero's* office, ask Ivan nonchalantly in passing, "Anything for the cleaners?" The results were discouraging. He considered buying him a new wardrobe, but that might offend the young man. He considered stealing his suit, but he slept in it. As a last resort, Ambrose presented him with a hand-carved olivewood rabbit whose bushy tail was a whiskbroom, and prayed that he would use it but Ambrose had no illusions. On the night of the party Ivan was as always coated in dust, lint, and feathers and resembled a hairy chicken plucker, while Winkie, shaved to the bone and dressed in royal blue, glowed like a burnished saddle.

The doorman saluted as they entered the hotel but Ambrose, hurrying after his silent assistant, was too distracted to exchange his usual smile. Going up in the tiny elevator, he stood behind the unkempt young man and, unable to control himself, picked at Ivan's lint in secret as he puffed nervously on his cigar. Before the door of their suite, Ivan, with a tranquil gaze, held his employer back momentarily in order to give him a cynically derisive clandestine chuckle. He then entered. Full of consternation, Ambrose rushed in after him.

"My God!" he shouted, seeing the room already crowded with well-groomed gentlemen in stunning tails, "we're late. This is horrible."

Ivan laughed compassionately. "Those," he explained, "are the waiters."

"But so many?"

"You wouldn't want us to have less than the Russians, would you?" Ivan glared at him reproachfully.

"I suppose not," muttered Winkie on second thought. Ashamed of himself, he gave up counting the waiters. "I just wasn't expecting anything like this." He tried to be casual as he looked around at the incredible transformation that had taken place in their office.

All of the furniture had been moved out and replaced by picnic tables surrounded by small potted almond trees. The entire suite was in bloom, a flowering grove of crystalline pink-and-white blossoms that clustered about the branches like rock candy.

"They're real, of course?" he inquired of Ivan dismally, thinking of the expense.

"Of course."

"Blooming early this year, aren't they? Quite a novelty. But couldn't you have gotten a bargain on pussy willows? I mean"— Winkie didn't want to seem unappreciative—"it's interesting."

"They're baked almonds from the Negev."

"Is that right," remarked Winkie, awed by nature's infinite variety. "I thought the baking went on afterward."

Ivan gave him a pitying look and, holding him by the wrist, led trusting Ambrose about the room like a decrepit horse he was taking out to shoot.

"I suppose volume buying cut the cost," Winkie mumbled hopefully to one of the uncomprehending waiters as he was shown everything. The stacked wooden cases of champagne, the glazed crocks of Beluga caviar, the pink suckling pigs with marasca eyes and baked apples in their mouths. The more Winkie saw the more restless he became.

On one wall was a large American flag with the words FUCK COMMUNISM written across it which made him particularly uneasy.

"Isn't that a little strong?" Ambrose asked hesitantly, anxious not to antagonize the young man anew.

Ivan sneered at him and doubled up his fists as if he were crunching beer cans. "I'm no appeaser," he snarled righteously.

"We've got to show Europe that we mean business. We're the leaders of the Free World, aren't we?"

"Whatever you say, my boy," soothed Winkie, no longer sure of his standards in the age of the Cold War.

Although the guests didn't begin to arrive until after eleven, they came in frightening numbers with big appetites, a Spanish armada of free-loading revelers. Winkie took one look at the whole damn crapulous crew and quietly left his place in the receiving line in order to save what he could. But no sooner would he stealthily hide away a case of champagne than it was uncovered amidst cheers and, in a trice, the corks were exploding like pistons. It was discouraging. Determined, Winkie tried for some minor economies. Picking up soiled napkins, turning off lights, presenting controversial discussion topics to keep the mouths moving without consumption. Failures all. He even slunk about the orchard collecting unfinished hors d'oeuvres and scraping off the left-over caviar, but gave this up also when a guest who was only resting between bites furiously snatched back his remnant from him. Badly rattled, the thrifty host departed *tout de suite*. Wedging his way into the bathroom, Ambrose shut the door and squatting down on the toilet seat, he cried. A dribble, a blubber, a burst. A monsoon of tears played havoc with the humidity of the room, fogging up the mirrors and seeming to condense on his bald head, for drops of pure sweet water trickled down into his eyes as if completing a natural cycle. The toilet paper was like oilskin and attempting to dry his eyes Ambrose succeeded only in lacerating his cheeks. Dimly aware of the pain, it occurred to him that he must be drunk.

Good manners had required a toast with the bankers, the contractors, the manufacturers of furniture and fluorescent lights, and though he had had only a *sorbo* with each, the *sorbos* had added up. Winkie thought of all the new friends he had made for America. He esteemed his young assistant's talent for planning and organization. It was not the sort of affair that he had had in mind, but Ivan had gotten full value for the Committee's money. When in a few days INTRA's complete delegation arrived, all Zaragoza would be at their feet. His little cry had done him good. Ambrose rose from the toilet seat renewed like the Phoenix and returning to the crowded party he found Ivan talking gravely to two men, one of whom was in clerical garb. Ivan introduced them as, "The Bishop of Zaragoza and Señor Garcia Alonso de Merida y Zumalacarregui, the Minister of Commerce, who has just arrived from Madrid."

The significance of their presence was not lost on Ambrose. In a rage of good fellowship, he kissed the Bishop's ring, saluted the Minister, and, while the two Spaniards looked on benignly, he enveloped his assistant in a fragrant bear hug and, shouting to be heard above the din, cried, "Dear boy. Tonight . . . tonight you've outdone yourself. Tonight . . ." Choked up and unable to go on, Ambrose fled.

"Fuck," snorted Ivan. Noting the confused look on the Bishop's face he smiled blandly and added, "Communism."

The Bishop nodded soberly.

It was a gay party. The later the hour, the more hilarious the crowd and Ambrose, now reconciled to the overhead, was in the thick of it. Tippling, laughing, leering, and leching, he had a glorious time. "She was pinched so much," he was whispering to an American producer who was in Spain to make a low-budget movie, "that her bottom was declared a national monument so that all might come and visit it in peace." The two men roared like maniacs and their eyes were wet with tears.

"They're all a bunch of filthy degenerates," cried the wife of the producer, coming over and taking an immediate shine to Ambrose. She was a pretty woman, doll-faced, one of those anonymous beauties who hover around well-groomed hair in barber shop posters. "I've been all over Europe," she informed Ambrose authoritatively, never at a loss for words, "and believe you me it's the same. You travel around and it opens your eyes. You begin to really appreciate what we've got back home. Take this place. If they hadn't had so much damn incest in their royal family with everyone sleeping in the same bed maybe they'd still have a king and be playing baseball now instead of killing dumb animals—"

Ambrose was fascinated by the way the black velvet gown that she wore hung from her nipples which, as she spoke, were in a constant state of erection.

"Look what happened to the French with their empire. They

started letting a bunch of queers sell those sex postcards full of perversion and obscenity and dirt and now look where they are. And the Swedes with their abortions! *Momenyou!* It's an object lesson to see these scum. Every American should have the experience and then maybe when they came back we'd have fewer creeps knocking the way we do things. Right?"

Ambrose was beyond caring. Although her speech was inflammatory, her body was more so. Bending over with dreamy eyes, he was about to salute her bosom with a playful nip when he was surrounded by a strumming and rattling troupe of strolling flamenco dancers who had been hired by Ivan especially for the occasion.

As they circled about him clicking their castanets, one of the dancers with long earrings and ferocious eyebrows that had been drawn in with a ruler came forward and riffled through her petticoats like a deck of cards. The producer's wife saw at once what was going on—the decline of the West. Giving her drink to her husband, she bounded into the ring in time to the music. Tossing their heads and slapping their hands, the two women flounced about the glowing host as if he were the spoils. Ambrose was delighted. Snapping off a sprig of almond blossoms, he put it roguishly between his teeth and, though unable to dance, he clasped his fingers behind his head and shuffled about, gloriously marking time while waiting to see which of the high-stepping ladies would win him.

"¡Olé!" shouted the delighted guests clustering around.

Ambrose gave them a nifty shuffle and waved back suavely.

The guests laughed and applauded.

Ivan watched from the doorway. He stood together with three grim visitors who had only just arrived. They each wore the same charcoal brown eerily iridescent raincoat crumpled with travel. They each had their hands jammed tightly into their pockets. Their facial muscles were tied up in knots and their yellow eyes were hooded and joyless. As they listened to what Ivan had to say, they did not appear to be breathing.

"¡Olé!" Urged on by the fiery thrum of the guitars the ladies were battling it out. "¡Anda, chiquillas!" They seethed about the floor stepping on one another's toes in a flamenco frenzy while Ambrose, off to one side and radiant, cut ponderous capers with bovine grace. He waved blissfully. To the producer. To the Bishop. To Ivan. To Senators Spingle, Motts, and Kravitz.

Ambrose struggled frantically to get his arm down before they saw him, but it was paralyzed in the air. He tugged, he pulled, he jerked. He bashed it in at the joint. It crumpled. A cold shiver pierced his brain like an icicle and his flushed face turned a sickly green. It came as no surprise to Winkie that he was a moral weakling. In a similar situation, a CIA agent would have taken his strychnine pill. Hobbling forward morosely on numb feet through the adulating crowd, Ambrose delivered himself up to the Senators. He was shockingly disheveled—striped tie askew, jacket awry—and with the bottom buttons of his shirt undone his paunch hung out like a hernia.

The scowling trio whipped their hands from their raincoat pockets with the precision of a firing squad and shot out the invitations to the party which they had received in Washington. The invitations began "BROUHAHAHAHA!!! Sponge on US."

Ambrose goggled. Pitifully high-pitched wretched obscure sounds came from his throat but nothing definite.

Ivan removed the twig of blossoms from his mouth.

"But," instantly squealed Ambrose, and put himself under solemn oath by raising his right hand, "I didn't—"

The Senators shook their heads in disbelief and spoke ominously like a Greek chorus. "Junket, Winkie, junket."

"No, no," spluttered Ambrose, near collapse. He peered longingly into one granite face after another and pleaded, "Good God, you mustn't jump to conclusions. It's not what you think. Consider my record."

"Caviar from behind the Iron Curtain," said Spingle.

"Employing our nuclear deterrent to fetch almond trees," said Kravitz.

"We've seen enough," said Motts.

Ambrose clung giddily to his assistant and moaned. "Tell them the truth, son. Tell them it isn't so." His mind appeared completely dismantled. He fell into a sudden drunken lethargy and then all at once roused himself. "For God's sake!" he cried out hysterically, "say something frugal, Ivan, before it's too late."

Stone sober, Ivan reasoned with the Senators. "As you can see, gentlemen, Mr. Winkie is currently exhausted. In order to save the government money he lives in a ridiculously small inexpensive room and since our arrival in Zaragoza he's been unable to get a decent night's sleep crammed into that tiny space with those two luscious full-grown secretaries of his."

Without warning, Ambrose collapsed into Ivan's arms, foaming at the mouth.

The Senators looked on interestedly as Ivan laid his superior out on the floor.

"You're a strong lad," said Spingle.

"Winkie has written good things about you," said Kravitz.

"You've got a future in government," said Motts.

"Is that right?" exclaimed Ivan, in modest surprise. "I hadn't given it much thought."

The three Senators discussed the matter among themselves. Breaking their huddle, they gathered about the recumbent form of Ambrose Winkie and angrily ripped up their invitations. Then turning to Ivan, Senator Motts as spokesman for the group announced, "The Zaragoza mission arrives in three days. Take over the helm. Cultivate the ground. We're leaving you in complete charge of *everything*."

"I suppose it's best," Ivan agreed reluctantly as he gazed down at the stricken Ambrose who was just beginning to stir.

"You're on the way up, Storch," the Senators assured him, and wheeling about like a drill team in perfect formation, they left.

Ambrose, as pale as death, raised himself up on one elbow. The scraps of invitation that rested on his eyelids like coins dropped to the floor. "Everything I've worked for . . ." he moaned distractedly. "You've been like a son to me. How could you, Ivan?" he asked, more hurt than bitter.

The new chief of the Zaragoza mission was touched. "Think of it this way, Ambrose," he advised, "I'm not taking, I'm giving. If something happens to fall my way that's only bread on the water. Giving *means* receiving. But the gift is really yours. Cheer up. Now you can do the birds full time."

Flabbergasted, Ambrose wet his pants in silence. When he was all through he began to cry as if his heart would break, making no attempt to conceal his tears.

"What's wrong now?"

Through his wine-parched and otiose lips, Ambrose sobbed out, "I think you're sick."

Ivan laughed good-naturedly. But having humored him long enough, he put his foot down. Ambrose was under it.

A cheer went up from the background. The guitars released their tension in an orgy of bravura thwacks and rumbles that resembled a twenty-one gun salute heralding the arrival of something big like a tornado or a movie star. It sounded very much as if Ambrose Winkie had just been won by one of the dancing ladies.

CHAPTER 20

🦎 The conversion of D.C.

The shy little nun who came to the door of the new Convento de la Sagrada Familia with a smile so sweet it seemed fitter for pancakes than a human face wasn't Sidney and that was the first disappointment. The second was the news that she had left. D.C. took the blow with remarkable stoicism, given his fragile condition. As the frightened nun rushed to bring him a glass of water, he fought his way up from his knees and leaned heavily against the doorpost. The utopian thought that Sidney's departure meant that all her worldly goods were probably still intact helped to clear his mind. If he could only locate them. Perhaps the nun would tell him, for she did not look like an anti-Semite. When she returned with the water, he informed her that his name was Widdemore (not Lopez) and he was to be trusted.

The nun had no reason to think otherwise, for she was really not shy but nearsighted. As a consequence, she leaned slightly forward with an expectant expression that made D.C. uneasy and he felt the need to nod repeatedly as she spoke: Sidney was an angel, a treasure, a pearl of great price, and she had been loved by all the convent. In the end, however, she did not have the vocation. She waited and prayed for the call, but it never came.

In her sweet innocence, she would watch every day for the post-man as if he might be carrying it. Once she did receive an envelope covered with brightly colored stamps showing pictures of pagan idols from Africa but she quickly tore it up and never mentioned it again. She was so quiet and independent. She never spoke of the great green letter D that she wore on her breast. At first, because she was an American, they supposed it to stand for *Democracia*. Later, when they came to know her better, they believed that it must mean *Delicada* or *Dulce*, for she was so dainty and agreeable, but no one knew definitely. The day that she went out the convent door they said a special rosary for her. They all felt that they had lost a sister. She lived now in the *tubo*, the old quarter, opposite the open market, but if he was looking for her he would probably find her in the army barracks doing works of charity. If not there, then the orphanage or the hospital. It was true that she lacked the special grace to become a nun but she was a good soul and had done the next best thing in unselfishly devoting her life to others less fortunate than . . . The nun leaned forward myopically and noticed with embarrassment that her visitor had vanished. Blushing so violently that her eyebrows turned strawberry, she hurried inside and quickly shut the door.

D.C., of course, knew the truth. The D was for Dimity and the varsity letter for modern dancing. The nun had told him all he wanted to know. Though weary, he was closing in on Sidney at last.

The ancient, narrow, labyrinthian streets of the old quarter, in which bicycles coming from opposite directions could barely go by one another without snarling their pedals, had been built originally to keep out the wind and keep in the citizens. D.C. soon discovered that he was a prisoner of the *tubo*. After passing the same stationery store for the fourth time, he felt like some experimental animal that had failed. He wondered nervously if he hadn't made a terrible mistake in not visiting the barracks first. But just when his last bit of strength was about to go up in panic, when he had ceased speculating on the pros and cons of superimposing himself on this cobblestone or that and had decided to let the chips fall where they might, he accidentally stumbled on the house opposite the market and in a state of wild exaltation he gushed into the dark hallway and up the stairs.

He knocked decisively—four arrogant raps. He tried again—three knuckle dusters and a lob—and it was a while before he realized that in the darkness he had only reached the first landing and was pounding on a blank wall. Chagrined, he moved on more cautiously. Groping his way to the top of the next flight of stairs, he got down on all fours in what seemed to be a feculent, adhesive, *sui generis* substance and crawled tentatively along the hall until he felt the outline of a door and knocked.

Sidney stood before him in a halo of light glowing like a radioactive isotope. She wore her white team sweater and a scarf of peacock blues and greens wound snugly around her neck to ward off the chill. In her hands she held a large pair of khaki trousers as if they were some sort of talisman. She gazed curiously out into the hallway and a tiny wrinkle of perplexity showed itself on her forehead.

Mum and cautious, D.C. advanced under her focal point, crawling forward on his belly like a commando to investigate whether the owner of the pants was still poaching on the grounds.

Sidney started as he brushed against her leg. "Richard!" she cried, artfully feigning annoyance to mask her pleasure. "What are you doing down there on the floor?"

Observing countless men's trousers with open flies draped promiscuously over the furniture in helter-skelter abandon, D.C. replied, "I'm fainting," and did.

Thirty-seven hours later the shock wore off. Somehow he was in bed, the mattress a spineless lump that dangled from a barred bedstead. His travel-stained feet hung saffron-colored over the end pilloried through the brass bars. Although only by scant inches, it was the first time since leaving Pamplona that he had slept off the ground and D.C. felt refreshed, invigorated, buoyant, and agreeably rapacious. His eyes fell on Sidney. In the moonlit room, she was seated beside a goose-necked lamp quietly basting the crotch of a pair of khaki trousers with a look of blissful contentment not unlike that of alimentary mystics dying of macrobiotic diets. D.C. had a new appreciation for the homely arts and crept soundlessly out of bed. On tiptoe over the cold floor, he stole up behind the little seamstress and lewdly seized her kumquats. Startled, Sidney cross-stitched his index finger with rapid thrusts.

"Oh Richard." She bit off the thread upon reaching his cuticle. "You're up. You're better. I was so worried about you."

D.C. gave her a surly nod.

"You poor dear," she said maternally, noting the finger in his mouth. "You must be starved. Hop back in bed and I'll bring you something nourishing to eat."

It was the first square meal that he had had in days. Manchego and bola and biscotel. As he ate, Sidney sat on the edge of the bed—her green mini-skirt endogenously high-rising—and fidgeted with the blanket while explaining her side of the convent.

"They just didn't want to pledge me, that's all there was to it. I did everything they said. Memorized every single saint, the holidays, the Renaissance altarpieces in Navarra from Allo to Valtierra. And I thought the girls liked me and all but I guess I was blackballed. It made me so miserable when I had to leave that I sat right down on the curb and cried." Recalling the unhappy time, Sidney sniffled and bit her cupid lips.

"And then what?" prodded D.C. Between mouthfuls, he slyly eased his leg over to the part of the blanket on top of which her hand rested.

"I felt so useless I wanted to die. I wasn't going to turn out silly like my mother running all over the world shooting innocent animals. I wanted to really *make* something of my life and not be just another wealthy heiress with two million dollars in tax-free municipal bonds."

D.C. sprang up in bed. "In your own name?" he asked incredulously.

"When I marry," she replied. Looking into his eyes with touching self-denial, she added, "But I'll never marry."

"You're young. Don't make any hasty decisions." D.C. paused and looked at her suspiciously. "They didn't do anything *unusual* to you in that convent, did they?"

"Oh no," Sidney insisted, "I'm not interested in marriage. Money can't buy happiness you know." She folded her hands peacefully in her lap and said with great conviction, "I want to devote myself exclusively to human suffering."

"That's a lot of territory," counseled D.C., coming out from under the blanket to discuss the matter. "Why don't you specialize in ringworm or seborrheac dermatitis?" While she thought it over, he proceeded deftly to examine the origins and insertions of all the principal muscles of her femur.

Sidney laughed gaily and wriggled away with the determination of a spawning salmon. She skipped to the table by the kitchen door on which she kept her pet goldfish, Webster, and settling her elbows about the bowl gazed into it metaphysically. "I don't know," she said, seriously mulling it over. "I don't think I'm the specialist type. I guess I'd rather be a sort of general practitioner like St. Francis."

There was something definitely Balthus about her, the way she spread herself around, her legs apart as if she were alone or indifferent, and always the tantalizing peek-a-boo of subtle shades of dark, erogenous flesh. "Sidney," he called softly, in a voice spastic with romantic tremors, "remember that night on the promenade deck? The two of us. Together. *Close!*"

Looking up from her fish bowl, Sidney smiled. "What happened to your friend, Ivan?" she asked, ingenuously.

"*That* bastard!" shouted the young lover, suddenly enraged. "A fair-weather friend! A wolf in sheep's clothing! An enemy of the people! Let us not sully the air with the name of that fork-tongued, muscle-bound car thief and slob. Sidney . . ." He closed his eyes, straining to recapture the chimerical mood. "Did you miss me?"

"Not really," she said, and giggled mischievously.

"Sidney," he coaxed, eager, beckoning, "come over here."

"Uh-uh," she refused, with a playful waggle of her concupiscible behind.

D.C. began to salivate copiously. "Sidney!" he screamed, and fell back on the bed. "I'm shivering."

The little angel of mercy was at his side in a flash. She saw the bloodless whites of his eyes and heard the black rattle of death in his throat. Stifling a cry, she reached for his hand which was shuddering on top of the blanket like an automatic weapon. It was icy. "Oh Richard," she groaned in despair, "I don't own a hot-water bottle."

Springing up, D.C. seized her around the waist and buried his nose in her major letter. "I'll be all right," he said bravely, "just hold me."

Sidney pushed the nursling back on his pillow. With lightning speed and nimble footwork, she tucked him in firmly under hospital corners and tried to comfort him. "Don't worry," she comforted frantically, "I'll think of something."

Crazed by the opportunity to alleviate human suffering but woefully inexperienced, the excited young girl ran into the kitchen and turned on all the burners full blast. Then dashing back, she ransacked the sparsely furnished apartment and collecting her few belongings and whatever else she could find, tossed everything on top of the patient. "Is that better?" she asked hopefully.

Under a bright mound topped by pastel-colored washcloths, Honey-Bunch panties, plaid cummerbunds, khaki trousers, and midnight-blue baby doll diaphanous nighties, D.C. lay buried like Hrothgar in his barrow. He stared dumbly at the ceiling where, directly above his head, two taped wires hung down in anticipation of a lighting fixture. He wondered if he had the strength to rise up and complete the circuit.

"Here," said Sidney, pulling off her scarf and tying it around his neck. "Are you still feeling chills?"

D.C. angrily rocked the pile above him. "What do you think?" he complained.

The anguished young girl clenched her tiny fist and beat on her lips desperately in a panic of life-saving holds from her Red Cross water safety manual. They wouldn't do. She scanned the room with dread. The situation looked grim. Only wood. There wasn't even a newspaper around in which to wrap him. As she hurriedly began removing her clothes and throwing them on top of the bed, Sidney felt very much like a doctor—dispassionate, prophylactic, her eye on the organ.

D.C. watched her progress spellbound. Nothing stood between his enchanted eyeballs and her captivating flesh but one frilly little yellow lace rose-bud bra. O frabjous day! Callooh! Callay! She hesitated, her elbows back, her fingers frozen on the hooks. D.C. shook the bed feverishly like a *pishka* and she held back nothing. O frabjous night! Out of sight.

"I don't have anything else to put on you, Richard," said the helpless, shivering, naked girl. "Please stop shaking. *Please*."

D.C. reared up remorselessly, cyclonically, palpitating, thrashing about, and the pile of odds and ends on top of him quaked and reeled, quivering like a haystack.

"Oh frogs!" moaned Sidney, almost in tears, and threw herself sacrificially onto the pile.

The weight of two million tax-free dollars was too much for the bed. It exploded like a star, sending dry goods spinning centrifugally out into the void. In no time D.C. had shaken Sidney down to the bottom where she lay tenderly in his arms with her mussed-up bangs and milk-white belly all warm and sugar-coated and smelling of sweet alyssum as they fucked.

Only the camel-bell sound of a streetcar way off and the steady *fssss* of the burning jets in the kitchen. On the hushed bed, the two lovers rested together yinyang in perfect harmony, quietly steaming. D.C. kissed her cozy ear meltingly. Rolling over on his back, he sighed with contentment and announced, "Now we'll have to get married, right Sidney?"

The pooped heiress stirred, her button nose in the pillow, and mumbled, "Wha?"

"A chic ceremony in some connubially recherché setting like Rockefeller Center or the U.N. A few dignitaries. Nothing garish. How does that sound?"

Sidney raised her head in horror. "Don't be silly, Richard. I mean I like you and all but I have my career to think of. Besides," she added modestly, taking note of his swift recovery, "you don't need me any more."

"Don't need you!" cried D.C. outraged. "Don't be ridiculous."

"Aren't you feeling any better?"

"Terrible. My health is shot, my medical history a nightmare. I'm rheumatic, epileptic, and a chronic Iberian swooner. You call *that* better?"

Sidney pushed herself up on her slim, supple arms in a graceful modern dance movement and gazed down into the young man's face with fresh interest. "I think you should see a doctor," she suggested in a cheerful voice, trying not to alarm him.

"Who needs a doctor? I hate doctors." Pulling her down on top of him, D.C. nuzzled in and whispered intimately, "But I could use a good nurse."

"Richard, no!" Freeing herself from his arms, she said firmly, "I *want* you to see a doctor."

"All right," he easily agreed, flattered by her interest, and once more he drew in her soft, pliant, excruciatingly caressable body full of untold Arcadian mysteries and delights. Not until she was locked tight in his zestful embrace did he inform her, "But only if it means we're engaged."

Sidney snuggled down. Brushing her raven hair back, she put her ear to his heart. "We'll see," she said equivocally as she began to listen. "It all depends."

D.C. was feeling superb; well fed, well rested, cleaned up—a potential bridegroom. He had even come to a temporary understanding with his clothes. When Sidney had first produced them in the morning he had turned deathly pale and ordered her to remove them from his sight lines. "I can't wear *those*," he said scornfully. But it seemed that she had burned his old rags in a ritual act of purification, a penitential *aubade*, and in the end he was forced to reconsider. The most recent owner of the jacket that he wore was a widower with nine children and cancer, for whom Sidney had mended the lining. The color had originally been blue but had turned a gaseous purple like certain automobiles left out in the sun too long. His pants were khaki and six inches shy of his ankles. Sitting in Dr. De la Ronchas' crowded waiting room with Sidney by his side quietly stroking his hand for encouragement amidst the thundering hawkers, the quixotic young man was now almost able to see something amusingly Bohemian in his antic costume. But if he could convince the plodding scientific mind that the degeneracy of his exterior mirrored the condition of his entire system, he was as good as married.

When it was their turn, they were shown into the doctor's examination room by a birdlike woman in civilian dress who might have been the doctor's housekeeper. She fussed over the young couple solicitously, told them not to give up hope, assured them that the doctor could work miracles (citing the framed diplomas on the wall as proof), and waved a thumbs-up good-bye.

D.C. chuckled to himself and strolled curiously around the room examining the pictures on the wall. The faces of children. Dark rings circling their sunken eyes typical of newspaper photographs of deceased parties. Taped to each one was some small object—a hatpin, a marble, a razor blade—that the child had gobbled up and Dr. De la Ronchas had skillfully fished out. D.C. counted seven crucifixes of assorted sizes. A popular item. If there had been no cheating and none of the hardware had been removed during autopsy, the doctor was plainly, as Sidney had said, a classy operator.

Sidney had never personally met Dr. De la Ronchas but she knew of his reputation from her many visits to the hospital. "You see, Richard," she called brightly, pointing to a huge diploma heavy with German text, "he did go to the University of Heidelberg. I told you."

D.C. came over, read the inscription, and said calmly, "Did you notice the date on that thing?"

"1941. What about it?"

"*1941*," repeated D.C. significantly. "Doesn't that bring anything to mind? Brown shirts, the Horst Wessel, Auschwitz, baked people."

"But all that was ages ago. Nobody remembers that war anymore. We weren't even born then. You can't be angry with the doctor for wanting to get an education simply because some ninny started a war. That's just not fair."

"For Crysake!" shouted D.C., livid with intolerance, "in '41 in Germany the only thing he could have learned was how to turn live human beings into lampshades and wallets. What's the matter with you? He's a Nazi. A hobnailedmesserschmittedblitzkrieging sadist. Let's get out of here."

"Please, Richard," protested Sidney, holding him back and trying to make him see reason. "I'm sure he hasn't done anything wrong. Everyone speaks so highly of him. Maybe it's only an honorary degree or something."

D.C. yanked his arm ruthlessly out of her grasp and was rushing away when all at once he saw what a preposterous thing he was doing and broke out in a cold sweat. He was amazed at himself. He hadn't realized the extent to which he had been perniciously influenced by the parochial thinking of Shammes Lopez. If De la Ronchas could produce a first-rate letter of rejection, what did he care about the good old days? "I'm sorry," he said stiffly, coming back looking like milk of magnesia. "You see I'm unwell. He's probably not a Nazi at all."

Although it no longer made any difference, D.C. was pleased to observe that he was right. Dr. De la Ronchas did not resemble a Nazi in the slightest, but he did look disturbingly like an Arab. Swarthy complexion, oily jet hair, and broad eyebrows that swept across his forehead like black fans. One hand hooked into the front of his starched white jacket, he looked at them intently, a hypnotic stare. "*Muy buenas,*" he said in a honeydew voice as he directed his eyes from one to the other not missing a trick, "and who is the patient?"

It was not a promising beginning. Immediately D.C. sought to rectify the good impression he had made by pouring out the tragedy of his disease-ridden youth while Sidney listened sympathetically. When he finished, the doctor plucked aimlessly at his eyebrows and said, "So." He held out his hand in the direction of a white stool. "Would you be so kind?"

Drawing the blinds and switching on a high-intensity lamp, he peered into the patient's ears, his mouth, his eyes, a hundred and one little nooks and crannies. "And you say you have been falling of late?" he inquired.

"Definitely," responded D.C., heartened by his interest. The doctor was on to something.

"Any spots? Do you have any spots before the eyes?"

"Oh yes. Big ones."

"Tinnitus?"

"A trifle."

"Vertigo? Syncope? A terrible burning in the urine?" asked the doctor, his eyes glittering.

"Oh more, much more," volunteered D.C. with a keen sense of attainment.

"I see," the doctor frowned. "Just a moment. There is one more test I should like to perform," and saying this he left the room.

Sidney gave D.C. a brave little smile but before she could think of anything positive to say, Dr. De la Ronchas had returned with his hand behind his back. "If you would please relax," he instructed the distrustful young man and no sooner had he spoken the words than he whipped out his hand, struck a tuning fork against a metal leg of the stool, and stuffed it into the patient's ear. G sharp!

"What the hell's the big idea!" shrieked D.C., hopping up and down and holding his ear in agony.

"As I suspected," reported the doctor objectively. He snapped off the lamp and opened the blinds. "You have not lost your hearing completely, Señor, but I fear it is only a matter of time."

Although his head was still humming like a transformer, D.C. was no longer in acute pain. "Then you've found something?"

De la Ronchas nodded and stared grimly at the young man. In his quiet, homespun way he seemed fairly bursting with bad news. "The morbid change in your hearing organ was the final symptom required for diagnosis. It did not come as a surprise. After excluding such possibilities as a tumor of the cerebellopontine angle, platybasia, carotid sinus syndrome, and trauma of the head, the conclusion was inescapable. You fall," he explained, as he wiped off the tip of his tuning fork with a tissue and placed it in his breast pocket, "because you are afflicted with Menière's disease."

"Oh no!" cried Sidney, covering her mouth.

"Menière's disease," said D.C. in admiration, rolling it around on his tongue. "Menière's disease." It had style, class, the unuttered promise of incurability. De la Ronchas was playing right into his hands. The quack.

"A curious affliction," the doctor went on intently, his eyebrows offering no hope. "With Menière's we find disturbances in the blood supply to the tissues and organs of the inner ear, the hearing and balancing mechanism. The exact cause of these disturbances as yet eludes us, which is regrettable. Your Menière's is a permanent, progressive, and debilitating illness. I caution you against taking it lightly."

Sidney turned as pale as a piano key.

"That sounds terrible," exclaimed the delighted patient. "A chronic disease with no cure."

"I didn't say that," bristled the doctor, annoyed at being misunderstood. "Yours is not the first case of Menière's that I have witnessed. In fact I am always finding cases. The raisin's skin is a grape to the armed vision. Some I have cured one way, some another. For extreme conditions, there is a simple operation, a destructive labyrinthotomy, which . . ."

"Forget it," snapped D.C.

". . . I perform reluctantly. Over the years, however, I have developed the popular treatment bearing my name with which I have relieved countless sufferers. To be sure it is not a complete remedy, but it is quick, painless, and has proved effective in five out of six cases."

"Why that's grand," D.C. applauded enthusiastically. "That's the one for me."

"Very well. Then you will enter the hospital at once."

"What gives you that idea?"

The doctor's manner was long-suffering. "I do not believe you understand. The vasodilating therapy which I employ requires alternating hot and cold showers intensively during a four-hour period under the strictest supervision. The temperature of the water must be varied constantly in exact accordance with your fluctuating body heat. Have I made myself understood?"

"The University of Zaragoza hospital?" asked D.C., tense in reconnaissance.

"The University of Zaragoza hospital," acknowledged the complacent doctor.

"I've seen it. Never mind."

Stunned silence. "The foremost hospital in all of Aragon!"

"Ha, ha," quipped D.C., sarcastically.

"Three hundred sixty-four beds," the doctor argued, positively incredulous.

"Richard," broke in Sidney, mediating, "it's for your own good. You've got to cooperate."

"Not a chance."

Taking the understanding young girl aside, Dr. De la Ronchas whispered in a voice sour with disapproval, "Negative attitude."

"I heard that!" shouted D.C. accusingly.

"We're trying to help you," insisted Sidney.

"I don't care," said D. C., pouting. "I don't like secrets. Whose side are you on anyway?"

The idealistic Sidney was shocked at this lack of trust. It was no picnic atoning for two million bucks. Although she was fond of D.C., she could tell that he really didn't want her help. "I'll go, Richard," she cried, heartbroken. "You don't need me."

"Wait!" begged D.C., wavering.

"Well?" demanded De la Ronchas confidently, squeezing his pressure point. "Are you now prepared to go to the hospital?"

The air was full of omens. D.C. felt like Nero when a thunderbolt hit the Temple of the Caesars decapitating all the statues at a stroke. Bad. The sacred shields used by the Leaping Priests had not been returned to the Temple of Mars. Bad. The sacrificial victim's intestines had a pink, healthy, flourishing look. Bad.

Sidney stood wretchedly by the door. "Please Richard," she pleaded, "do it for me."

The money was tempting but D.C.'s mind was like a fist. "Never!" he cried irrevocably.

After four hours of constant immersion that shriveled his fingers and loosened his scalp, D.C. was laid out on a hospital bed to dry. His long hair streamed down into his face and the small emerald bubbles that formed on his lips were wafted away each time he exhaled. By the bedside Sidney sat quietly chewing on the edge of her scarf as she watched over him with her fingers crossed. A nurse came into the room wearing a big nun's hat that ballooned out in front of her like a flying jib. Propping the waterlogged patient up, she slapped him around until he could raise his arms in self-defense.

"Shave, Señor?" she offered cordially.

Bleary-eyed, D.C. ran his hand over his soggy stubble, smiled wanly at Sidney, and gave his consent.

The nurse wrapped a towel around his neck and returned with a bowl of hot water, soap, a shaving brush, and a straight razor. Setting her equipment down on the high table next to the bed, she wet the brush and proceeded energetically to lather up the left side of the patient's head.

"Aren't you starting a little high?" D.C. asked feebly.

She flipped open her razor expertly, muttered something unintelligible, and with a single stroke eliminated D.C.'s left sideburn. Two more swipes and she had carved out an immense arc around his ear that left it naked and shivering. Removing the towel, she wiped her hands with satisfaction, collected her tools, and made for the door.

"But what about the other side?" D.C. called after her in alarm.

She looked back, clucked sadly in reply, and left.

D.C. put his hand to his hairline and felt nothing. "What's going on around here anyway?" he complained, fully aroused.

Sidney jumped up. "No, Richard. You're not supposed to get out of bed," she informed him pedantically.

"I have to empty my bladder," was his snide comment, but the moment he put his weight on his legs they collapsed under him like melted cheese. He sat immobilized, sneering down at his feet which dangled uselessly over the edge of the bed.

"You poor dear. Don't worry. Dr. De la Ronchas is sending someone for you," she reassured him as she brushed the hair out of his eyes.

D.C. liked the feel of her pearl-smooth hand on his forehead, the tender way in which she straightened out his hospital gown, the botanical smell of her lips as she kissed his cheek, and so it seemed to him exceedingly strange that he should be cursing at the top of his lungs, pealing forth vile, fanatical, madcap oaths without letup until the doctor's man arrived.

"What took you so long?" D.C. fumed as the old orderly helped him on to the portable table he had rolled in.

The orderly pointed to his mouth and made a few non-sounds to indicate that he was a mute, smiled benignly, and strapped the patient down.

"You don't have to do that," D.C. explained. "It's just down the hall."

"Be brave, Richard," implored Sidney, waving after him and trying unsuccessfully to hide her tears as he was wheeled out of the room.

"For God's sake, I'm only going to the bathroom!" he insisted.

The table rolled along on soapbox-derby wheels and the old man ran hard to keep up.

"Slow down," cautioned D.C. restlessly as they approached the bathroom door. "You've passed it!" he screamed in terror as they flew by. Struggling frantically to get off, he tore at the black leather strap around his chest. The strap turned over. On top of a swastika that had been burned into the leather it was stamped West Germany. D.C. felt as if he were about to have a nosebleed. An awful, overpowering, disillusioned weariness—the retribution meted out to romantic audacity—numbed his stuff. Sidney had swindled him into the hospital and signed him over to the authorities to do with as they pleased. Under the claim of necessity she had worked out his final solution. Done in by a visionary teenager. The showers were only to soften him up before the invasion. He had been sold out! Cashiered! Paid off!

The free-wheeling table crashed through the swinging doors of the operating room and was caught by two attendants, Laurel and Hardy. Dr. De la Ronchas, dressed in a pea-green cap and gown, came over to have a look.

"See here, Ronchas!" bellowed D.C., outraged, "this thing has gone far enough."

"What do you mean?" asked the doctor softly, while wrapping

the hanging ties around his cap and making a small bow in front.
"You said five out of six cases were helped by your treatment. Five out of six you said."

"Yours is the sixth," he reported regretfully. "I am not eager to perform this operation, yet it must be done." He motioned to the attendants who wheeled the table into the center of the room and positioned it under a large, swivel-necked spotlight, slipping caster cups under the wheels to prevent it from rolling away during the excitement of the operation.

It was a demonstration room. The students peered down at him as if it were "Dr. Tulp's Anatomy Lesson." Already they were lifted out of their seats by curiosity and the operation hadn't even begun. Eager bastards! Always bucking for grades. D.C.'s mournful eyes picked out a priest among them, no doubt a medical student, but the opened notebook on his lap looked so much like a Bible that it made him sick. Through the swinging doors entered De la Ronchas' brilliantly gowned assistants, a flashy lot. They were either color-coded or a minor league pickup team wearing their own uniforms. Hardy, the fat attendant, carried over a beat-up garbage can that smelled like the red tide of the Pacific and set it down under his nose.

"Doctor, you're making a grotesque mistake," pleaded D.C., in a frenzied last-ditch effort to escape.

"Be tranquil," advised De la Ronchas. "Your life is in good hands."

"But aren't you going to wash them?"

"I wear gloves," replied the nettled doctor, resentfully snapping on a pair of rubber ones. "*Dämmerschlaf*," he ordered.

"What?" D.C. eagerly inquired, hoping it meant that the doctor had had a last minute change of heart.

He hadn't. D.C. shrieked. From behind someone had just stuck a needle into him.

While they waited for the anesthetic to take effect, the medical team kneeled down on the operating room floor. They were praying but there was nothing that D.C. could do about it. A rebellion was going on in his nerve endings turning him into a neutral observer.

"*Señores,*" announced Dr. De la Ronchas, getting up, "*vamos a ver.*" He tied on his surgical mask and led his assistants to the operating table.

A blinding light went on and D.C. heard the doctor say, "I notice that you are circumcised." The head bent over him was mounted on a green umbrella and there hiding out behind the mask was the inevitable Pock Mark. Under the circumstances D.C. felt that it was good to see a familiar face.

Dr. De la Ronchas cut into D.C.'s flesh just behind the left ear —a sharp scalpel, a beautiful incision—and deftly removed the outer wall of his aditus to expose his middle ear. The tiny bone called the incus was dead ahead, just where it should be. Several students up front applauded. So far so good. A yellow-gowned assistant held a suction hose to D.C.'s head, slurping up the blood in noisy asthmatic gulps while the doctor sized up the obstacle. In order to gain access to the vestibule of the inner ear he had to drill a small horizontal canal through the incus, and D.C.'s was an unusually delicate one, only slightly larger than a thorn from a rose bush. A gambler, De la Ronchas was willing to try anything once. He called for his powerful motor-driven burr and with a light hand resolutely blasted away.

D.C. recognized the sound of Valley Forge, George Washington's rag-covered feet tramping around on his ear drum. It will never work, said George. Never, never, never, never, never. It can't be done, Schlemovitz. Assimilation without identification is anarchy! A man without a past is a man without a country! Give me history or give me death!

Shutting off his burr, the doctor put a jeweler's glass to his eye and squinted into the hole he had made. The vestibule lay before him like the dark side of the moon. Elated, he snapped the glass from his eye and, turning, struck his head against that of his grape-colored right-hand man who himself was trying to get a peek.

"*¿Tiene los escombros?*" the doctor asked irritably.

His assistant's eyes dove under his surgical mask in shame. He had been so engrossed in the actual drilling that he had failed to collect the flying debris, the microscopic bone chips and dust that were needed to fill up the canal after the destruction of the labyrinth. Dropping to the floor, he produced an elfin dustpan and brush from under his gown and penitently proceeded to sweep up whatever he could find as the doctor observed him in rigid silence. Incredulous, De la Ronchas circled about the stooped figure, and seeing what was going into the dustpan, he lost his appetite. He returned to the operating table in an unsettled state of mind and, snapping his fingers impatiently, called for his needle. An anxious nurse hurried forward on low heels with a three-inch platinum needle, but in her haste to place it in his outstretched palm she pierced his rubber glove. Plucking it out like Androcles, the doctor glared homicidally at the trembling hulk and she fled. Struggling for composure, De la Ronchas took the needle between his thumb and index finger—holding it as if it were a pencil—and tried to thread the canal. Once . . . twice . . . the more he jabbed about, the more rattled he became.

On a distant skateboard, rumbling like an oncoming subway, Death was hot-dogging it over to D.C. The old fata morgana was sailing along dressed in a black alpaca coat and hat and sporting a yellow Star of David on his right sleeve. Fat-cat hodaddy hanging five, hanging eight, hanging ten, he flipped out and came up smiling Chub, Warner M.

"*Fashtaist mame loshen?*" queried Chub.

D.C. closed his eyes in resignation. "A *bissel,*" he replied faintly, and temporarily gave up the ghost.

The doctor's gown was wringing wet and perspiration flowed over his glabella and down the sides of his nose as if they were rain gutters. He barked and the chastened nurse flew over, tentatively soaked up the drippings with sterile gauze, and got out of his way just as soon as possible. Crouched over in extremity, Dr. De la Ronchas leered at the opening. He cleared his throat of vibrations, steadied his aim by taking hold of his wrist with his left hand, flicked his eyes to heaven, lunged forward, and truly hit the bull's-eye. Ave Maria! Then slowly . . . painstakingly . . . with excruciating care, with ineffable control, he fed the needle into the canal. The point passed through the bone, into the vestibule, and gently nudged up against its anterior wall. One slip now, one involuntary twitch, and he would strike the facial nerve. De la Ronchas held his breath.

"*¡Cuidado!*" cautioned someone in the gallery.

The doctor boggled, wheezed eerily, and glared over his shoulder in search of revenge. The students sat with downcast eyes, taking notes ferociously. De la Ronchas snorted in scorn and resumed the operation. Withdrawing the needle from where it had lodged in the patient's seventh cranial nerve, he pressed it toward the medial wall of the vestibule and signaled for the destruction of the labyrinth to begin. At once an assistant hooked up the end of the needle to the portable Volksreizmittel electrosurgical unit while another selected a dial setting of 18 and turned on the juice. Three quick doses and it was all over. D.C.'s sea-shell-elegant membranous labyrinth had been therapeutically fried, third-railed into health. De la Ronchas seemed satisfied. Handing over his needle, he distastefully accepted the floor scrapings and plugged up the canal, saving the few authentic bone chips till last and thereby achieving an excellent cosmetic result. He examined his work critically and found it acceptable. Peeled off his gloves. Untied his mask. Grape-gown would sew up the patient. The gallery rose in tribute and gave the doctor an uninhibited, wildly enthusiastic, standing ovation. Glancing contemptuously at them as he passed, De la Ronchas stalked out of the operating room with their cheers ringing in his auditory canals.

As soon as the doctor came through the swinging doors, Sidney, who had been crying in the hallway for over two hours, rushed up to him expectantly.

"I do *not* like to operate," De la Ronchas stated decisively, still a bit wound up. "I have *never* cared for it. Ever since my first cadaver..."

"Is he all better, Doctor?" Sidney interrupted, as jittery as a sparrow.

The doctor removed his cap and used it to dry off his face, his hands, the back of his neck. He surveyed the frail, hollow-eyed, tear-stained teen-ager in cool silence, judging her capacity for pain.

"What is it?" pleaded Sidney, terrified at seeing the blood on his gown.

"Understand," he warned, "I am not apologizing. I never apologize. Under the circumstances events went as well as could be expected."

"He's dead," Sidney concluded.

"Not at all."

"I know he is. I feel it in my knuckles. I have E.S.P."

"He is *not* dead," insisted the miffed doctor irascibly. "I have never lost a Menière's. My record is irreproachably spotless."

"He was so young. His whole life before him and all. Like me." Sidney bit hard on her finger to hold back the tears.

"Narcissistic hysteria," diagnosed the doctor. "*Mira*," he said sternly, shaking some sense into the young girl. "Without fear of contradiction I swear to you that the operation has been a partial success. I have thoroughly eliminated the tinnitus, the nystagmus, the vertigo."

Sidney smiled gratefully at him through watery eyes full of admiration.

"However," the doctor went on empirically, "we must bear our crosses. Your husband will now be totally deaf in his left ear. Yet his hearing was going anyway so that is no great loss. The paralysis of his facial muscles is fortunately restricted to but a single side of his face which will leave one perfect profile. Enough for anyone. Of greater concern to me is his center of gravity. I believe it has been subtly altered by this operation. My professional opinion is that henceforth your husband will always walk at a 45° angle to the ground. He will not fall anymore because of Menière's, Señora, but, considering his angle, I suggest that he be watched around the clock."

The agony of her husband reduced to an acute pulp settled in Sidney's joints, stiffening them like calcium deposits, and as the students burst noisily out of the operating room and crowded past her, they were hushed by her motionless, inviolable figure, gazing sightlessly ahead, mantled with a tragic grandeur.

To a Spaniard, only death merited such heroism. "I will not argue with you anymore," said the exasperated doctor, striding off. "Go in and see for yourself."

Sidney had never felt so needed before. Although she hated to limit herself, here was someone who was the epitome of everything that she wanted in life, who summed it up like a historical marker. Seeing a priest come out, she impulsively grabbed on to him and explained the unusual situation. She argued Jesuitically that if death-bed conversions were binding, post-operative marriages fell into the same category. Snared by her logic, the priest waived the formalities and together they rushed into the recovery room where almost before D.C. had come out of the anesthetic, the two lovers were pronounced man and wife.

CHAPTER 21

🐚 A scheme so heinous that it naturally succeeds, or Pearson is re-bagged.

"Your spade work did it, Ivan."

"Absolutely!"

"We never could have done as well without you."

"You've opened up the territory, young man. When we get back to Washington, Senator Pettidrooper will hear of this. The government can be proud of employees like you. But if some-day . . . if someday you should ever choose to do anything in the private sector of our economy I want you to know that there will always be a place for your talents at Ackermann's Tool and Die. My card for future reference."

"And mine."

"And mine."

Fifteen happy businessmen in white shirts and nylon socks, star sapphires on their pinkies and Florsheims on their toes, were clumped together in the doorway of INTRA's Zaragoza offices at the Grand Hotel to say farewell to the bearded whizz-kid whose contacts had made their trip so successful. Pocketing their invitations, Ivan fidgeted uncomfortably with the two-foot-high trophy that they had just presented to him (a testimonial of their affection) as he waited to shut the door.

"Couldn't you have gotten one more appropriate to the occasion, Krump?" protested Ackermann, distressed by the sailboat topping the golden column of the trophy.

"It was all they had," whined Krump, shrugging his shoulders impotently. "But I'm sure Ivan knows how we feel about him anyway."

"I know," said Ivan, rattling the doorknob.

"You see." Krump was relieved. "How much longer will you be staying on, Ivan?"

"A couple of days," Ivan estimated. "I have a few odds and ends to wrap up here first. Then on to Washington to make my final report. But if I don't get started soon"—he laughed engagingly and forced them out the door—"it may be weeks."

"So long, old buddy."

"See you in Washington."

"Hope your friend feels better."

"Say Ivan," called a big red-headed wag with several pounds of inflamed mustache drooping from his upper lip, "as long as you're hanging around why don't you go out to the base and help them find what they're looking for. If you come up with it they'll make you a general."

"But no one knows *what* they're looking for," Krump advised in a worried voice.

Red whacked Krump playfully with his order-laden briefcase. "That's what makes it tricky," he giggled piercingly. "You think it's easy to become a general?"

Ivan slammed the door. He knew what the Air Force was looking for. The question was how to use the information. Three days before, a Globemaster transport heavy with United States canned goods, fresh lettuce, and moisture lotion destined for the Zaragoza PX had crashed into a hillside about a half-mile away from the base. Nothing remarkable. An accident. They happened every day. The *Heraldo* carried a small article on an inside page. But since then strange things had been going on at the crash site. A thousand men wearing what appeared from a distance to be polyethylene bags on top of their uniforms (as if their garments had all been recently dry-cleaned) were combing the area and no one was permitted to enter it without authorization. Floodlights had been set up in a giant perimeter around the wreckage which MPs patrolled with congenital sneers and killer dogs, firing their machine guns at anything that moved. Air-tight security. Even the phlegmatic *Heraldo* had become curious.

Having sorted out the facts, Ivan decided to delay his departure. If an orphan didn't use his wits and take advantage of his opportunities, though he might become an angel in the next world, he would never become a general in this one. He removed fifteen business cards from his pocket. Unwilling to die of boredom, he tweaked the stack in half and dropped the embossed pieces into his wastebasket. The crash of the transport wasn't yet an international incident, but Ivan was confident that he had the material to work with.

"Still brooding?" he asked, entering Ambrose Winkie's old office.

Huddled in a corner of the slip-covered couch with his legs drawn up under his chin was Pearson Causley looking better than ever. His face had filled out and with his overseas cap tilted back on his head he exuded a he-man, out-of-doors, home-on-the-range robustness. Coiled up, he resembled Teddy Roosevelt preparing to charge. His gaze was vacuous, but so remarkably vacuous that it bordered on intensity and he seemed to be lying in wait like some sly, patient, heavy-lidded predator. Lackadaisically rubbing his chin on his knees, Pearson mumbled, "Sort of."

"Want to come for a walk?"

"I guess not."

"You've been holed up in here since you arrived. Personally, I couldn't care less. I like strong smells. But don't you want some exercise?"

"Why?"

"How about a rubber of twenty-one?"

"I don't think so."

"Poker?"

". . . I don't know."

"Euchre? Écarté? Napoleon? Gaigel? Zioncheck? Crapette?

Boat House Rum?" Irritated, Ivan offered him a host of squelching possibilities.

Unable to cope with them, Pearson sighed heavily and suggested, "Maybe a little later."

"Suit yourself," said Ivan with such complete indifference that it was difficult to believe that he was the one who had first raised the subject. Although he had been mildly curious to see how the Army had altered his old school chum, Ivan found the incapacitated reality painfully distasteful. If by the purest chance Pearson's arrival had turned out to be a blessing in disguise, the disguise was nevertheless odious.

"You could give that stuff to the hotel," Ivan recommended, suppressing his rancor. The taut laundry line that Pearson had strung across the room supported his efflorescent khaki shorts, socks, and handkerchiefs. "I'll cover the bill," he volunteered.

Pearson cringed. "I'm used to doing my own," he declared, childishly possessive, as if his scooter were being threatened.

Ivan poker-faced him in silence.

Grinning sheepishly, Pearson avoided his friend's eye and buried his chin between his knees. "I like to do my own," he confided. "By hand they come out fluffy."

Ivan made no comment. Idly he picked up one of Pearson's jewel-like combat boots from where it stood glittering at attention before the pleated skirts of the couch.

The ex-soldier's eyes popped out of their sockets like those of a gored soprano. "You'll smudge it," he shrieked temperamentally, and snatched the boot away from his friend. Using the short end of his tie, he erased the fingerprints with fanatical devotion and returned the polished gem to the floor. He glanced across at Ivan whose expression accused him of losing his cool. Pearson flattened himself back into his snug corner of the couch.

"Thanks for letting me sponge off you like this," he offered in repentance, making up. "Don't think I'm not grateful. If I hadn't been able to track you down I don't know what I would have done." He pushed his cap down low over his forehead and added with an affecting simplicity, "You and D.C. are my only real friends on the outside."

"I told you," chided Ivan, covering that wearisome ground again, "we lost touch."

"That's right," acknowledged Pearson apologetically. "But you were the one I really wanted to see. You always could figure out the score. I thought maybe you might help me decide what to do now that I've been demilitarized."

"I've been working on it," Ivan revealed.

"It's not easy. I mean to come out after you've been in the service for a while. You sort of get accustomed to things being done a certain way. But I'll find myself soon. Don't worry, it's just a question of getting my feet on the ground and when I do I'll pay you back . . . every cent."

"I hope so," said Ivan firmly.

Pearson relished his friend's dry humor and his laughter came out in short, constipated blurts, a repetitive sound that might have been the last vestigial evidence of his stutter. But all at once and for no apparent reason he sank into a disquieting hebetude and only gradually did something like vitality—uneasiness—creep into his face.

"You know," he said in a vague way, sorting out his thoughts like cinder blocks, "it's odd. For years you live with certain ideas about yourself and then one day you find out that they're not you at all. It's Pythagorean, like discovering you're wearing somebody else's pants. I guess the reason I never realized that I was a joiner is that no one ever asked me to join anything before. It's not a sell-out. I liked the Army. . . . No kidding, I really did. It was like a home to me. Better than mine. Regular hours! No loose ends! Security! You went by the book and there was only one that you had to read." Pearson caressed the chevrons on his arm. "I was a corporal," he recalled wistfully.

Ivan, who had been massaging his gums as his friend spoke, now wet them down with his tongue making powerful, obscene, sucking noises. "You've changed," he observed philosophically.

Cautious of what civilian life held for a changed man, Pearson replied, "It's hard to say."

"Definitely," exclaimed Ivan, shaking his beard with patriarchal authority and brooking no opposition. "The Army's been good to you. You look healthy. You don't stutter any more. You've got a fresh *Weltanschauung*. And you've picked up some post-graduate credits in your major. Pigeon," he concluded, "you're a new man."

"I loved my work," admitted Pearson. "The equipment we had! The things we made!" He was becoming positively animated. "The whole team volatizing together! It was wonderful."

"Ah, yes," exclaimed Ivan, as if reminding himself of something. "Speaking of your accomplishments, are you certain that Zyrian was aboard the plane that crashed?"

"Zyrian," repeated its maker with parental fondness. "The last word! The ultimate weapon!"

"But was it aboard?"

"Absolutely," cried Pearson, with sensational definitiveness. Eyes luminous, metabolizing exorbitantly, he was all professional. "It can only be Zyrian. We're stockpiling it around the world just in case. You see," he explained with snappy military gestures, "we always move it in transports rather than bombers as a cover. Allays suspicion. We smuggle it in with the PX supplies as sporting goods."

"I see," said Ivan, slowly nodding his head in appreciation.

"Packed in volleyballs," disclosed Pearson, tickled with the ingenuity of it.

"Remarkable!" Ivan urged him to continue.

"Since it permeates most everything the big problem was finding a shipping container," he informed him confidentially. "That is it *was* a problem until one day some guy brought his lunch in a Baggie and it worked. Held our weapon like a tuna fish sandwich. A real breakthrough and after that we hit on the idea of making the bladders of our balls two-ply polyethylene. Gee . . ." a nostalgic quiver in his ruddy lips, "I miss the old gang."

"Exactly how dangerous is Zyrian?" prodded Ivan.

Pearson seemed pleased with the question. "Maybe this will give you some idea. It's SOP for a plane to carry *four* twenty-megaton nuclear bombs, but we allowed only *one* regulation-size volleyball per shipment."

"And what if they never find it?"

Pearson scoffed at the Nervous Nelly. "We'll find it," he

reported confidently. "It probably rolled away on impact and some kid picked it up. There's nothing to worry about. I mean there are all kinds of built-in safety devices on the ball. Seamless construction, reinforced rubber surface, heavy-duty combination-locked pin in the pin hole. A fully tested piece of equipment."

"But what about prolonged exposure to the elements?" persisted Ivan critically.

"Prolonged exposure," echoed Pearson. He wavered like a broken calla lily and cast his eyes about balefully as if suddenly realizing that he was no longer the handmaiden of Mars. ". . . I don't know," he muttered helplessly. Drained by uncertainty and as colorless as his gas, the ex-soldier fell into a profound, unmitigated, thanatoidal sleep.

Ivan's next step was to pay a visit to the commander of the base, his Zaragoza friend Colonel Bouchbelt. Going out of town in the taxi, a picturesque bullet-ridden relic of the Spanish Civil War, he sat in the rear on a throne-like seat that raised him close to the roof and studied the terrain. Erosion honeycombed the land. Ivan looked with contentment on Nature's handiwork, a marvelous web of intricate gulleys and underground caverns any one of which might have concealed septillions of puny man-made spheres without a trace. As the taxi drew near to the base, a stilted red-and-white–checkered water tower could be seen hovering over it like an archetypal volleyball, an immane totem mocking the search.

The soldier on duty at the guardhouse was a sharp-looking little fellow with a white scarf, a white holster, and a big brown gun. He listened to Ivan's account of his business but made no secret of the fact that he didn't believe a word of it. Keeping Hairy Beatnik under surveillance, he picked up his phone and called headquarters. The Colonel was too busy to see anyone. Ushering the pariah back into his waiting taxi, he slammed the door and placed his hands on his hips as haughty as a puffin. "I had you pegged for a queer bill right away," he said smugly. "You talk too good English. Beat it," he ordered the driver, who stripped the gears mercilessly in his haste to get away. Ivan leaned back in his seat and chuckled softly to himself. He had found out what he wanted to know. Bouchbelt was at the crash site and Zyrian was still on the loose. *"Prisa! Prisa!"* he called to the wild-eyed driver as the taxi left the paved approach to the American base and thundered on to the Spanish cobblestones. Ivan was very eager to get back to the hotel.

The following morning when he lifted his *persianas* at the Grand where he now comfortably resided, Ivan witnessed a huge, angry, tumultuous, placard-carrying crowd passing in the street below. There were people of all ages and of both sexes, waving their fists and shouting as they went. It was but one of many similar demonstrations spontaneously organized by the police that occurred throughout the city that day. The signs read *FEO* AMERICANS and GASSERS GO HOME and when a group tired and broke up, the officers collected the signs and distributed them in another part of town. The *Heraldo* was officially grim and tight-lipped but before the day was over the Russians had once again walked out at Geneva, the President had pleaded ignorance, Colonel Bouchbelt had sworn that there was no present danger to public health or safety, and at the Teatro Argensola they were singing:

Under mounting pressure, the Colonel hurriedly summoned his senior officers to the subterranean war room whose low ceiling and insulated walls compounded the sense of urgency that they all shared. For more than two hours they met in secret session, brain-storming furiously, hacking their tortuous way through countless layers of ramifications until at last they came to a decision that pleased everyone. It was so ravishingly simple that it was amazing no one had thought of it before. They would merely send another fully-laden Globemaster into the air carrying a dummy volleyball, deliberately crash it in the identical spot, and watch to see where the ball bounced. The Colonel, who was not given to compliments, dismissed the meeting by saying, "Thank you, gentlemen," which for him was tantamount to ecstatic delirium.

Every available man was put into the field and from a high tower that had been hastily erected at the crash site, Colonel Bouchbelt directed the operation with gusto. Using a bull horn, he promised an immediate court-martial to any blockhead who dared to lay a finger on the ball before it came to rest. "Look sharp, now!" he bellowed, as the enormous plane started its dive and three parachutes broke out into the clear. "A weekend pass to the man who spots it first." Highly motivated, the soldiers pressed forward, their hands stuffed in their armpits as a precaution, and tightening their circle around the rubble of the first plane, they left barely any room for the wreckage of the second. Demographically speaking, the human density was immense and the plummeting transport seemed to be heading straight for the population center. The plane's engines had been shut off and it made surprisingly little noise as it descended, its black snub nose swelling syphilitically and covering the crowd like a gruesome shadow. One impressionable soldier looked up and screamed, but the rest, with supreme confidence in technology, kept their disciplined eyes glued sublimely on the tiny clearing in their midst. "Hold your ground!" exhorted the Colonel. It appeared that the carnage would rival the Crusade of the Innocents, but at the very last moment the plane veered as if someone were still at the controls and slipped silently into the empty pocket with freakish accuracy. A mushroom-shaped cloud rose lazily above the wreck as it thunderously disintegrated, debris falling like Cartesian reality in a precisely calculated pattern inches short of the bystanders. It was a miracle of planning, not a scratch on anyone. While pieces of metal still glowed with the heat, the eager soldiers rushed forward into the fuliginous mess in quest of the ball. By nightfall they were still there, milling about the ice-cold wreckage with tired eyes as they shuffled their way disconsolately through the charred lettuce leaves. Perched high on his lonely tower, the Colonel stood small and remote against the darkening sky, forgotten like a burning cigarette.

Ivan allowed twenty-four hours to go by in which he sat back and watched Spanish-American relations disappear before phoning his friends. By the time Colonel Bouchbelt burst through the door of Ivan's suite several people were already there hashing over the situation. The Colonel brushed blindly past them and confronting Ivan demanded to know "Where is it?" with a weird, slide-whistle, rising inflection.

Ivan glanced over the Colonel's shoulder at the two monstrous civilians who had come in with him and who now leaned with their backs against the door blocking the exit while casually munching on Indian nuts, shells and all. "Patience," he advised gently.

"You said you had it and that's why I'm here. This is no game, Storch," warned Bouchbelt, whose sense of humor even under normal circumstances was limited to a single story of an old buddy who had fired his ejection seat before opening the canopy of his plane. "I want that ball and I want it now!"

"All in good time. I believe you know these gentlemen."

The Colonel, who had grown up in the lumbering country of northern Oregon, longed to impale Storch on a hooked peavey but looking about, he saw that they were not alone. Also in the room were the Spanish Minister of Commerce (Señor de Merida) and the Bishop of Zaragoza, both of whom wore sinisterly curved dark glasses, and the American ambassador, the ex-polo champion and ever youthful S. Dudley Warble, who appeared depressed and uncomfortable in his kid gloves and velvet collar. Bouchbelt nodded belligerently.

"Before we begin," proceeded Ivan, scrutinizing the scene with the consummate poise of a seasoned diplomat, "I want to know what Sammy Jay and Tod Lee are doing here?" He had remembered their lithoidal faces from the sports pages when they played on the line for Texas Pentecostal Holiness—left mugger and right crusher, respectively.

The Colonel seemed angered that Ivan knew his friends. "CIA," he owned up crossly.

Without a word, Señor de Merida picked up his briefcase and started for the door.

"They'll have to go," Ivan told Bouchbelt, and clinging to the minister's thrashing coattails, he growled, "Get rid of them!"

In his four-button blue jacket with its four, buttoned patch pockets, Colonel Bouchbelt stood foursquare, the very image of obdurate symmetry, until his eye fell upon the pained expression pinching the face of S. Dudley Warble. "All right," he gave in. "But not too far away boys, *understand?*"

Sammy Jay and Tod Lee winked back slyly to show that they did, and hulking out into the hallway, they crouched down beside the three Spanish secret policemen who already had their ears to the wall.

When they were gone, Ivan apologized gallantly to Señor de Merida for the Colonel's undiplomatic behavior, an apology heartily endorsed by the Ambassador, while Bouchbelt, the statesman in spite of himself, winced in silence. "Now," said Ivan, "I think we can begin." Unlocking the deep bottom drawer of his desk, he dried his hands on the rear of his shabby pants and tenderly removed the volleyball inside.

"Aaaah!" said Ambassador Warble with pleasure.

"Aaaah!" said the Minister with relief.

"Slowly," said the Bishop, spiritually helping Ivan ease the ball out of the drawer.

"But how did *you* get it?" the exasperated Colonel demanded to know, as if the young man weren't qualified. He approached the ball with impenetrable suspicion.

"Your curiosity is natural enough," said Ivan tolerantly, and held the Colonel off by throwing a nasty straight-arm in his face. "But don't be hasty." Cradling the ball under his arm, he turned to Señor de Merida. "Merely for the sake of argument," he suggested in a sportive mood, "let's say that this isn't the missing gas bag. What do you think of that?"

The Minister who was built like a tooth—large crown and

spidery underpinning—teetered perceptibly. "Do not jest, Señor." Scowling. "My government insists that your country live up to its original agreement for the use of our bases or if not we will be forced to take the necessary steps."

"*Your* bases!" shrilled Bouchbelt derisively.

"*Our* bases," contended the crimson-faced Minister, stamping his foot. "There are *no* Amercian bases in Spain. There are only Americans."

"You're perfectly right," pacified Ambassador Warble, and he bathed Bouchbelt in the molten fury of his unutterable displeasure.

Calmly pursuing his hypothesis, Ivan asked the Colonel, "And you?" He patted the ball gingerly. "If this isn't the one you're looking for?"

The Colonel appeared sick. "I don't want to talk about it," he replied spitefully.

Ivan laughed with indulgence for he understood the military mind's low threshold for idle speculation. He took the ball from under his arm and held it in his hands. "All things considered," he said presently, addressing the Ambassador and loading his words like dice, "I think you'll find everything in order." And with that he flicked his wrists and the ball shot across the room Warble-ward.

"Aggggh!" gasped the alarmed Bishop, clutching his throat.

The Ambassador, whose right arm had instinctively swung back as if he held a spectral mallet, recovered in the nick of time, to trap the missile against his pump-slosh-palpitating heart. It wasn't that he believed the volleyball was dangerous but he simply hated to fumble a good pass. He turned the ball over in his hands and smiled affluently. "Yes," he concurred, "this looks fine, Mr. Storch."

Colonel Bouchbelt wanted to see for himself. He marched forth-rightly up to the Ambassador, bent forward, and ran his eyes over the ball. He pointed to the trademark. "It isn't a Voit," he cackled contemptuously.

Ambassador Warble staggered and paled over, the color even seeping out of his eyes, eyes that had once been a sunny, vivacious, springtime green and now resembled martini onions.

"I DON'T CARE!" bellowed Bouchbelt, defensively, calling on a higher allegiance. He grabbed the ball away from the grim Ambassador. "It doesn't feel like a Voit. It doesn't look like a Voit." He slammed the ball down on the floor. "And it doesn't bounce like a Voit. This ball," he summed up fervently, exhilarated by his heady commitment to truth, "is not a Voit."

Struggling to maintain his self-control, Warble twisted the silver eagle on Bouchbelt's shoulder as if it were his nose. "This isn't loose, is it, Colonel?"

The Colonel whimpered as if it *had* been his nose. "But it's not our ball," he said plaintively.

"You're mistaken," Warble advised him with frosty finality.

Once again Señor de Merida started for the door.

"Please," said Ivan, restraining him and snatching the volley-ball out of the Colonel's arms. "I believe I can clarify the situation. The alleged gas in question," he quickly explained to the impatient Minister, "is colorless, odorless, and tasteless. Therefore by all popular standards it doesn't exist. Am I correct?"

"Perhaps," hedged the skeptical minister.

"On the other hand there is the palpable container. What the public wants is something it can see, it can smell, it can sink its teeth into. The public demands a volleyball and"—holding it up in triumph—"here it is."

"But it seems it's the wrong one," Señor de Merida cynically pointed out to him.

"Only at first glance," Ivan asserted coolly. "A careful examination will convince you that it's the *right* one." Ivan threw the ball to him. "It may not bounce well in this room or on the cobblestones outside but just imagine how it's going to skip along on your new high-speed superhighway to Madrid."

"I begin to see the drift of your thoughts," said the Minister in admiration, looking the ball over with keen interest. "But do you see any of our new mighty warplanes flying over our new superhighway?" he wondered, tossing the ball to the Ambassador.

"I see them," exclaimed Warble prophetically. "Can't you see them, Colonel?" He rammed the ball into Bouchbelt's insensitive stomach.

The Colonel looked up sullenly. "Airacobras," he replied, and heaved the ball at Señor de Merida who squeezed it in delight. Bouchbelt took a quiet sadistic pleasure in knowing that nowhere on earth were spare parts available for these vintage craft.

"Airacobras," repeated the enraptured Minister and passed the ball off to his friend the Bishop to see what he could make of it.

No longer fearful, the Bishop flirted openly with the ball, dribbling it between his feet soccer-style and unabashedly cavorting about the room.

Ivan's discerning ear detected the rustle of paper counterfeiting silk under his swirling cassock. An insignificant vanity but an endearing one. "Perhaps the Bishop would like a new cathedral?" he offered voluptuously.

"Marvelous!" cried the flushed, breathless Bishop, and cleverly snapping the ball up with his instep he butted it back to the Ambassador. "Do you think"—panting—"that we might break the ground next month? I have my birthday," he disclosed shyly.

"God mustn't be kept waiting," replied Warble considerately and flipped the ball to Ivan who passed it to the Colonel who hurled it to the Minister who fed it to the Bishop and so it went, from hand to hand, sailing about the room like a divinely ordered planet making its harmonious appointed rounds.

Overflowing with melic concord, the blissful Señor de Merida rushed around the circle embracing the Americans. "*Amigos mios*," he cried, clasping them one after the other. Bouchbelt submitted with ill-concealed distaste. "Henceforth there shall be no secrets between us," the Minister swore optimistically, and to prove good faith at least on his part he produced the mysterious letter that had unmasked Zyrian and presented it to Ambassador Warble. "Anonymous letters are worthless letters," he poohpoohed. "There is no foreign gas in Spain."

With extreme cordiality, mutual backslapping, and polyphonic expressions of undying devotion, the two Spaniards departed and the incident was closed.

"Well, Colonel," observed the Ambassador when they were alone, "*you* certainly turned out to be a dim-witted, hydrocephalic, fumbling, fog-bound, pea-brained horse's ass."

"Goddamned foreigners," muttered Bouchbelt, and it was evident from the way in which he avoided the Ambassador's glare that he considered everyone but himself in this category.

Warble made a curt mental note to have the Colonel disemboweled as soon as possible and turned toward Ivan like the dappled dawn. "Your country is proud of you," he gushed. "Your handling of this situation has been nothing short of brilliant. I don't know how I can thank you enough, Mr. Storch."

"You'll come up with something," Ivan assured him pleasantly.

"A diplomatic coup!" marveled the Ambassador. He studied Ivan solemnly and out of the blue asked, "Are you a registered member of either one of our two great political parties?"

"Not officially."

"But which one do you favor," he pursued cunningly.

"The one in power," Ivan responded without a moment's hesitation.

The Ambassador removed his glove and laid his bare palm on Ivan's shoulder as if he were knighting him. "I believe I can help you," he said beaming.

Colonel Bouchbelt appeared jealous. In his vexation he muttered to himself, producing a babel of terrible, deformed, homuncular thoughts and cracked his knuckles as if each one were an Ivan. "If I ever find out who wrote that letter I'll—" Bouchbelt subsided. As still as a dry gulch. He had blown his mind in a single mighty surge of psychic expansion and as his eyes blazed forth with sudden intelligence a tiny scab fell from his heart. "There's been a leak in security," he reported to the Ambassador.

"Well done!" said Warble, damning with faint praise, and he shared the joke with Ivan.

"And *there* it is," snarled the Colonel, putting the finger on the Ambassador's queer-eyed favorite. "How did he know that Zyrian was colorless, odorless, and tasteless?"

Despite its unlikely origin, the question was a good one. "How *did* you know about that?" inquired Warble sympathetically, more curious than anything else.

Although his well-trained limbs were totally composed, Ivan's mouth seemed to disappear into his beard like a hermit. It wasn't that he had failed to anticipate this question—for in fact he had created it—but the beauty of its ontology had momentarily taken his breath away. His pleasure was a clear-channel station to the source, as pure as machinery. He could no more be explained as self-seeking than you could dismiss a clock as ambitious or a mountain or the dynamo innocence of the sea. "I'm sorry," he apologized, and raised his good eye. "What did you say?"

"The gas, Mr. Storch. How did you happen to know the properties of the gas?"

"Oh that," answered Ivan off-handedly. "My friend told me all about it."

Warble felt a malignant lump in his throat. "But that's classified information," he pointed out in a gentle voice so as not to alarm the young man.

"COCK AND BULL!" Bouchbelt thundered incredulously. "What friend?"

Apparently insulted, Ivan threw open the door to the inner office and growled, "That one."

The Colonel looked in at the soldier curled up like a fetus and felt such absolute funereal disappointment that he couldn't speak. The transference of his anger was a slow, agonizing process. "Boys," he called, somewhat melancholy at first, but getting his full voice, "BOYS!"

Without bothering to turn the knob, Sammy Jay and Tod Lee simply overran the door and hurtled monstrously into the room. Following the Colonel's instructions, they dragged the dazed soldier to his feet and bent his wrists like bananas.

"Who are you?" grunted Pearson in acute pain, but unable to suppress his curiosity.

"*We'll* ask the questions," snapped Sammy Jay testily. He let Tod Lee go first, but Tod Lee couldn't think of any. Sammy Jay ground his heel into the floor, brooding. Stumped. "Aw shit," he admitted forlornly, "we're from the CIA. What's this deal all about anyhow?"

"He's a traitor. A disgrace to the uniform he's wearing," charged the Colonel righteously, spitting on the prisoner.

Warble shook Ivan's hand. "As you've so eloquently demonstrated, Mr. Storch, loyalty to country comes before all other loyalties." Stalking up to the captive, the Ambassador struck him across the cheek with his glove. "You spy," he said reproachfully.

Despite his throbbing wrists, Pearson smiled back with real warmth.

Warble was astonished. Bemused by anarchy. Unrepentant lout, thought the irate Ambassador. "Take him away," he said in disgust.

"Hold on." Ivan went to the desk and picked up the typewriter that was there. "You'd better take this." He stuffed it under Sammy Jay's arm. "It may be the one on which that letter was written."

"That's quick thinking," exclaimed Warble, his voice stirred with tribute. "Very good!"

Ivan tapped his head with his index finger. "Twenty-four hours a day," he said wryly.

The Colonel turned away, sickened by their intimacy, and snarled, "Come on!"

Crunching the typewriter under his arm and tightening his clamp on the prisoner, Sammy Jay nodded his heavy-headed thanks to Ivan and notified him respectfully, "This is sure gonna make you a big firebird back home."

"I know," Ivan said.

As Pearson was being led away, he and Ivan looked at one another. "Don't feel bad," called Pearson kindly, nestled between the two giants. "I wasn't equipped for the real world anymore. I just couldn't get the hang of it. You were right, the Army made a new man out of me."

Although Colonel Bouchbelt would have preferred the smart aleck, he seemed pleased that he was not leaving empty-handed.

Alone, Ivan wandered into the inner office that had known so many of his old friends. He hadn't noticed that Pearson in his hurry to leave had gone off without his boots, but there they were glittering on the floor and Ivan had to admit that they made him feel just a little sad. The hard truth was that Pigeon had been educated out of his environment. He had undergone an ecological mutation. But once again he had given himself up to the destructive element and he seemed to be blooming in it. Love produces love concluded Ivan and he was happy for him. Knowing how much his friend prized his boots, Ivan picked them up and gathering together all of the forgotten clothes from the line he started to make a package. He would drop it off at the local post office on his way back home to America. It was the least he could do for a friend.

CHAPTER 22

Deus ex machina.

Nine A.M. of the vernal equinox. It was time to take inventory. Behind the blue-paneled bar reserved for First-Class passengers, the bartender was counting bottles and noting down what was left as he always did at the end of a crossing. The only other people in the room were three onion skins—two women and a man—who sat around a blue plastic-topped table looking related by rimless glasses and no chins. The two women were talking loudly to one another as if they were trying to overcome the noise of the man's multi-band portable radio but there was nothing coming from it at the moment.

"Mother"—playing with the handle of her empty coffee cup—"you *must* fly back with us from New York. I won't take no for an answer."

"Not a chance," replied Mother. She shook her head of thin curls that were as brown as daughter's but lacked their spring. "I'm going straight home. I've had enough traveling. I'm bushed. Don't forget I'm a year older than last year. Besides," she added, "*he* doesn't really want me to come."

"Yes, she's one year older than last year," he said quietly while absorbed in extending the radio's already soaring antenna until it just cleared the ceiling.

"Harry *wants* you to come, Mother. And you could see Zev and Bitsy. I won't take no for an answer."

"I'd like to see the dogs"—she toyed with the idea—"but I don't intend to stick my nose in where it's not welcome."

"It won't be any picnic for her in that stuffy little room," Harry reported factually without looking up from the dial of his radio.

"Don't be ridiculous, Mother. It's all settled. You're coming home with us."

Suddenly the radio came alive. "CRRRACKLE monster killer GARP GARP again. Gloria GARP a CRACKLE and talented fourteen-year-old CRIK was CRACKLEDDD in Central Park and is officially listed as CRACKLE 21. Her throat was ZINGED-CRRRACKLECRIKCRRRACKLEGARP BEEP BEEP."

"Listen!" cried Harry excitedly. "I've got New York."

"Would you please make that a little lower, Harry?" said his wife irritably. "Do you hear that, Mother? New York! If the fog doesn't hold us up we'll be there in a few hours. Excited?"

"We've got radar," Harry pointed out wearily.

"Damn right!" replied Mother. "I can't wait to get some good down-to-earth American cooking instead of a lot of glop on everything."

"I know *exactly* what you mean," said her daughter knowingly. She got up. "We'd better get back to the cabin, Mother, and finish our packing. Are you coming, Harry?"

Harry collapsed his antenna and followed.

Outside all of the exposed decks were damp and deserted. The fog was so thick that the fog horns themselves seemed lost in it, their mooing muted and far off. From the Captain's bridge it was impossible to see even the covered hatches directly below, yet the ship maintained its headlong speed, slicing through the murk like an artful skier through blown snow. In front of the hatches, in front of the forward masts, in front of the sloping breakwater shield, at the unprotected prow of the ship stood a brazen solitary figure shrouded in fog. It was Ivan. Either he couldn't bear to be cooped up any longer or he wanted to be the first one to arrive. He was wearing a superb tan raincoat with complicated flaps and belts and buckles, the kind that suggests countless secret recesses full of guns and tape recorders. In addition to his new raincoat, the most spectacular alteration in Ivan's appearance was his handsome, shimmering, steel-flecked beard. It had vanished, gone like a stage prop, skimmed off. His naked jaw was ruggedly handsome, flat as a driving iron. There was nothing to hide. It looked as if he had a strong bite. The lower half of his face was the color of mothballs but this was only temporary. Even in the fog with his collar turned up he looked remarkably spruce.

Fit as a fiddle. Since boarding the ship at Algeciras, he had been working out down in the gym, four walls covered with $8\frac{1}{2}$ x 11 celebrities in black frames autographed "To Hans who fixed my back. Best ever." Ivan paid no attention to them as he rowed, peddled, and pulled his way home, throwing out excess energy like war surplus, and now and then laughing out loud as he put more and more distance between himself and a loaded American volleyball lost somewhere in the Old World. Europe was a thing of the past. He was heading toward the future and prospects were excellent.

Was he lonely? Alone is not necessarily lonely. He was Dynamic Storch who had separated himself out of the middle-class glue, and rowing, peddling, and pulling, he was bound away for the new territory. The world couldn't hit a moving target. From his position at the prow, the entire ship was behind him like a giant invisible rocket hurtling him forward. He was burning through, an ablative personality shedding layers for survival.

Out there, somewhere dead ahead, lay the New Jerusalem, impossible to see, a magic city that glowed when viewed through an amber umbrella handle. The city was humming and the hum grew louder. The noise seemed to hover over Ivan's head like a helicopter but despite his efforts to pierce the fog nothing was visible. Suddenly down through the clouds came a *deus ex machina*, which was very unusual for an Atlantic crossing during the thrift season. When just above Ivan's head, the *deus* tugged on the line that he was suspended by and came to a jiggling halt. He floated effortlessly through the air somewhat ahead of the ship and slightly off to one side, an unstoppered jinni in blue coveralls and a white crash helmet. Dangling urbanely in his harness which resembled an elegant breeches buoy, the short canvas pants studded with topaz-colored stars, he seemed to be shouting some friendly greeting but the roar overhead obscured his words. Ivan strained to hear the message.

"You are Cancer the Crab. Your element is arrogant power. Your planetary influence is the moon. Sign of emotional generosity. Your colors are red, white, and blue. Your song 'God Bless America.' Your gems are pearls, moonstones, and crystal. Tangerines contain your biochemical salts. Your symbolic number is one."

"What's that?" called Ivan dubiously, and cupped his hand behind his ear.

The *deus* jerked on his line again and was lowered until he hung eye to eye with Ivan on the sea side of the ship's railing. He had a hatchet head and shrewd-looking almond-shaped eyes. "You see I've looked into you, Mr. Storch," he said candidly. "I'd know you anywhere."

"Senator Pettidrooper," guessed Ivan, showing no surprise. "I've been expecting you."

Ivan's quick identification of him seemed to confirm something in the Senator's mind and he gazed into the young man's heart penetratingly. It was Saul setting eyes on David for the first time long before the jealousy and the rage. An epic meeting.

"Where's the beard?" the Senator bluntly inquired.

"I shaved it off," Ivan told him in a free spirit of cooperation. "I'm not afraid of taking risks."

"I know. I've been following your career with interest. What are you aiming at, Mr. Storch?"

Taking his hands from his pockets, Ivan gripped the ship's railing and leaned over it intently. "Clear thoughts," he answered in a husky voice, "and the golden rule."

Pettidrooper approved. "In that case your future is in politics."

"Politics," considered Ivan.

"The very essence of the give-and-take spirit at the heart of American life."

"I think I'd like that," said Ivan modestly.

"Then you're to be groomed!" announced Pettidrooper, his

voice ringing above the engine and the sea and the foghorns. Thrusting a glittering object into Ivan's hand without explanation, he tugged decisively on his line and slowly ascended. "It will take time. We'll have to get started at once. Meet me in Washington on the Hill. You have a limitless future, Mr. Storch. Not this November but soon . . . soon . . . soon."

"On the Hill," confirmed Ivan loudly. Feeling a little foolish because there was no longer anyone there, he stopped waving and wiped the mist from his face. Pettidrooper, the thaumaturgical Senator, had vanished like an hallucination. Ivan became aware of his clenched hand and one by one he carefully unlocked his fingers as if he expected a rare butterfly to flutter out. There in the palm of his hand lay a silver ballpoint pen on which was engraven the Great Seal of the Senate of the United States. Pettidrooper had thoughtfully left his calling card.

All morning it had been drizzling in New York but no matter what the season it was always Christmas on the pier, a colorful extravaganza of expectant hubbub. Behind a portable, white picket fence people wearing plastic rain hats squirmed about in .ticipation, impishly jabbing one another with furled uml. ellas to pass the time. At the rear of the pack, waiting patiently like a solitary bicycle outside a school yard, was Schlemovitz, his eye glued to the cigarette in front of him. When the lady who was smoking it was through, the ex-millionaire retrieved the butt and took the last few exhilarating puffs. Clearly Schlemovitz had fallen on evil days. Without a raincoat, he stood with his frayed collar up and the lining of his jacket hung gray out the bottom. The crown of his once-splendid hat was currently mashed in, its ribbon crinkled, its brim sagged. His damp wispy hair was pasted over his ears like white guitar strings over the sound hole. From top to bottom he looked as if he had been through the wringer. He had. With a queen's gambit all-purpose counter check, Mrs. Schlemovitz had cleaned him out and run off like a gypsy to zigzag in the classy arms of S. Fish, the dancer. "Schlemovitz," he told himself bitterly as he bent over and scooped up a fresh butt, "the heart of woman is a twisted pump." But after a few calming mentholated drags he raised his eyes and added in repentance, "They should only be happy."

Everyone was waving madly as the colossal ship was tugged into place and the thick mooring lines made fast. The ship's horn went through Schlemovitz's empty stomach like a javelin and, shivering in the dampness, he warmed his hands in his pockets and watched the gangplanks slide out. Scanning the deck, he picked out a young girl with a pink babushka as his son's new wife. A frail-looking little thing but sweet. Her picture had been in the paper. But where was the boy? Schlemovitz pressed forward obliviously treading on toes.

"Can't you wait till I'm finished?" complained an irate smoker who had seen the scavenger at work.

Schlemovitz stopped and stared at him dumbly.

"Just hold your horses. You'll get the butt when I'm through, I promise."

Schlemovitz glowered and guttural noises came from his lips.

"Sure, sure," said the smoker nervously, intimidated by the old man's revolutionary eyes. "Go ahead. You take it." He held out the cigarette.

"Keep your charity," exploded Schlemovitz contemptuously, and with a haughty toss of his battered hat, he moved on.

A thick clump of excited reporters, photographers, and curious onlookers blocked his way. They were bunched around someone who was hidden from view. Eager faces strained forward to get a glimpse of what it was all about, men and women on tiptoe, on crates, on pocketbooks, on luggage, gaping children on shoulders or held aloft. Regardless of who he was, everyone appeared resolved to see every inch of him and be a part of the excitement.

Determined not to lose sight of the girl, Schlemovitz pushed through.

"Is it true, Mr. Storch, that you caught him single-handed?" a woman reporter was asking in an urgent, breathy, captivated, take-me-I'm-yours sort of voice, her notebook all but forgotten as she goggled at the virile celebrity.

Schlemovitz could see him now, a fancy raincoat and big-business hornrims over the eyes. "Storch." The name meant nothing to him but there was something oddly familiar about the face. "A big shot," thought Schlemovitz, dismissing the idea as he squirmed past, "no wonder, they all look alike."

On the deck the girl was gradually making her way toward the gangplank in the tide of debarking passengers. She was radiant, laughing and talking with someone small beside her who was screened by the guard rail so that Schlemovitz could see only the hair. It looked familiar. Crouching in the crowd so as not to be seen, he watched her as she came to the head of the gangplank and the hair broke out into the open. Instantly his bony knees dislocated and Schlemovitz would have gone down if he hadn't been hemmed in all around. He was smothered, suffocating, sapped. *Hysterica Passio! Eli Eli!* The mother had him by the throat. His boy! His son! Bent forward as if he were leaning the wrong way on Klopman. An immigrant in a faded jacket. A wounded deserter in short khaki pants. Schlemovitz watched in miserable silence as she placed a napkin on his head before crossing the open area between ship and shore. While she held his arm protectively, he put his foot down on the gangplank as if he were stepping into a hot bath. His face was queer, undecided, a sneer on the port side, a smile on starboard. "The boy needs rest," Schlemovitz consoled himself. "It's hard work being a newly-wed." He crept closer.

Up the gangplank rushed a long-legged chauffeur in gun-metal gray livery. He tipped his visor to the couple, snapped open his large black umbrella, and solicitously helped the injured party down to a waiting wheel chair. It was a wonderful machine, all chrome and cushions, with wire wheels, balloon tires, and a crescent-shaped silver horn mounted on the arm rest. A Rolls Royce of wheel chairs. Schlemovitz could see that his son had come into money. The boy would never recover from it. Tears basted the old man's eyes and migraine roasted his brains.

The chauffeur was a friend of the family rather than a mere employee and he fussed over the new member with sincere fondness. He laid a mink lap robe over the invalid's knees and placed a karakul shawl over his shoulders. From a holder attached to the side panel, D.C. removed a gold-tipped cigarette and before he could find a match the chauffeur had attentively lighted it. Leaning back triumphantly in his wheel chair, the invalid smoked like a king. His son was an American through and through, a polluted go-getter who had gotten. Schlemovitz dried his eyes in retaliation.

Stepping up on the small platform behind the wheel chair, the chauffeur inserted two flashlight batteries and started the motor. Although he had a terrible pock-marked complexion, he seemed to know his business. As Sidney walked beside the moving chair holding her husband's hand and petting him, the skilled chauffeur guided it smoothly through the admiring crowd.

Schlemovitz turned away from the departing rich with blisters on his tongue and a kind of croaking. "Poison," he said, "a poison in the blood like noodles, a cancer in the flesh like worms. If thine eye offend thee pluck it out. Pluck it out. PLUCK IT OUT!" Schlemovitz was shouting now and people all around were craning their necks to see the raving maniac. "You knew, Albert, and I didn't believe you. This earth, my home, a pint-sized pimple in a second-rate solar system stuck off in some miserable corner of the universe. It needs an enema. AN ENEMA! One last, great, screaming, suicidal douche until the pressure blows off the poles and water gushes out of its navel. Raise high the red bag, Lovely, and let the new wave flow."

All at once the sky blackened over moodily. Bystanders turned away from the mad old man who was groveling about on the floor and looked beyond the ship with expectant faces, muted and drawn together as people usually are before a storm. Schlemovitz, unable to find any tobacco in the immediate vicinity, gave up the search and, getting to his feet, he gazed out at the heavens with satisfaction. In the distance lightning flickered soundlessly through the dirty clouds like a new broom. He had seen enough. Unbuttoning his jacket, he held it open. Pinned to the loose lining like notices on a bulletin board were a dozen charred butts among which were represented many of the nation's leading brands. With the air of a connoisseur dipping into his private stock in honor of a special occasion, he carefully made his selection. While he was about it, a booming, mind-breaking, sudatory blast of thunder rattled the pier, shook up the citizens, and scattered them about like waste paper in all directions. "Take heart, Schlemovitz," he told himself as he calmly lighted up, "it won't be long now."